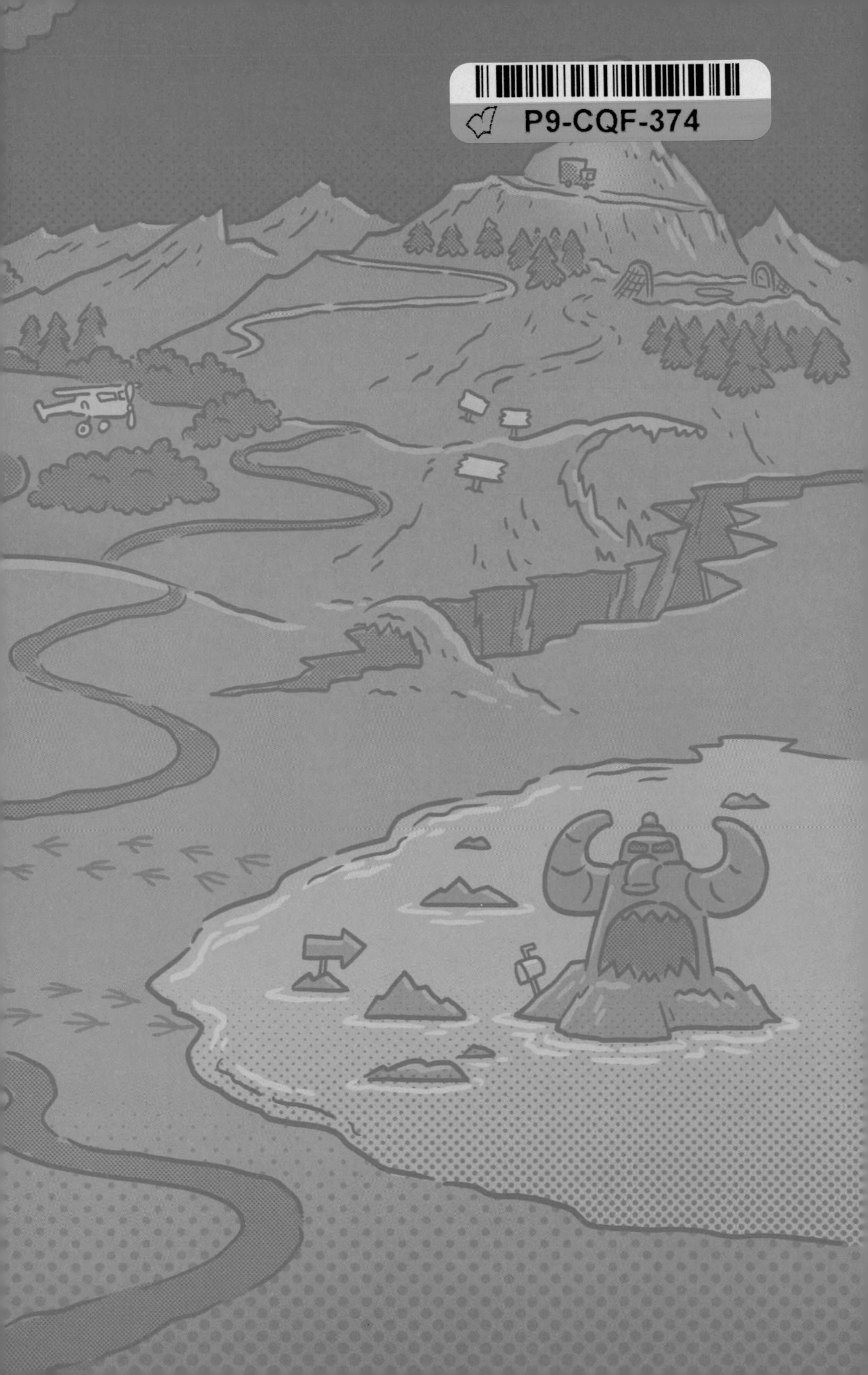

# DINO MIGHTY!

## THE HEIST AGE

BY **DOUG PALEO**

ILLUSTRATED BY **AARON BLECHA**

**ETCH**

**HOUGHTON MIFFLIN HARCOURT**

BOSTON   NEW YORK

ALL RIGHTS RESERVED. FOR INFORMATION ABOUT PERMISSION
TO REPRODUCE SELECTIONS FROM THIS BOOK, WRITE TO
TRADE.PERMISSIONS@HMHCO.COM OR TO PERMISSIONS,
HOUGHTON MIFFLIN HARCOURT PUBLISHING COMPANY, 3 PARK
AVENUE, 19TH FLOOR, NEW YORK, NEW YORK 10016.

ETCH IS AN IMPRINT OF HOUGHTON MIFFLIN HARCOURT
PUBLISHING COMPANY.

HMHBOOKS.COM

ILLUSTRATED BY AARON BLECHA
THE ILLUSTRATIONS IN THIS BOOK WERE SKETCHED
IN PENCIL AND THEN CREATED DIGITALLY.
THE TEXT WAS SET IN FENNARIO AND KIDPRINT.
THE DISPLAY TYPE WAS SET IN GRANDSTANDER.
COVER DESIGN BY AARON BLECHA AND PHIL CAMINITI
INTERIOR DESIGN BY PHIL CAMINITI

THE LIBRARY OF CONGRESS CATALOGING-IN-PUBLICATION
DATA IS AVAILABLE.

ISBN: 978-0-358-33157-5

MANUFACTURED IN CHINA
SCP 10 9 8 7 6 5 4 3 2 1
4500825589

# CHAPTERS

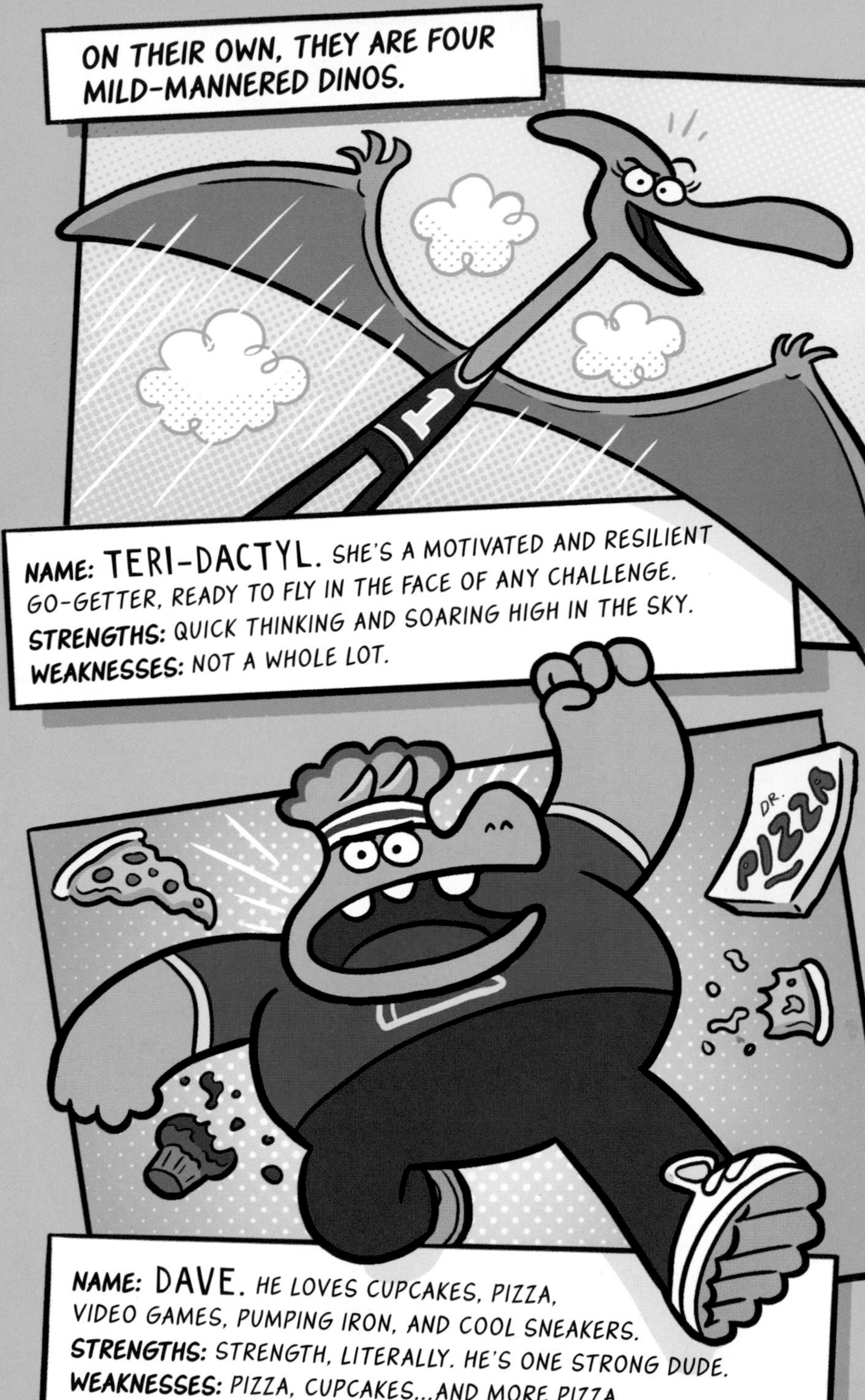
ON THEIR OWN, THEY ARE FOUR MILD-MANNERED DINOS.
1
NAME: TERI-DACTYL. SHE'S A MOTIVATED AND RESILIENT GO-GETTER, READY TO FLY IN THE FACE OF ANY CHALLENGE.
STRENGTHS: QUICK THINKING AND SOARING HIGH IN THE SKY.
WEAKNESSES: NOT A WHOLE LOT.
DR. PIZZA
NAME: DAVE. HE LOVES CUPCAKES, PIZZA, VIDEO GAMES, PUMPING IRON, AND COOL SNEAKERS.
STRENGTHS: STRENGTH, LITERALLY. HE'S ONE STRONG DUDE.
WEAKNESSES: PIZZA, CUPCAKES...AND MORE PIZZA.

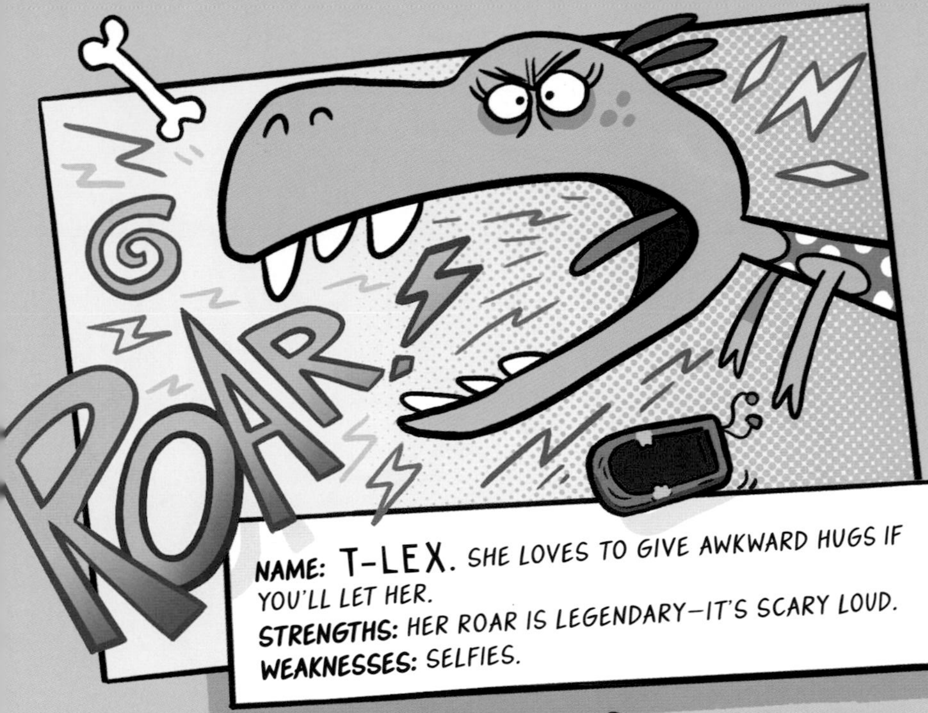
ROAR!
NAME: T-LEX. SHE LOVES TO GIVE AWKWARD HUGS IF YOU'LL LET HER.
STRENGTHS: HER ROAR IS LEGENDARY—IT'S SCARY LOUD.
WEAKNESSES: SELFIES.

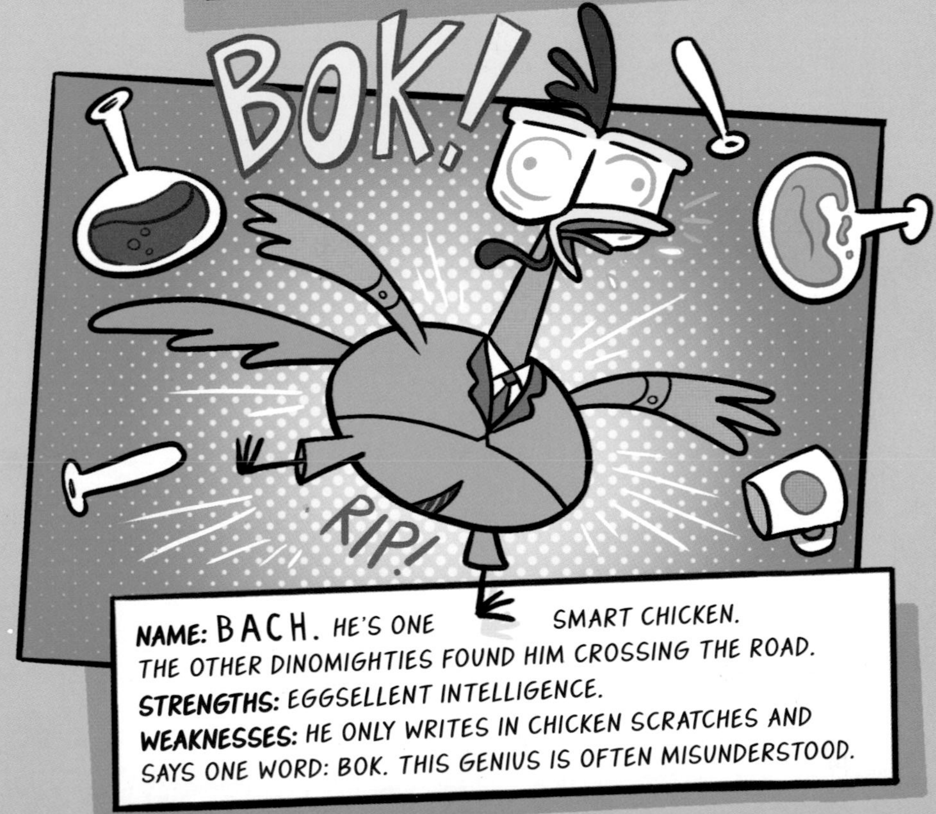
BOK!
RIP!
NAME: BACH. HE'S ONE SMART CHICKEN. THE OTHER DINOMIGHTIES FOUND HIM CROSSING THE ROAD.
STRENGTHS: EGGSELLENT INTELLIGENCE.
WEAKNESSES: HE ONLY WRITES IN CHICKEN SCRATCHES AND SAYS ONE WORD: BOK. THIS GENIUS IS OFTEN MISUNDERSTOOD.

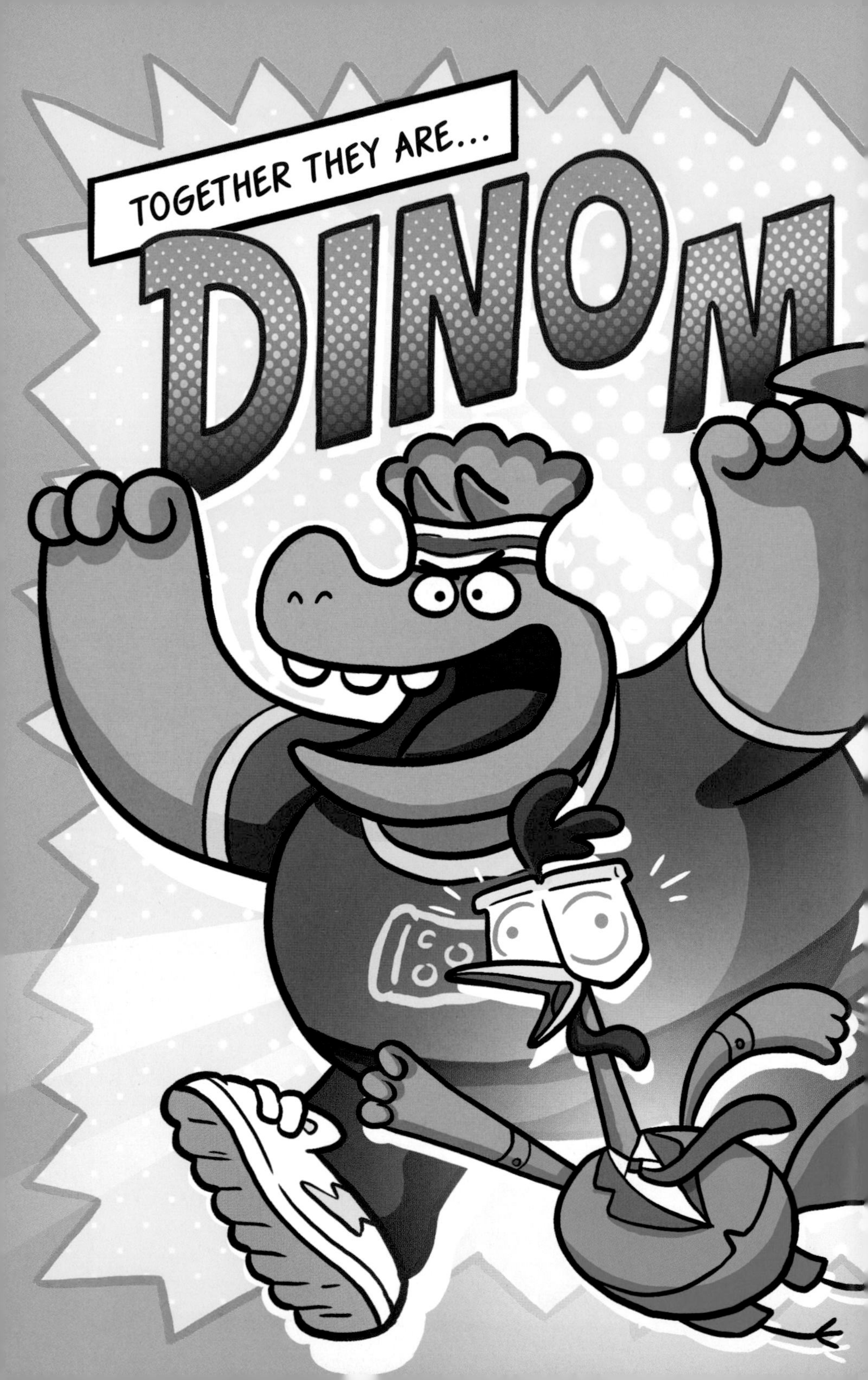
TOGETHER THEY ARE...
DINOM

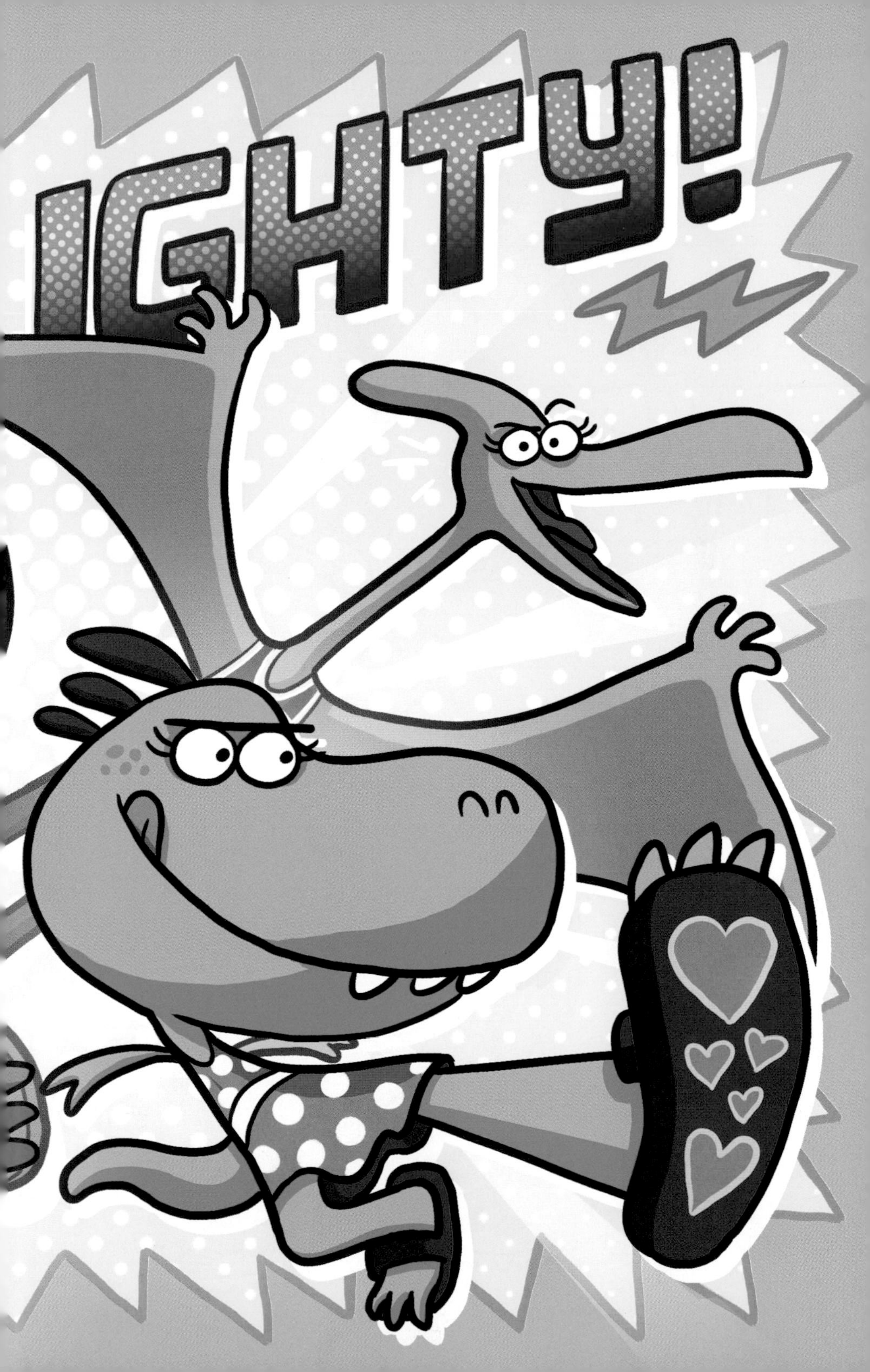
IGHTY!

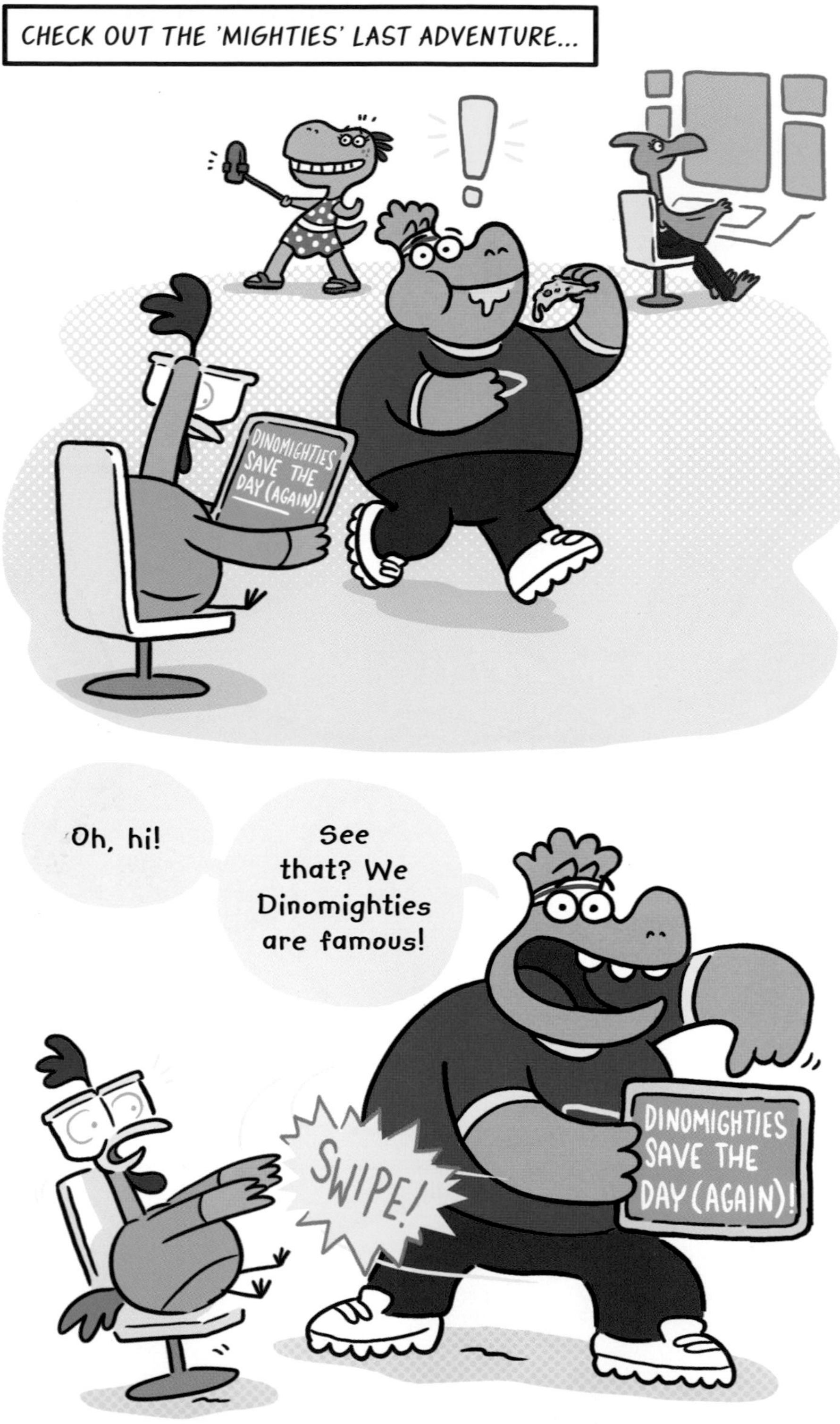
CHECK OUT THE 'MIGHTIES' LAST ADVENTURE...
DINOMIGHTIES SAVE THE DAY (AGAIN)!
Oh, hi!
See that? We Dinomighties are famous!
SWIPE!
DINOMIGHTIES SAVE THE DAY (AGAIN)!

Some might even call us hometown heroes!

We keep Dinotown safe from the top bad guys on the nemesis list.

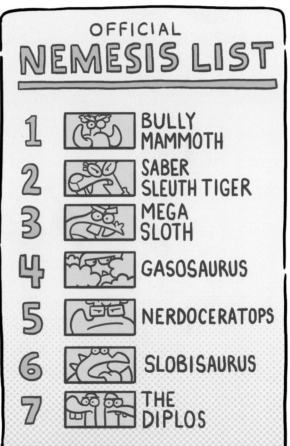

OFFICIAL
# NEMESIS LIST

1  BULLY MAMMOTH

2  SABER SLEUTH TIGER

3  MEGA SLOTH

4  GASOSAURUS

5  NERDOCERATOPS

6  SLOBISAURUS

7  THE DIPLOS

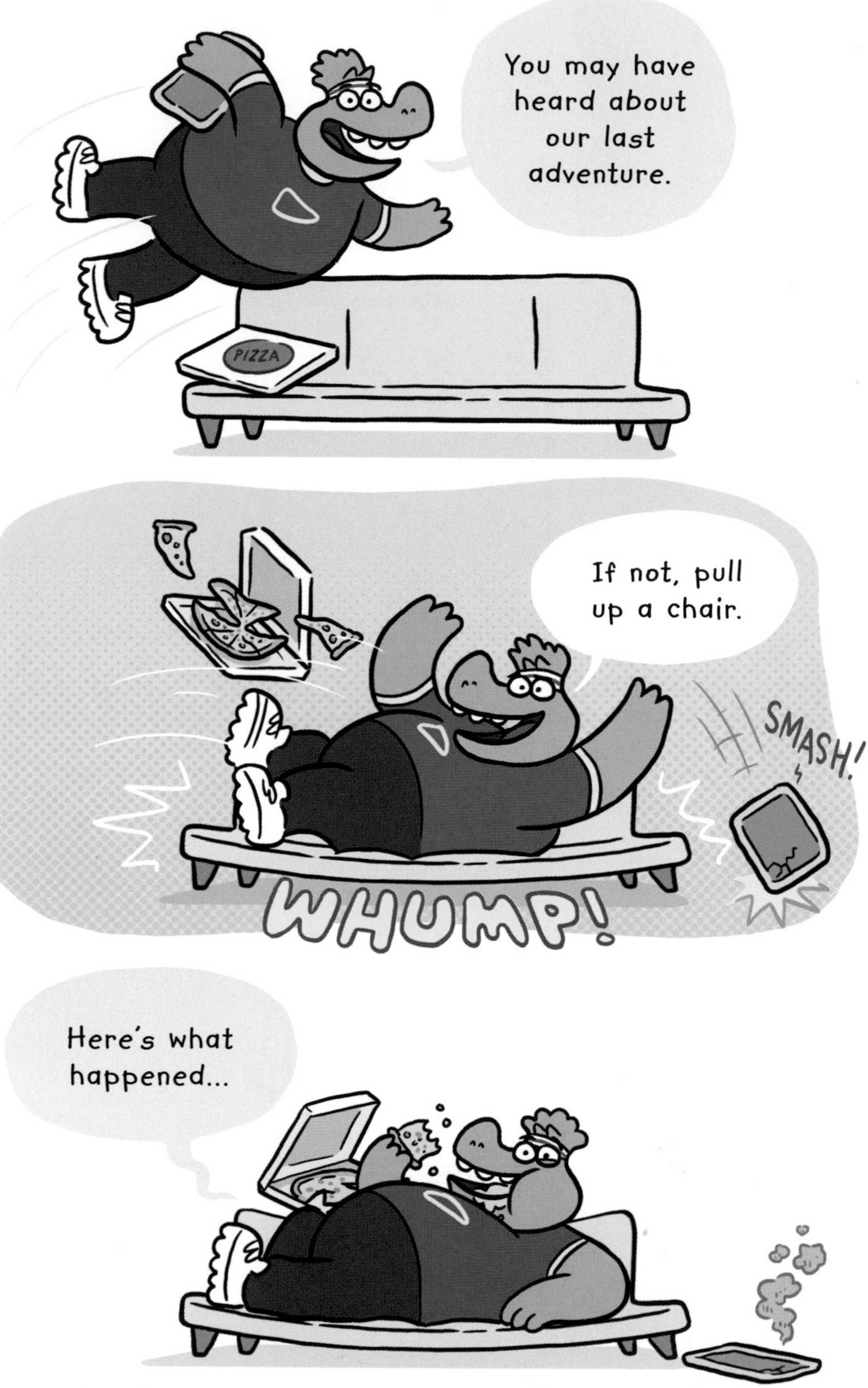

You may have heard about our last adventure.
PIZZA
If not, pull up a chair.
SMASH!
WHUMP!
Here's what happened...

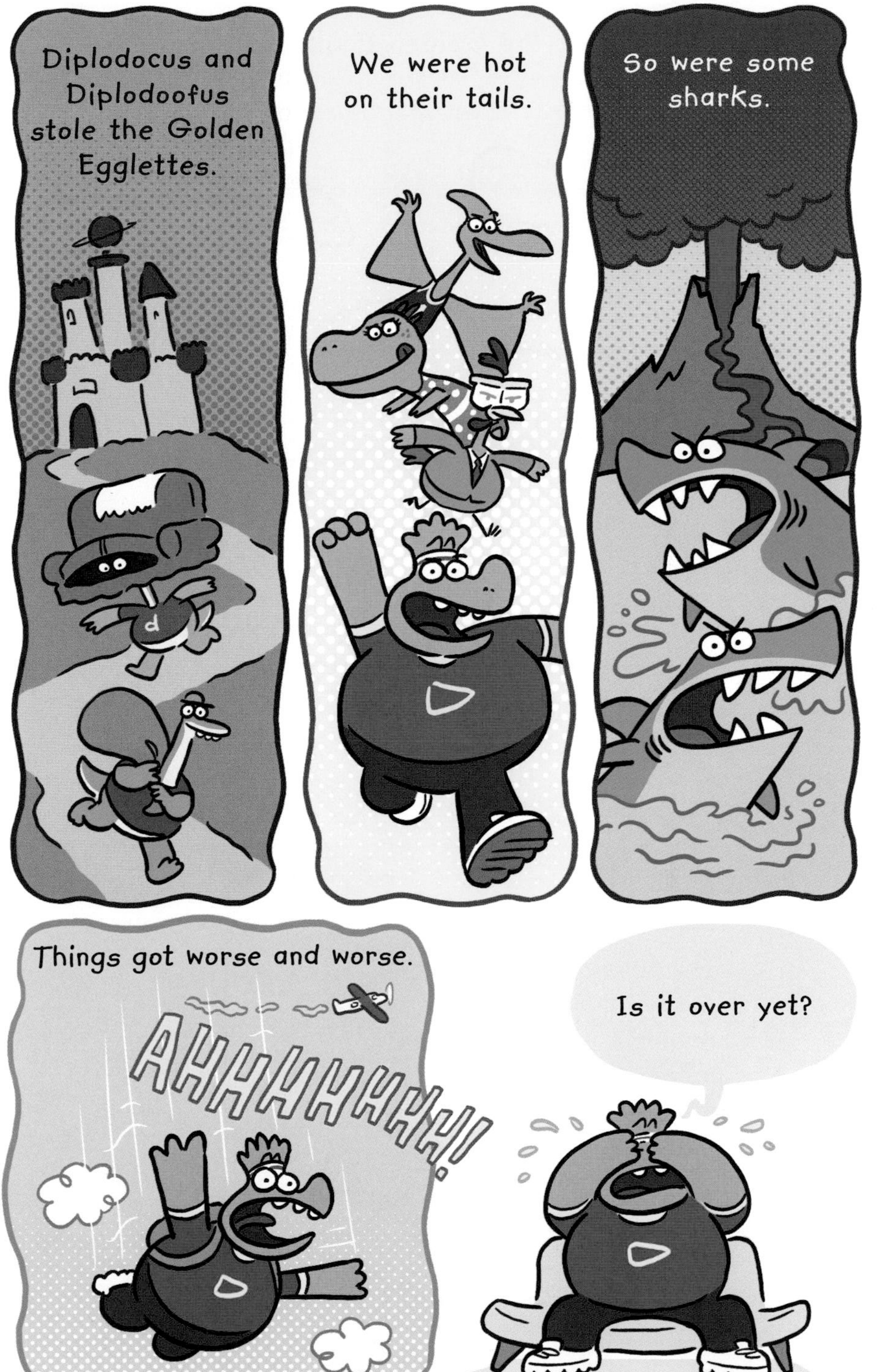
Diplodocus and Diplodoofus stole the Golden Egglettes.
We were hot on their tails.
So were some sharks.
Things got worse and worse.
AHHHHHHHH!
Is it over yet?

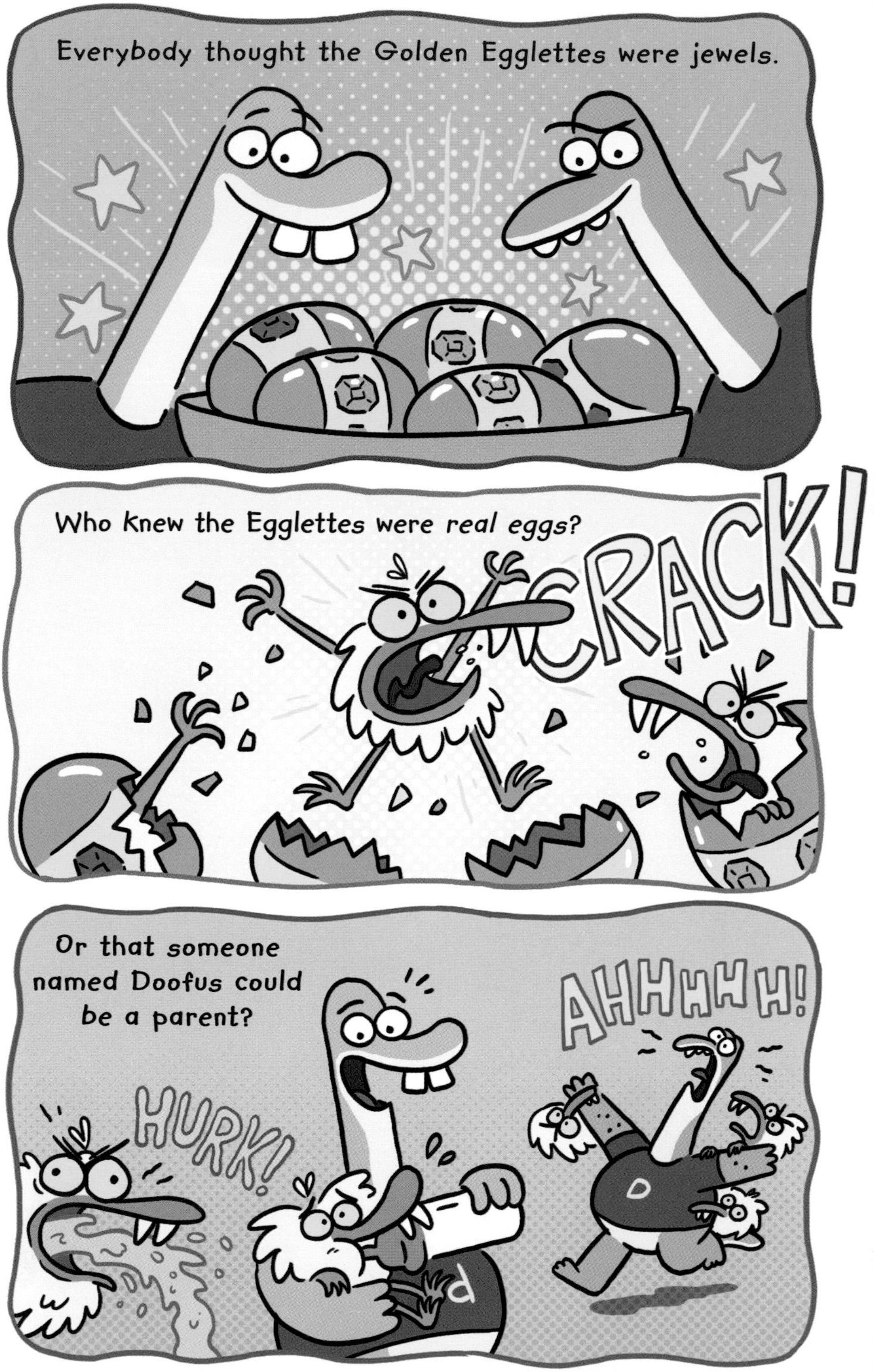
Everybody thought the Golden Egglettes were jewels.
Who knew the Egglettes were *real eggs*?
CRACK!
Or that someone named Doofus could be a parent?
AHHHHHH!
HURK!

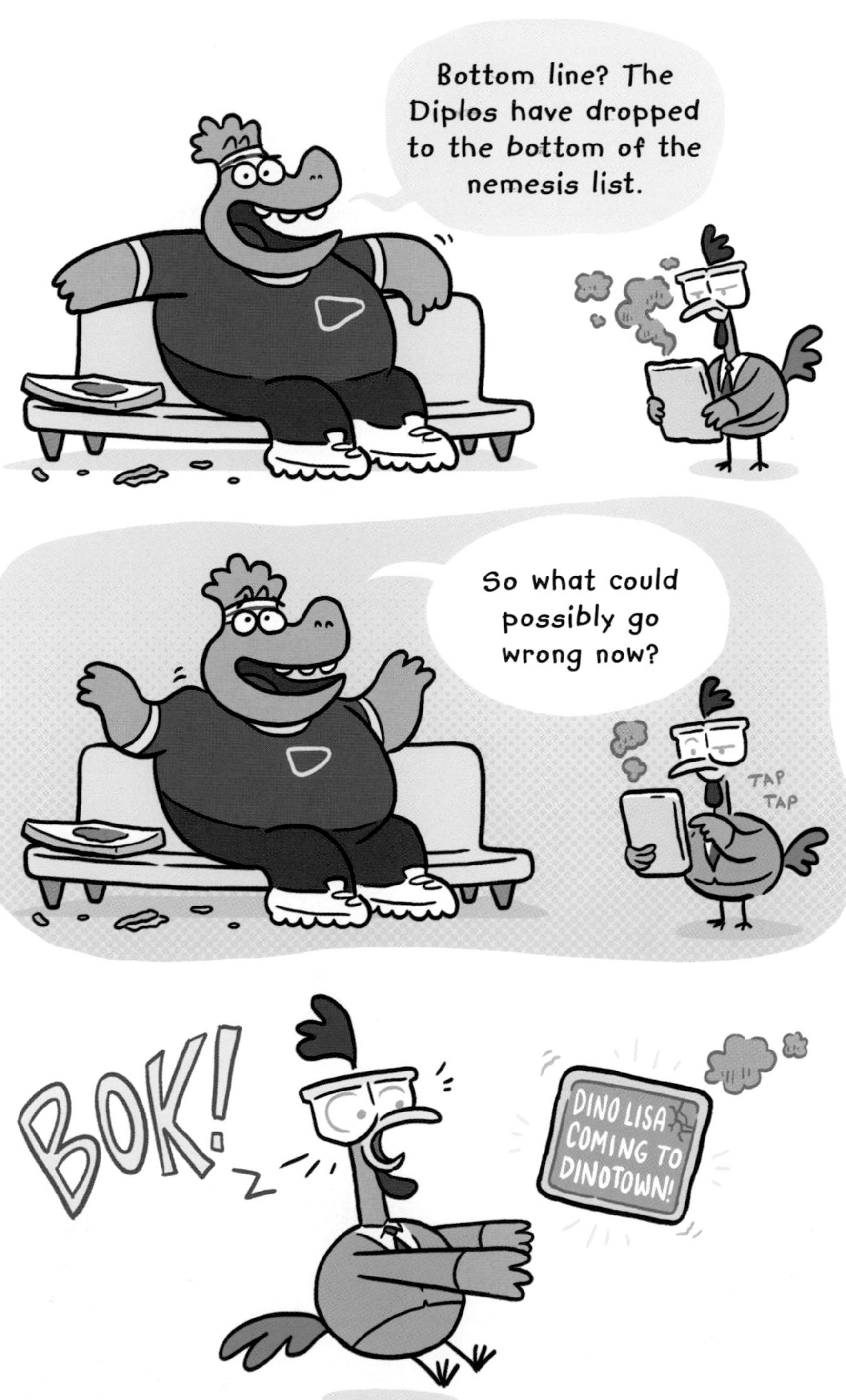
Bottom line? The Diplos have dropped to the bottom of the nemesis list.
So what could possibly go wrong now?
TAP TAP
BOK!
DINO LISA COMING TO DINOTOWN!

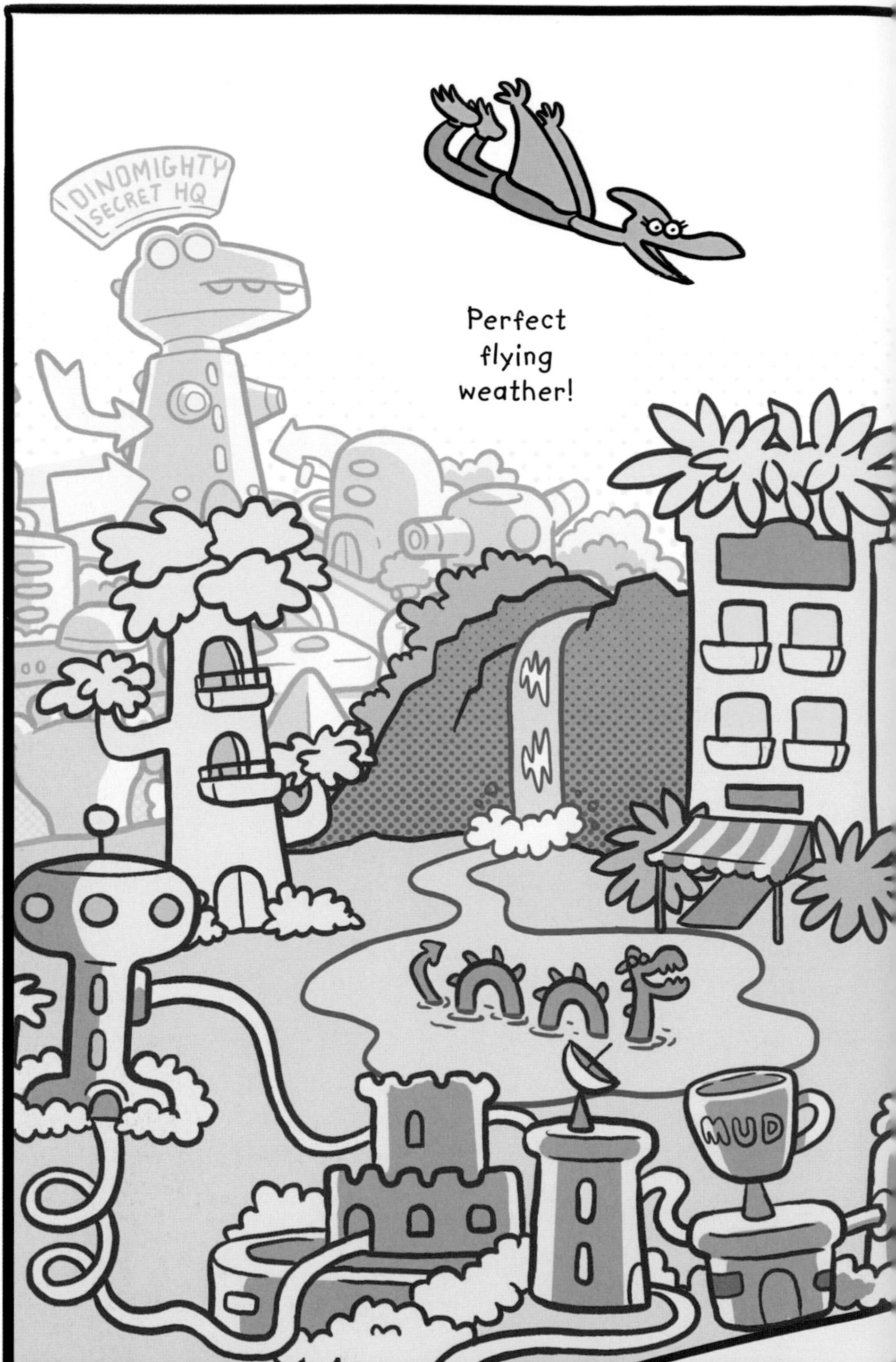
DINOMIGHTY SECRET HQ
Perfect flying weather!
MUD

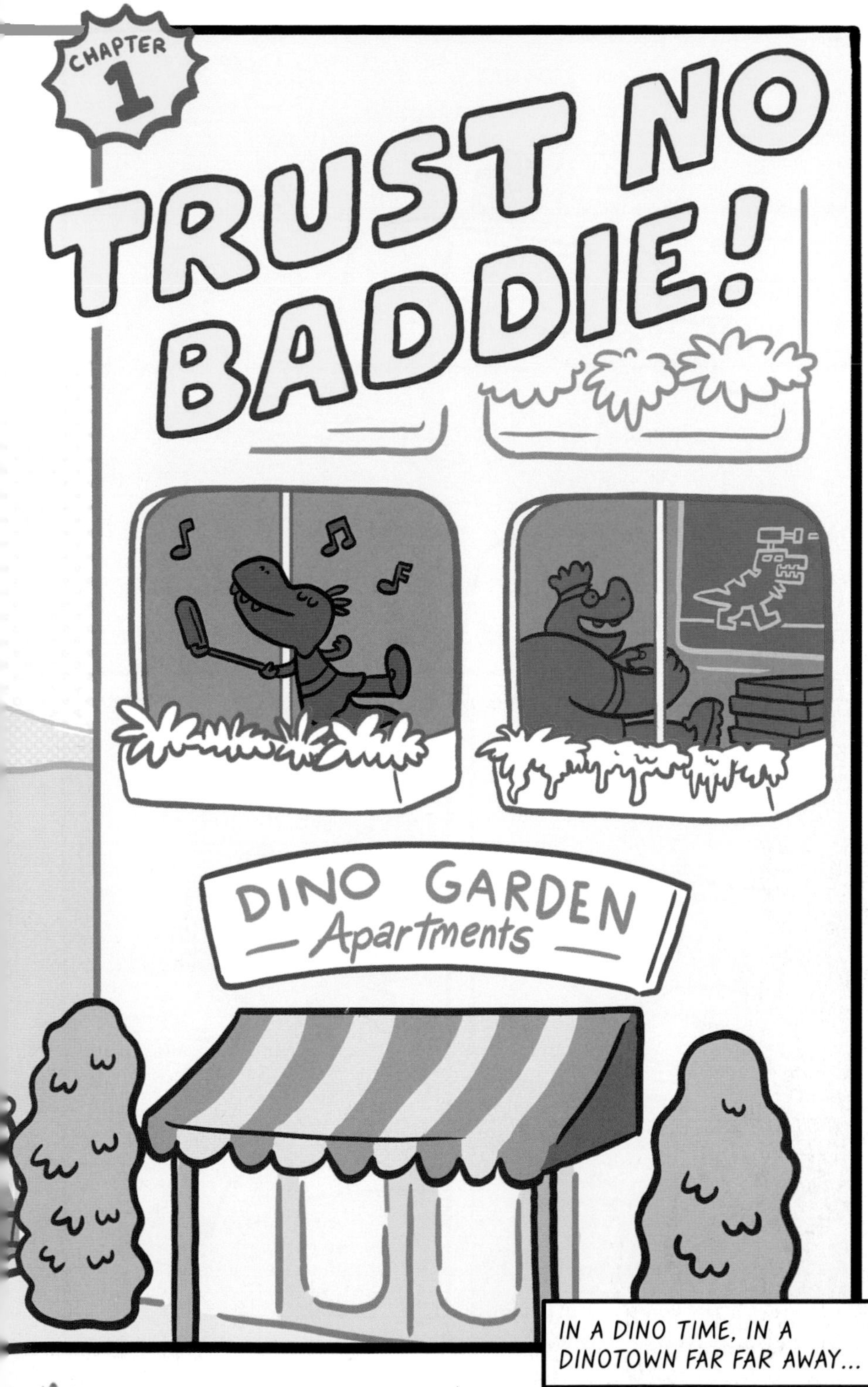
CHAPTER 1
TRUST NO BADDIE!
DINO GARDEN Apartments
IN A DINO TIME, IN A DINOTOWN FAR FAR AWAY...

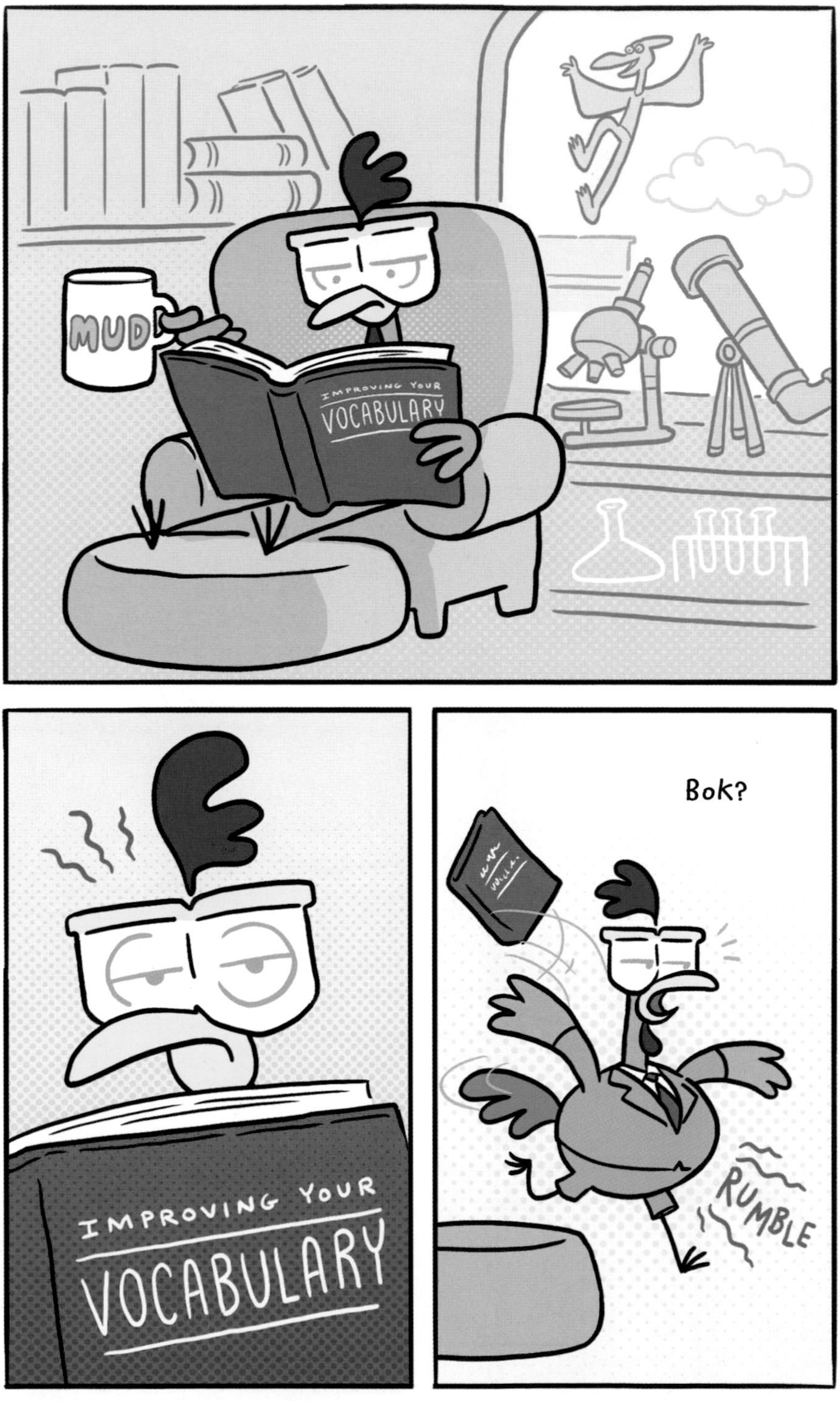
MUD
IMPROVING YOUR VOCABULARY
IMPROVING YOUR VOCABULARY
Bok?
RUMBLE

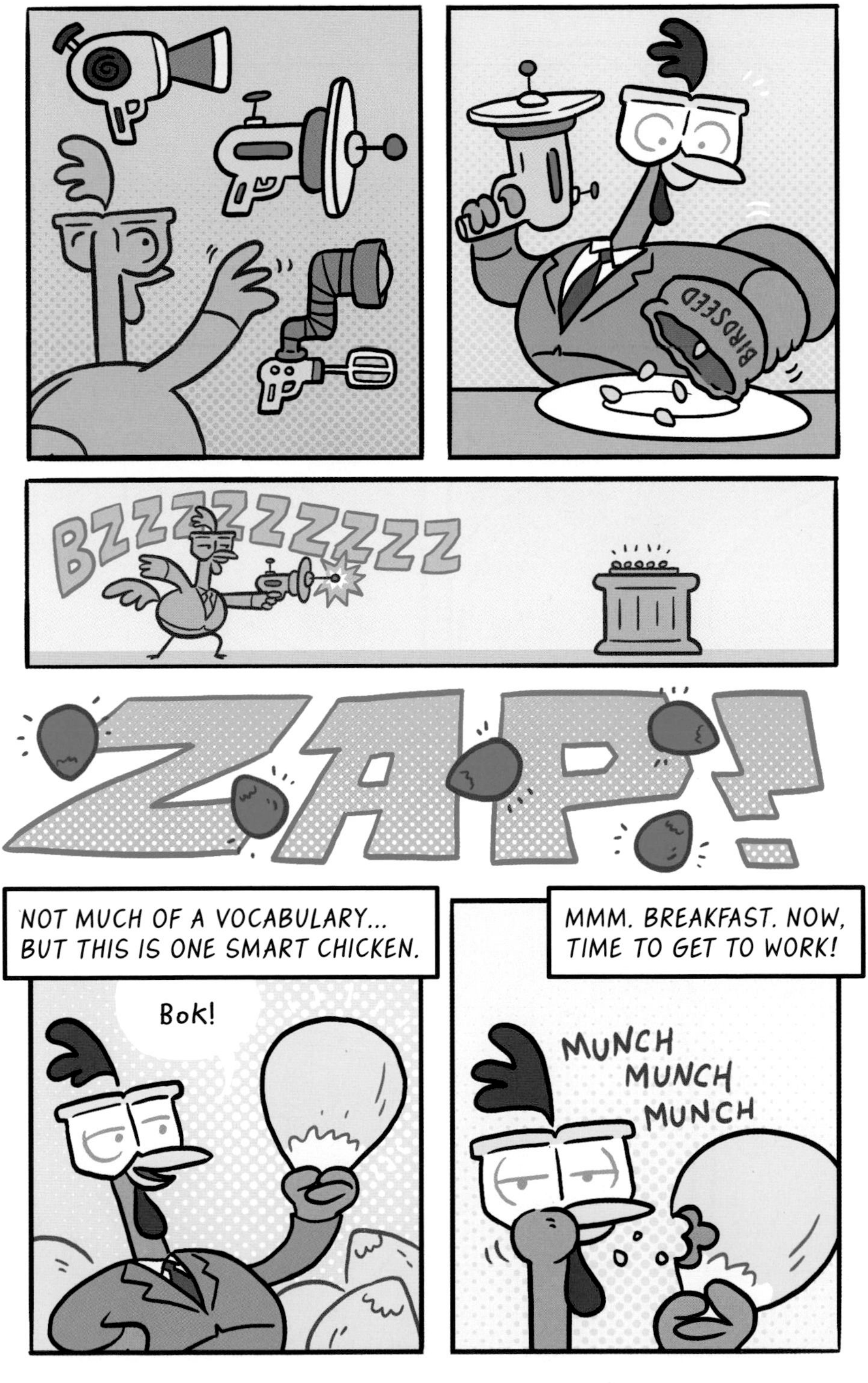
BIRDSEED
BZZZZZZZZZZ
ZAP!
NOT MUCH OF A VOCABULARY... BUT THIS IS ONE SMART CHICKEN.
Bok!
MMM. BREAKFAST. NOW, TIME TO GET TO WORK!
MUNCH MUNCH MUNCH

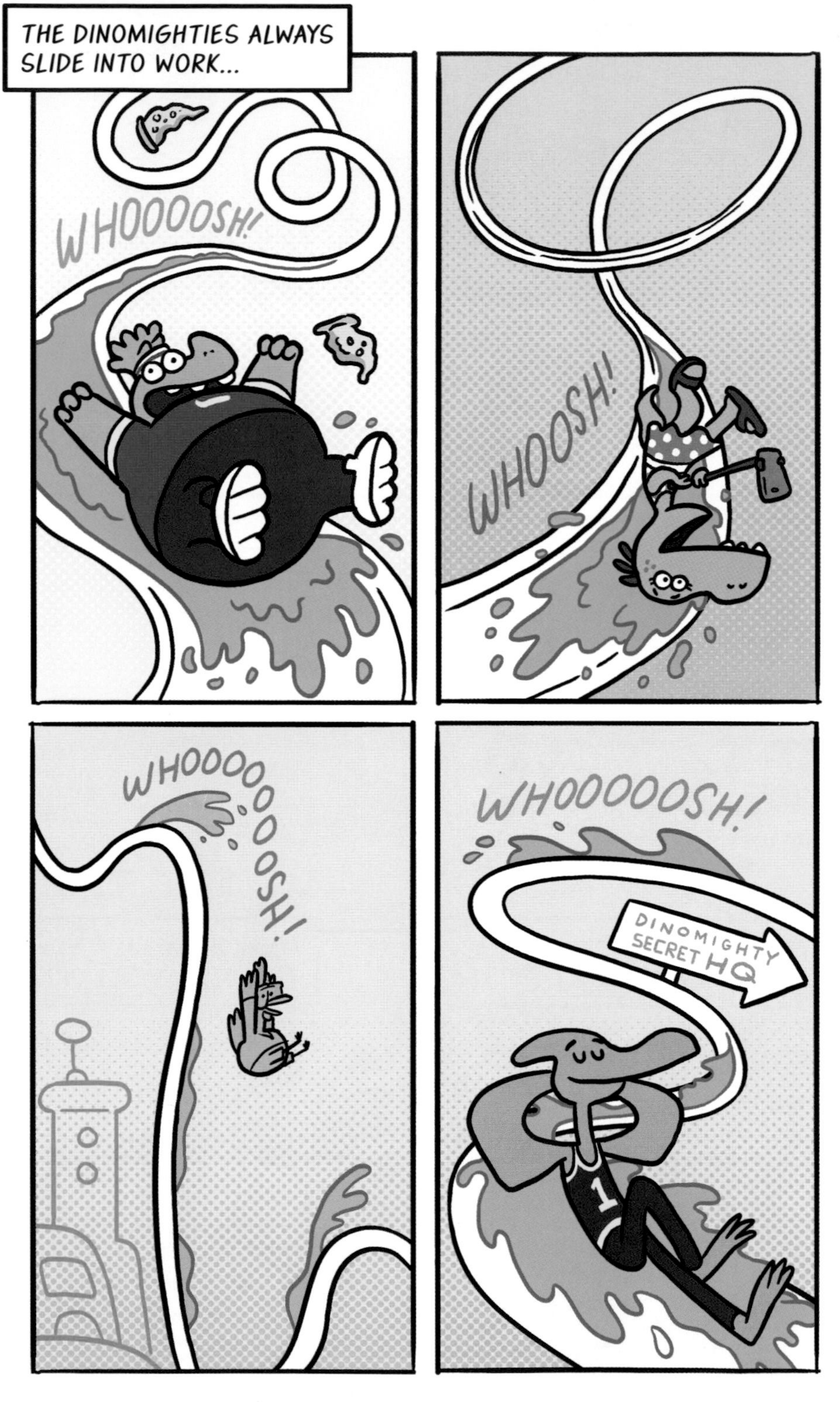
THE DINOMIGHTIES ALWAYS SLIDE INTO WORK...
WHOOOOOSH!
WHOOSH!
WHOOOOOOOOOOSH!
WHOOOOOOSH!
DINOMIGHTY SECRET HQ

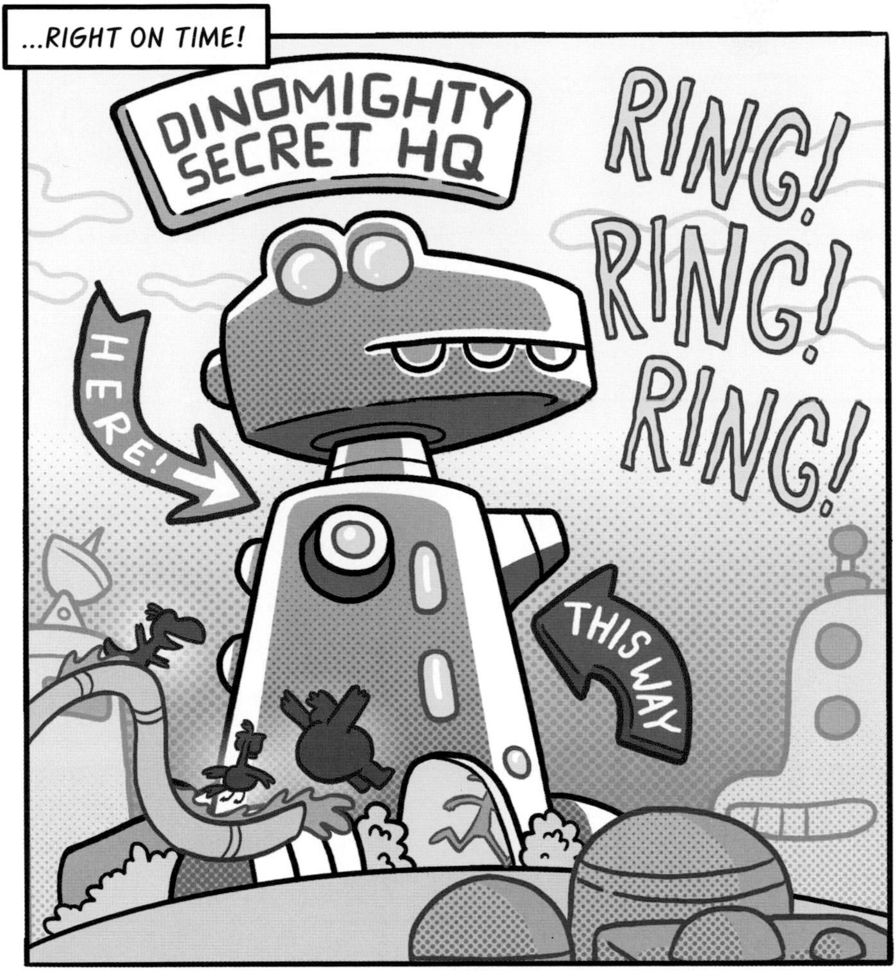
...RIGHT ON TIME!
DINOMIGHTY SECRET HQ
RING! RING! RING!
HERE!
THIS WAY

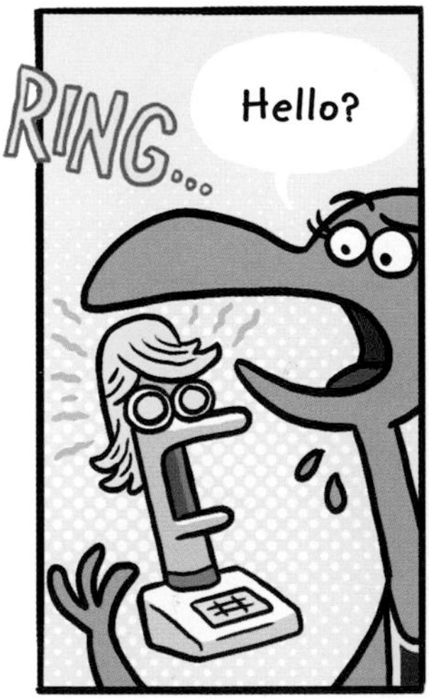
RING...
Hello?

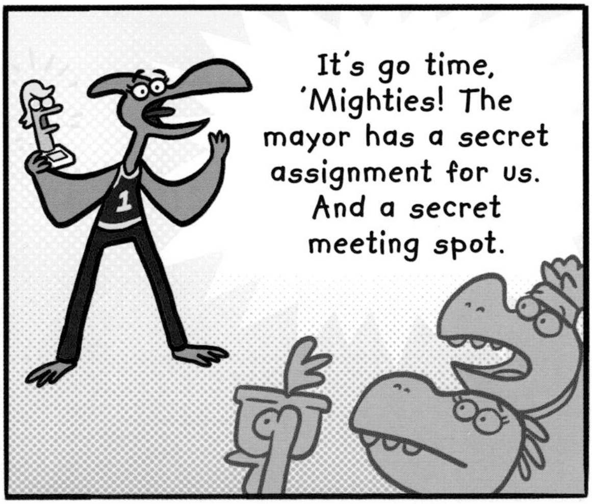
It's go time, 'Mighties! The mayor has a secret assignment for us. And a secret meeting spot.

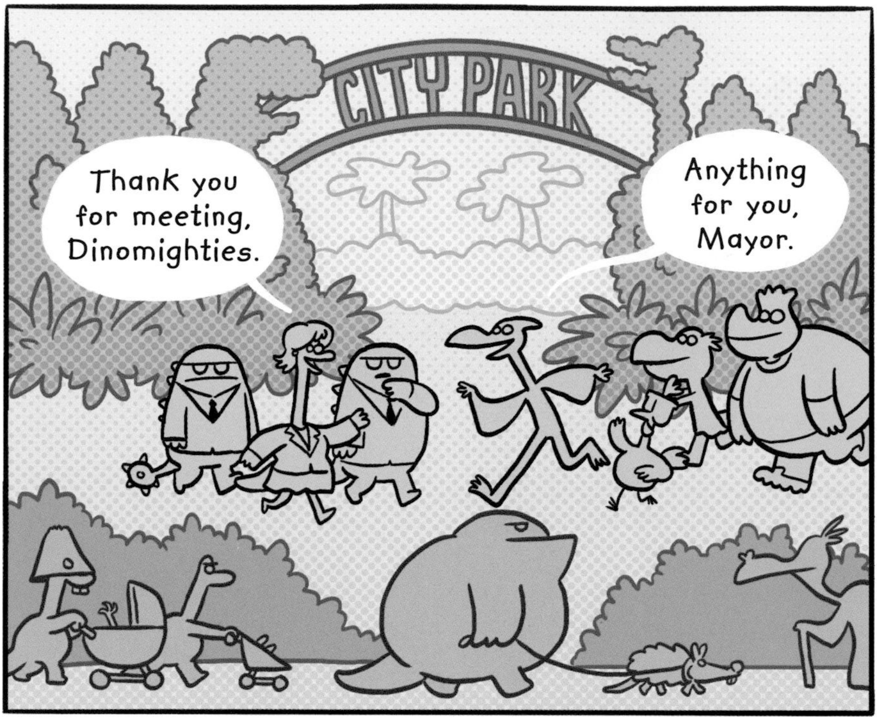
CITY PARK
Thank you for meeting, Dinomighties.
Anything for you, Mayor.

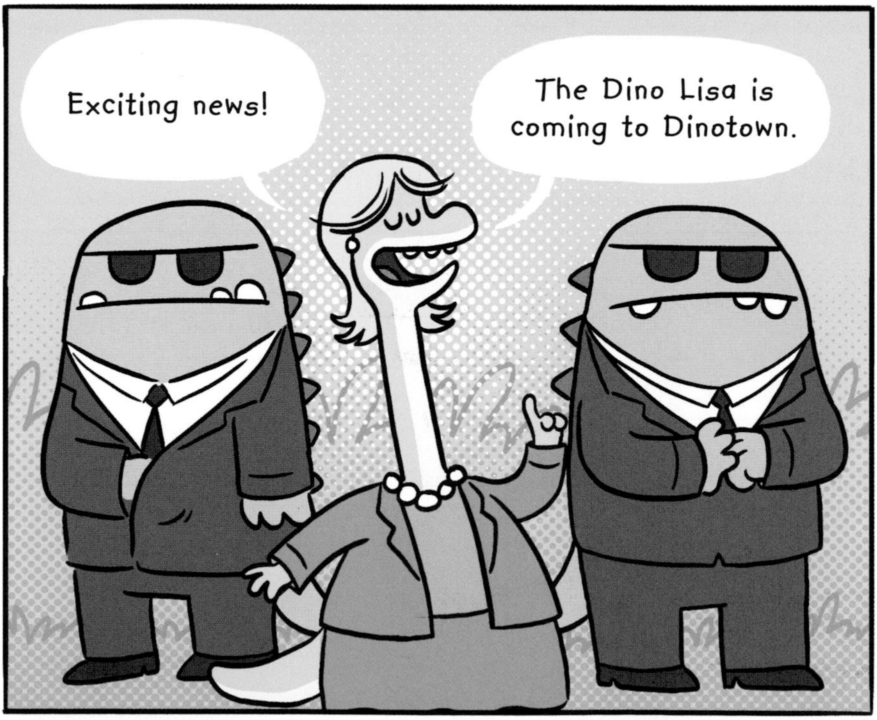
Exciting news!
The Dino Lisa is coming to Dinotown.

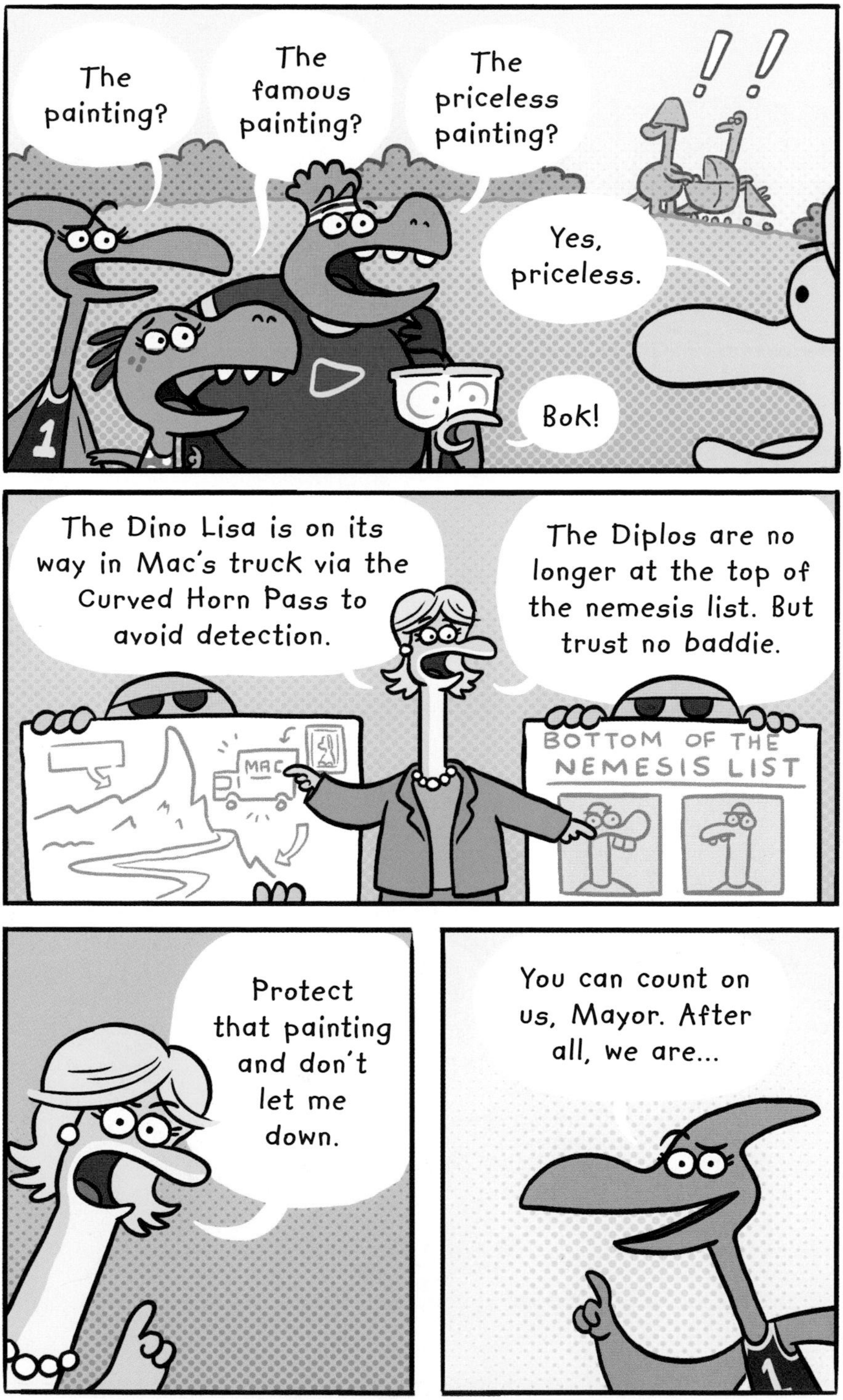
The painting?
The famous painting?
The priceless painting?
Yes, priceless.
Bok!
The Dino Lisa is on its way in Mac's truck via the Curved Horn Pass to avoid detection.
MAC
The Diplos are no longer at the top of the nemesis list. But trust no baddie.
BOTTOM OF THE NEMESIS LIST
Protect that painting and don't let me down.
You can count on us, Mayor. After all, we are...

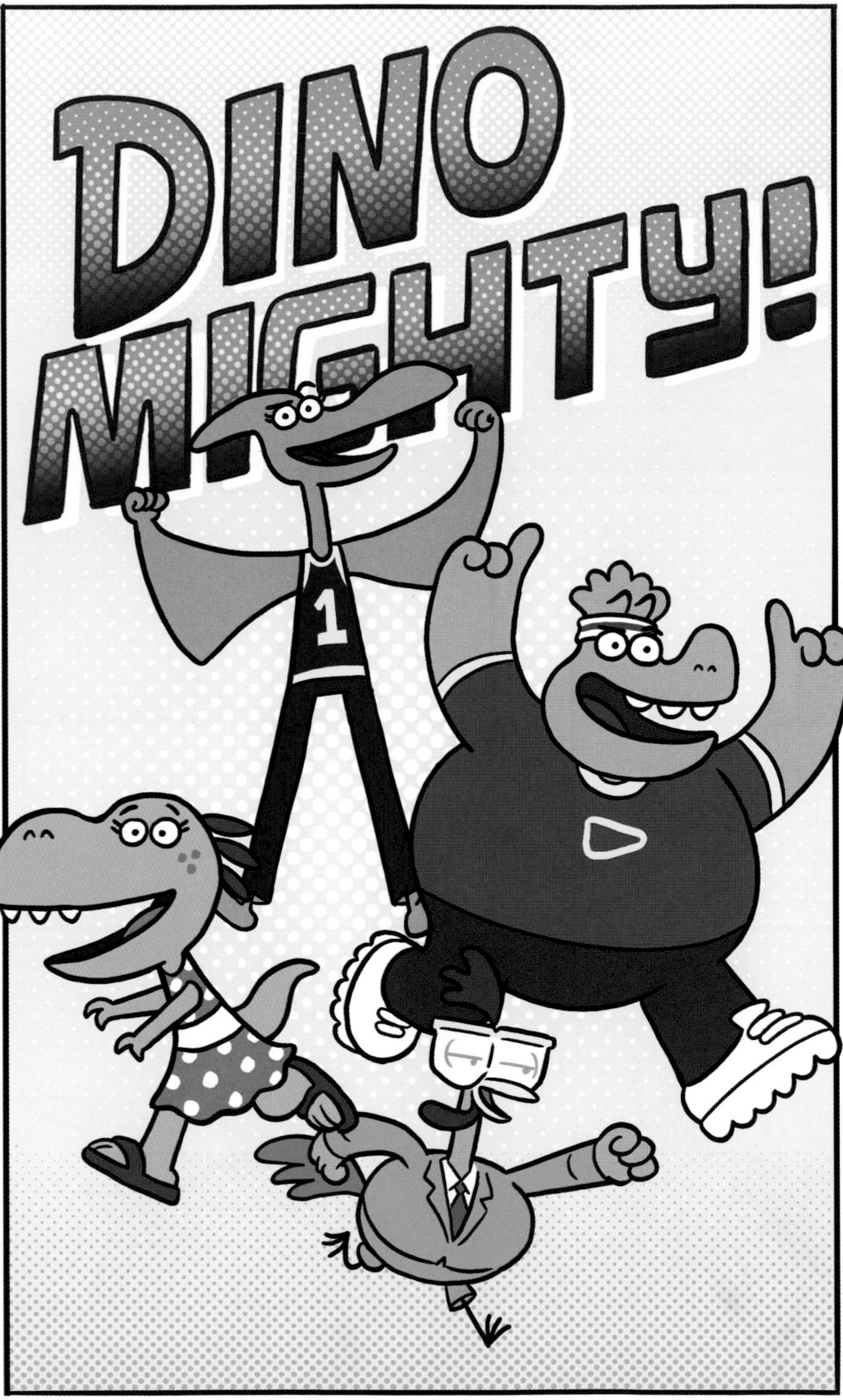
DINO MIGHTY!

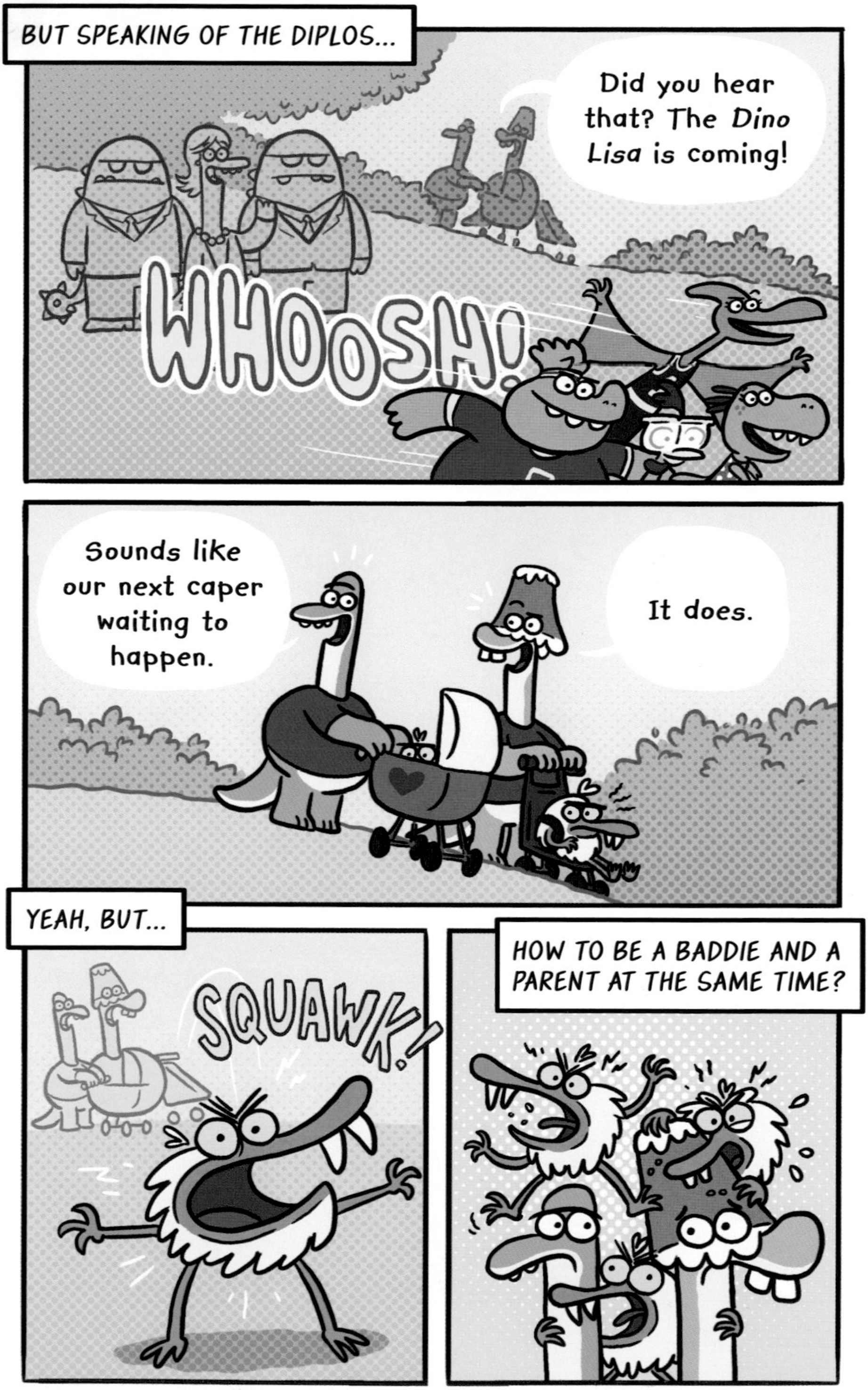
BUT SPEAKING OF THE DIPLOS...
Did you hear that? The *Dino Lisa* is coming!
WHOOSH!
Sounds like our next caper waiting to happen.
It does.
YEAH, BUT...
SQUAWK!
HOW TO BE A BADDIE AND A PARENT AT THE SAME TIME?

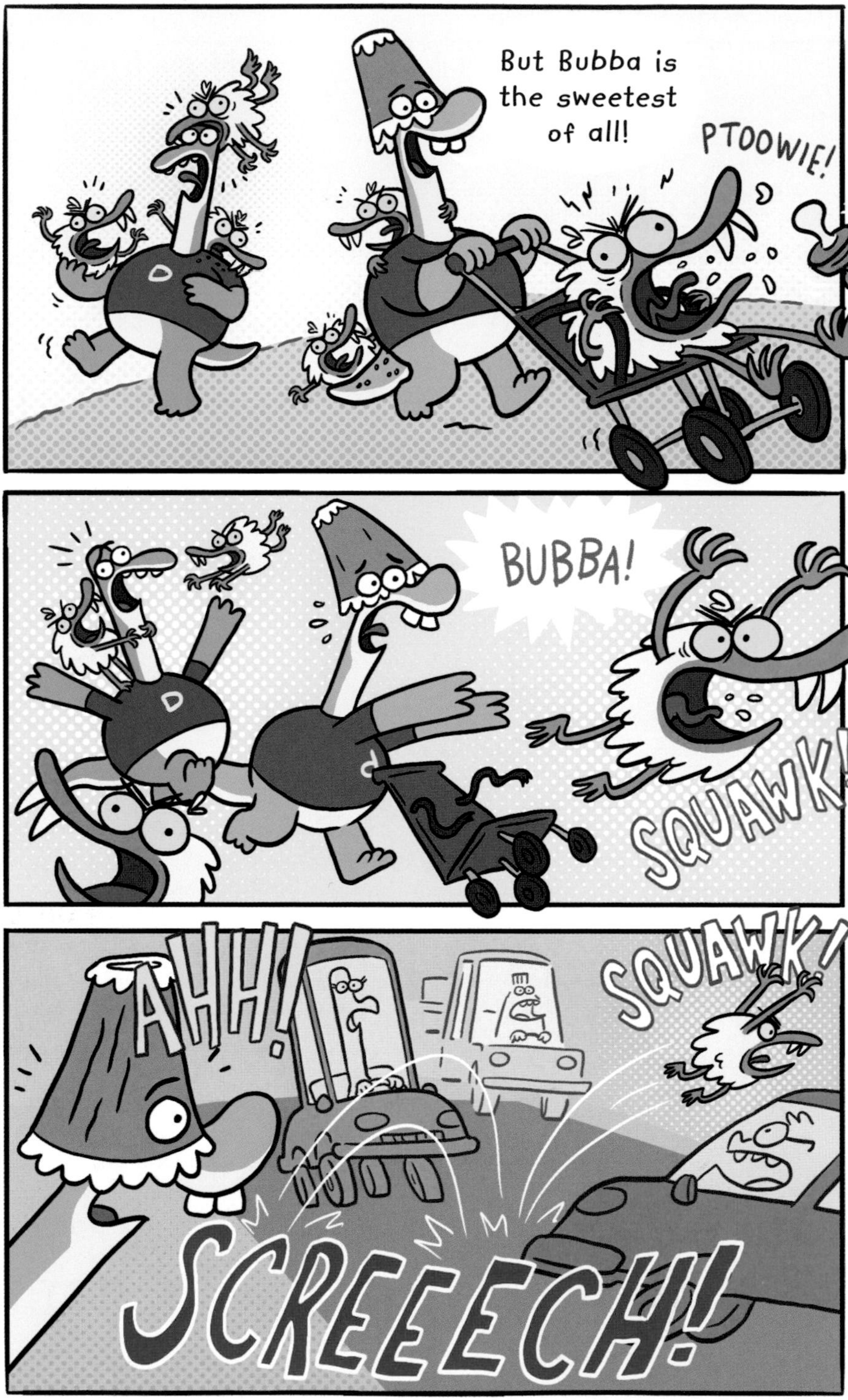
But Bubba is the sweetest of all!
PTOOWIE!
BUBBA!
SQUAWK!
AHH!
SQUAWK!
SCREEECH!

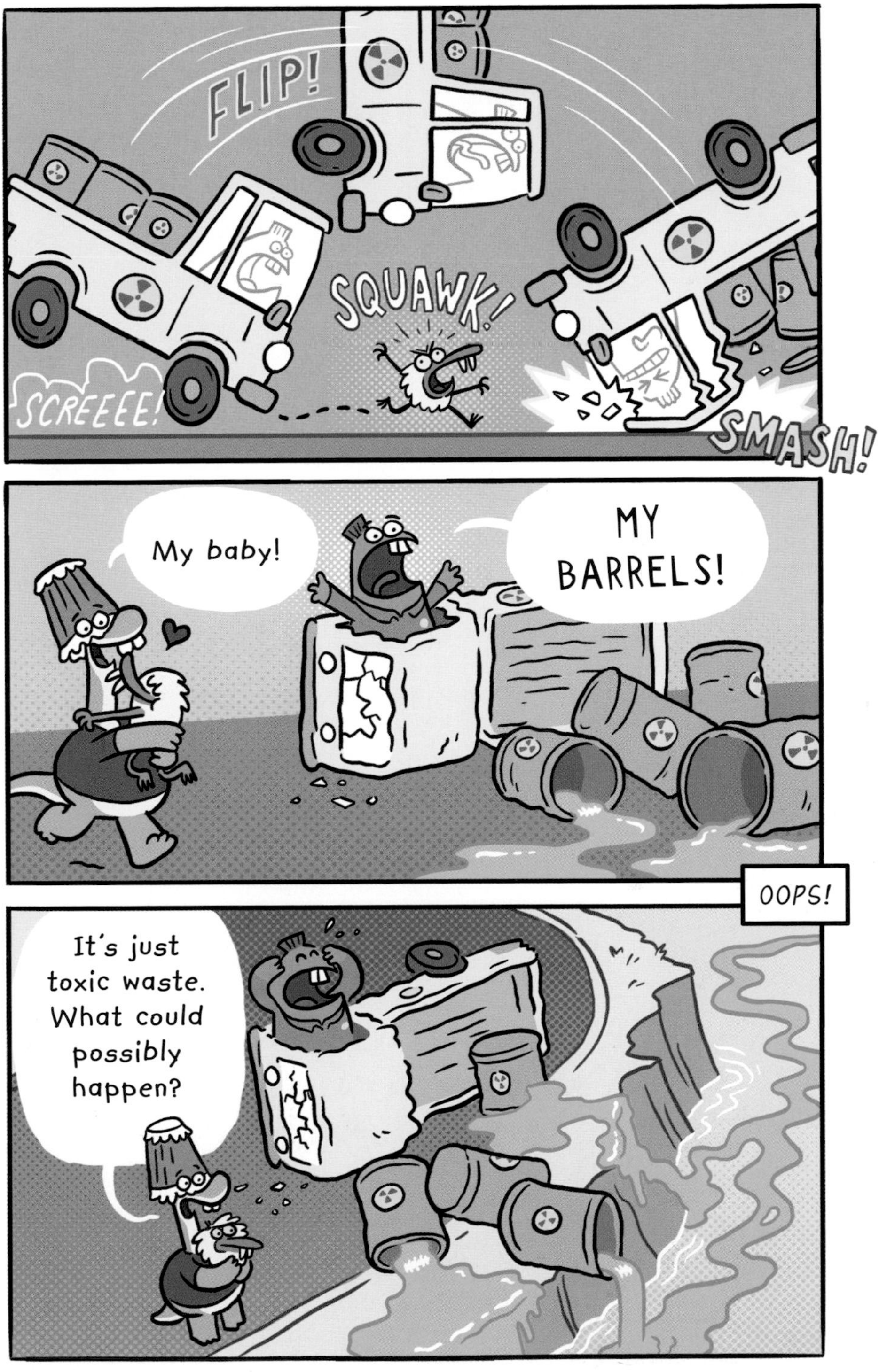
FLIP!
SQUAWK!
SCREEEE!
SMASH!
My baby!
MY BARRELS!
OOPS!
It's just toxic waste. What could possibly happen?

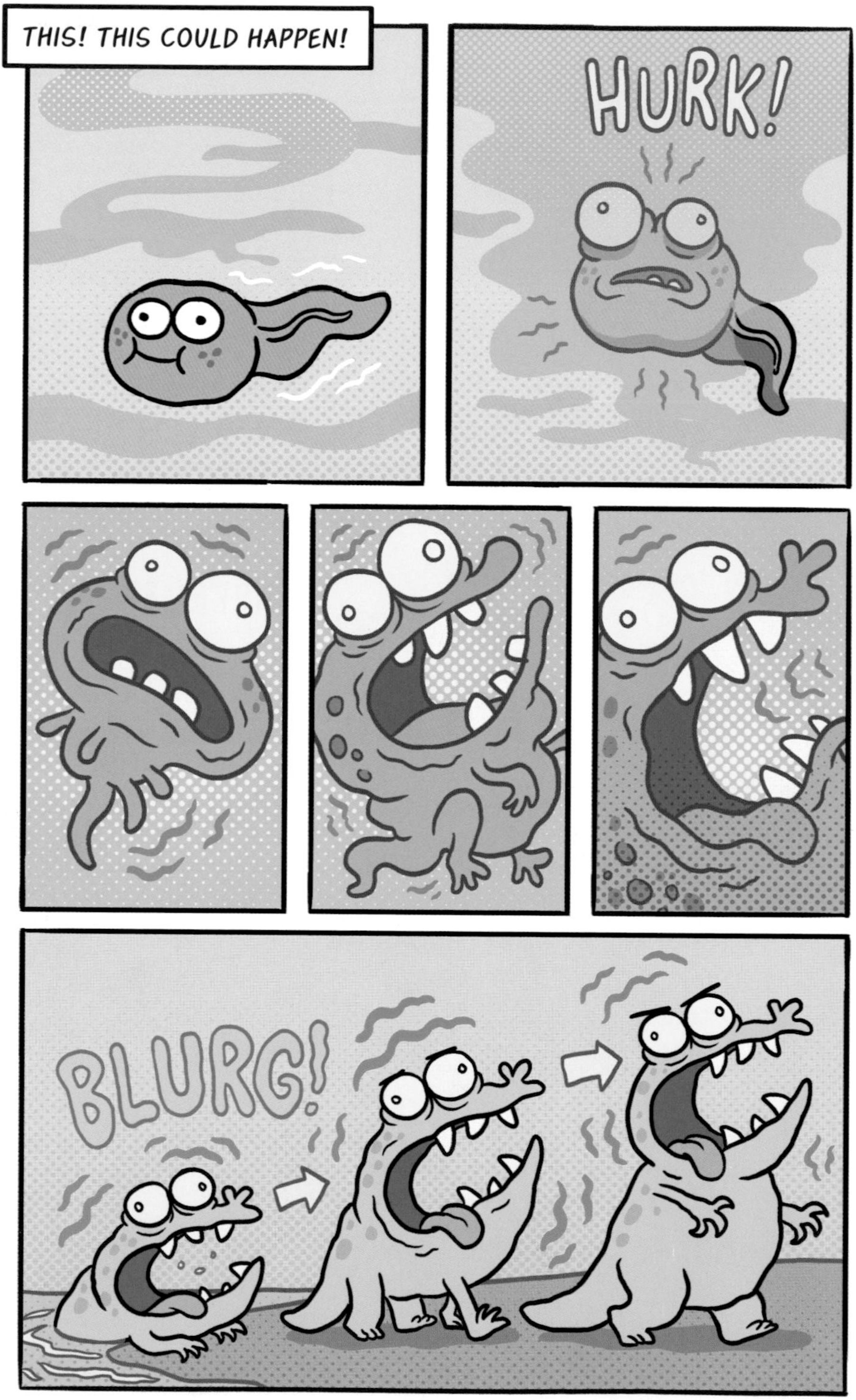
THIS! THIS COULD HAPPEN!
HURK!
BLURG!

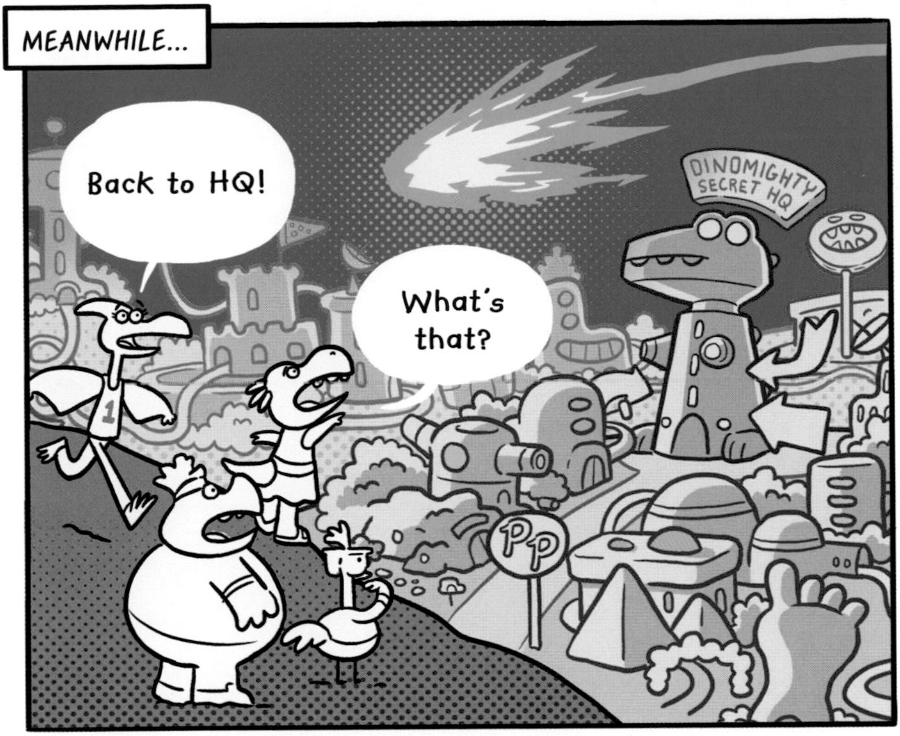
MEANWHILE...
Back to HQ!
What's that?
DINOMIGHTY SECRET HQ
PP

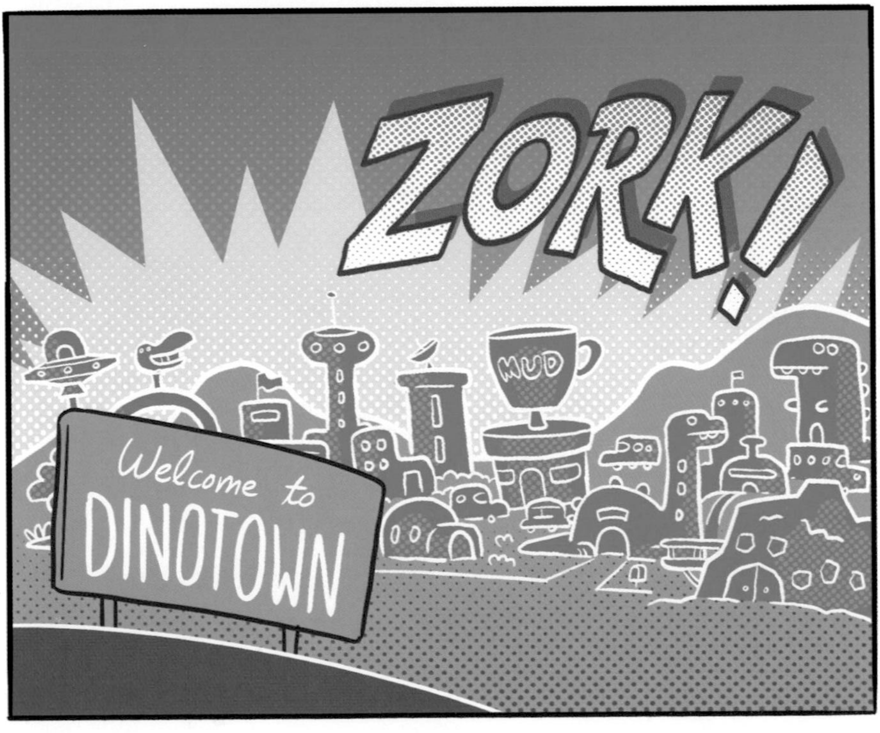
ZORK!
MUD
Welcome to DINOTOWN

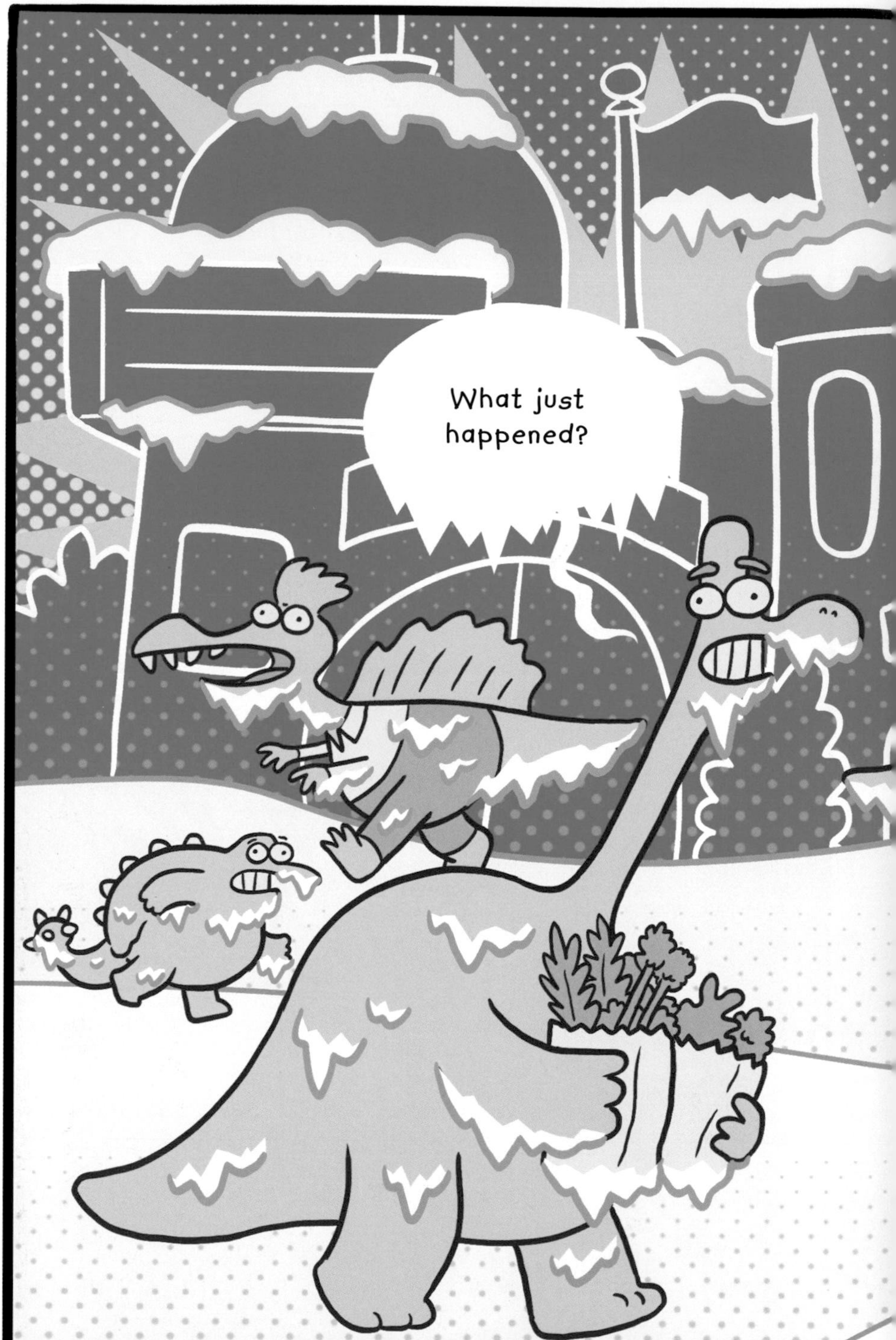
What just happened?

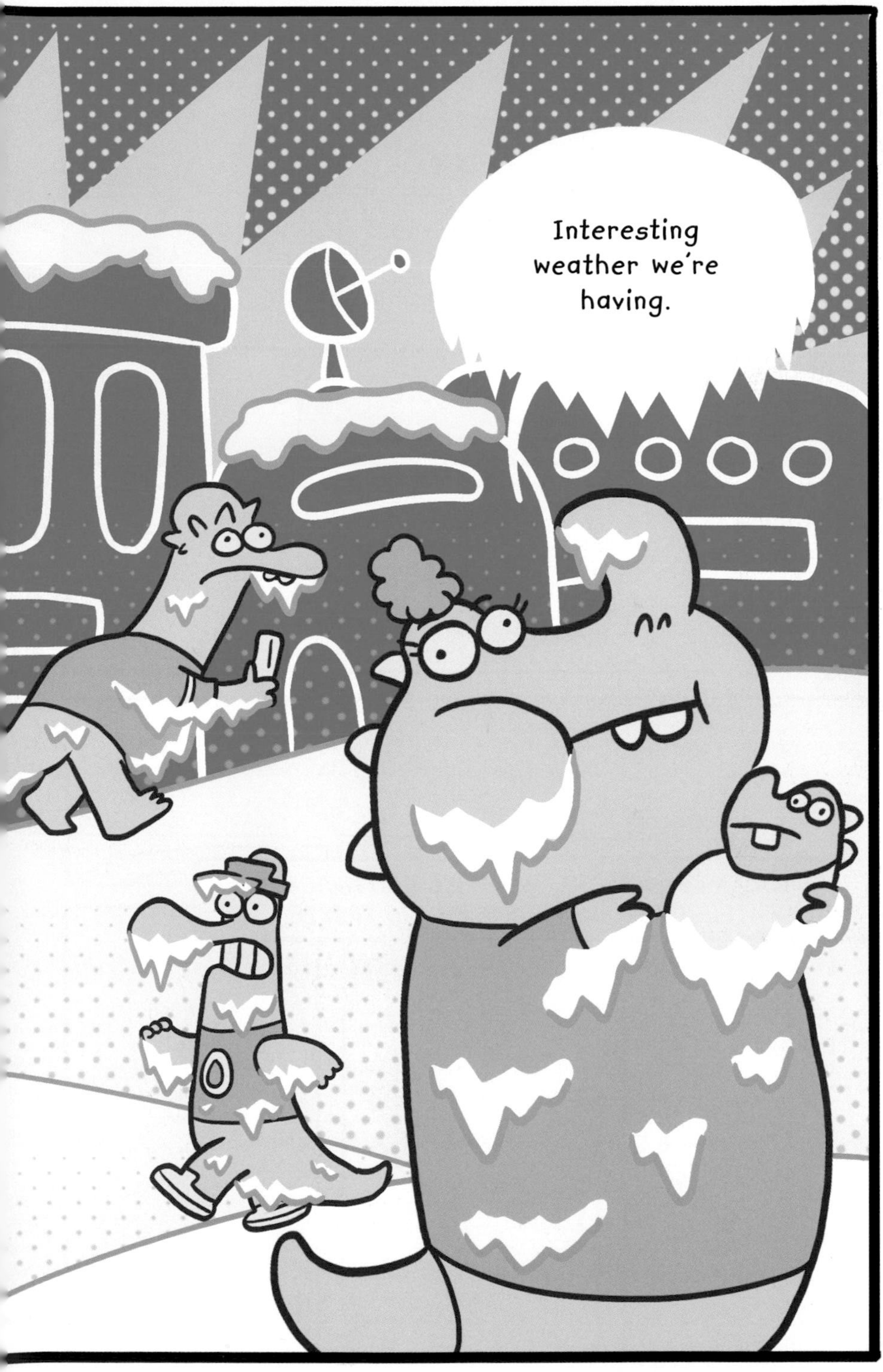
Interesting weather we're having.

Back to headquarters! NOW!

CRACK!

WATERSLIDES

CANNONBALL!

IF THERE WAS A REASON THE 'MIGHTIES SHOULDN'T JUMP ON THEIR WATERSLIDES RIGHT AFTER A BIG FREEZE...

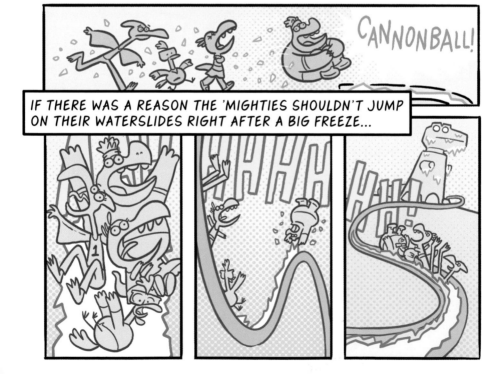

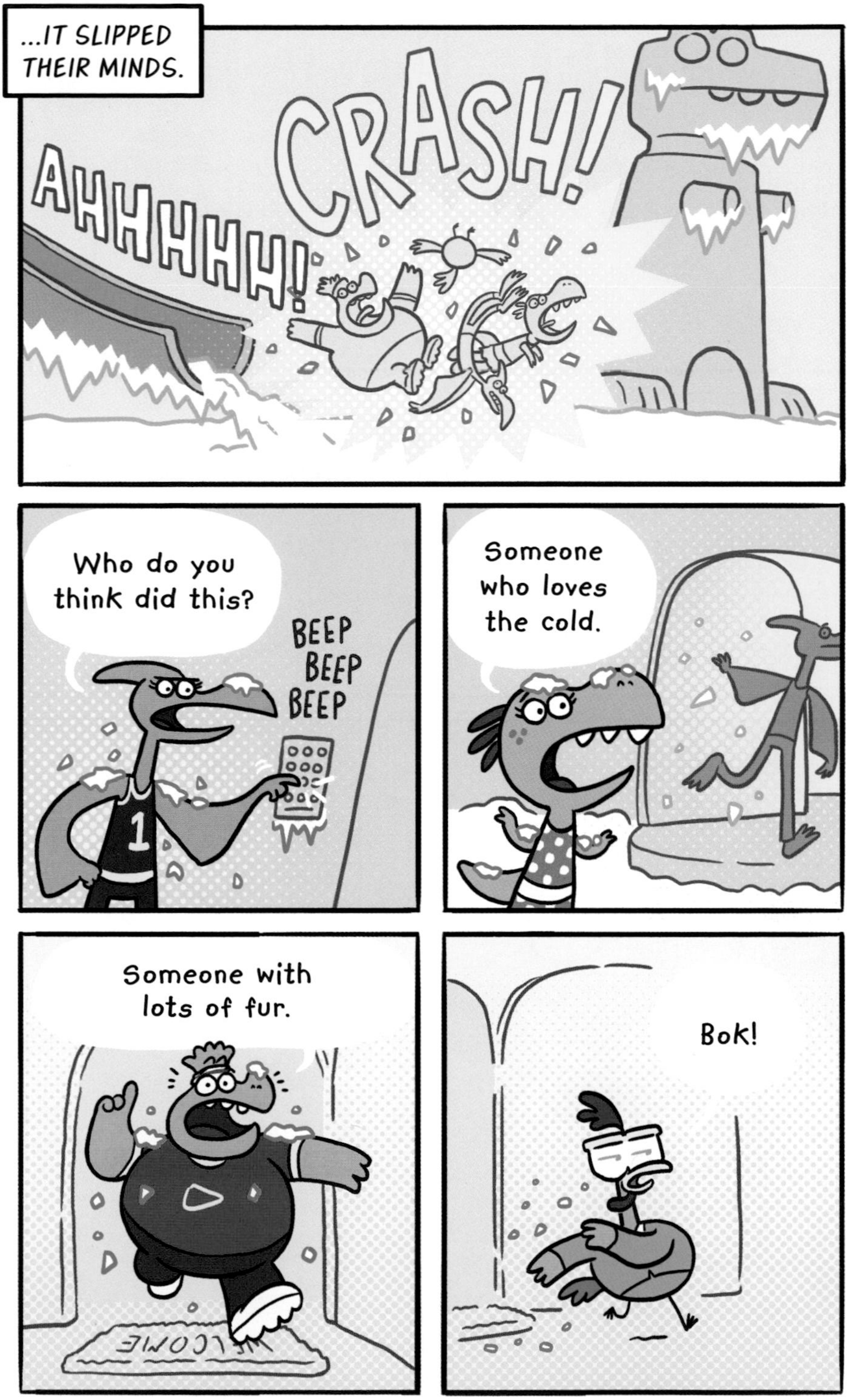
...IT SLIPPED THEIR MINDS.
AHHHHHH!
CRASH!
Who do you think did this?
BEEP
BEEP
BEEP
Someone who loves the cold.
Someone with lots of fur.
Bok!

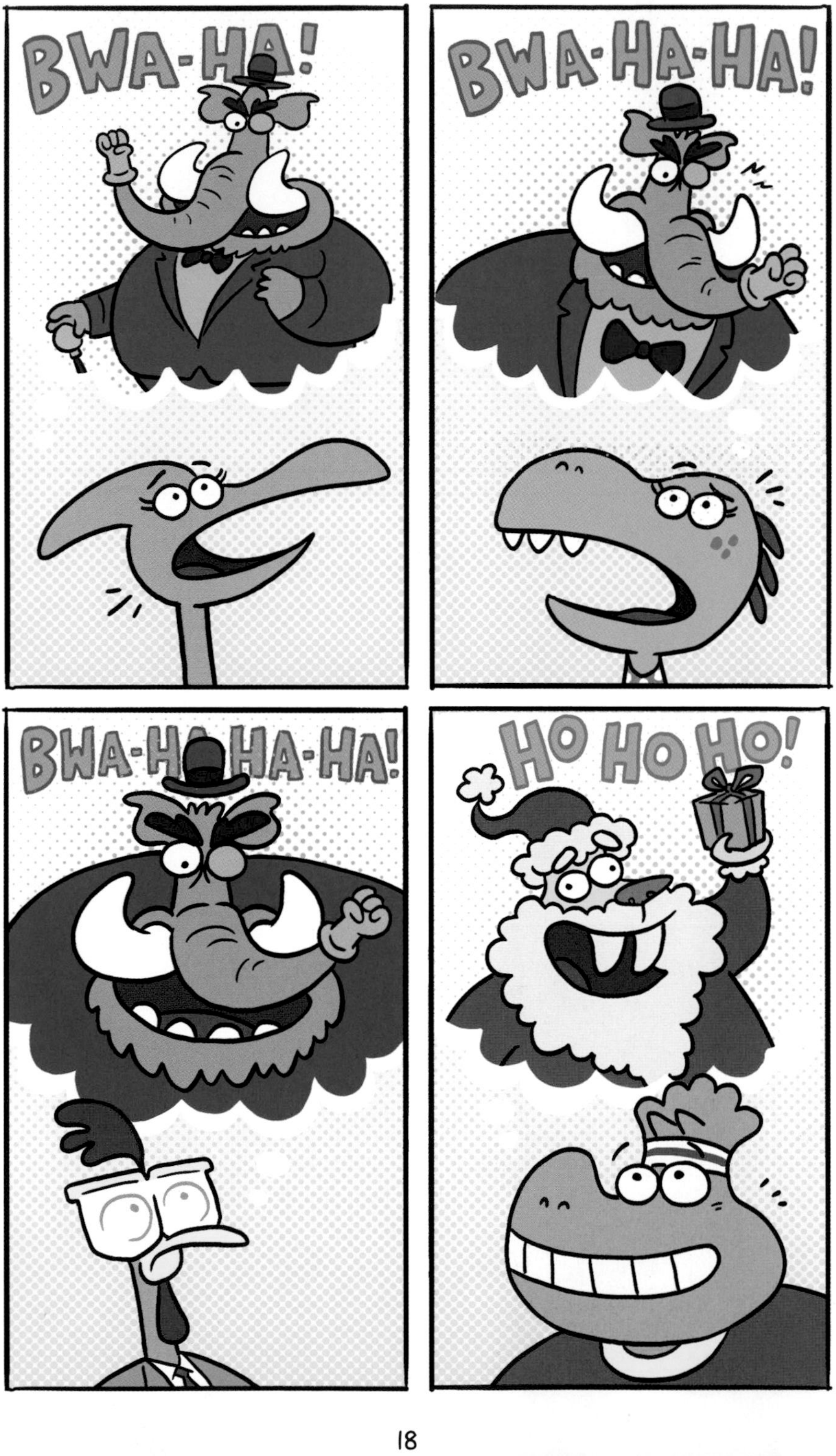
BWA-HA!
BWA-HA-HA!
BWA-HA-HA-HA!
HO HO HO!

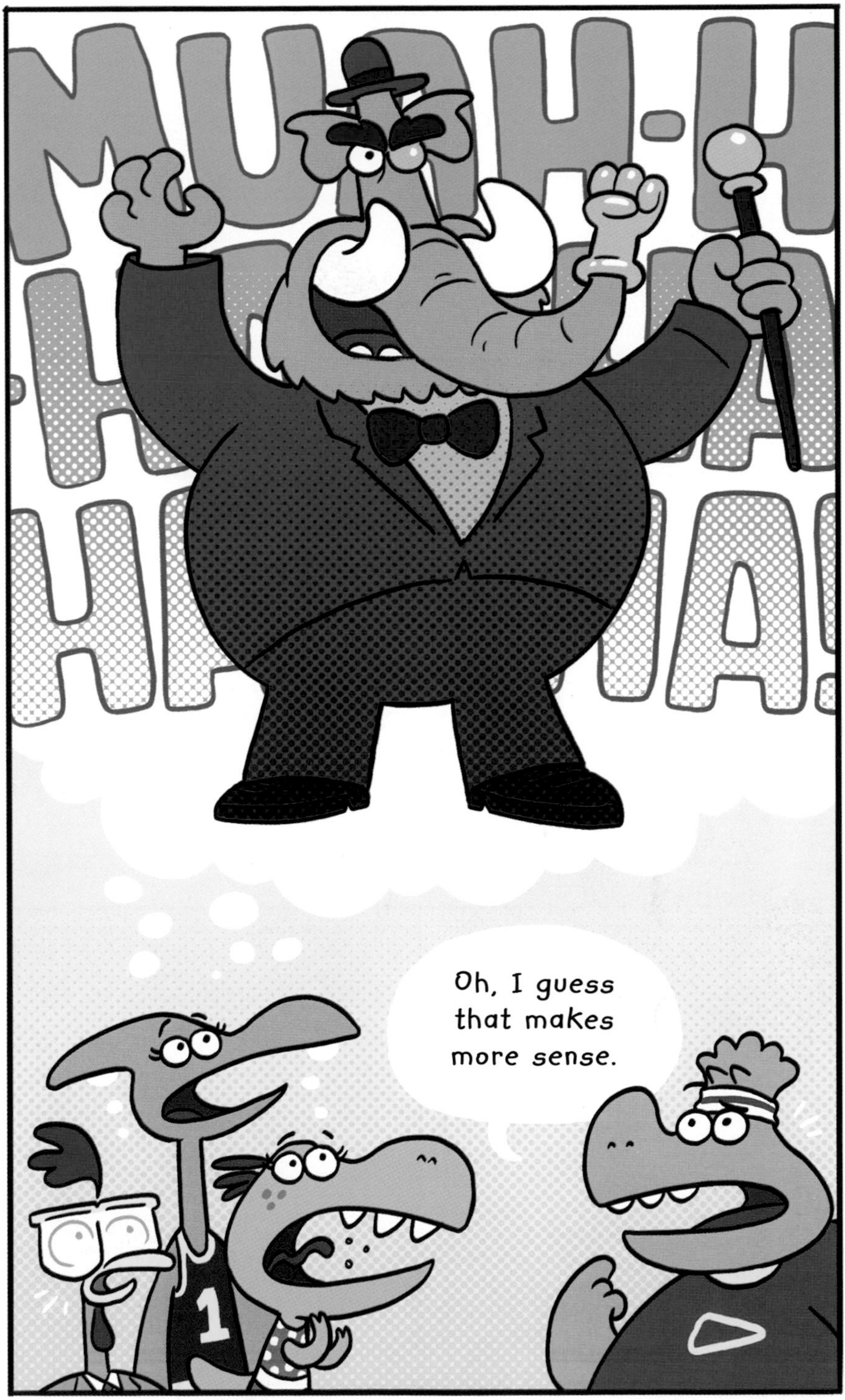
Oh, I guess that makes more sense.

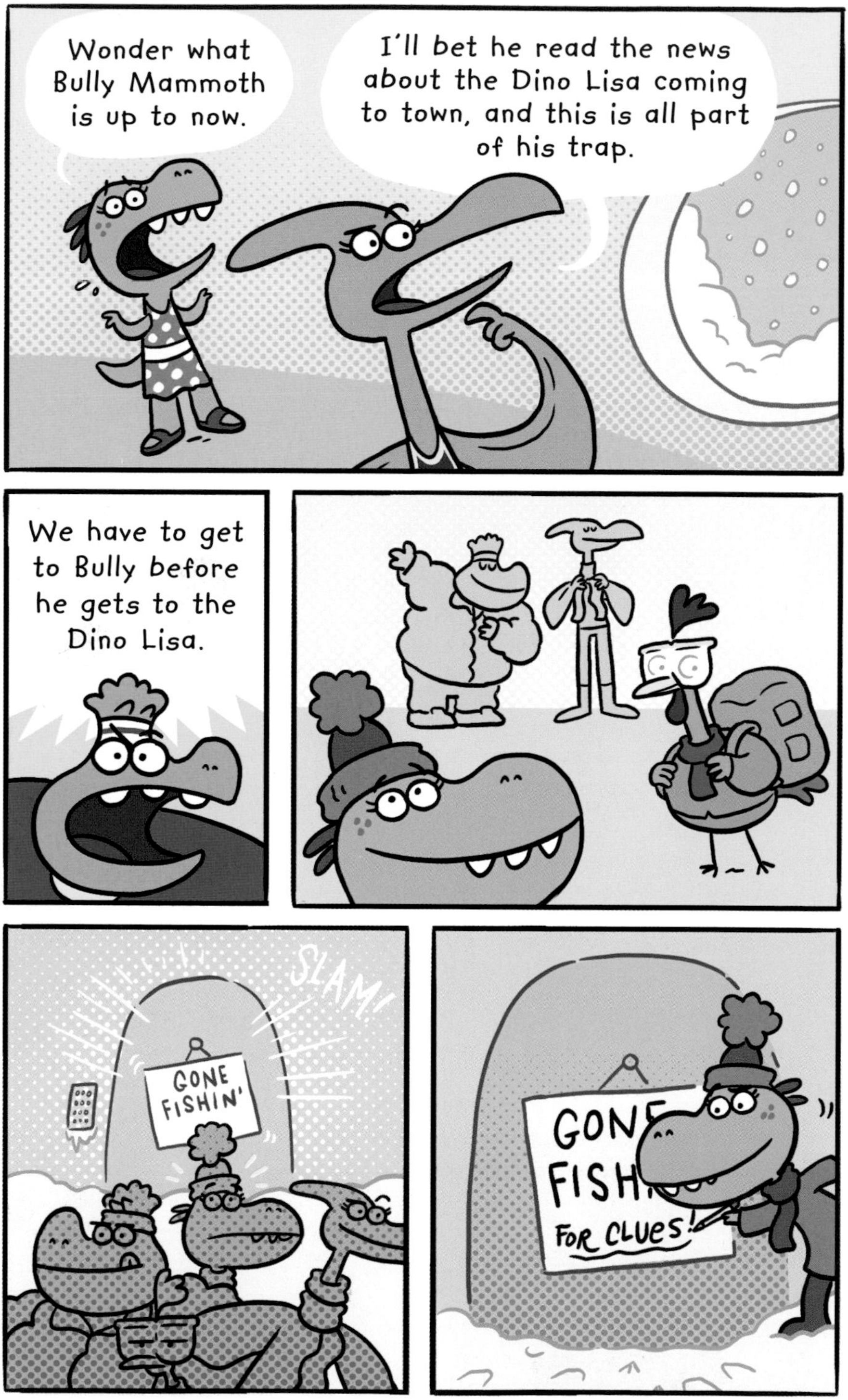
Wonder what Bully Mammoth is up to now.
I'll bet he read the news about the Dino Lisa coming to town, and this is all part of his trap.
We have to get to Bully before he gets to the Dino Lisa.
SLAM!
GONE FISHIN'
GONE FISH... FOR CLUES!

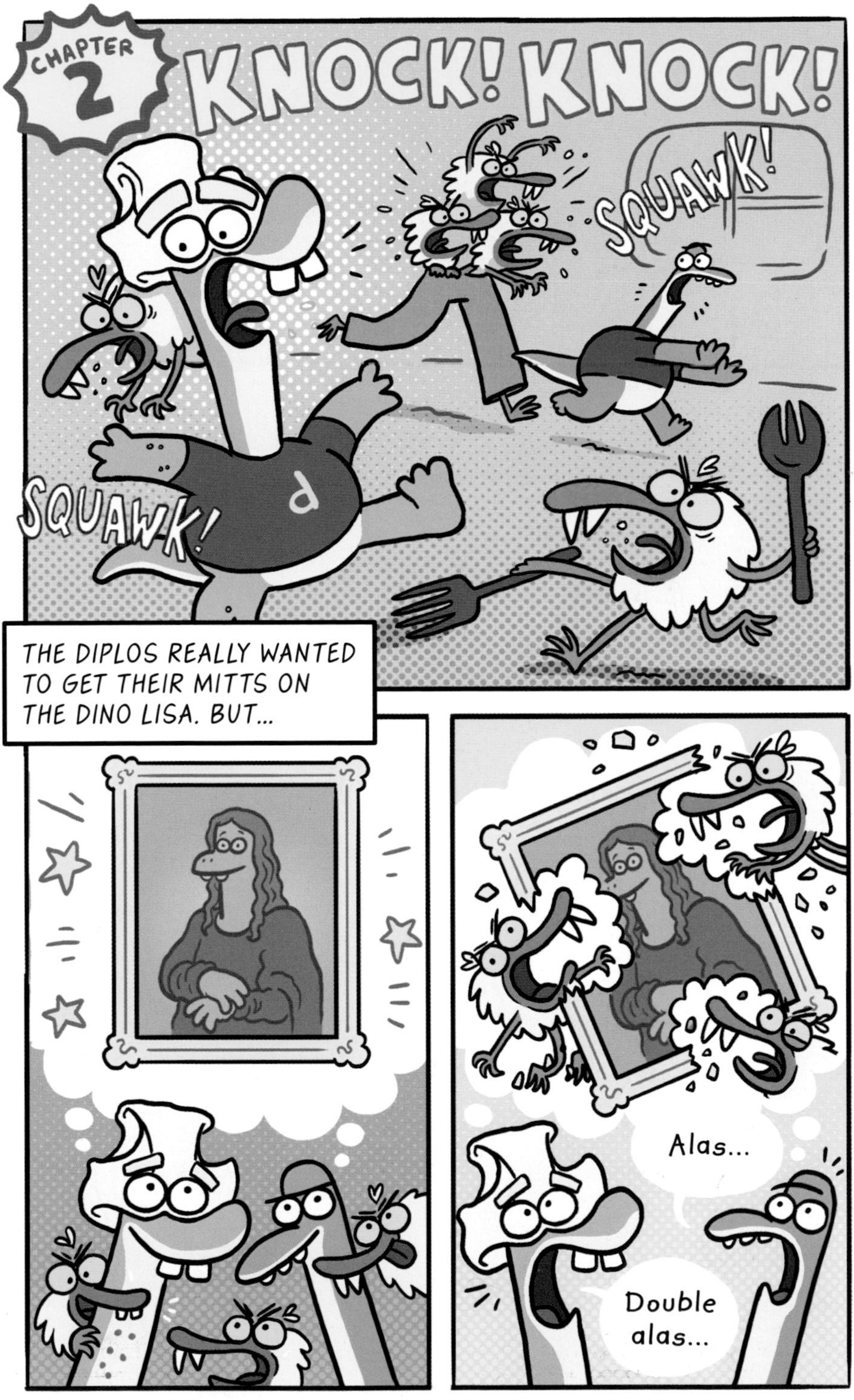
CHAPTER 2
KNOCK! KNOCK!
SQUAWK!
SQUAWK!
THE DIPLOS REALLY WANTED TO GET THEIR MITTS ON THE DINO LISA. BUT...
Alas...
Double alas...

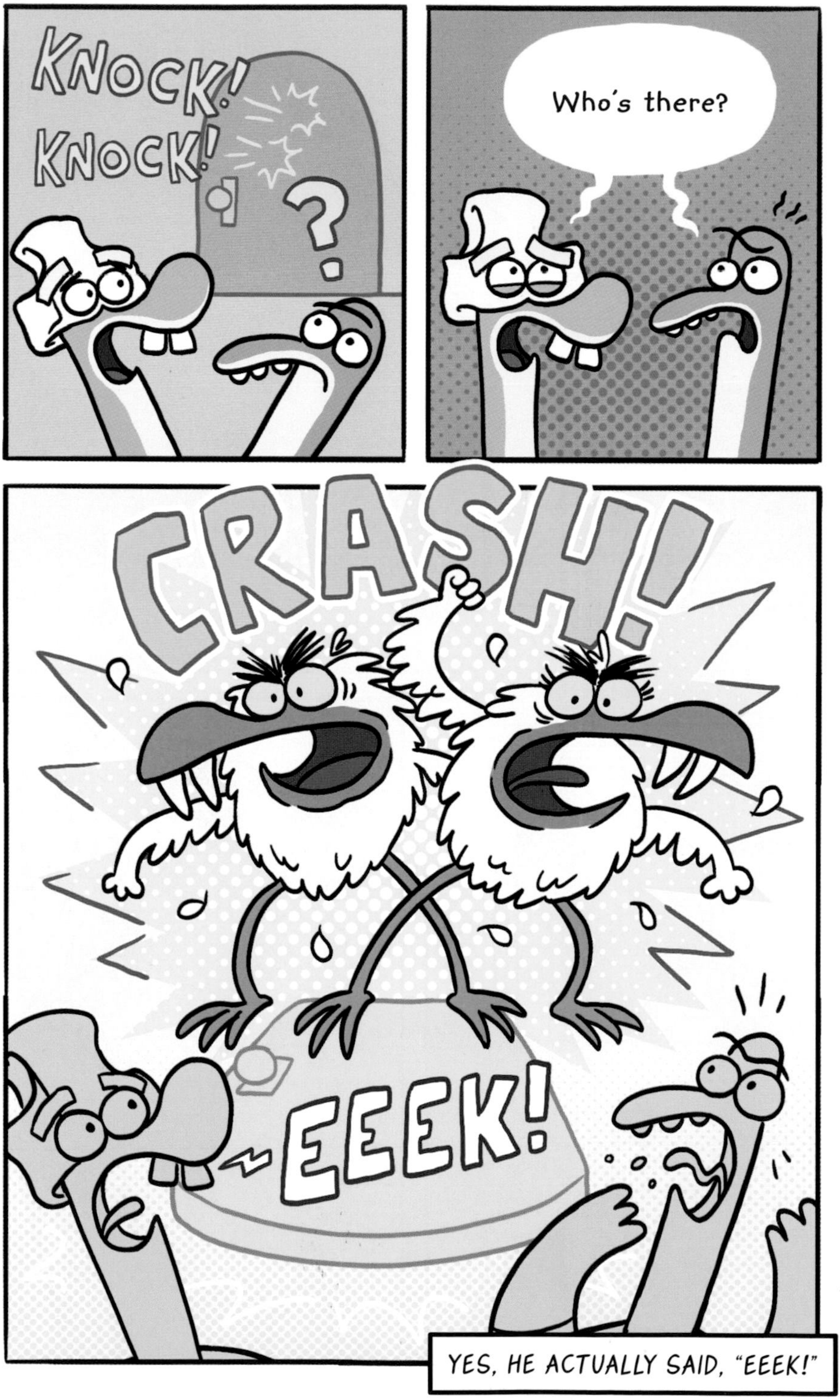
KNOCK! KNOCK!
?
Who's there?
CRASH!
EEEK!
YES, HE ACTUALLY SAID, "EEEK!"

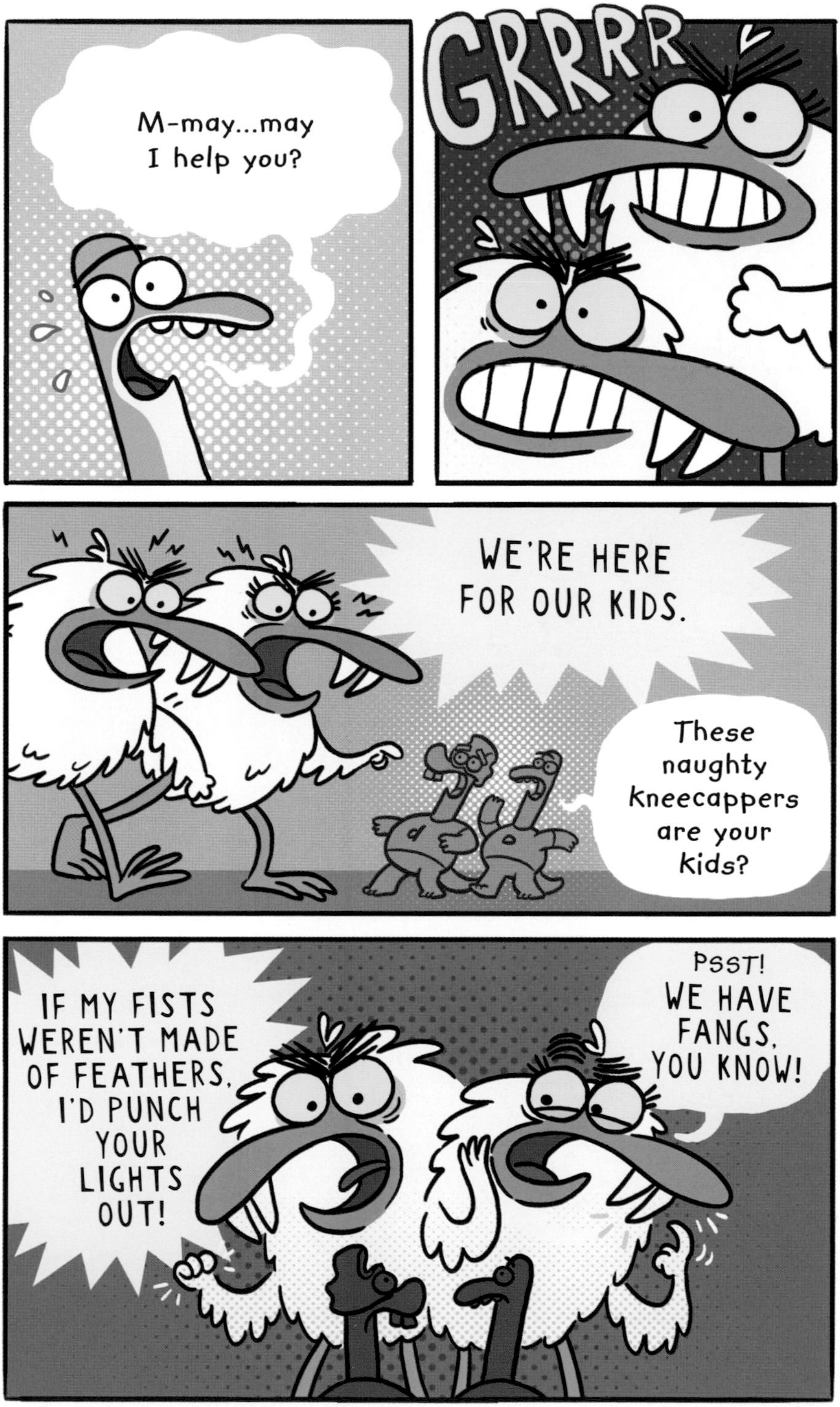
M-may...may I help you?
GRRRR
WE'RE HERE FOR OUR KIDS.
These naughty Kneecappers are your kids?
IF MY FISTS WEREN'T MADE OF FEATHERS, I'D PUNCH YOUR LIGHTS OUT!
PSST! WE HAVE FANGS, YOU KNOW!

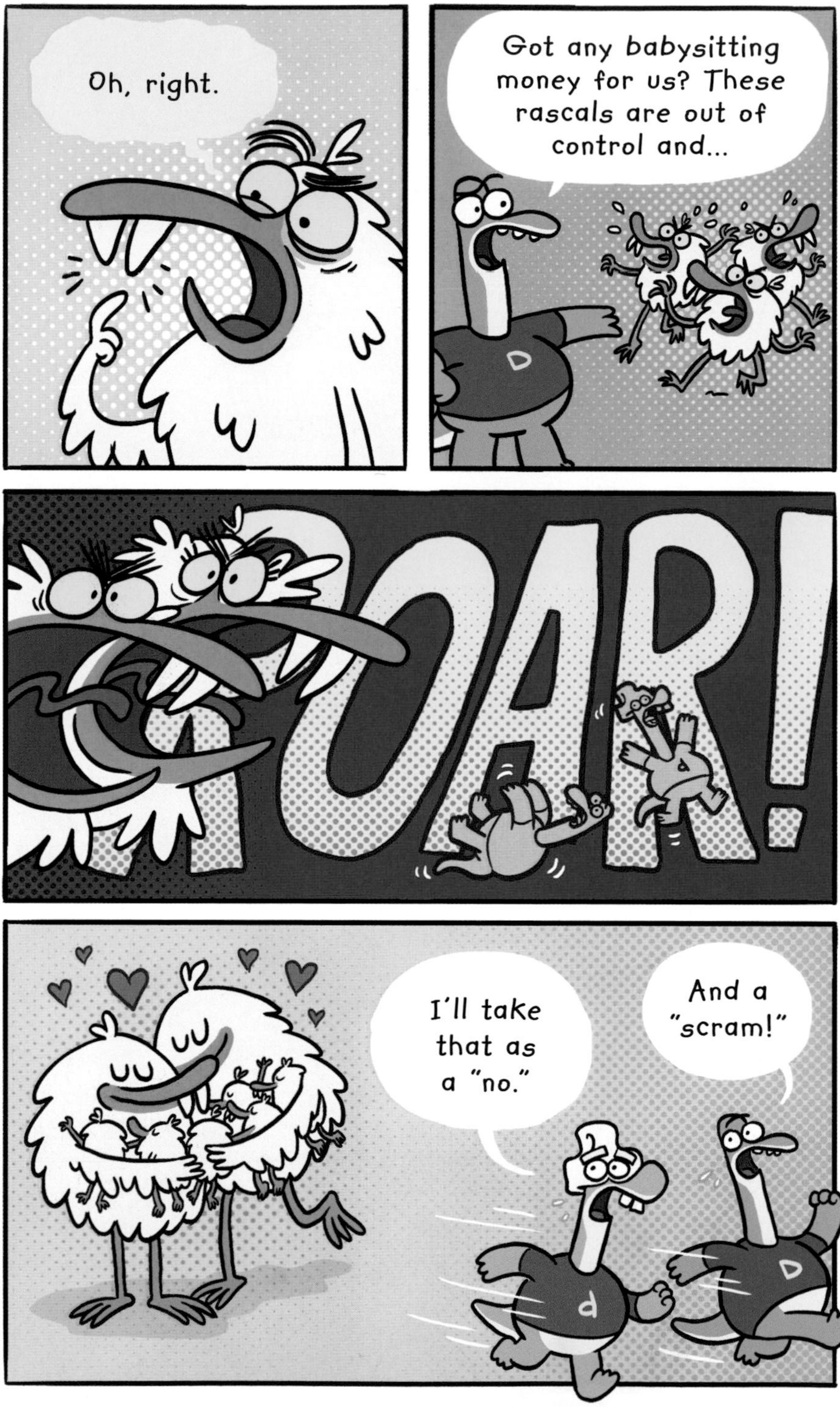
Oh, right.
Got any babysitting money for us? These rascals are out of control and...
ROAR!
I'll take that as a "no."
And a "scram!"

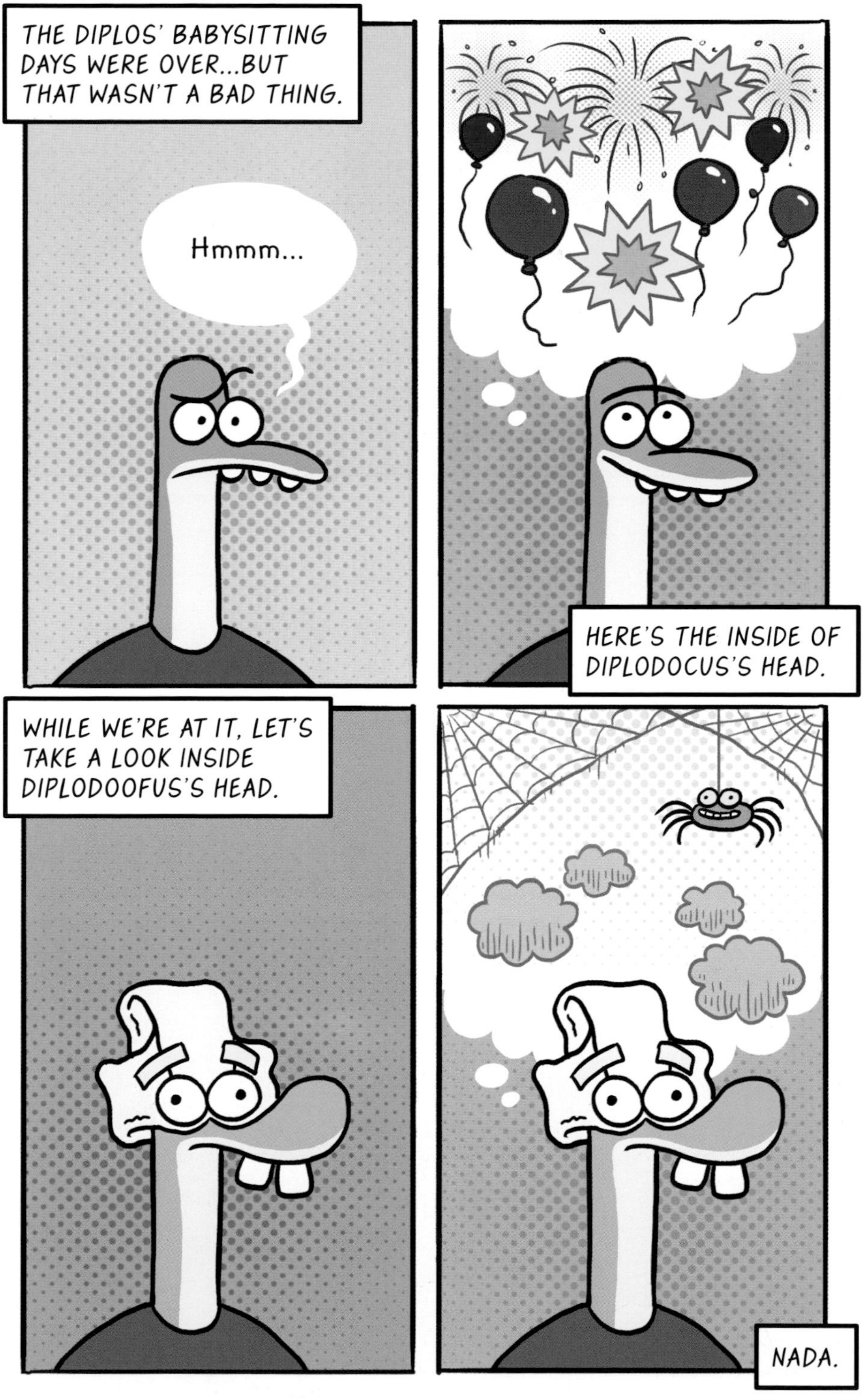
THE DIPLOS' BABYSITTING DAYS WERE OVER...BUT THAT WASN'T A BAD THING.
Hmmm...
HERE'S THE INSIDE OF DIPLODOCUS'S HEAD.
WHILE WE'RE AT IT, LET'S TAKE A LOOK INSIDE DIPLODOOFUS'S HEAD.
NADA.

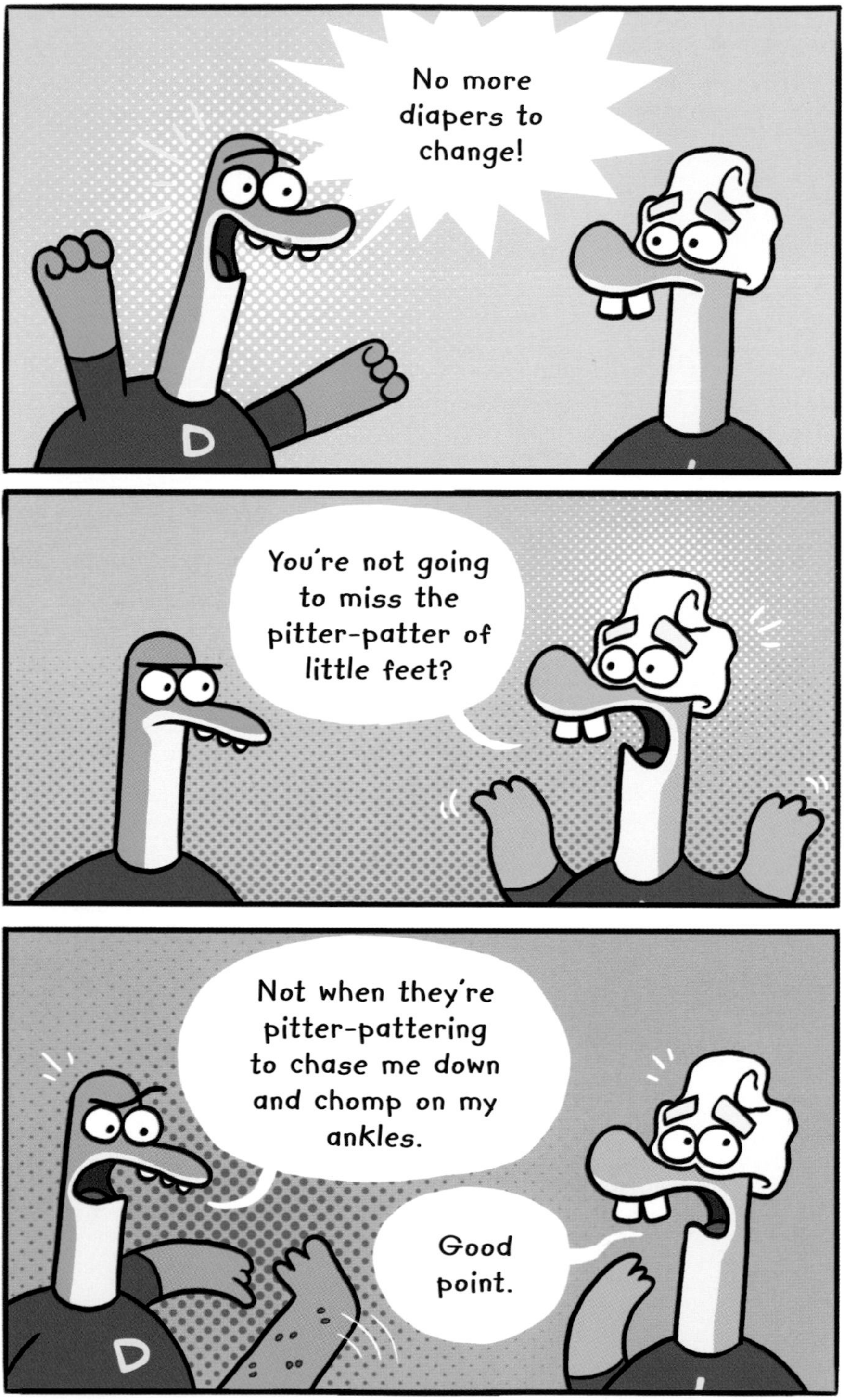
No more diapers to change!
You're not going to miss the pitter-patter of little feet?
Not when they're pitter-pattering to chase me down and chomp on my ankles.
Good point.

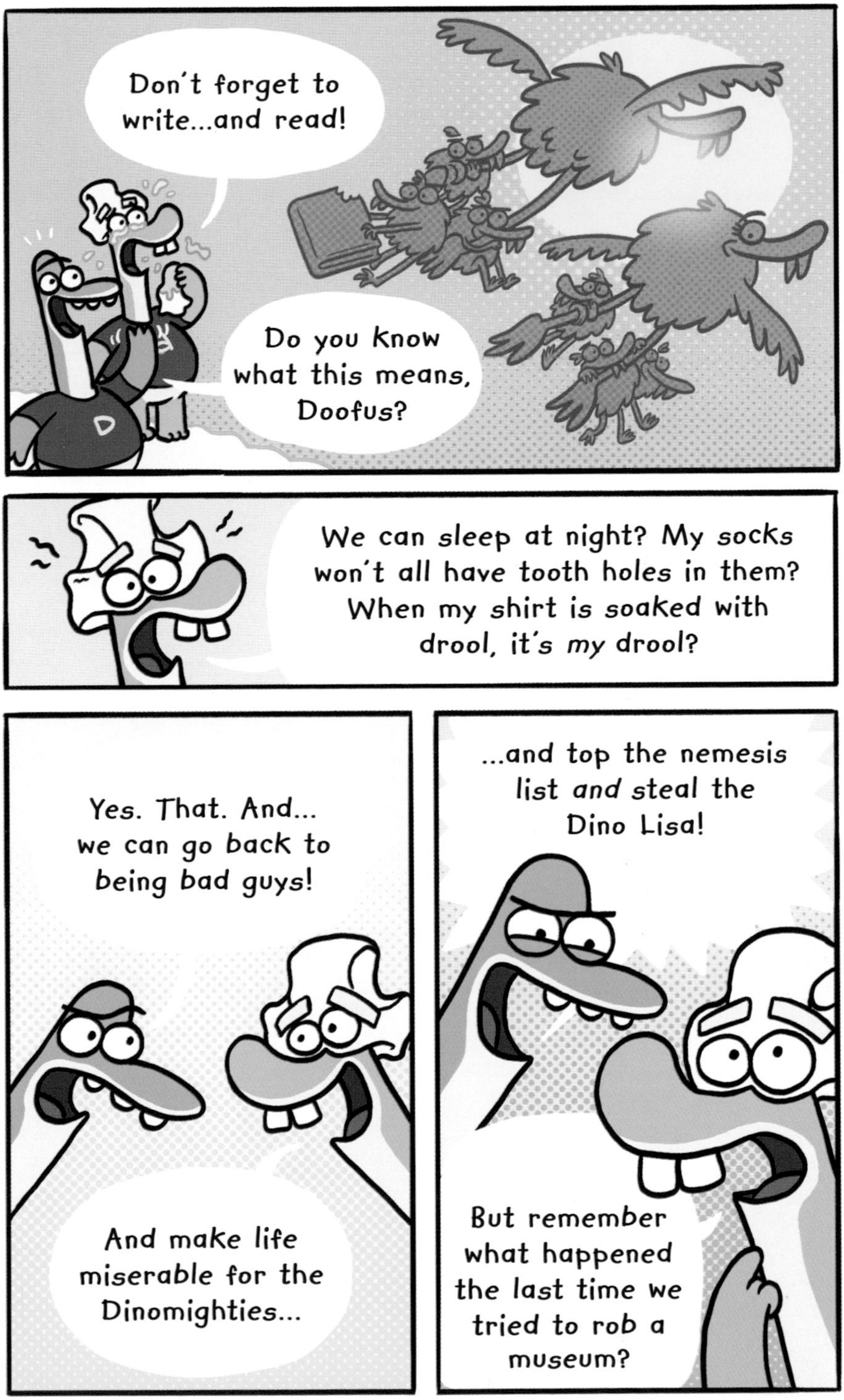
Don't forget to write...and read!
Do you know what this means, Doofus?
We can sleep at night? My socks won't all have tooth holes in them? When my shirt is soaked with drool, it's *my* drool?
Yes. That. And... we can *go back* to being bad guys!
And make life miserable for the Dinomighties...
...and top the nemesis list *and* steal the Dino Lisa!
But remember what happened the last time we tried to rob a museum?

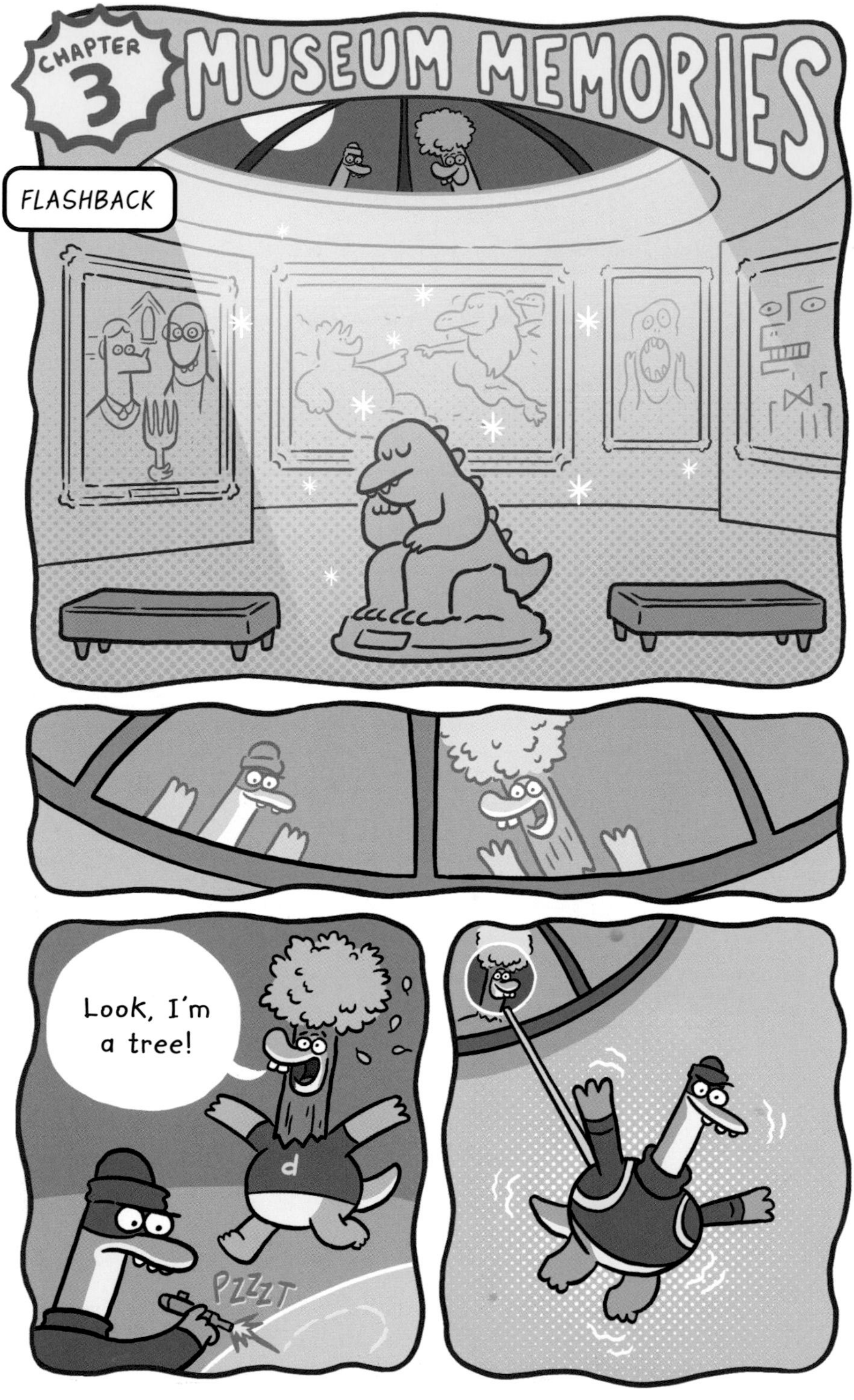
CHAPTER 3
MUSEUM MEMORIES
FLASHBACK
Look, I'm a tree!
d
PZZZT

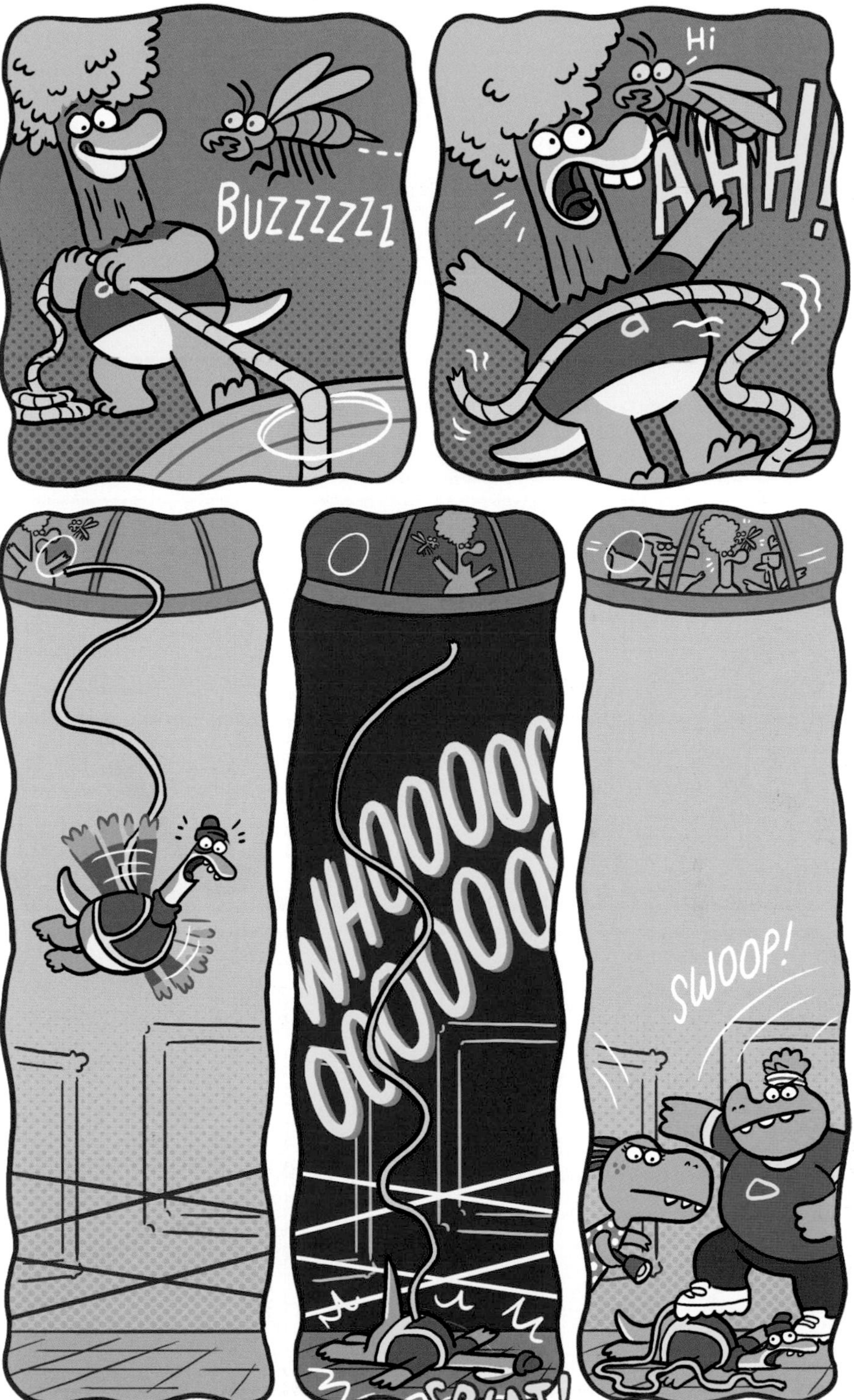
BUZZZZZZ
Hi
AHH!
WHOOOOOOOOOOOOO
SPLAT!
SWOOP!

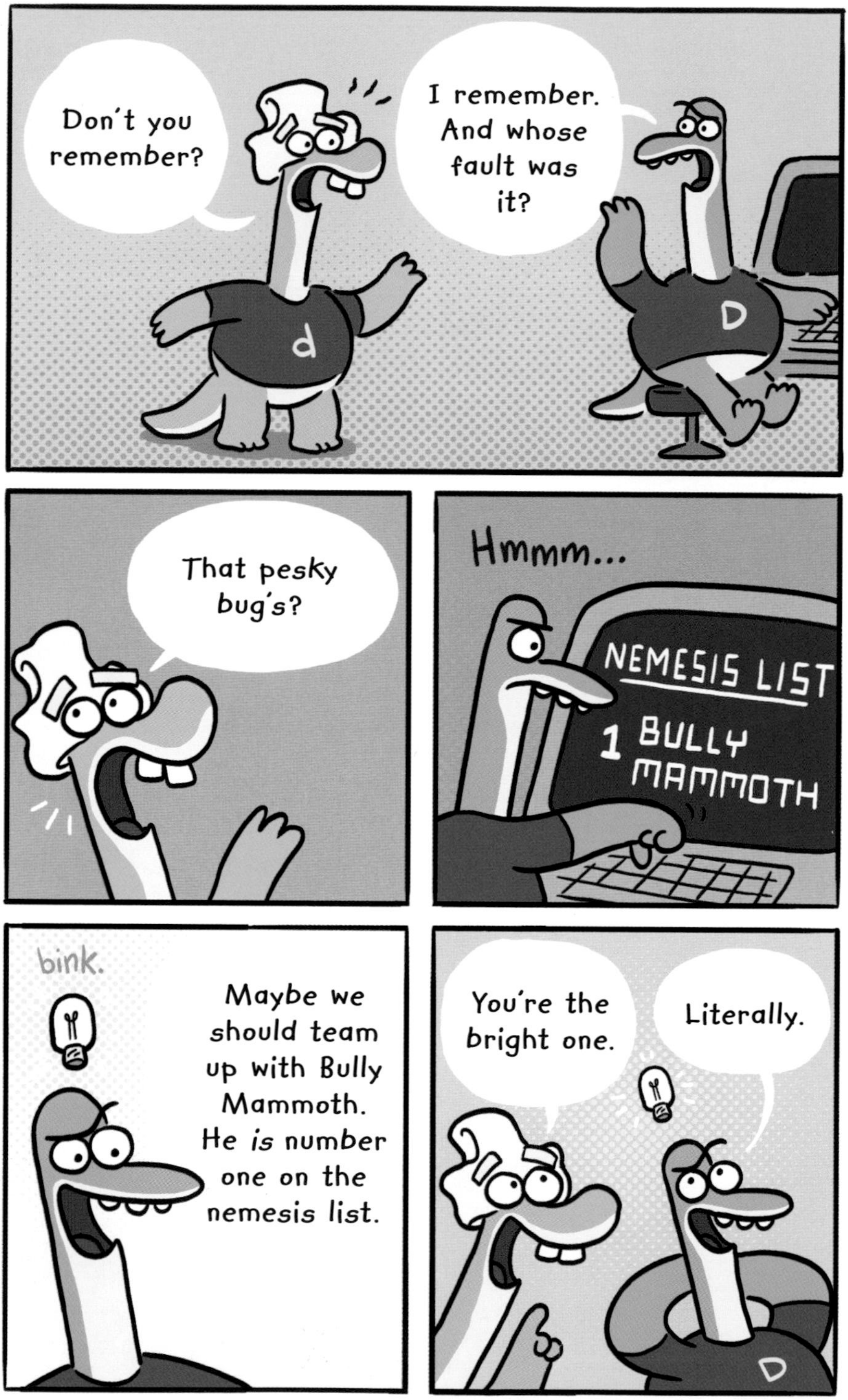
Don't you remember?
I remember. And whose fault was it?
d
D
That pesky bug's?
Hmmm...
NEMESIS LIST
1 BULLY MAMMOTH
bink.
Maybe we should team up with Bully Mammoth. He *is* number one on the nemesis list.
You're the bright one.
Literally.
D

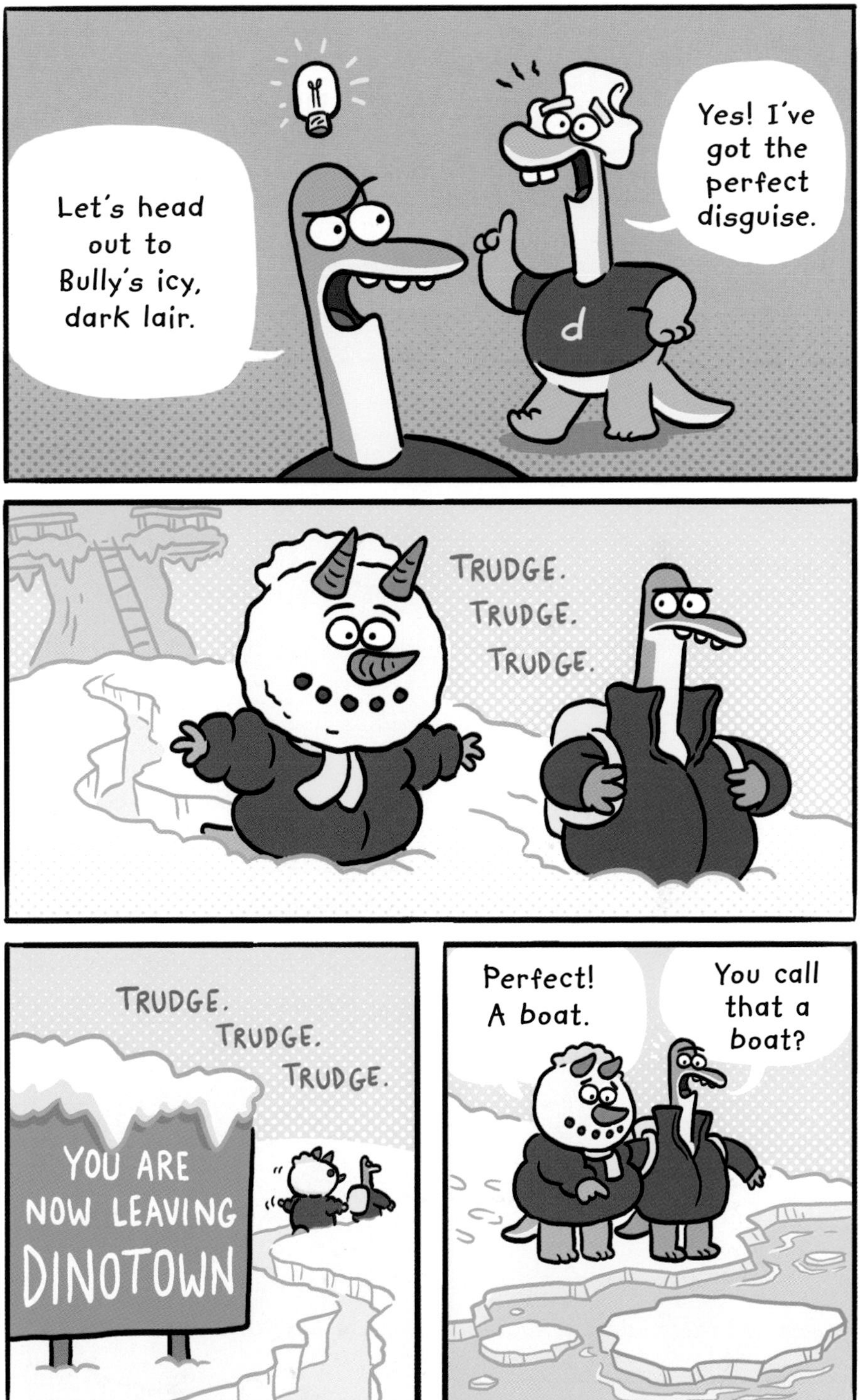
Let's head out to Bully's icy, dark lair.
Yes! I've got the perfect disguise.
TRUDGE. TRUDGE. TRUDGE.
TRUDGE. TRUDGE. TRUDGE.
YOU ARE NOW LEAVING DINOTOWN
Perfect! A boat.
You call that a boat?

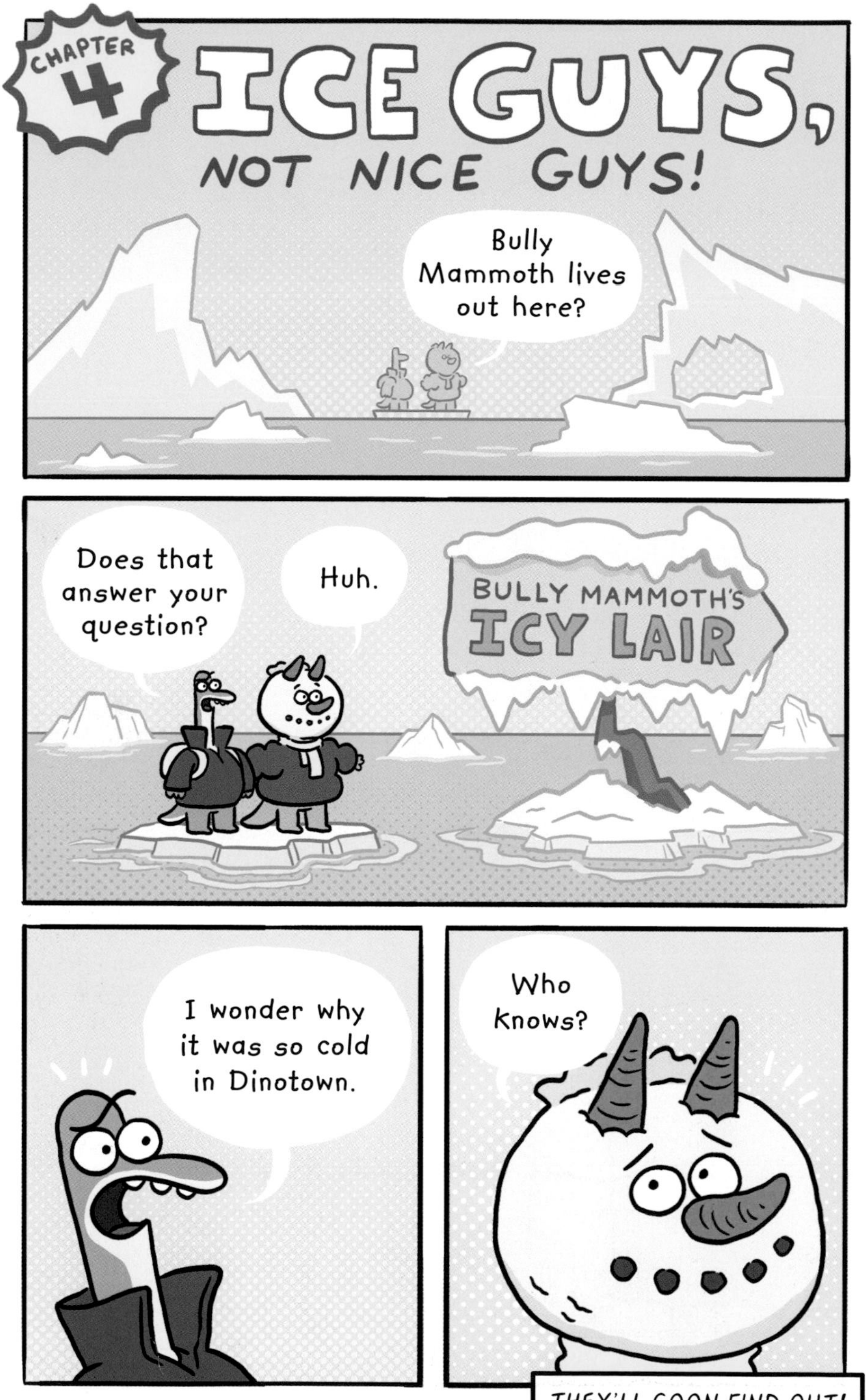
CHAPTER 4
ICE GUYS, NOT NICE GUYS!
Bully Mammoth lives out here?
Does that answer your question?
Huh.
BULLY MAMMOTH'S ICY LAIR
I wonder why it was so cold in Dinotown.
Who knows?
THEY'LL SOON FIND OUT!

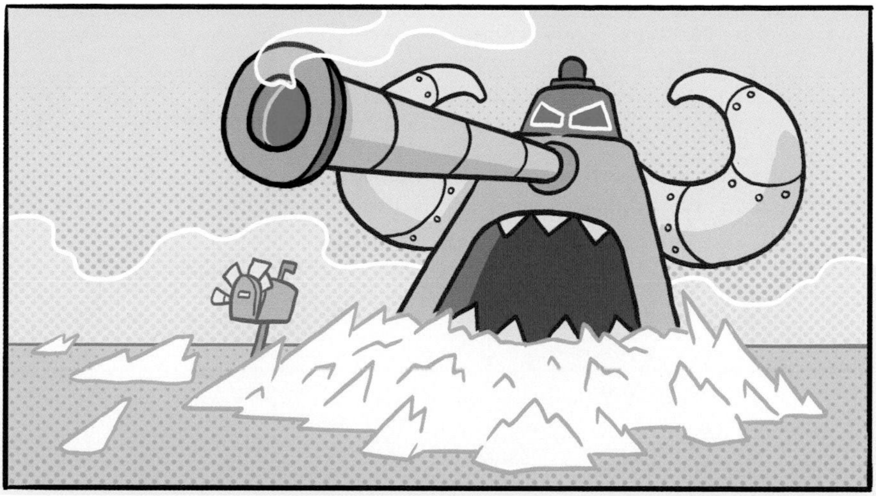

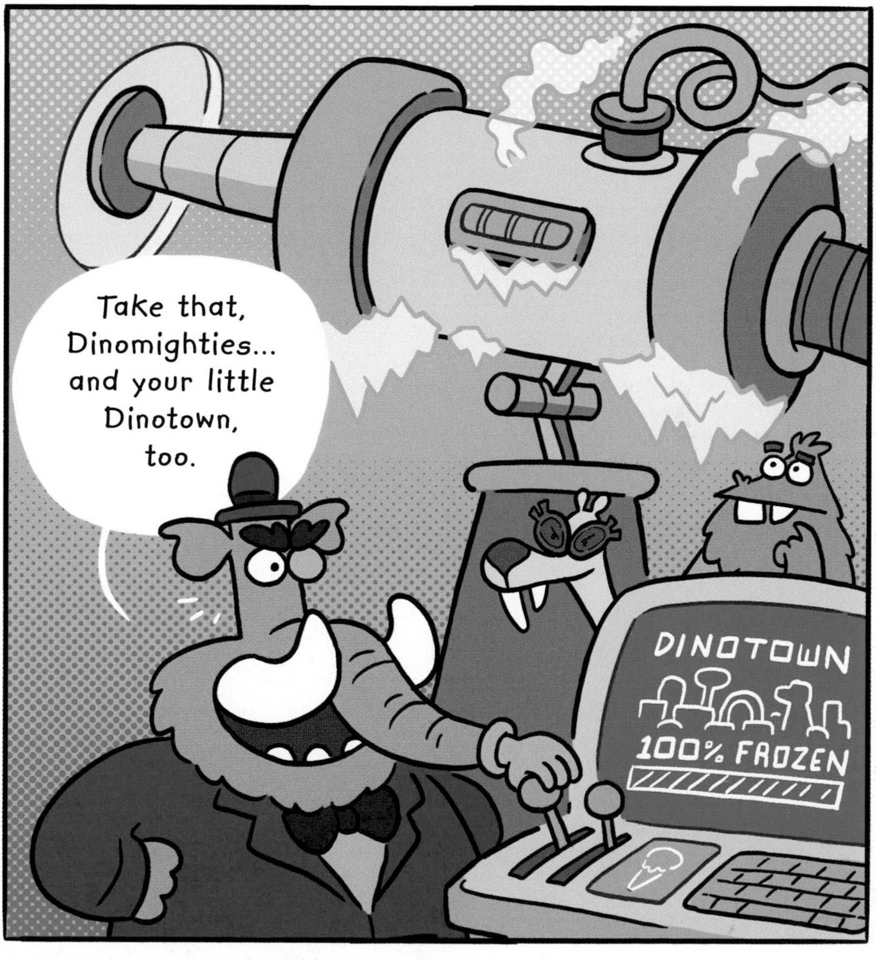
Take that, Dinomighties... and your little Dinotown, too.
DINOTOWN
100% FROZEN

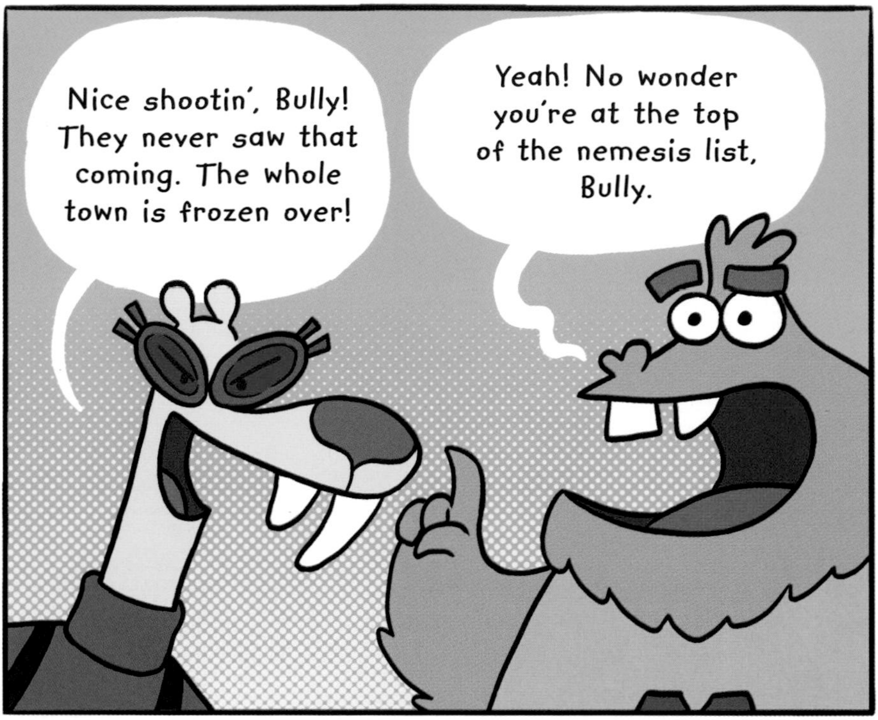
Nice shootin', Bully! They never saw that coming. The whole town is frozen over!
Yeah! No wonder you're at the top of the nemesis list, Bully.

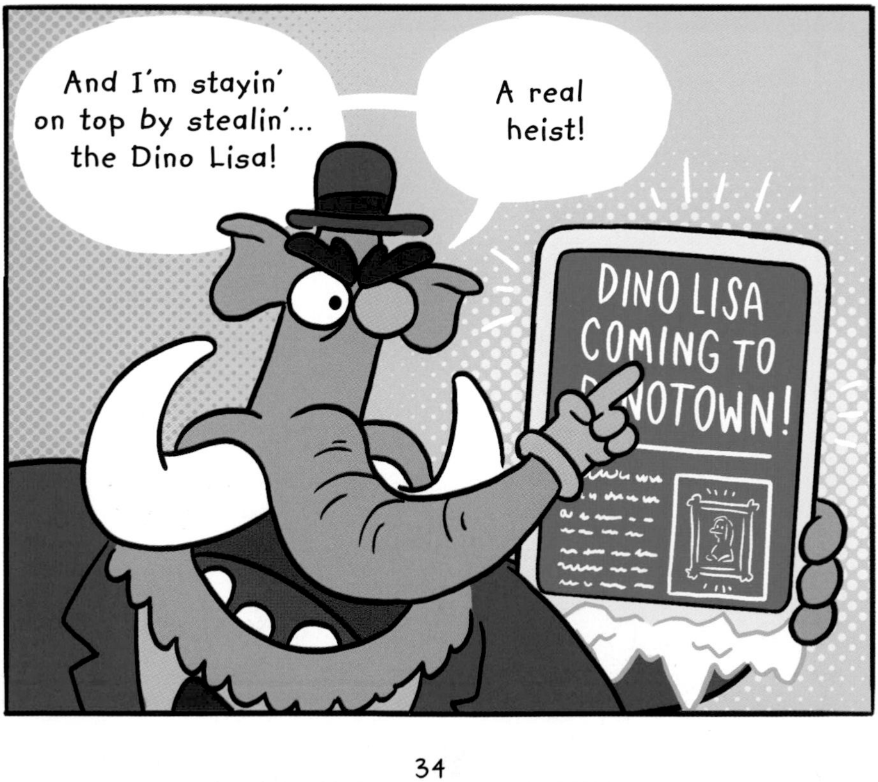
And I'm stayin' on top by stealin'... the Dino Lisa!
A real heist!
DINO LISA COMING TO

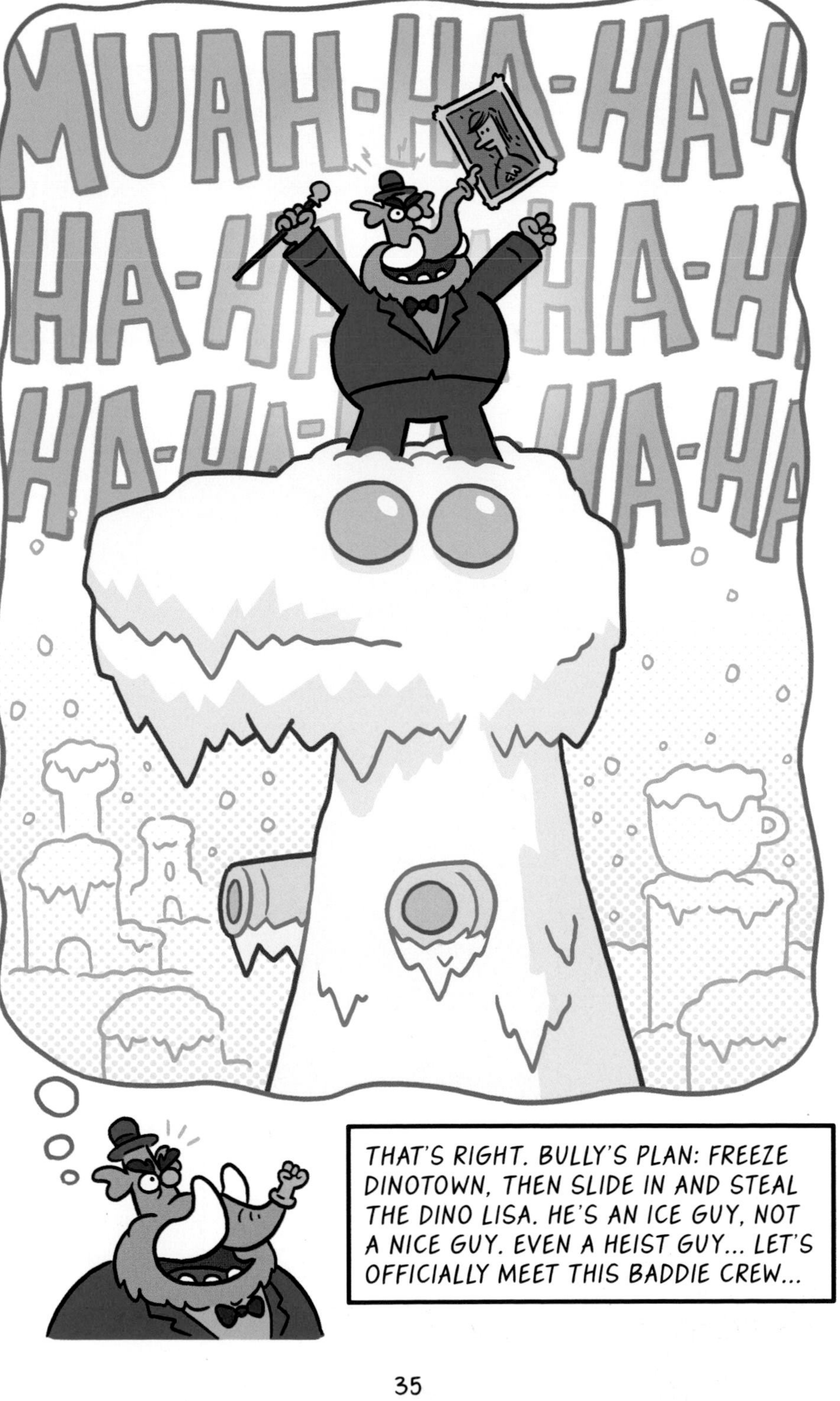
MUAH-HA-HA-HA
THAT'S RIGHT. BULLY'S PLAN: FREEZE DINOTOWN, THEN SLIDE IN AND STEAL THE DINO LISA. HE'S AN ICE GUY, NOT A NICE GUY. EVEN A HEIST GUY... LET'S OFFICIALLY MEET THIS BADDIE CREW...

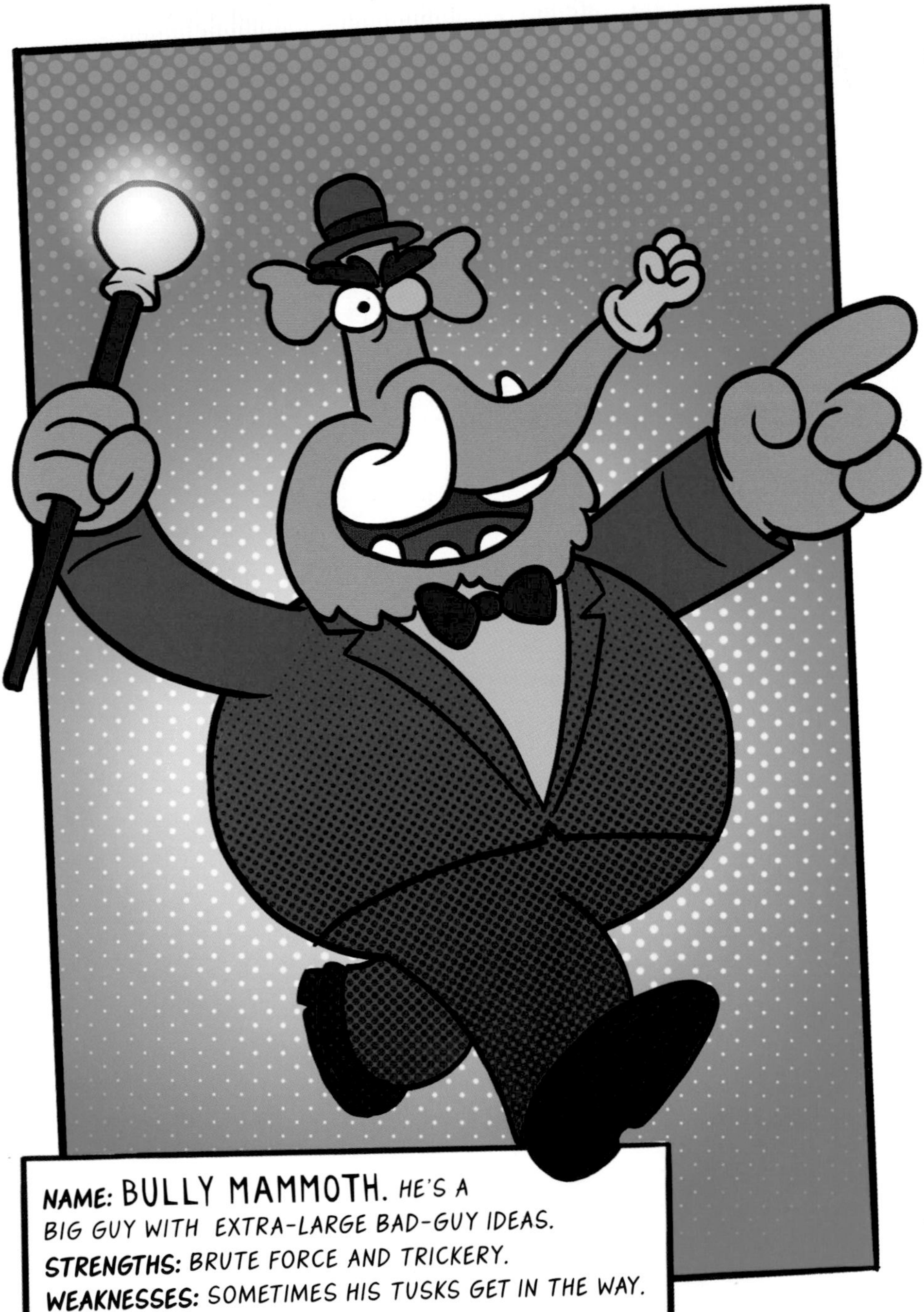

**NAME:** BULLY MAMMOTH. HE'S A BIG GUY WITH EXTRA-LARGE BAD-GUY IDEAS.
**STRENGTHS:** BRUTE FORCE AND TRICKERY.
**WEAKNESSES:** SOMETIMES HIS TUSKS GET IN THE WAY.

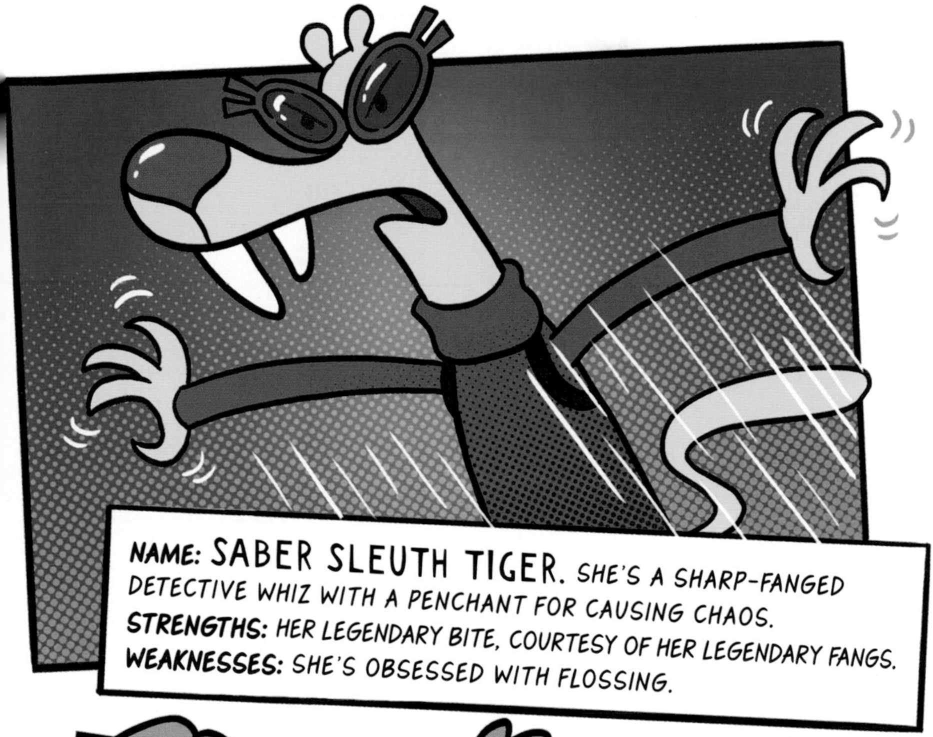
NAME: SABER SLEUTH TIGER. SHE'S A SHARP-FANGED DETECTIVE WHIZ WITH A PENCHANT FOR CAUSING CHAOS.
STRENGTHS: HER LEGENDARY BITE, COURTESY OF HER LEGENDARY FANGS.
WEAKNESSES: SHE'S OBSESSED WITH FLOSSING.

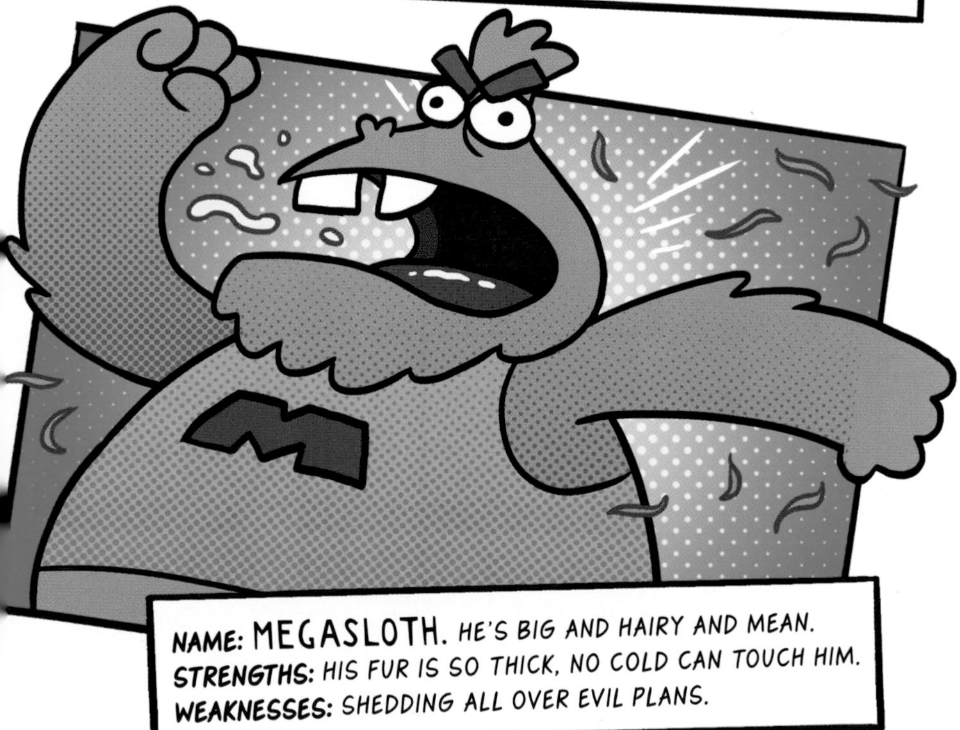
NAME: MEGASLOTH. HE'S BIG AND HAIRY AND MEAN.
STRENGTHS: HIS FUR IS SO THICK, NO COLD CAN TOUCH HIM.
WEAKNESSES: SHEDDING ALL OVER EVIL PLANS.

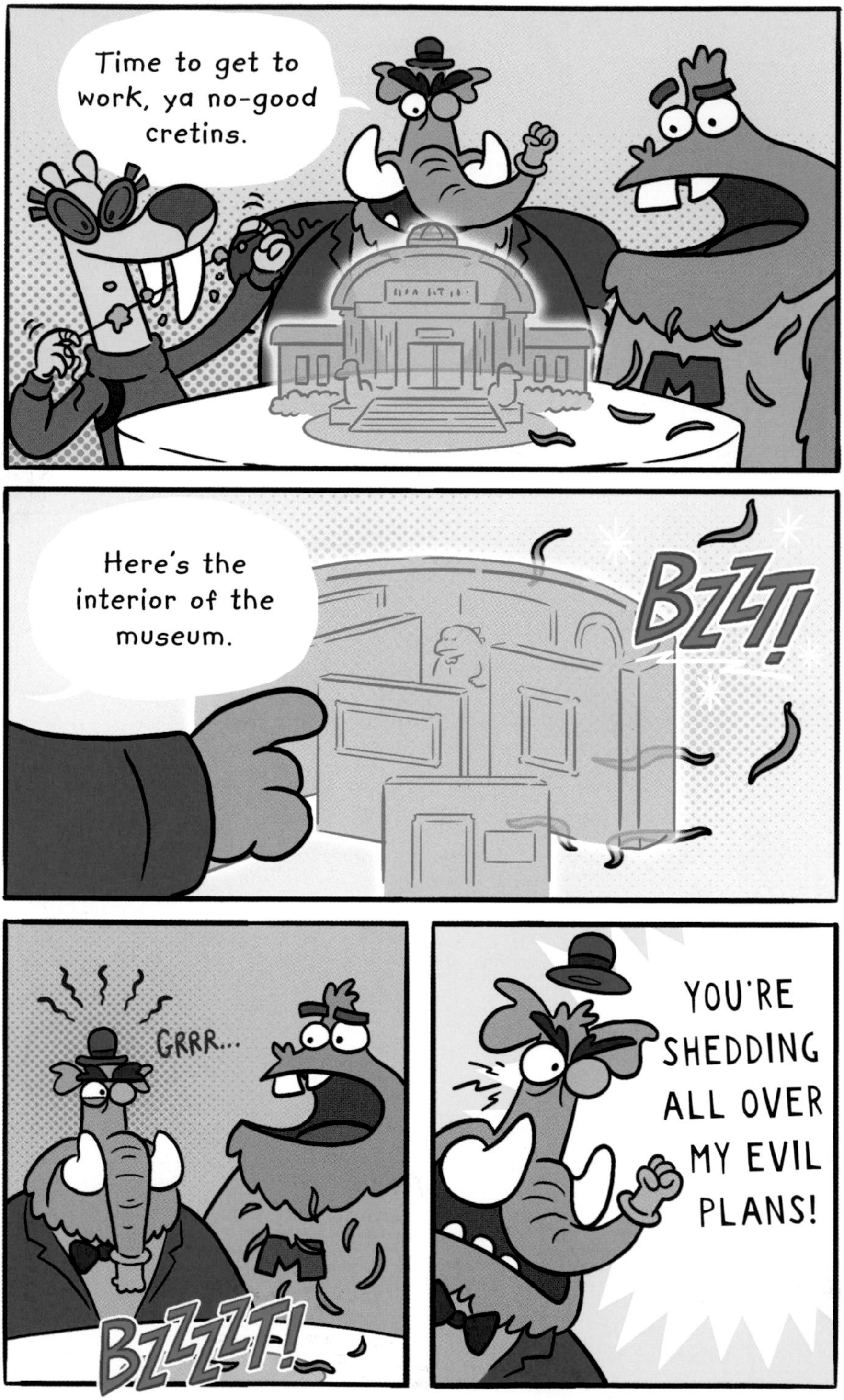
Time to get to work, ya no-good cretins.
M
Here's the interior of the museum.
BZZT!
GRRR...
M
BZZZZT!
YOU'RE SHEDDING ALL OVER MY EVIL PLANS!

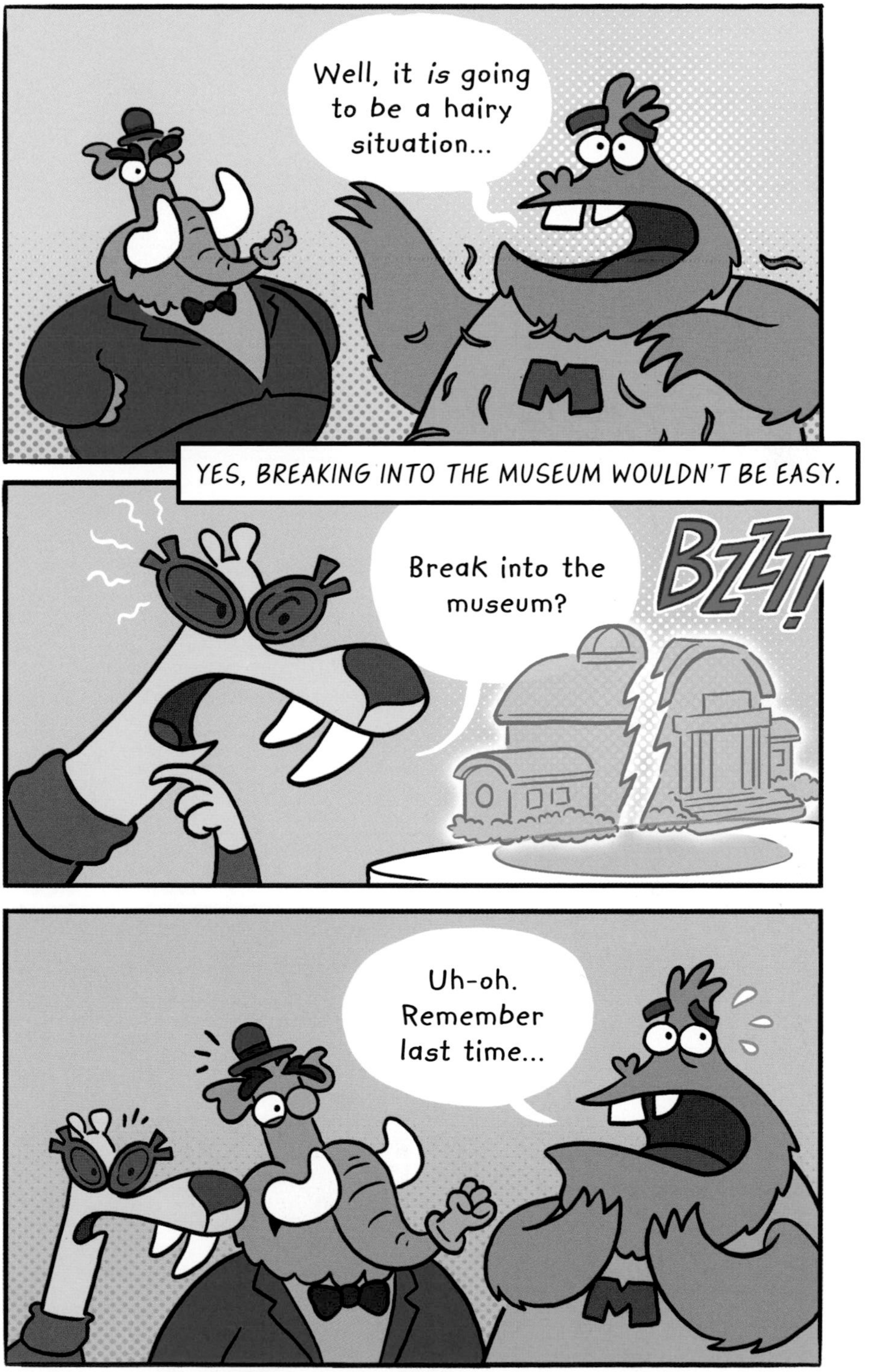
Well, it *is* going to be a hairy situation...
YES, BREAKING INTO THE MUSEUM WOULDN'T BE EASY.
Break into the museum?
BZZT!
Uh-oh. Remember last time...

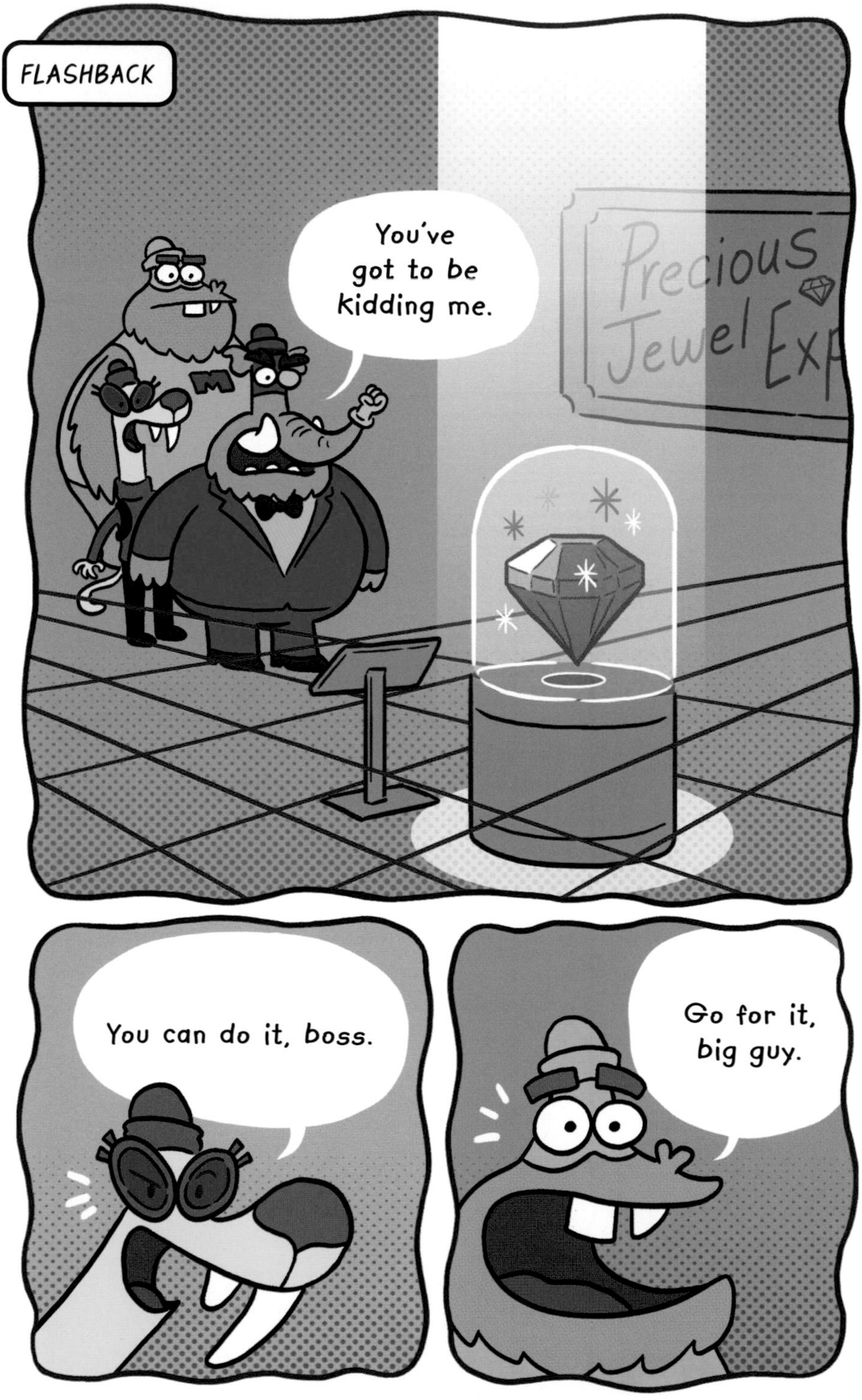
FLASHBACK
You've got to be kidding me.
Precious Jewel Exp
You can do it, boss.
Go for it, big guy.

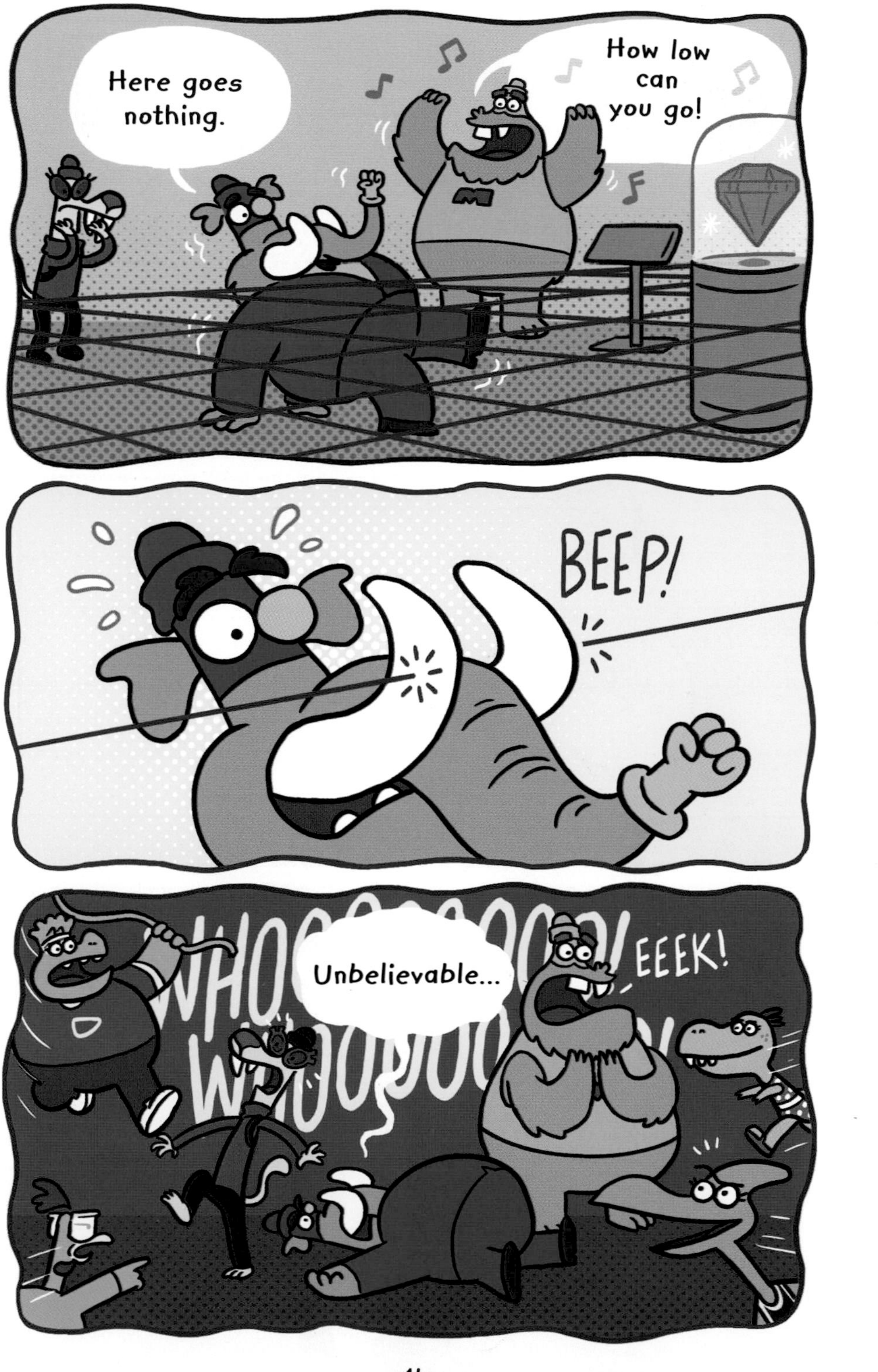
Here goes nothing.
How low can you go!
BEEP!
Unbelievable...
EEEK!

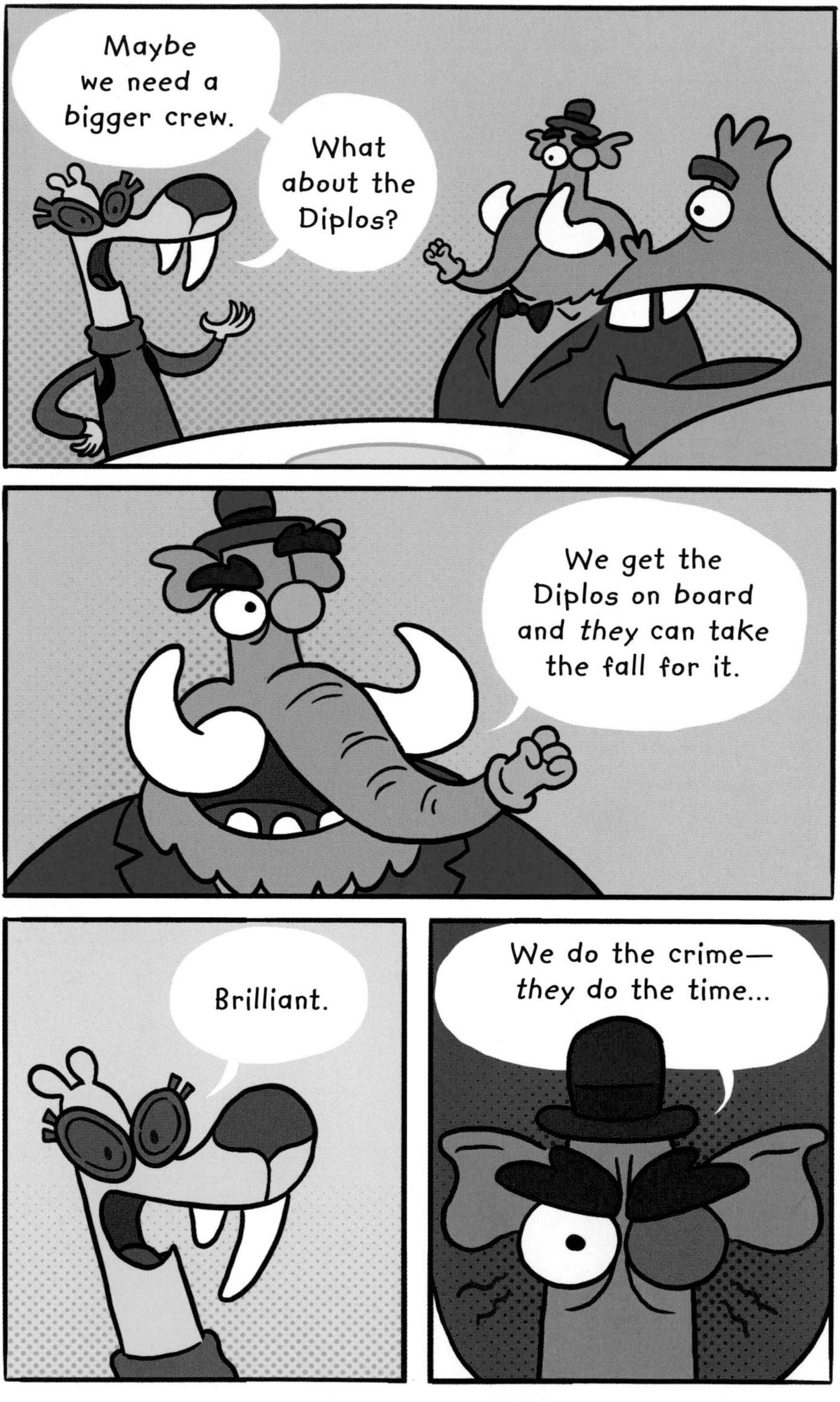
Maybe we need a bigger crew.
What about the Diplos?
We get the Diplos on board and *they* can take the fall for it.
Brilliant.
We do the crime—*they* do the time...

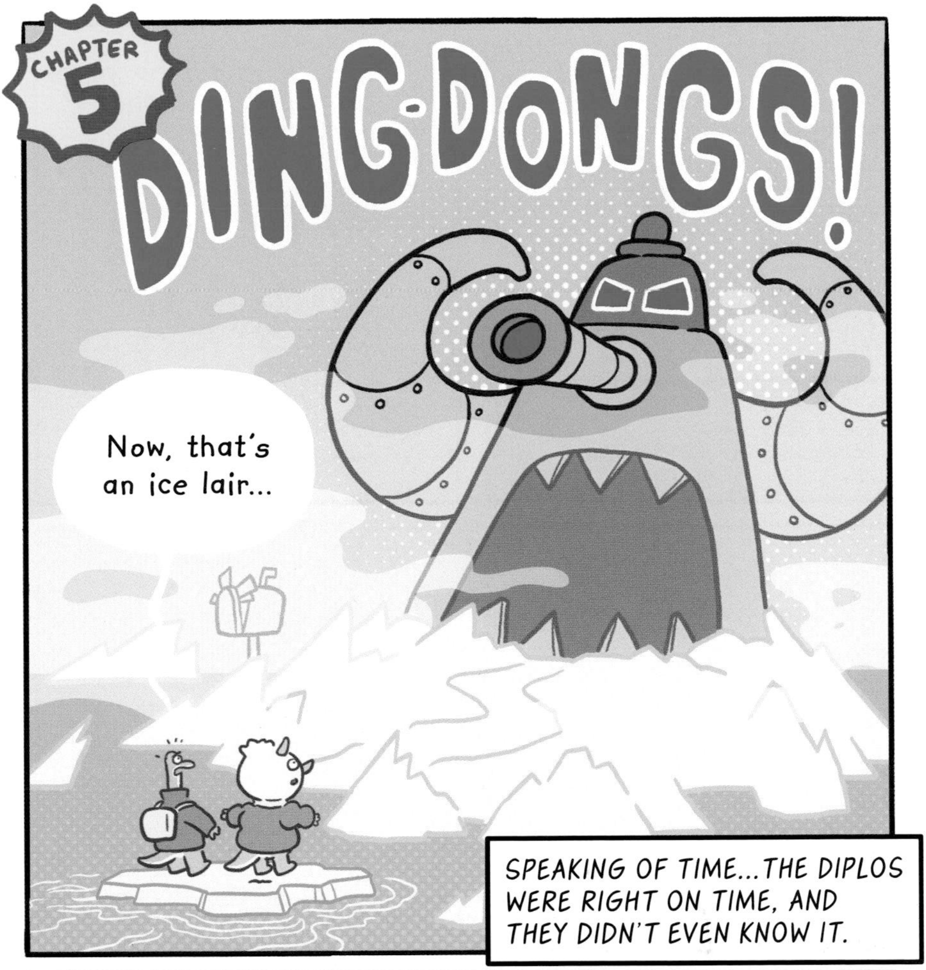
CHAPTER 5
DING-DONGS!
Now, that's an ice lair...
SPEAKING OF TIME...THE DIPLOS WERE RIGHT ON TIME, AND THEY DIDN'T EVEN KNOW IT.

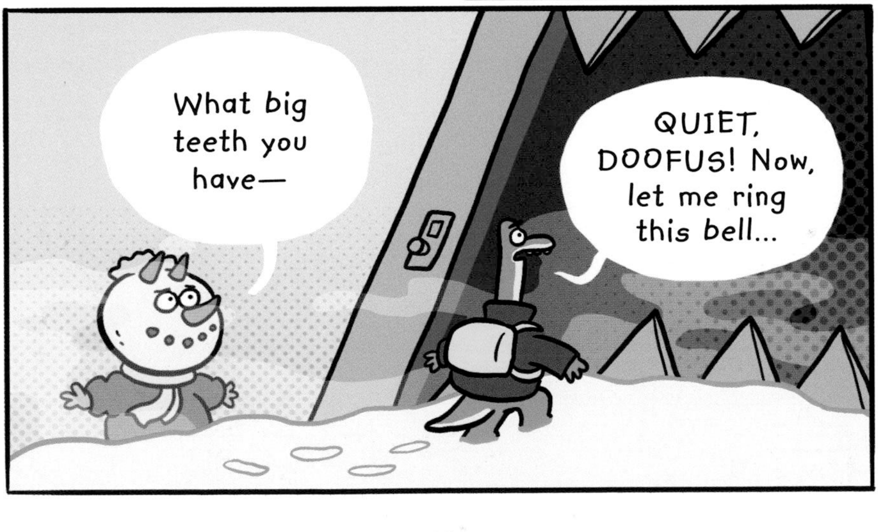
What big teeth you have—
QUIET, DOOFUS! Now, let me ring this bell...

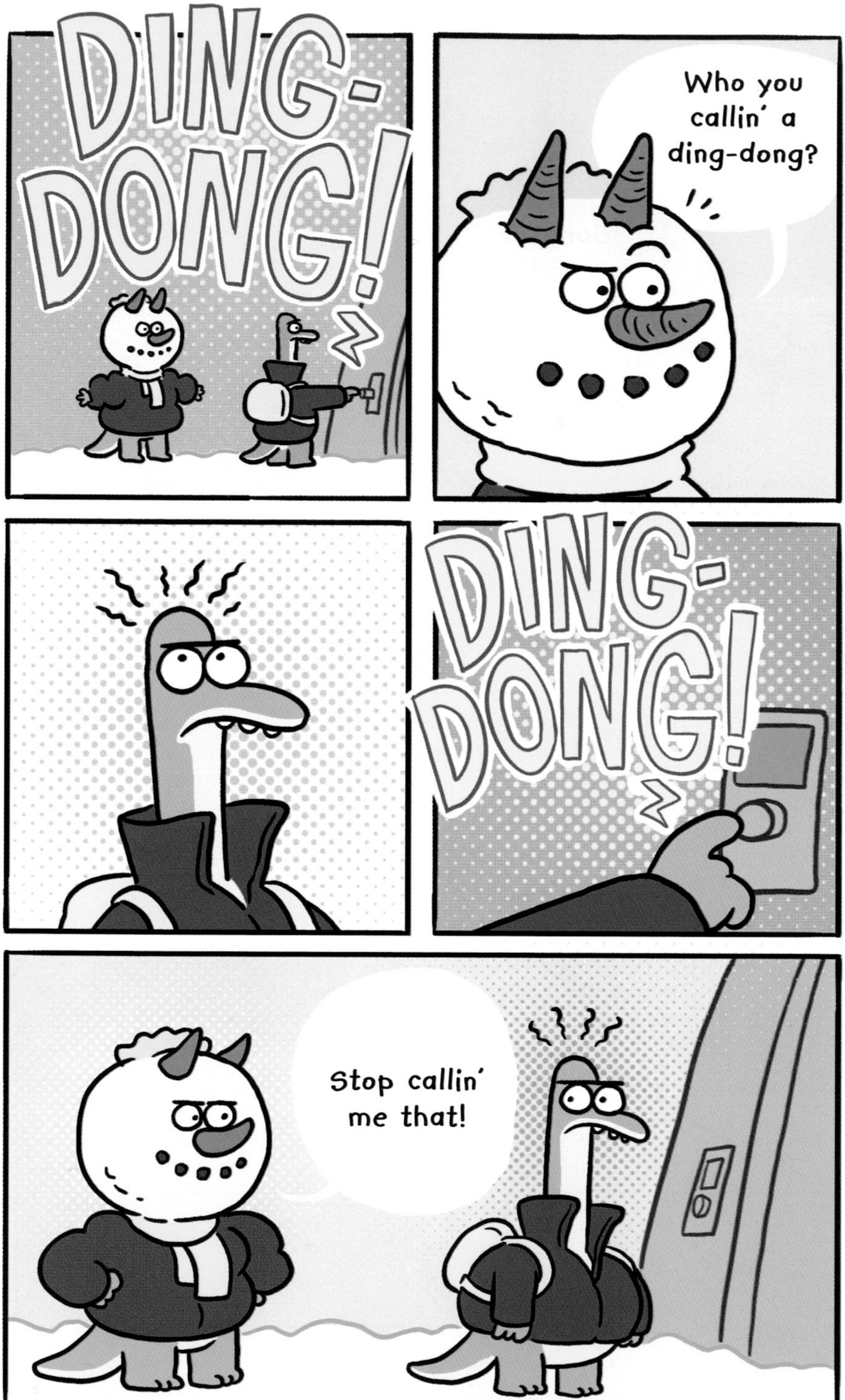
DING-DONG!
Who you callin' a ding-dong?
DING-DONG!
Stop callin' me that!

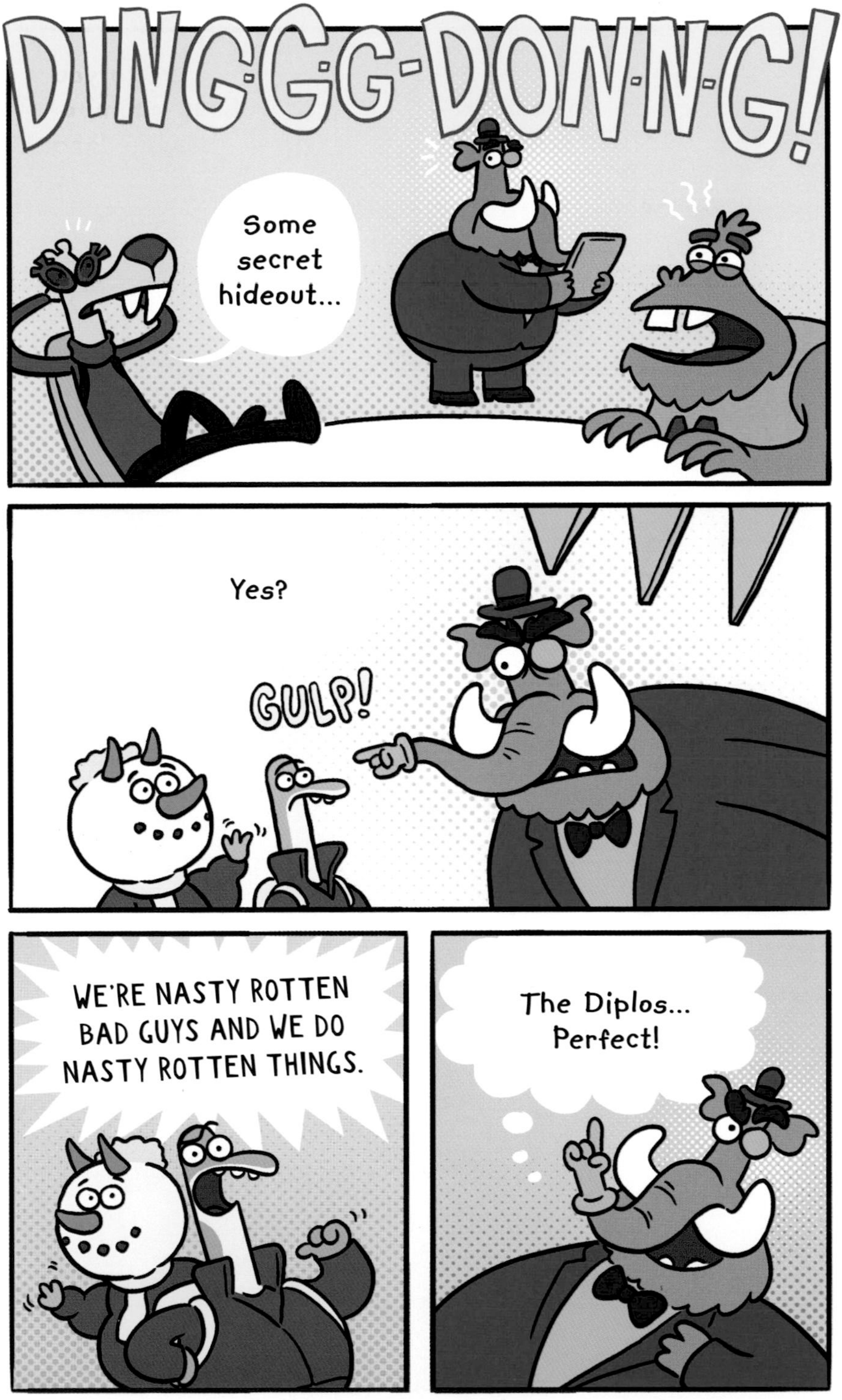
DINGGG-DONNG!
Some secret hideout...
Yes?
GULP!
WE'RE NASTY ROTTEN BAD GUYS AND WE DO NASTY ROTTEN THINGS.
The Diplos... Perfect!

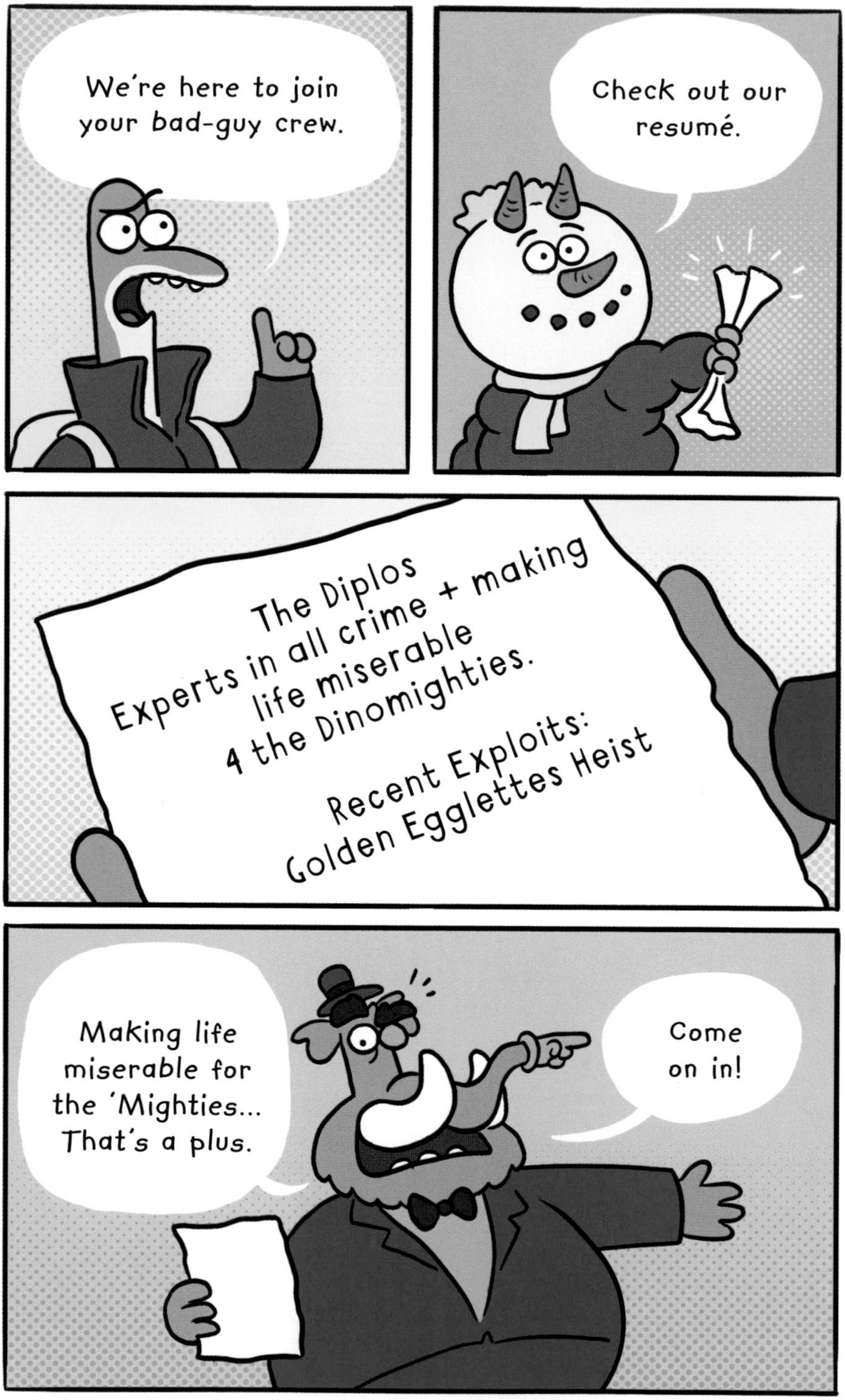
We're here to join your bad-guy crew.
Check out our resumé.
The Diplos
Experts in all crime + making life miserable 4 the Dinomighties.
Recent Exploits:
Golden Egglettes Heist
Making life miserable for the 'Mighties... That's a plus.
Come on in!

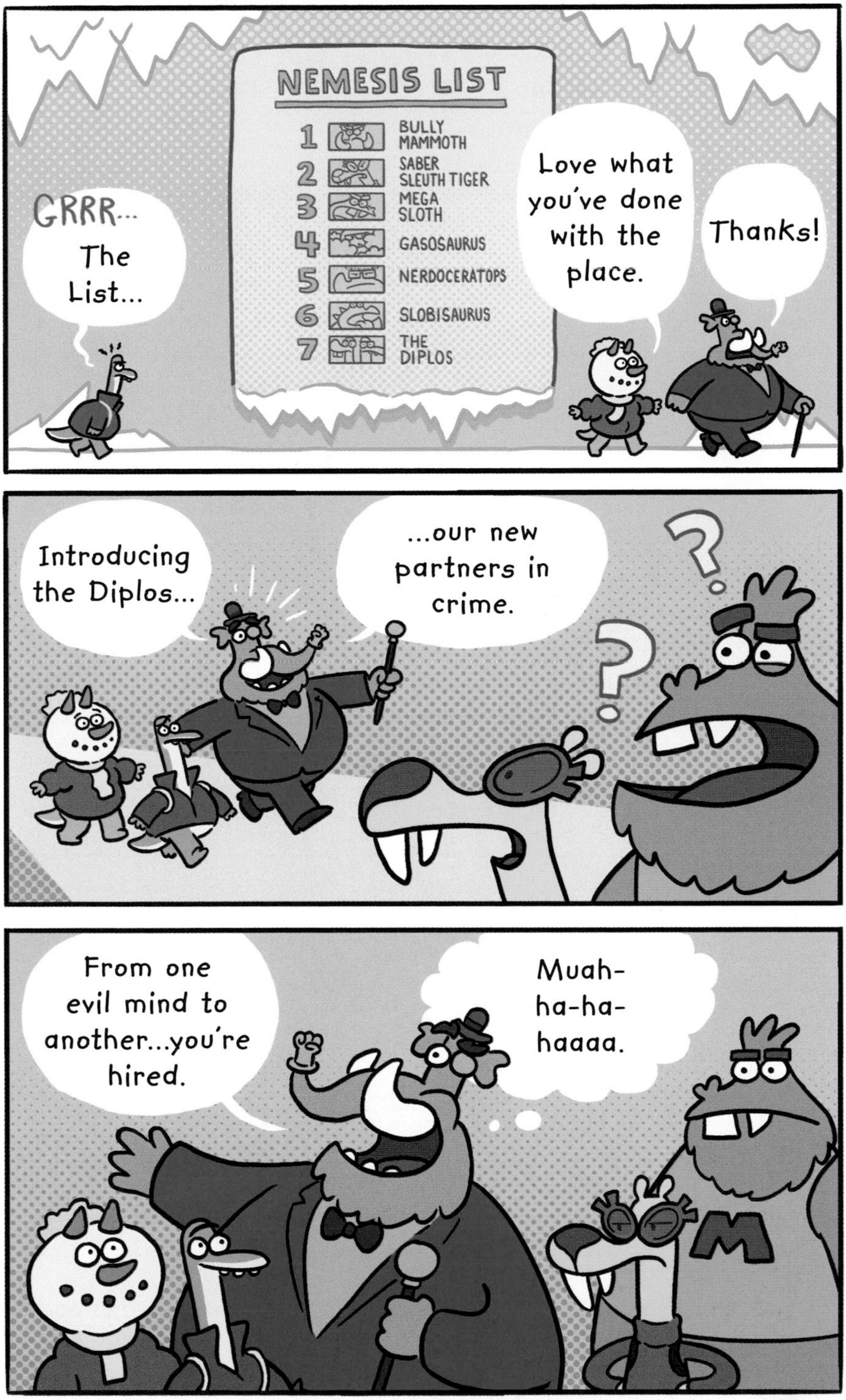
NEMESIS LIST
1 BULLY MAMMOTH
2 SABER SLEUTH TIGER
3 MEGA SLOTH
4 GASOSAURUS
5 NERDOCERATOPS
6 SLOBISAURUS
7 THE DIPLOS
GRRR...
The List...
Love what you've done with the place.
Thanks!
Introducing the Diplos...
...our new partners in crime.
From one evil mind to another...you're hired.
Muah-ha-ha-haaaa.

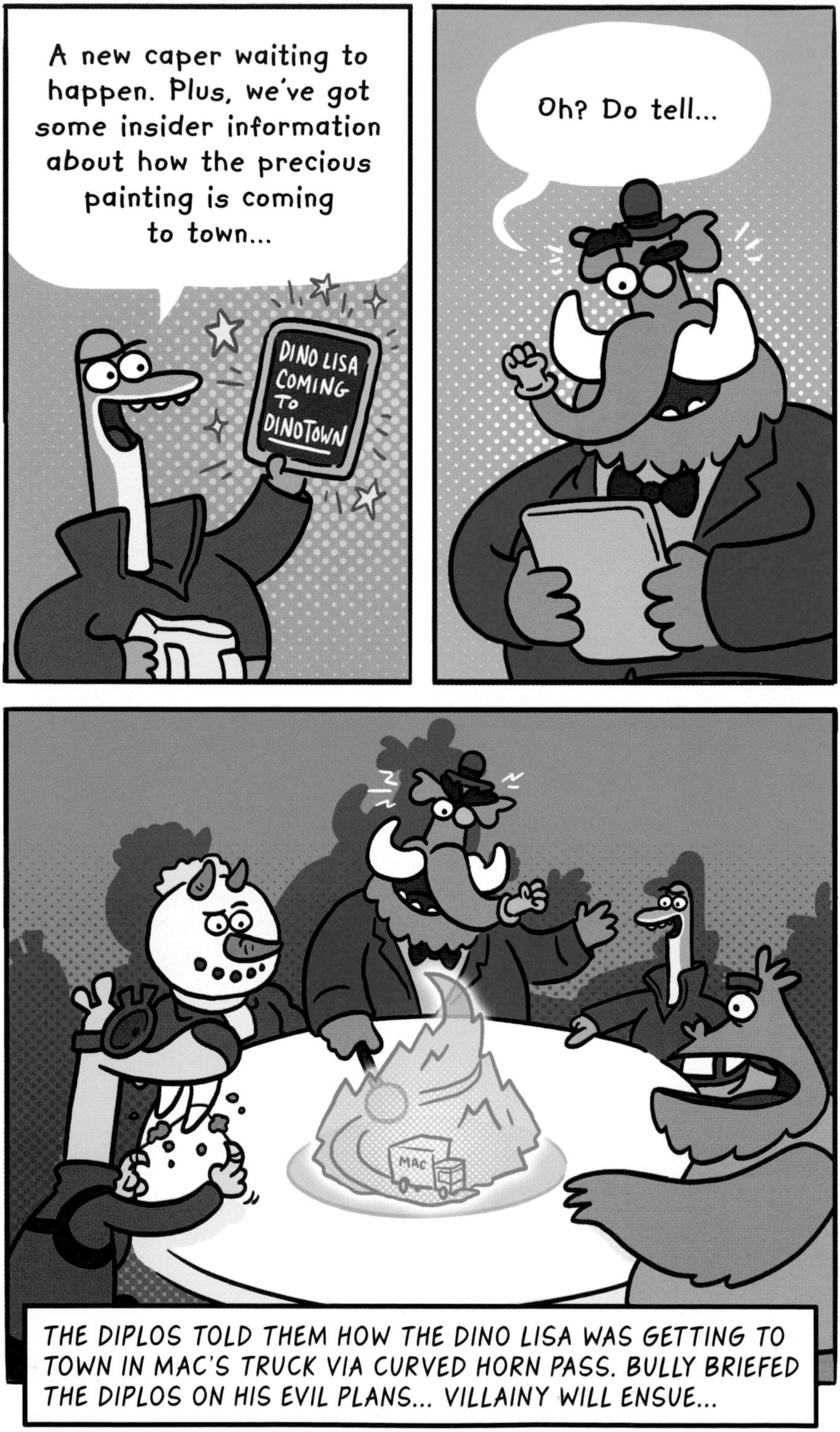
A new caper waiting to happen. Plus, we've got some insider information about how the precious painting is coming to town...
DINO LISA COMING TO DINOTOWN
Oh? Do tell...
MAC
THE DIPLOS TOLD THEM HOW THE DINO LISA WAS GETTING TO TOWN IN MAC'S TRUCK VIA CURVED HORN PASS. BULLY BRIEFED THE DIPLOS ON HIS EVIL PLANS... VILLAINY WILL ENSUE...

# CHAPTER 6 THE BOOGEYDINO

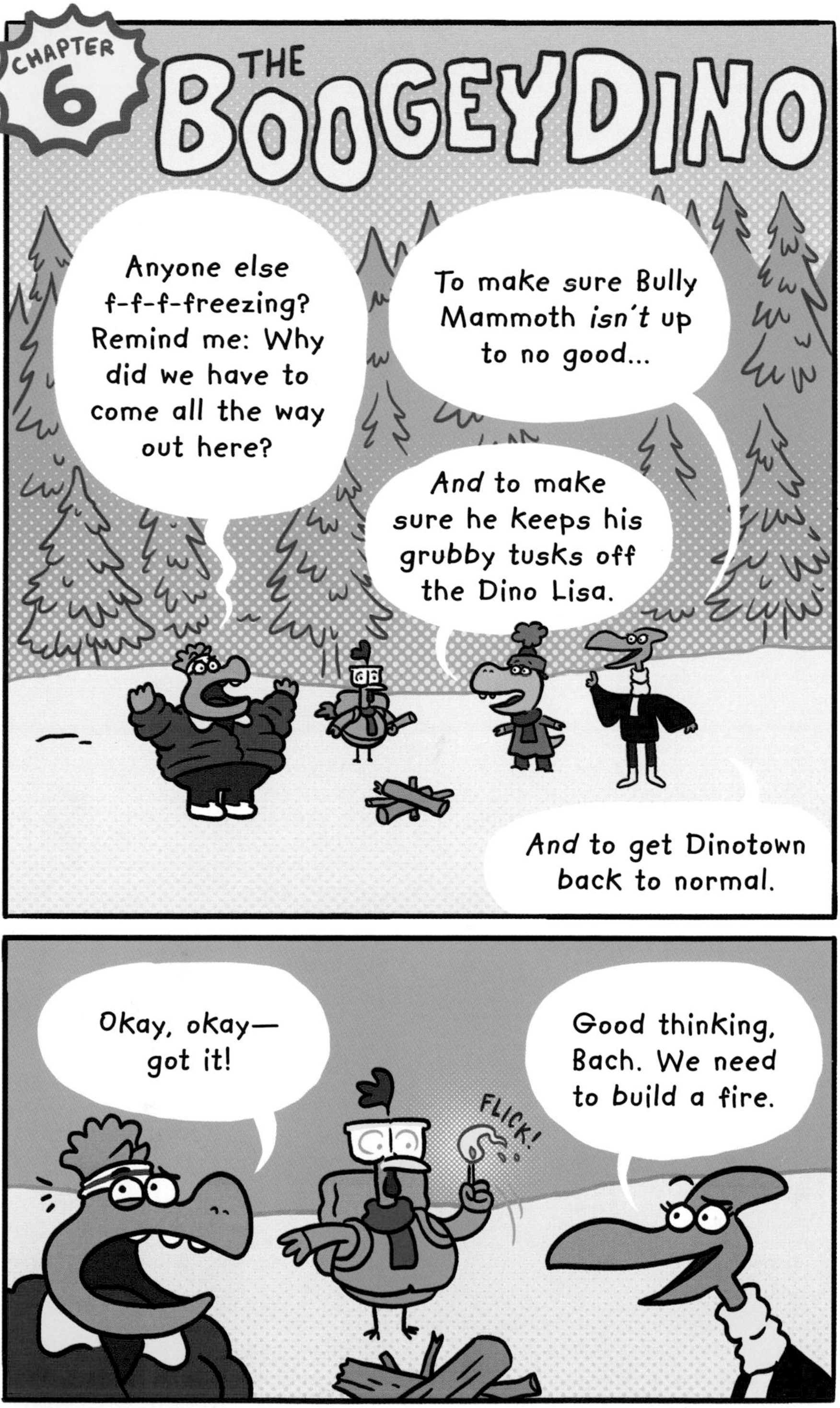
Anyone else f-f-f-freezing? Remind me: Why did we have to come all the way out here?
To make sure Bully Mammoth *isn't* up to no good...
*And* to make sure he keeps his grubby tusks off the Dino Lisa.
*And* to get Dinotown back to normal.
Okay, okay— got it!
FLICK!
Good thinking, Bach. We need to build a fire.

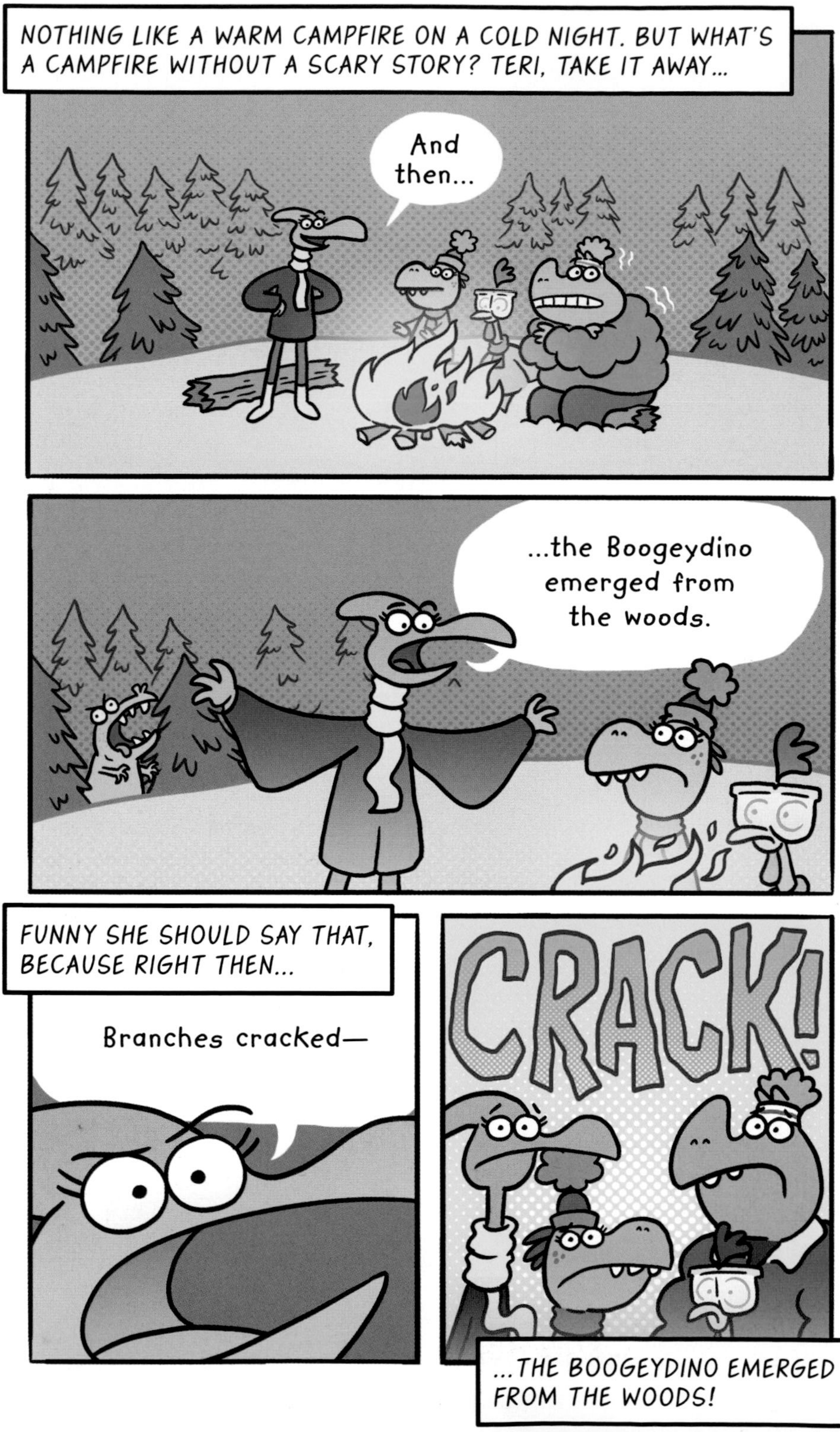
NOTHING LIKE A WARM CAMPFIRE ON A COLD NIGHT. BUT WHAT'S A CAMPFIRE WITHOUT A SCARY STORY? TERI, TAKE IT AWAY...
And then...
...the Boogeydino emerged from the woods.
FUNNY SHE SHOULD SAY THAT, BECAUSE RIGHT THEN...
Branches cracked—
CRACK!
...THE BOOGEYDINO EMERGED FROM THE WOODS!

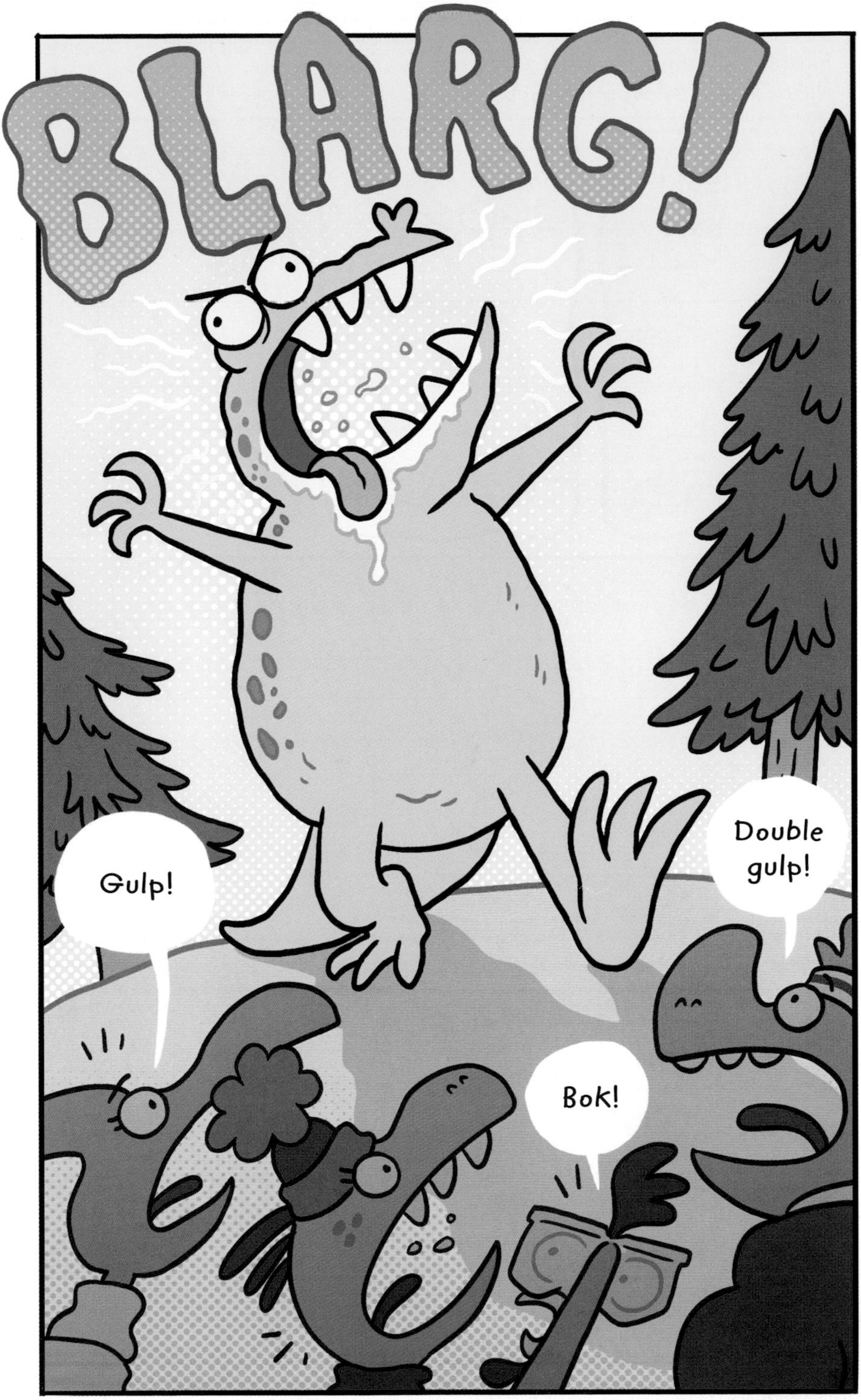
BLARG!
Gulp!
Double gulp!
Bok!

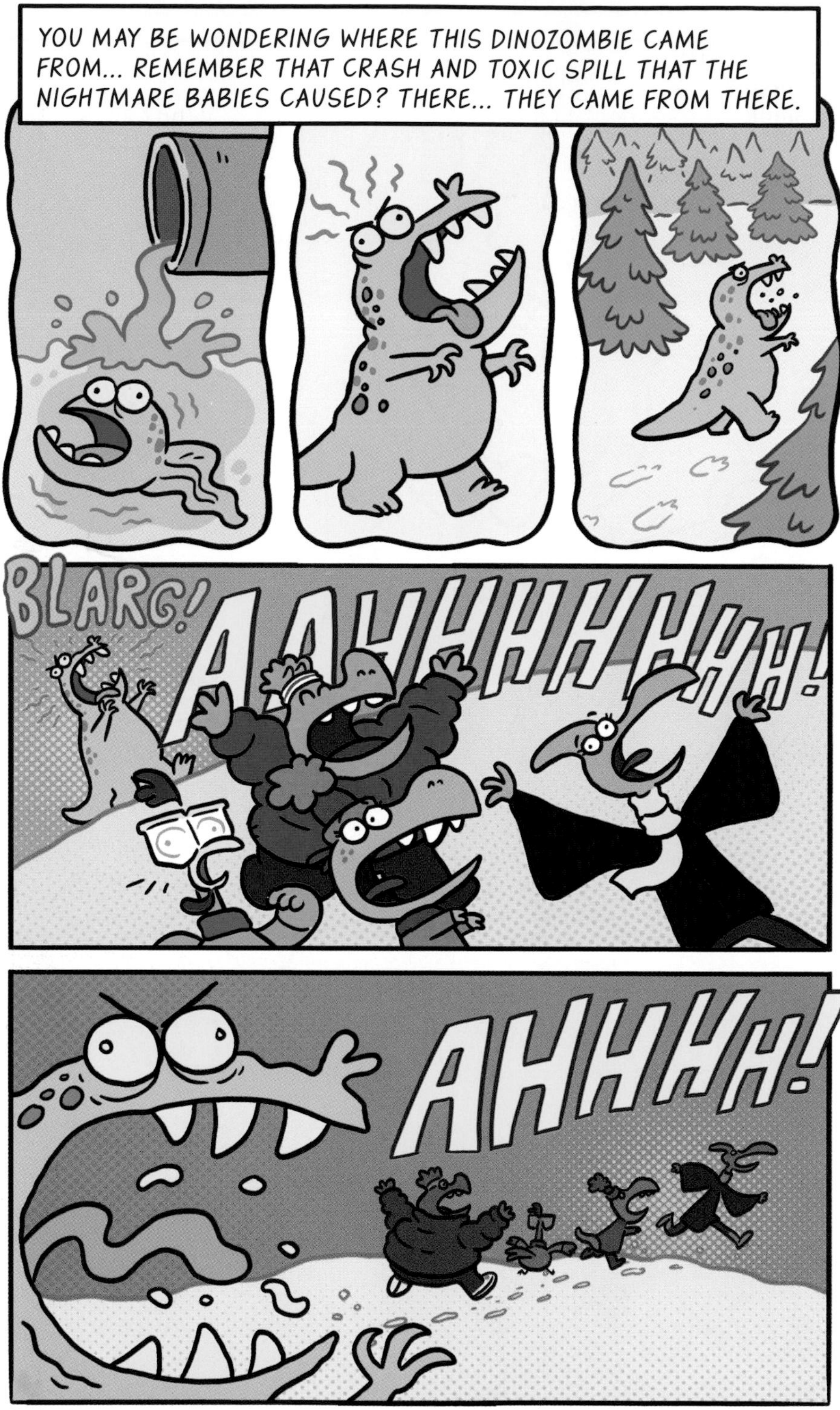
YOU MAY BE WONDERING WHERE THIS DINOZOMBIE CAME FROM... REMEMBER THAT CRASH AND TOXIC SPILL THAT THE NIGHTMARE BABIES CAUSED? THERE... THEY CAME FROM THERE.
BLARG!
AAHHHHHHHH!
AHHHH!

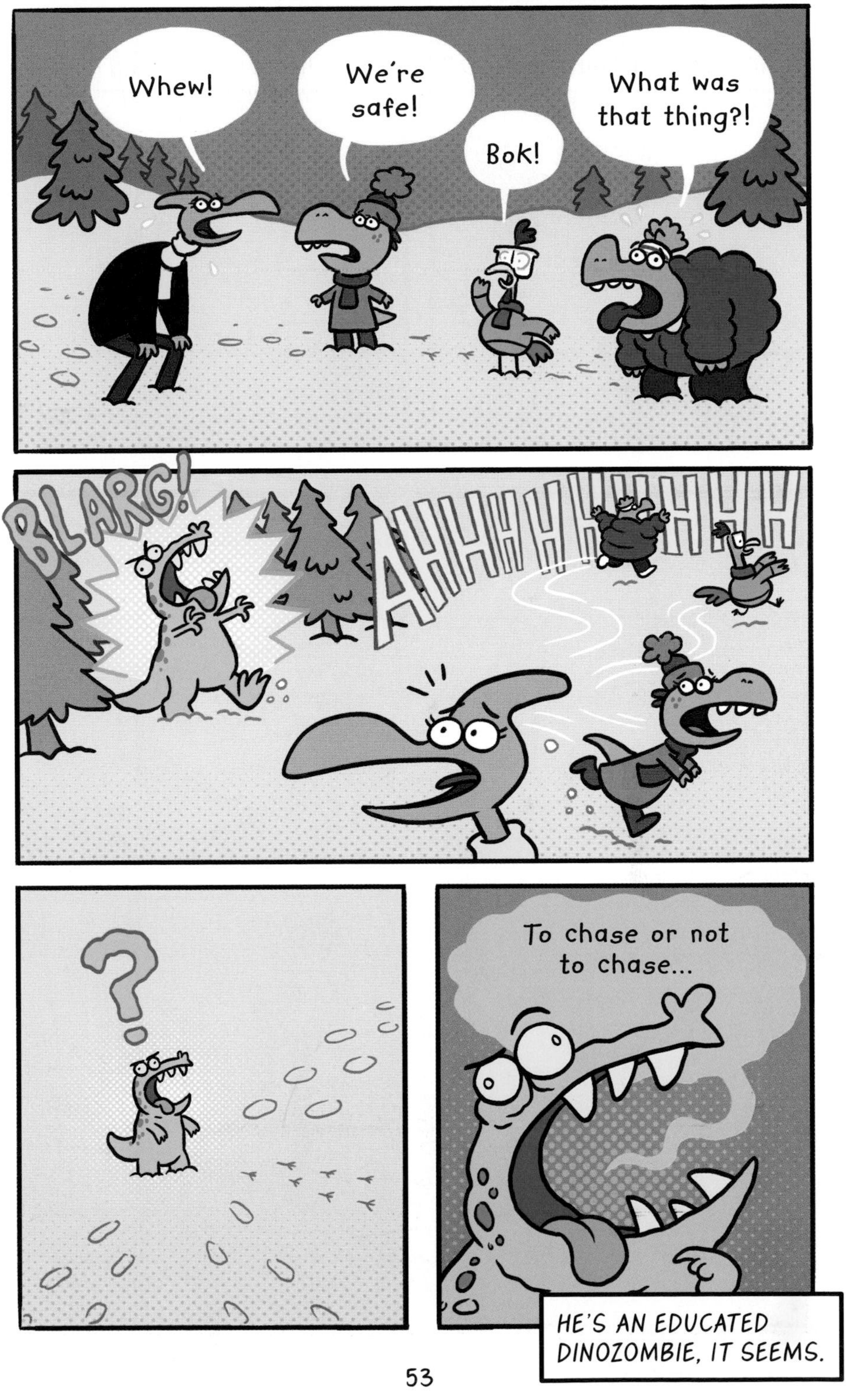

Whew!
We're safe!
Bok!
What was that thing?!
BLARG!
AHHHHHHHHHHHHH
?
To chase or not to chase...
HE'S AN EDUCATED DINOZOMBIE, IT SEEMS.

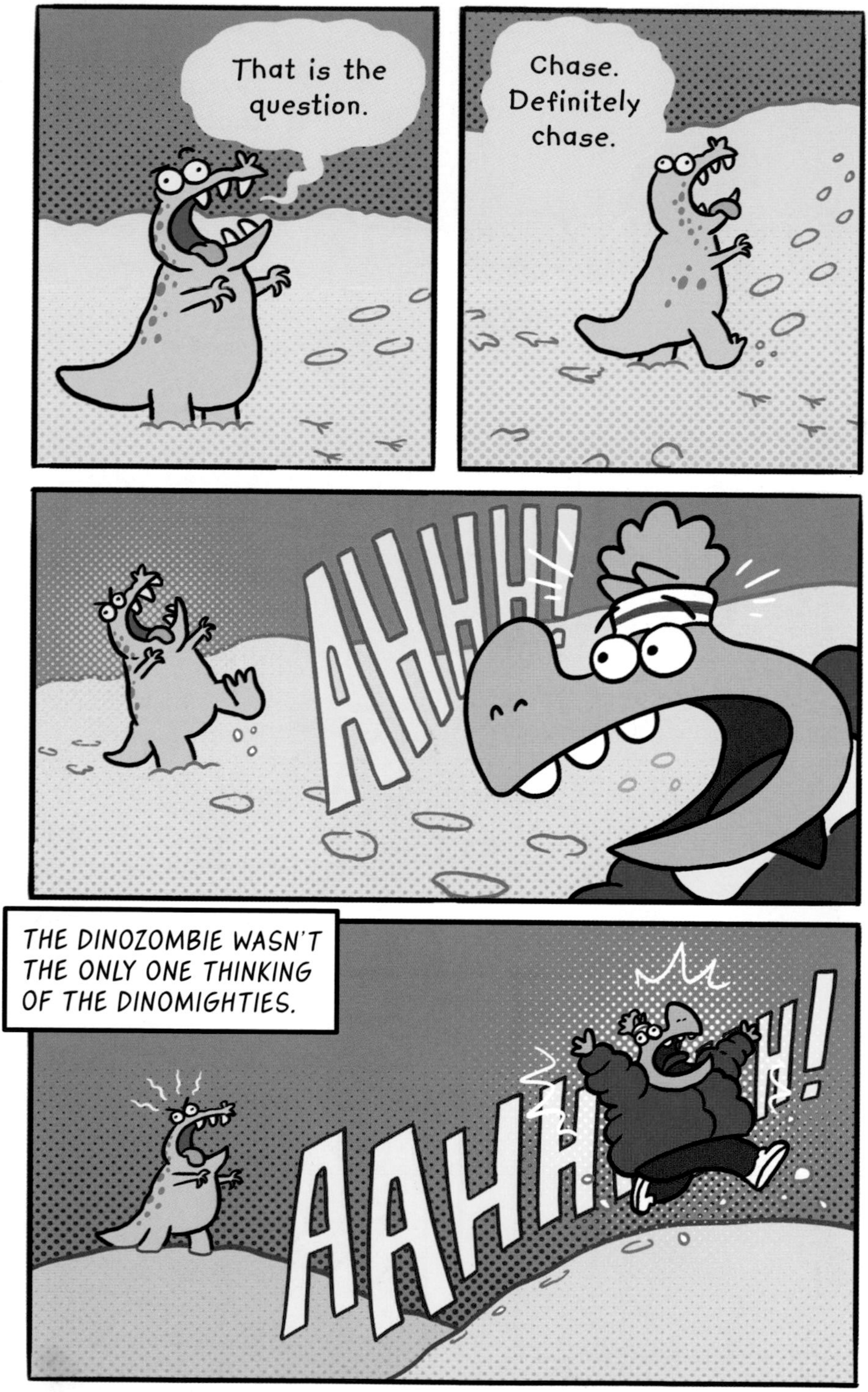
That is the question.
Chase. Definitely chase.
AHHH!
THE DINOZOMBIE WASN'T THE ONLY ONE THINKING OF THE DINOMIGHTIES.
AAHH H!

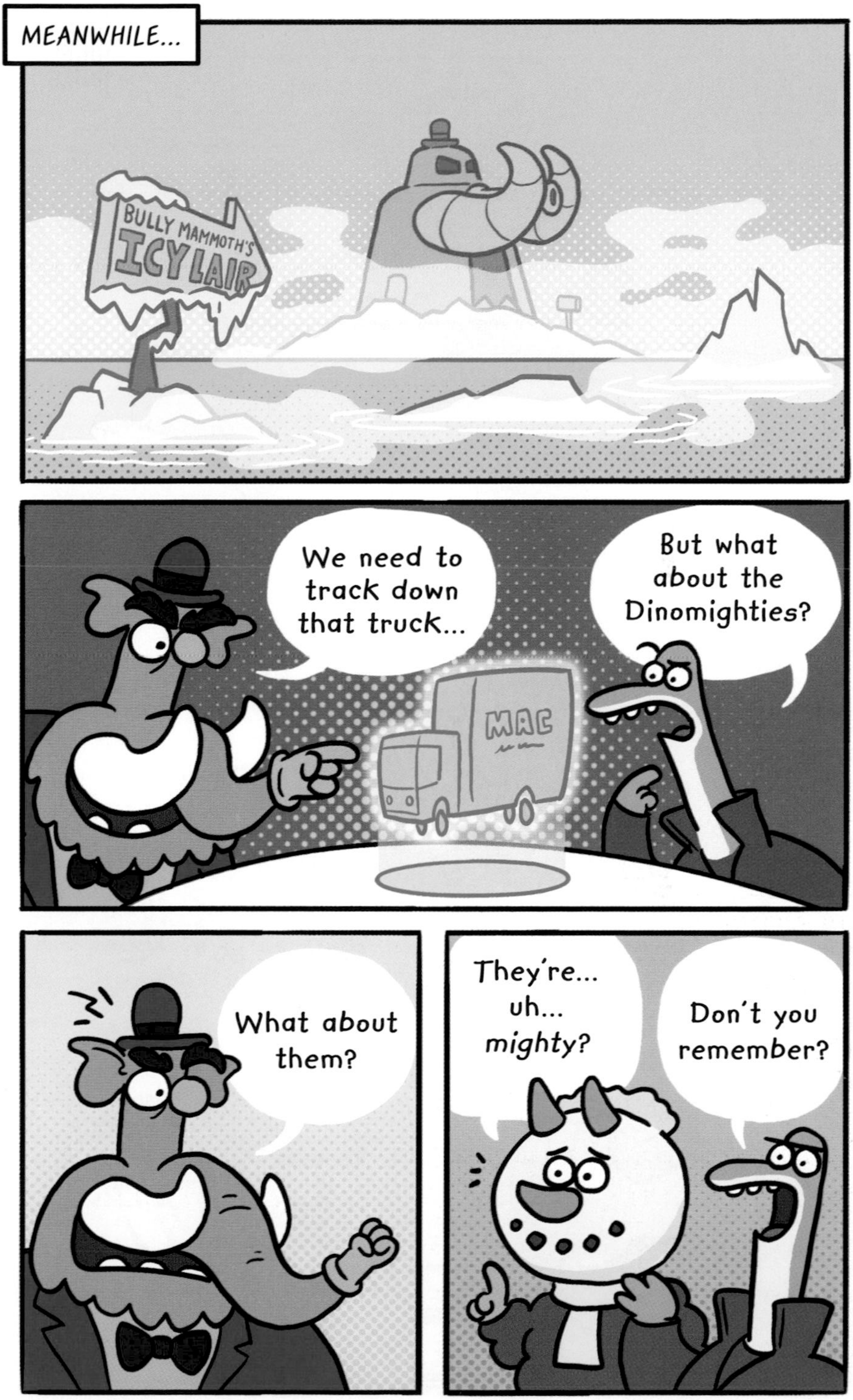
MEANWHILE...
BULLY MAMMOTH'S ICY LAIR
We need to track down that truck...
But what about the Dinomighties?
MAC
What about them?
They're... uh... mighty?
Don't you remember?

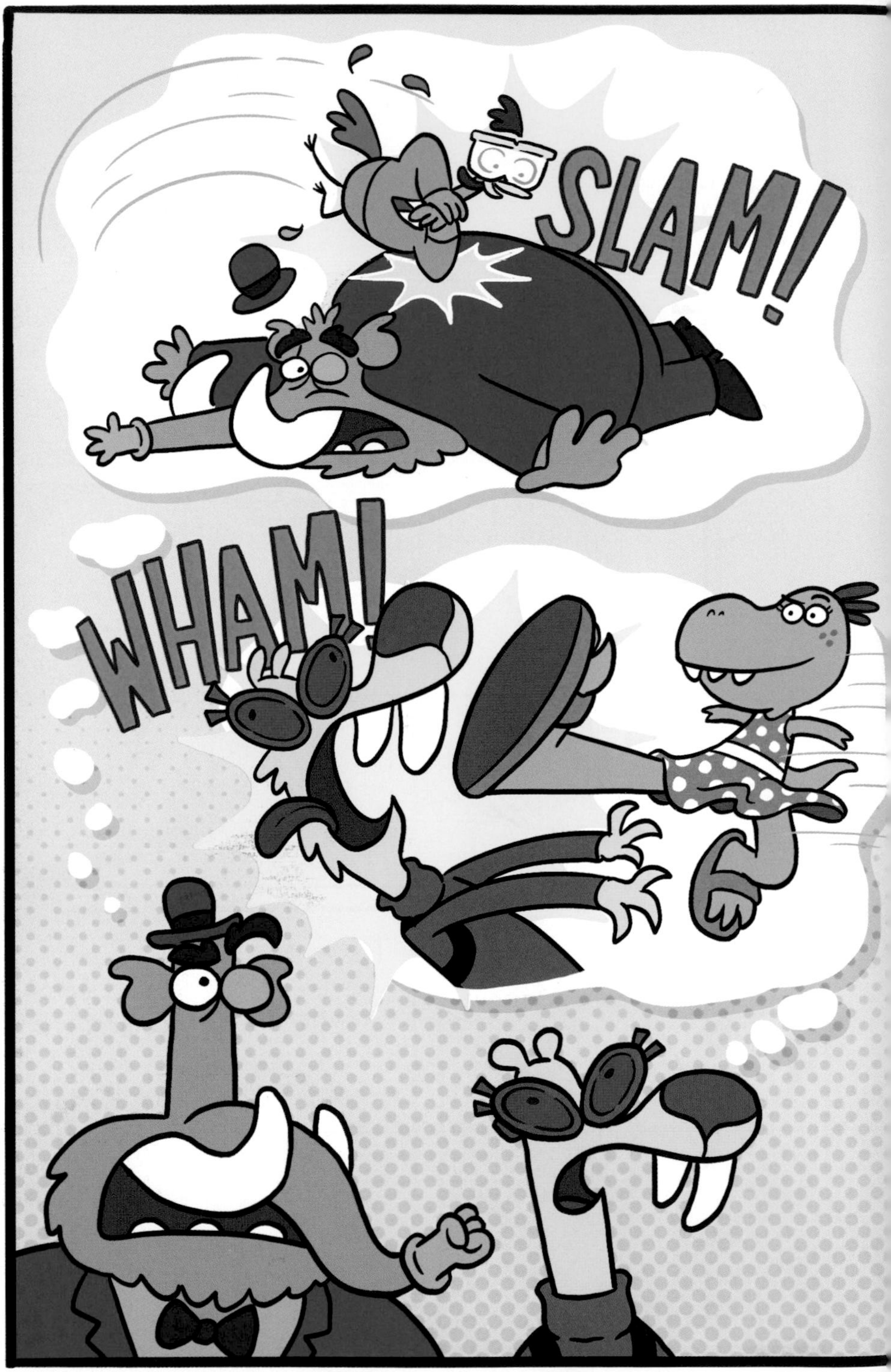
SLAM!
WHAM!

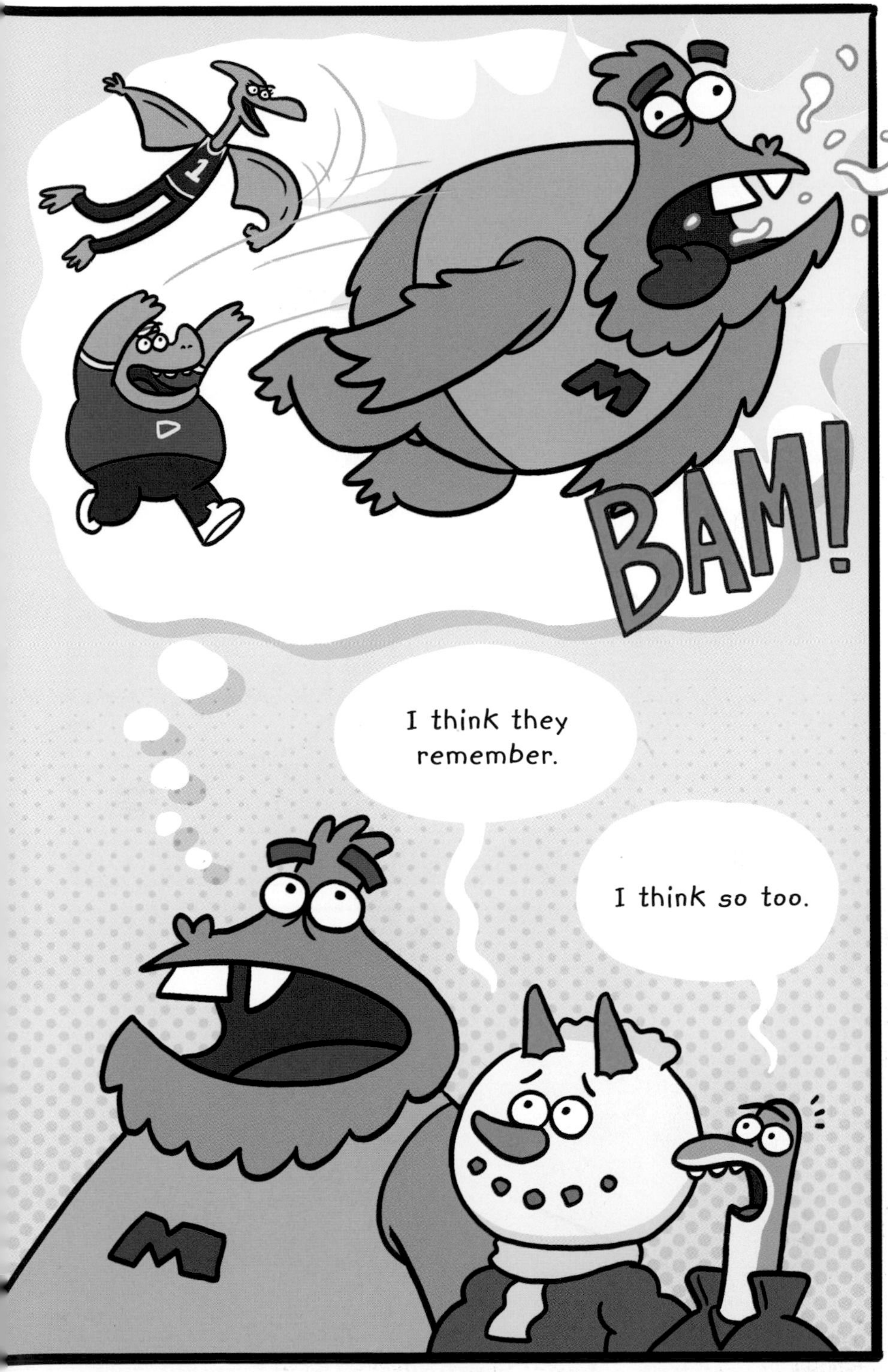
BAM!
I think they remember.
I think so too.

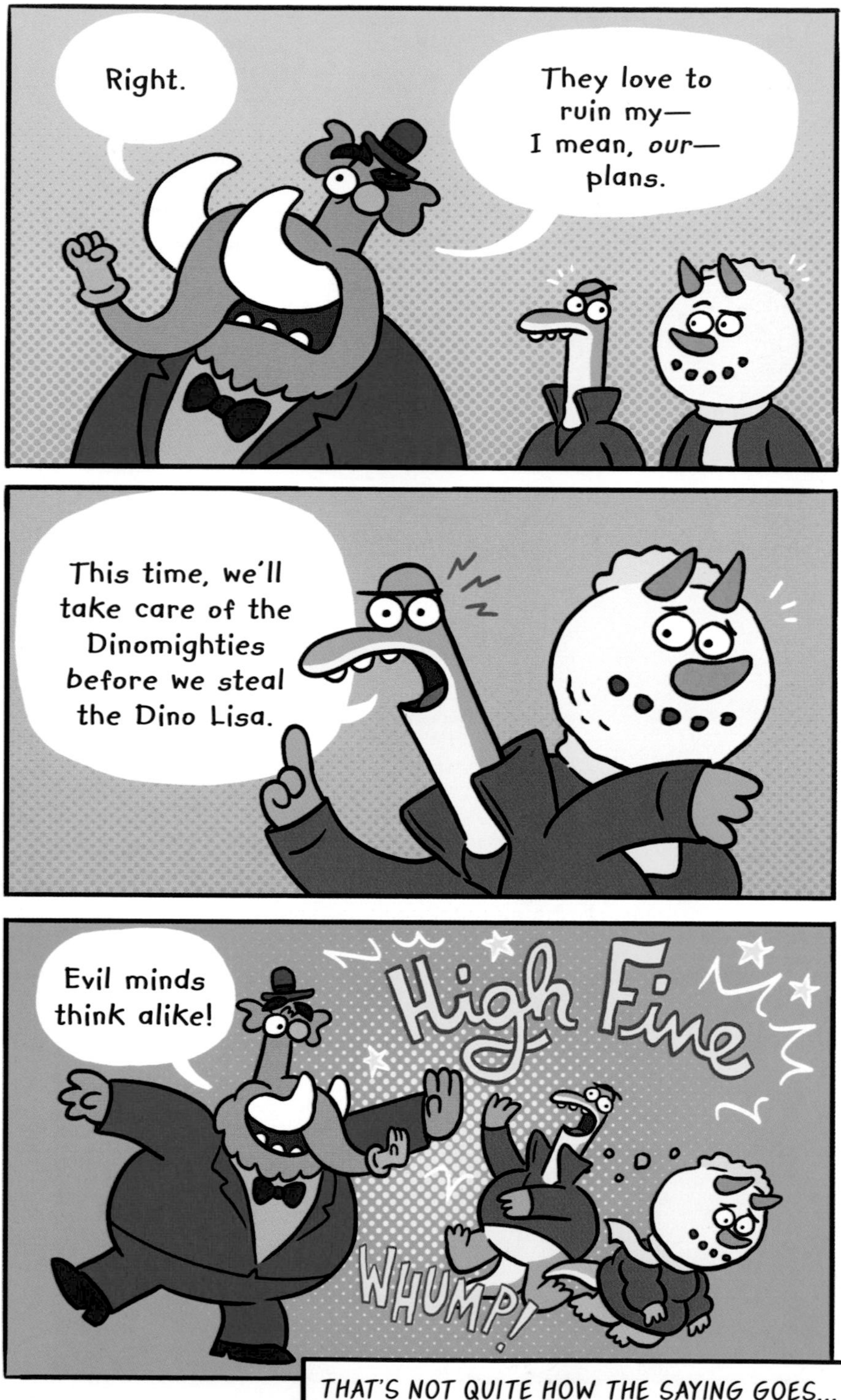

Right.
They love to ruin my— I mean, *our*— plans.
This time, we'll take care of the Dinomighties before we steal the Dino Lisa.
Evil minds think alike!
High Fine
WHUMP!
THAT'S NOT QUITE HOW THE SAYING GOES...

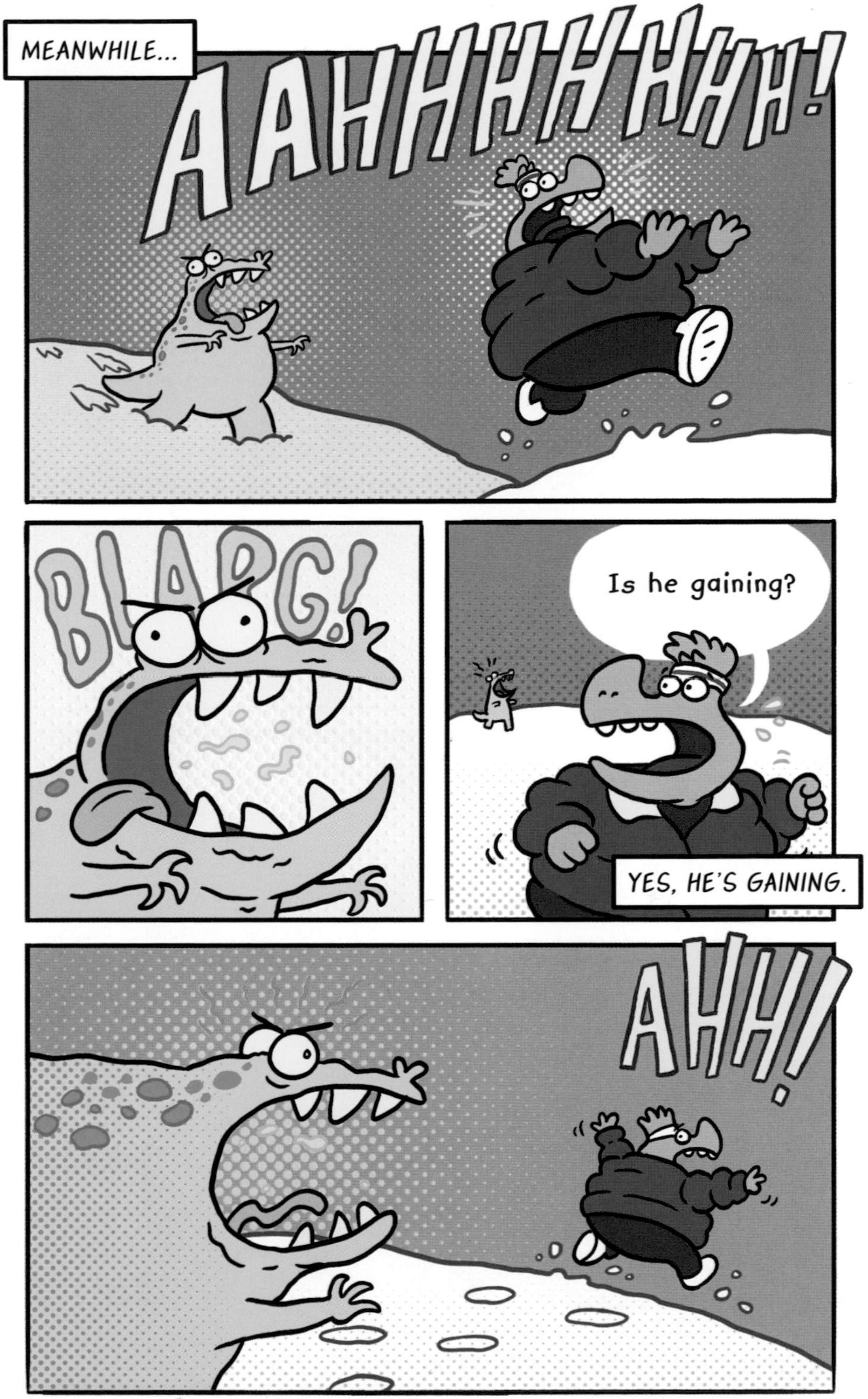
MEANWHILE...
AAHHHHHHHH!
BLARG!
Is he gaining?
YES, HE'S GAINING.
AHH!

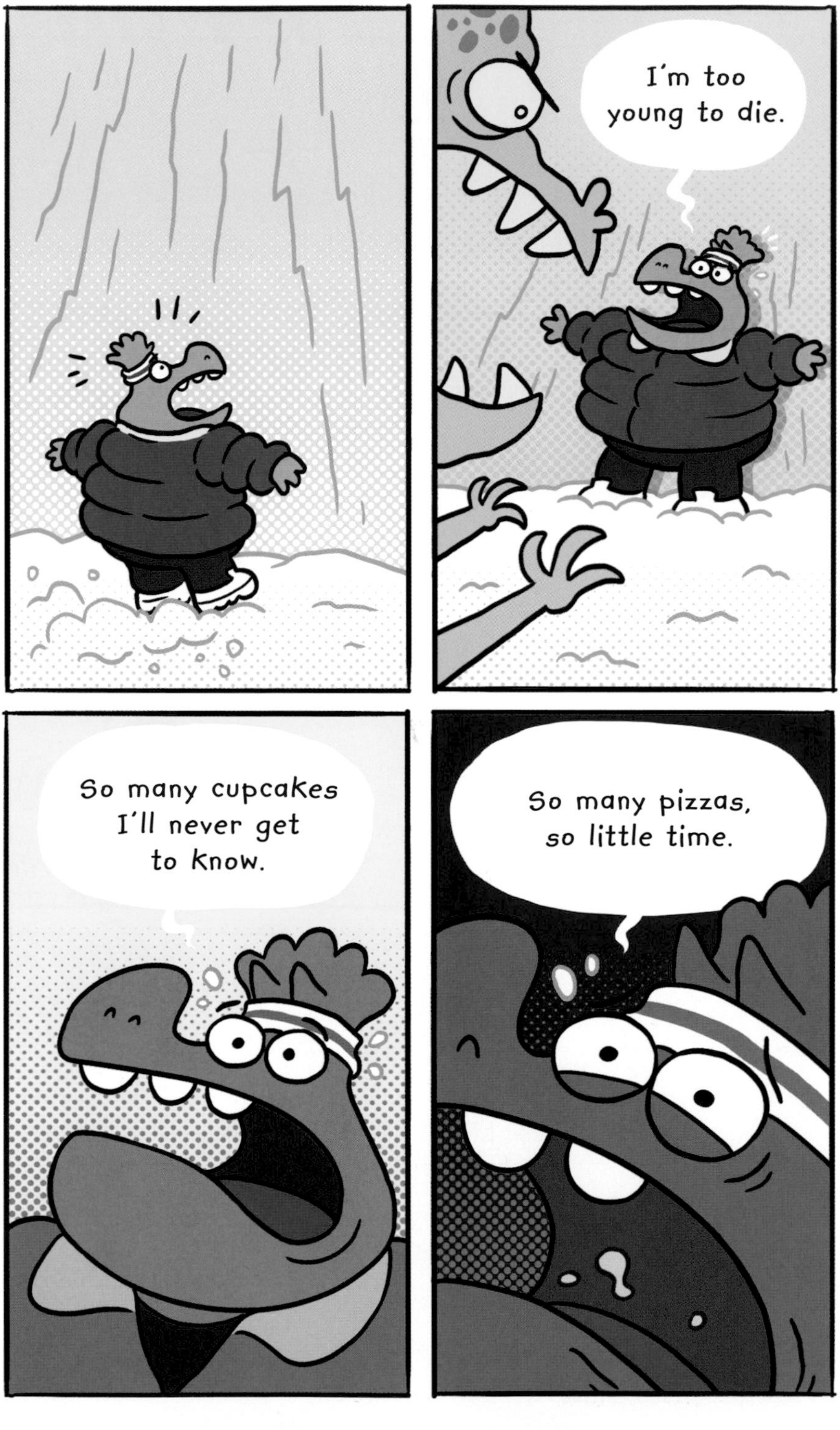
I'm too young to die.
So many cupcakes I'll never get to know.
So many pizzas, so little time.

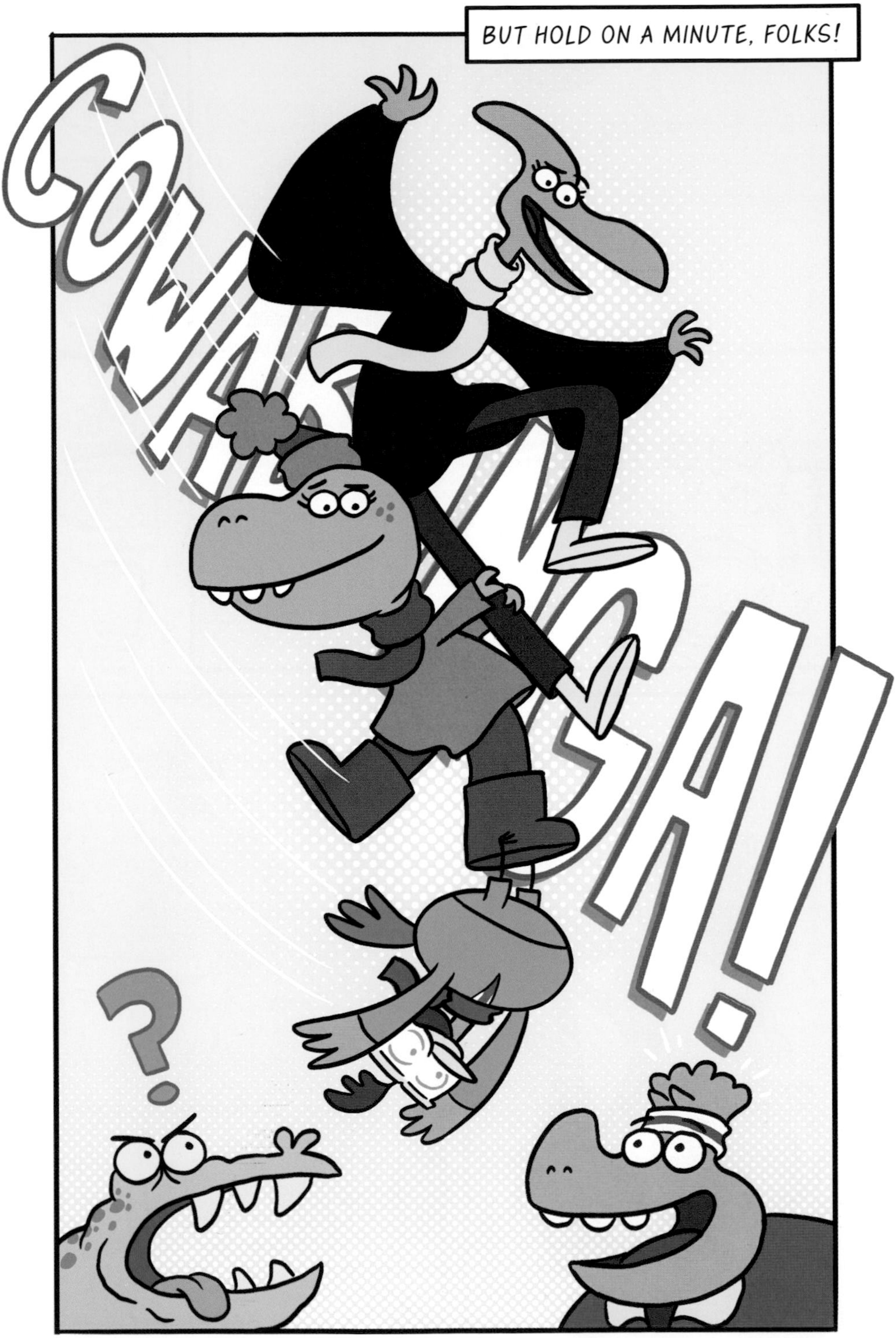
BUT HOLD ON A MINUTE, FOLKS!
COWABUNGA!
?

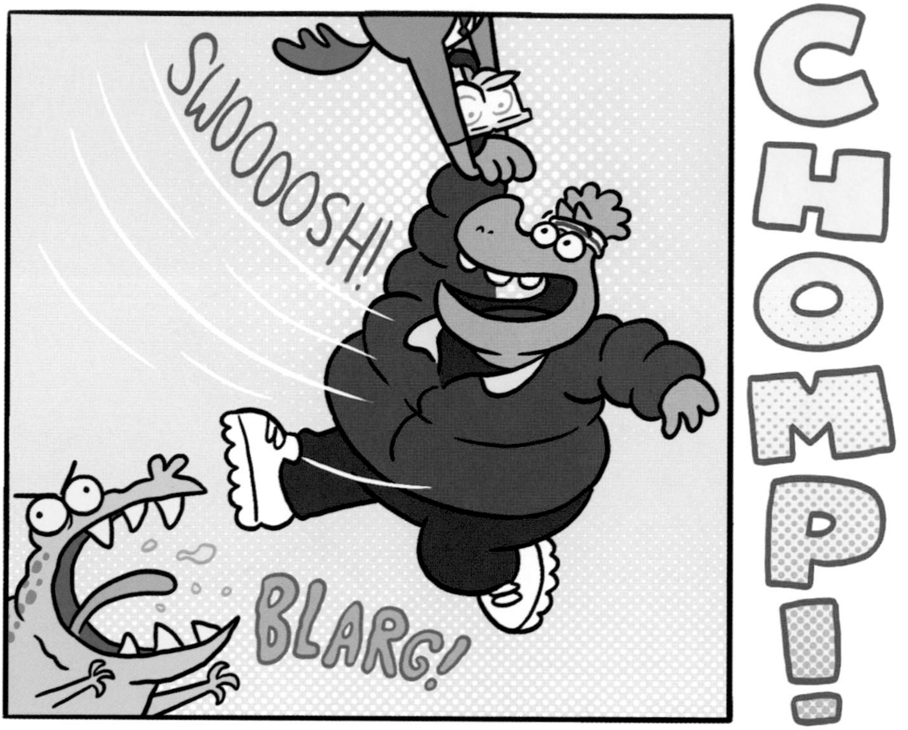
SWOOOOSH!
BLARG!
CHOMP!

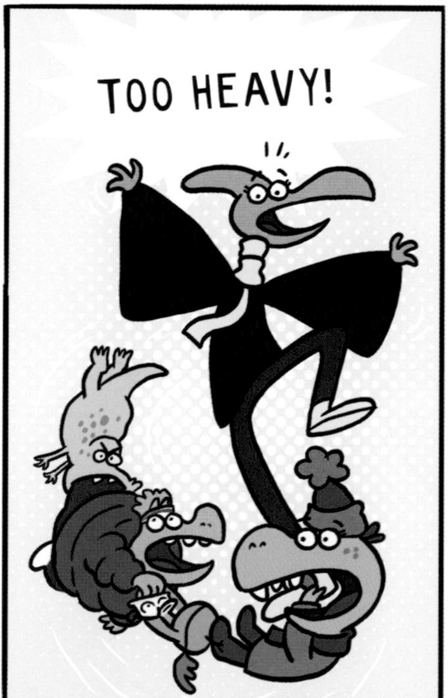
TOO HEAVY!

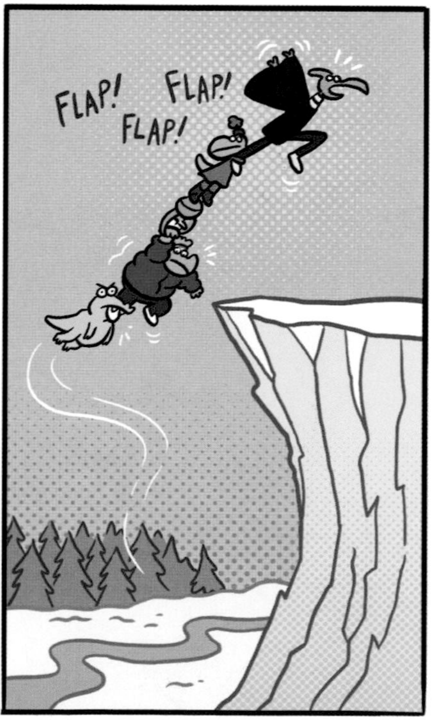
FLAP! FLAP!
FLAP!

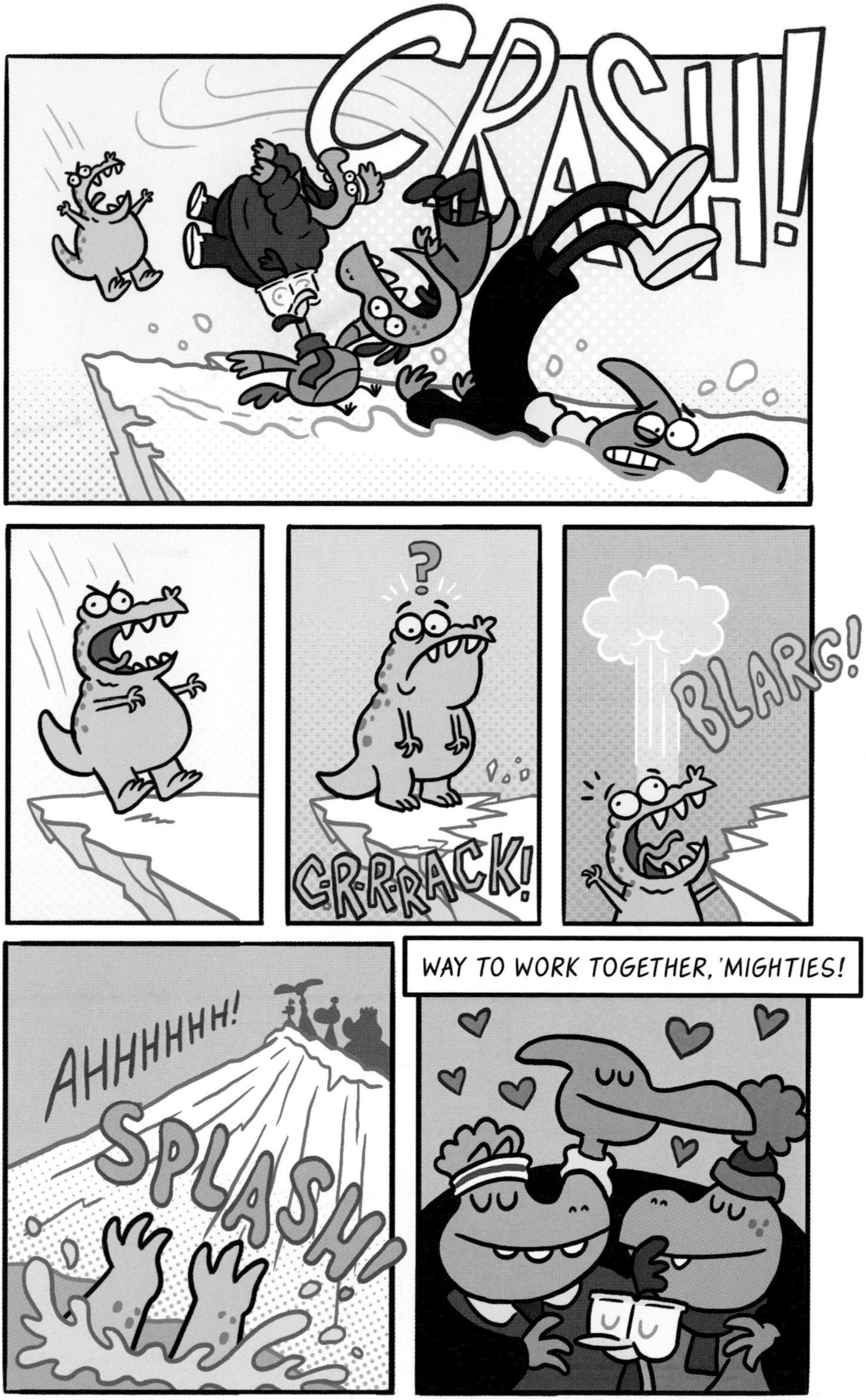
CRASH!
?
C-R-R-RACK!
BLARG!
AHHHHHH!
SPLASH!
WAY TO WORK TOGETHER, 'MIGHTIES!

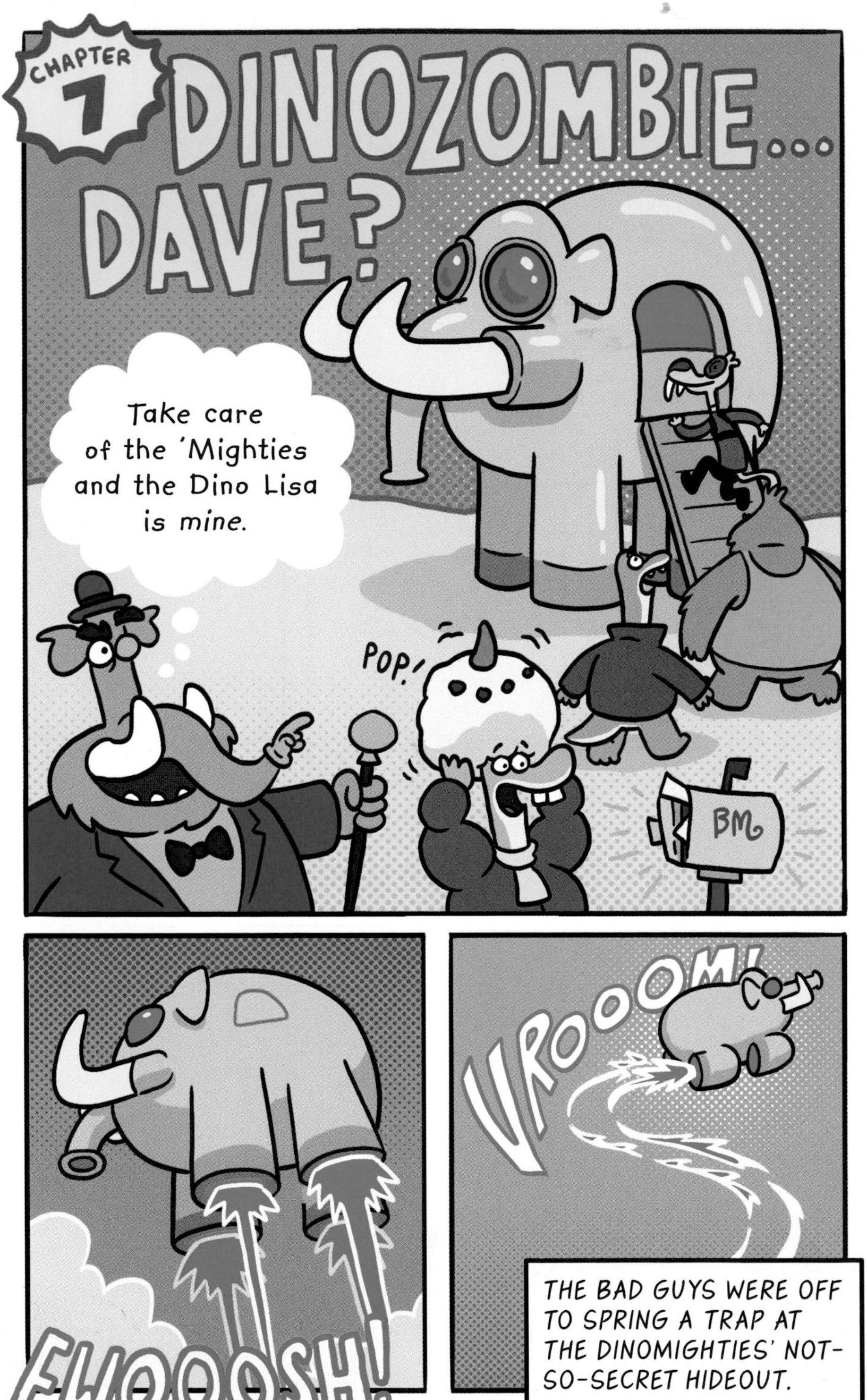
CHAPTER 7
DINOZOMBIE... DAVE?
Take care of the 'Mighties and the Dino Lisa is mine.
POP!
BM
FWOOOSH!
VROOOOM!
THE BAD GUYS WERE OFF TO SPRING A TRAP AT THE DINOMIGHTIES' NOT-SO-SECRET HIDEOUT.

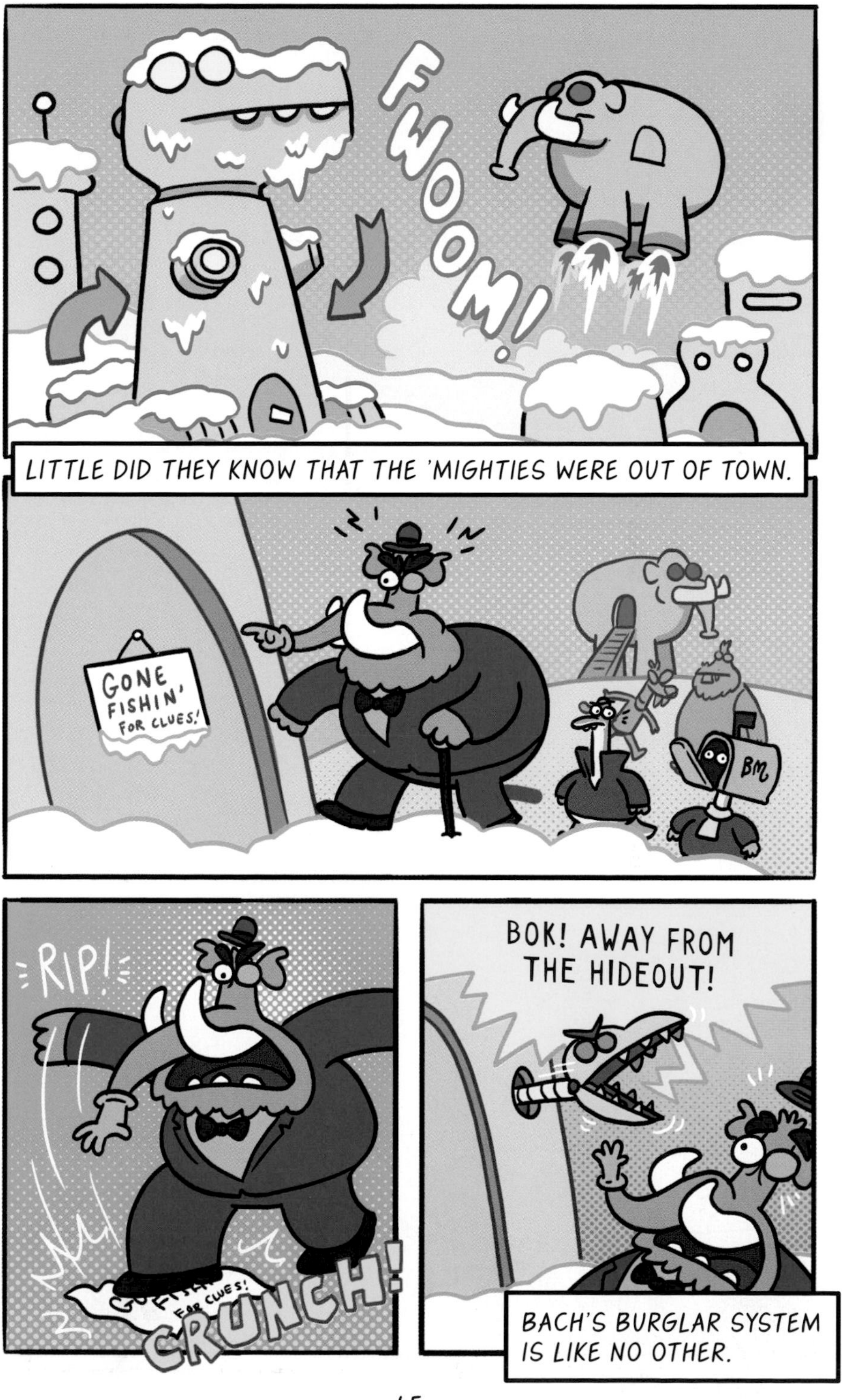
FWOOM!
LITTLE DID THEY KNOW THAT THE 'MIGHTIES WERE OUT OF TOWN.
GONE FISHIN' FOR CLUES!
BM
RIP!
FOR CLUES!
CRUNCH!
BOK! AWAY FROM THE HIDEOUT!
BACH'S BURGLAR SYSTEM IS LIKE NO OTHER.

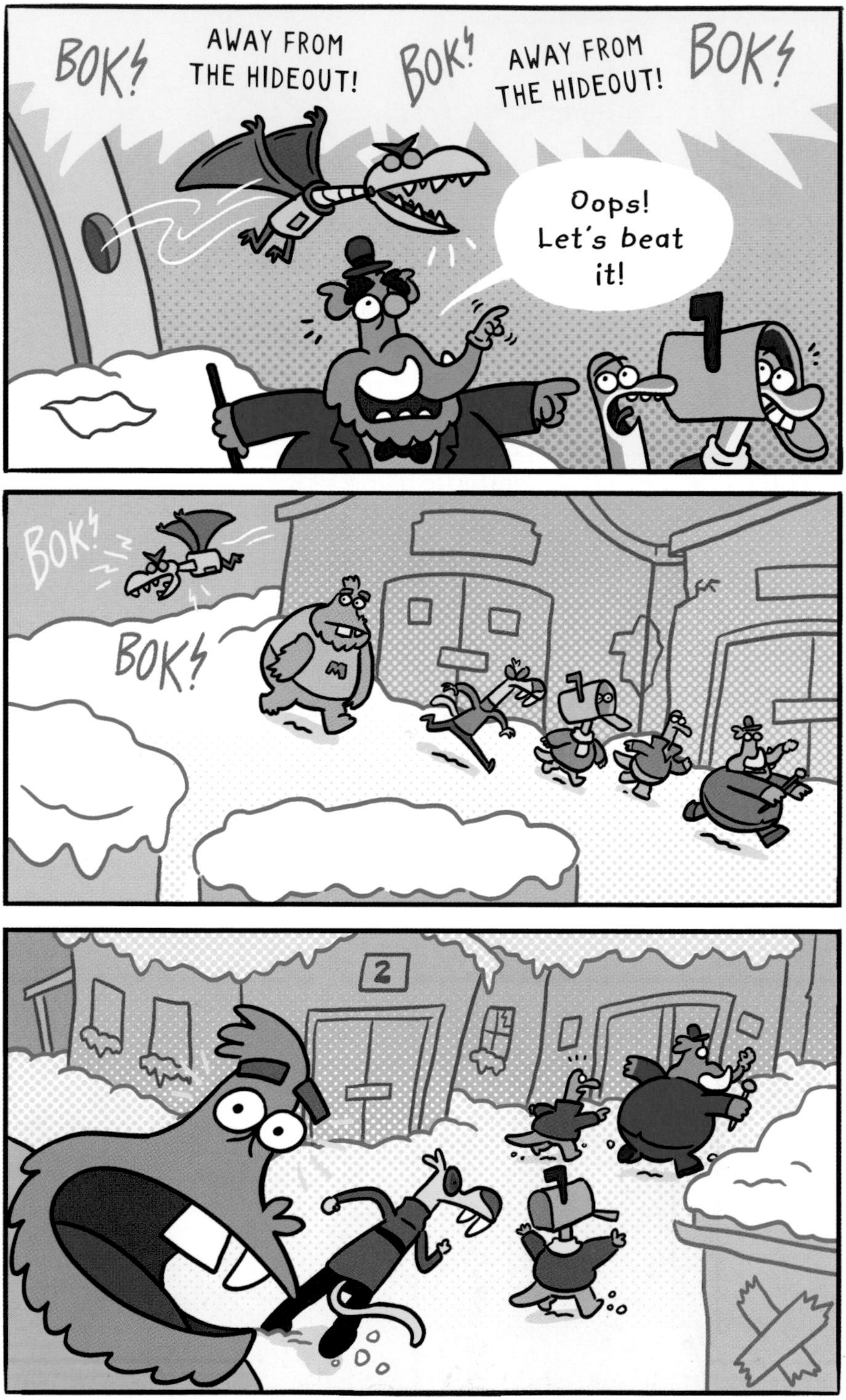
BOK!
AWAY FROM THE HIDEOUT!
BOK!
AWAY FROM THE HIDEOUT!
BOK!
Oops! Let's beat it!
BOK!
BOK!
2

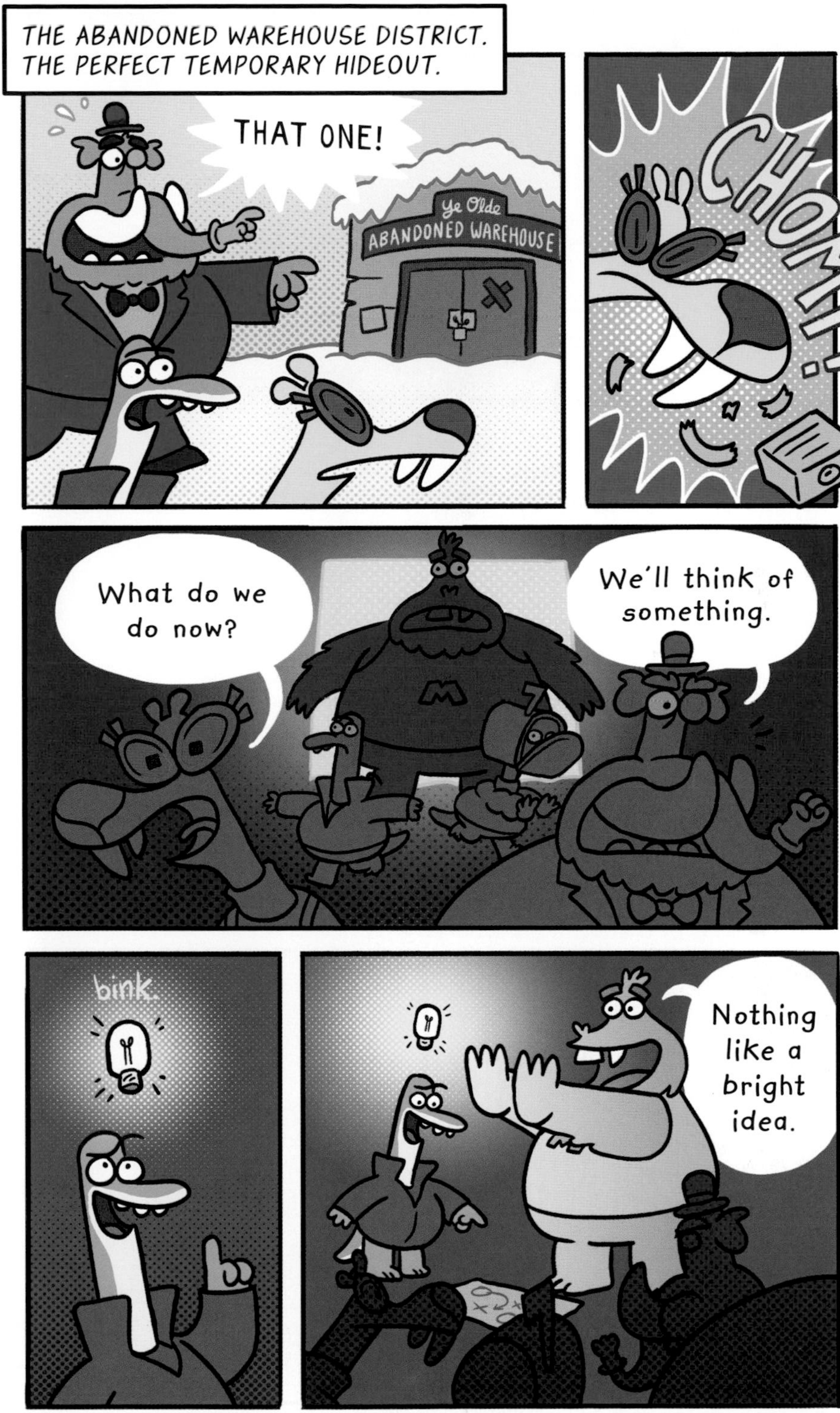
THE ABANDONED WAREHOUSE DISTRICT.
THE PERFECT TEMPORARY HIDEOUT.
THAT ONE!
Ye Olde
ABANDONED WAREHOUSE
CHOMP!!
What do we do now?
We'll think of something.
bink.
Nothing like a bright idea.

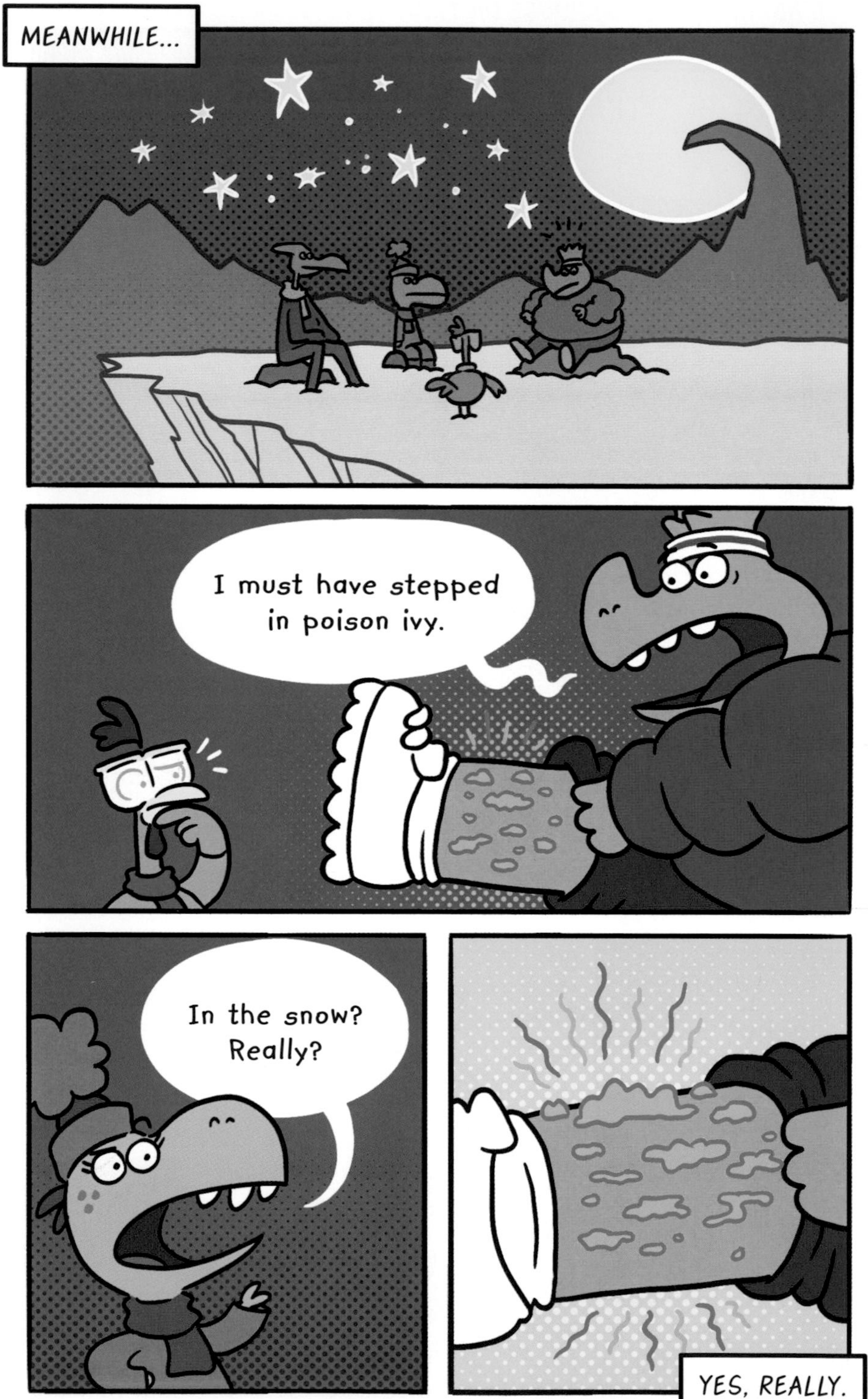
MEANWHILE...
I must have stepped in poison ivy.
In the snow? Really?
YES, REALLY.

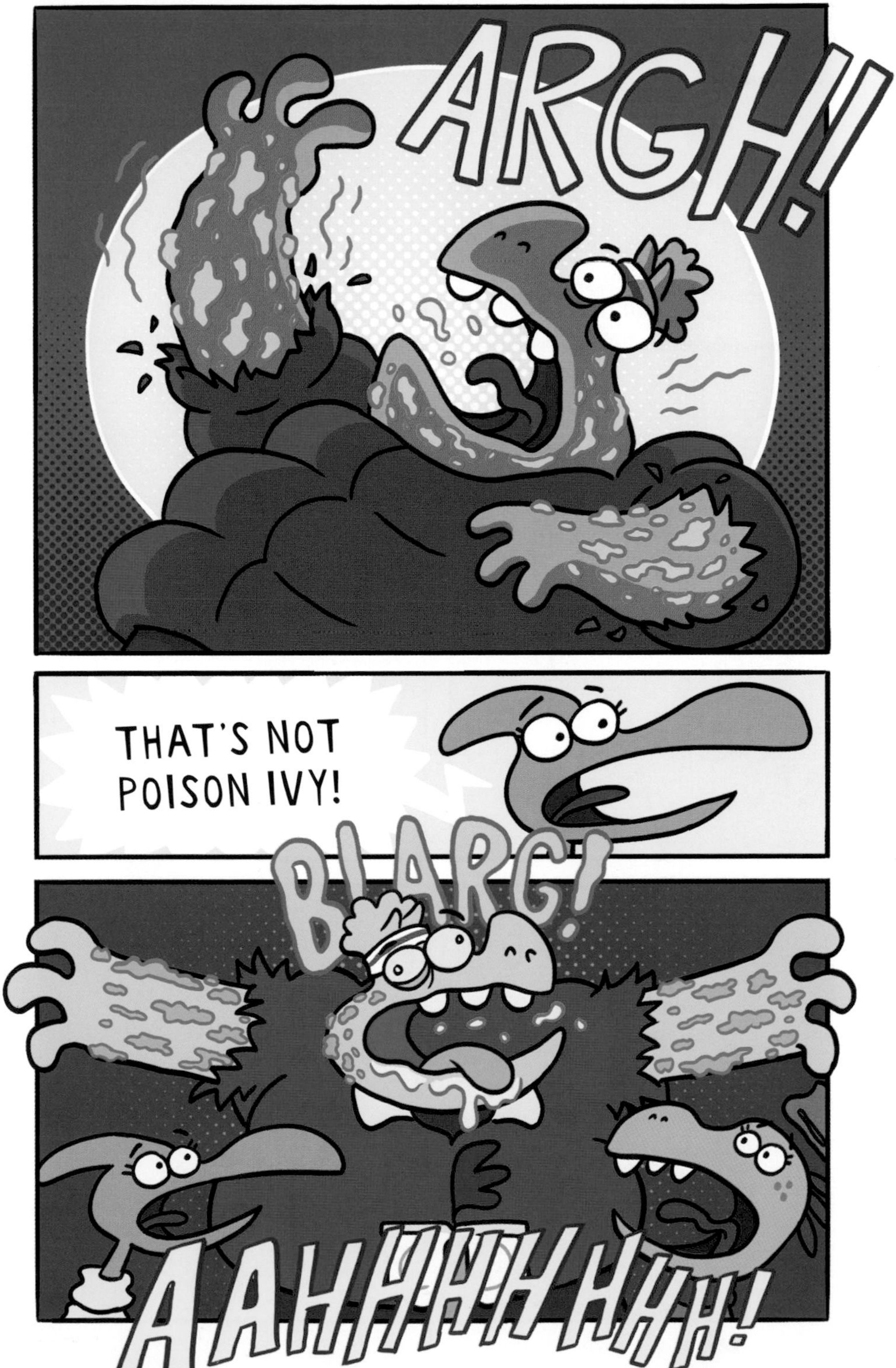
ARGH!
THAT'S NOT POISON IVY!
BLARG!
AAHHHHH HHH!

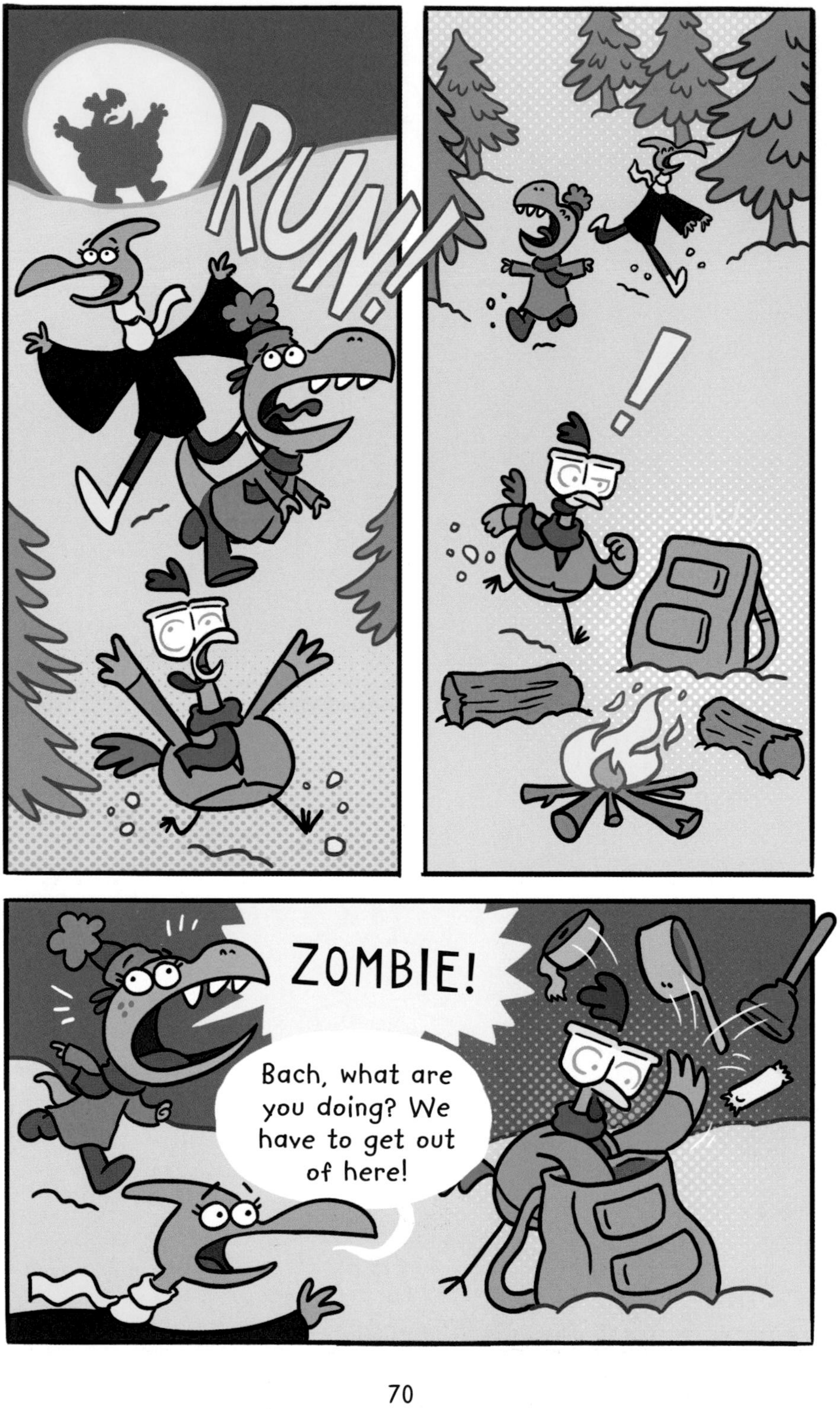
RUN!!
!
ZOMBIE!
Bach, what are you doing? We have to get out of here!

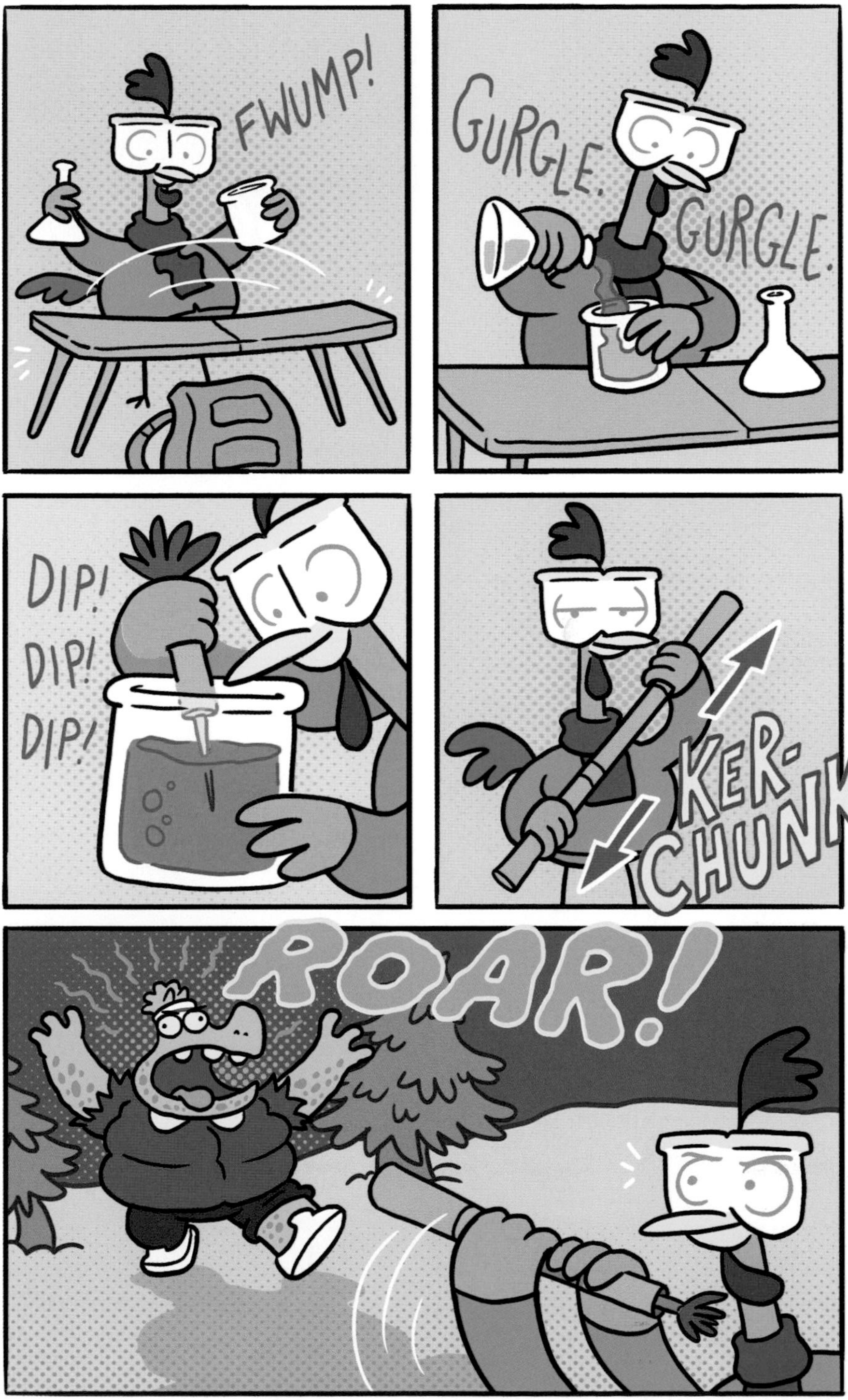
FWUMP!
GURGLE.
GURGLE.
DIP!
DIP!
DIP!
KER-
CHUNK!
ROAR!

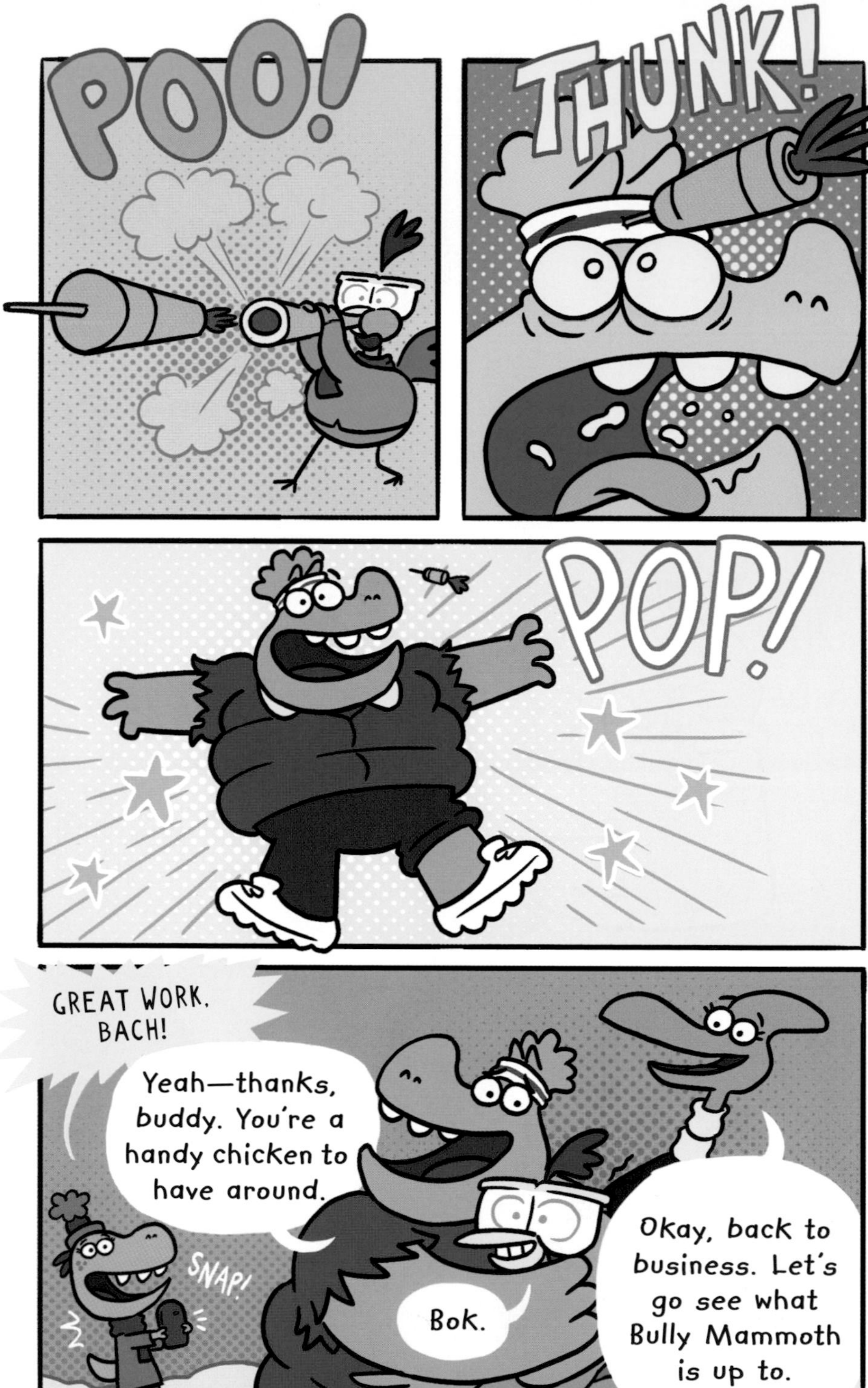
POO!
THUNK!
POP!
GREAT WORK, BACH!
Yeah—thanks, buddy. You're a handy chicken to have around.
SNAP!
Bok.
Okay, back to business. Let's go see what Bully Mammoth is up to.

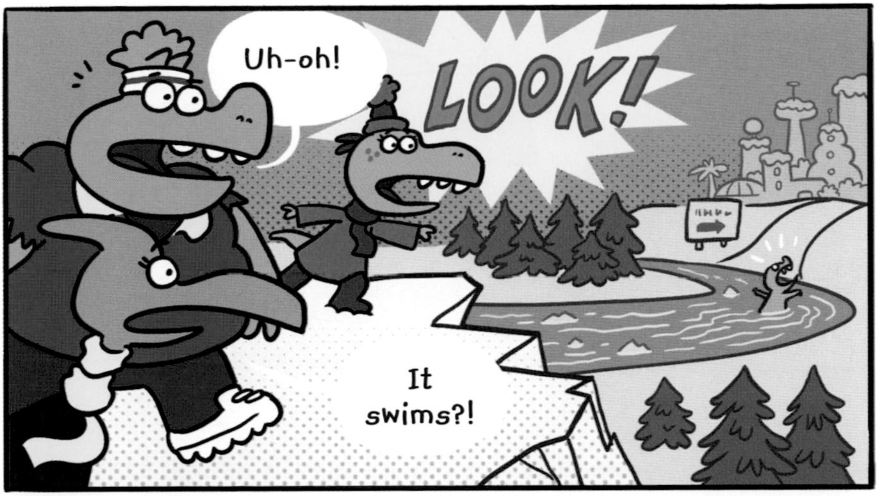
Uh-oh!
LOOK!
It swims?!

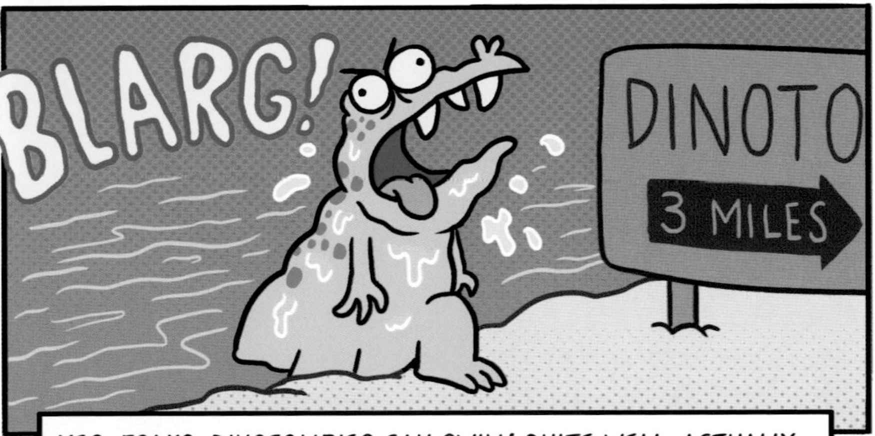
BLARG!
DINOTO
3 MILES

YES, FOLKS, DINOZOMBIES CAN SWIM! QUITE WELL, ACTUALLY...

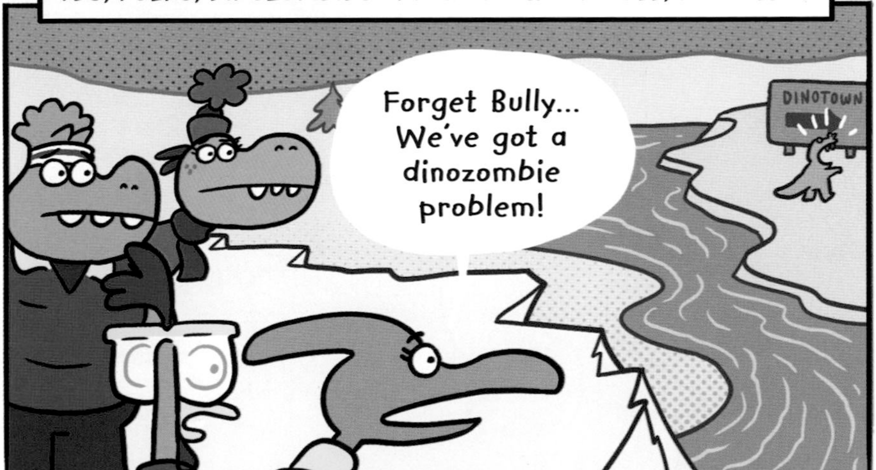
Forget Bully... We've got a dinozombie problem!
DINOTOWN

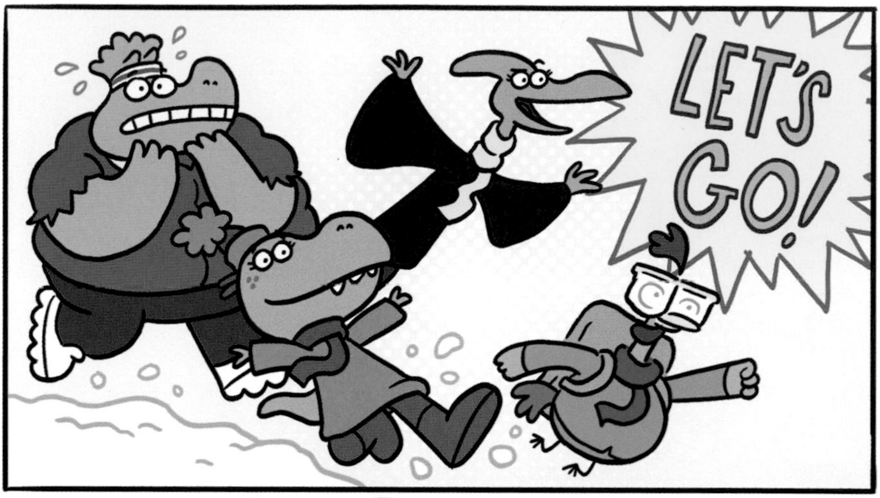
LET'S GO!

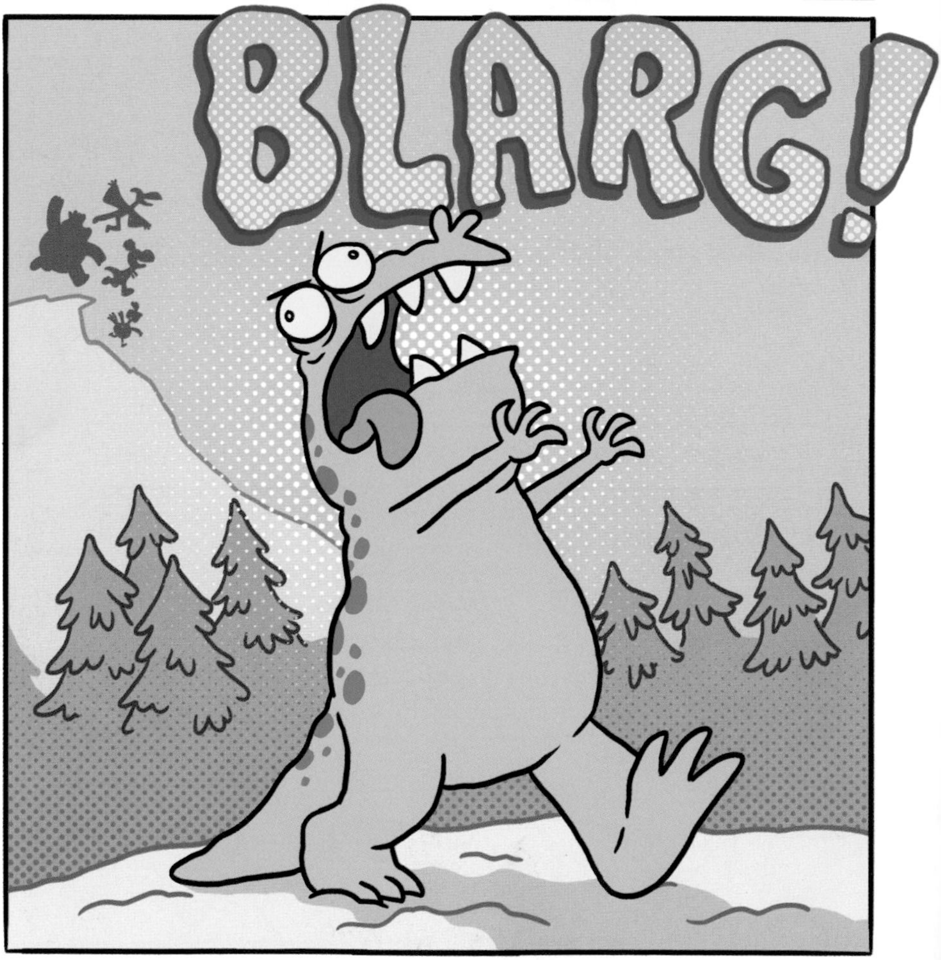
BLARG!

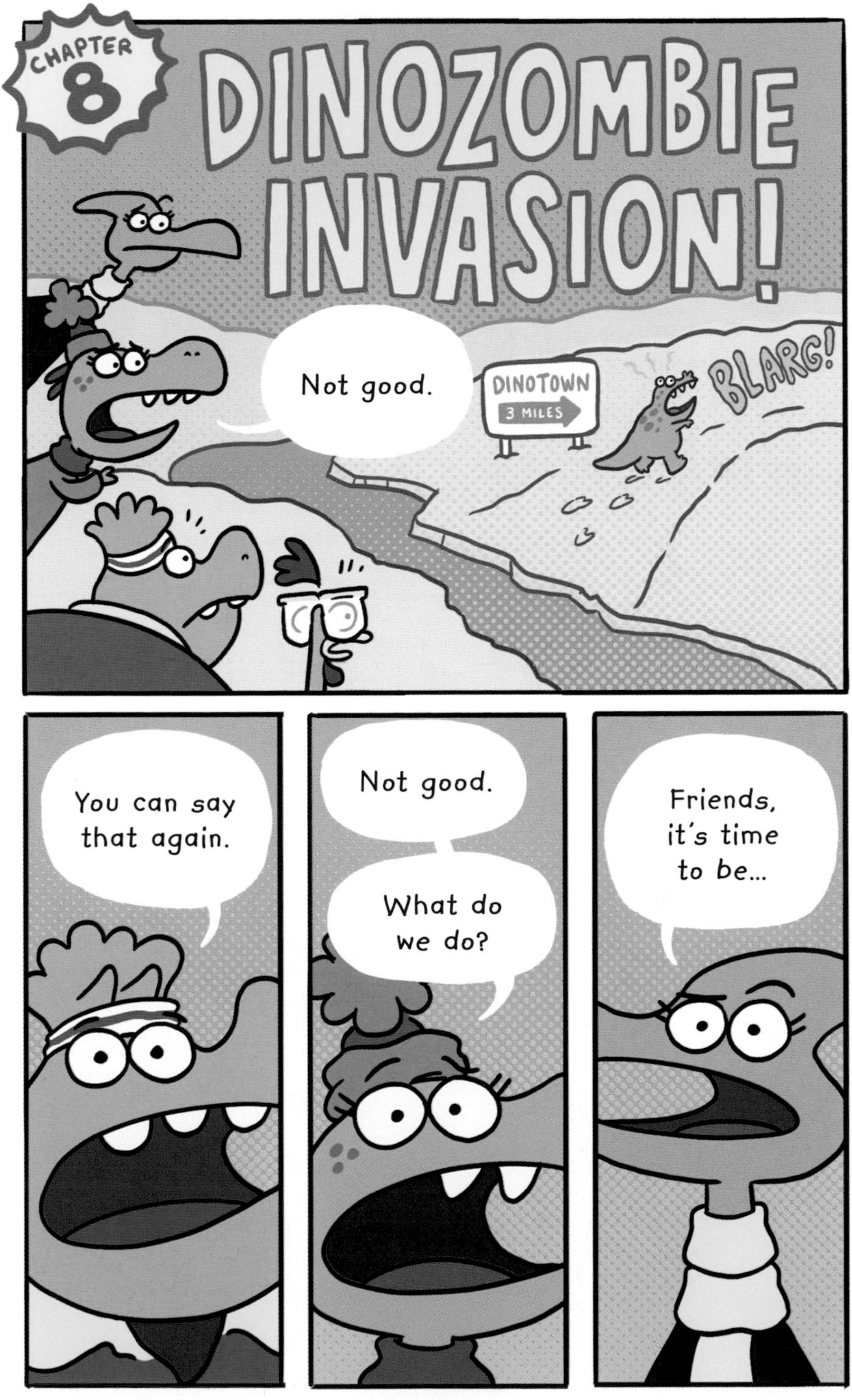
CHAPTER 8
DINOZOMBIE INVASION!
Not good.
DINOTOWN
3 MILES
BLARG!
You can say that again.
Not good.
What do we do?
Friends, it's time to be...

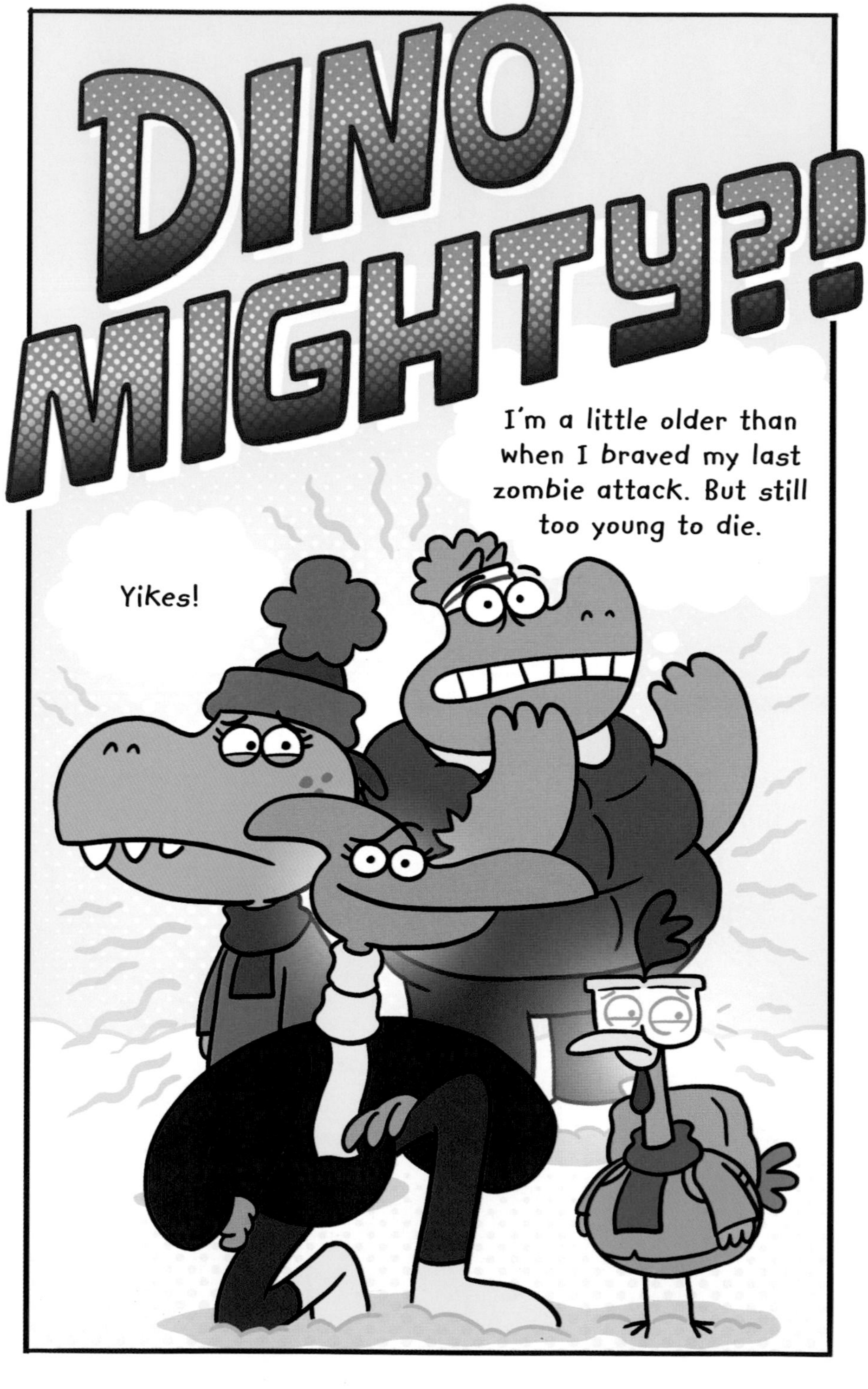
DINO MIGHTY?!
I'm a little older than when I braved my last zombie attack. But still too young to die.
Yikes!

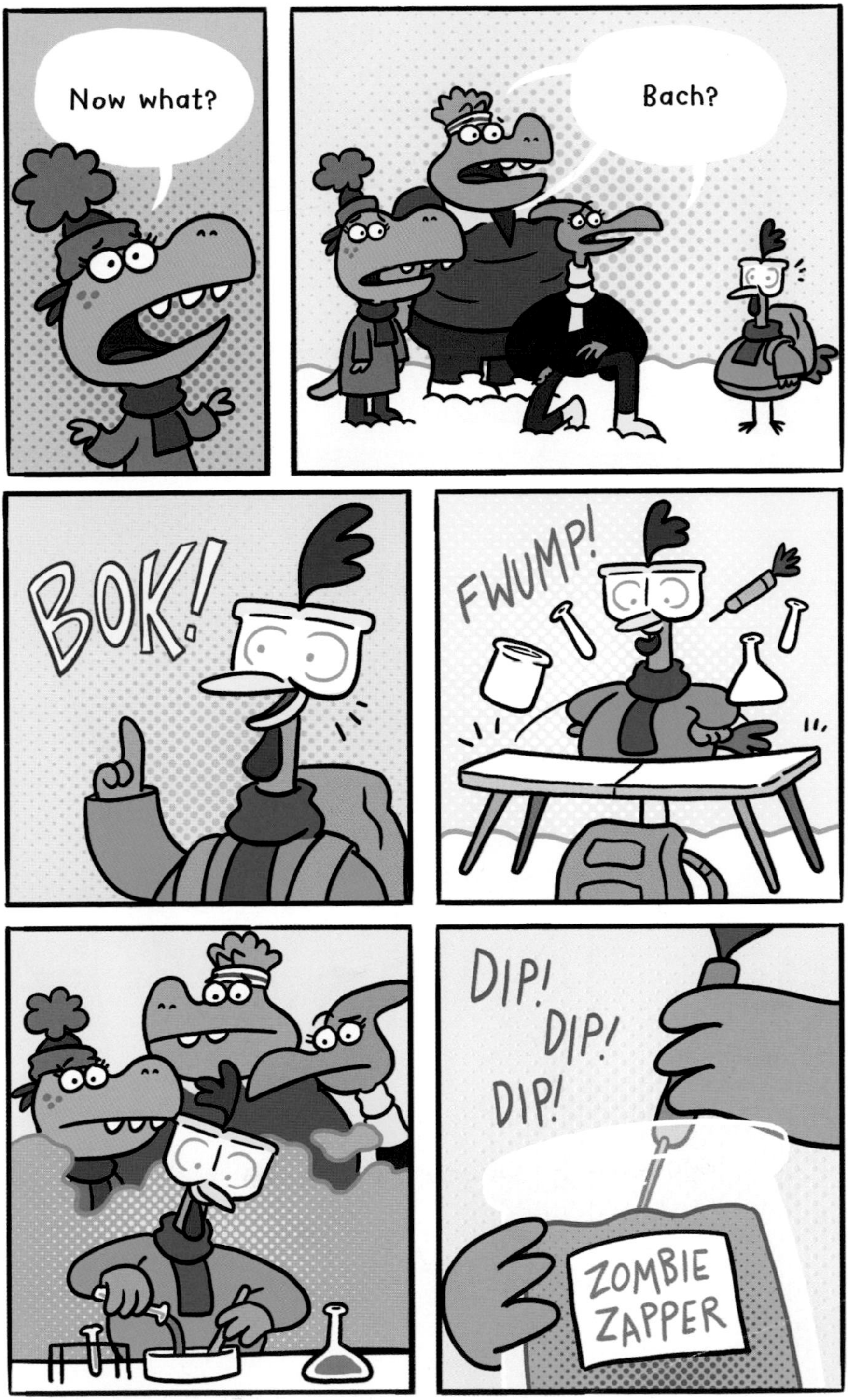
Now what?
Bach?
BOK!
FWUMP!
DIP!
DIP!
DIP!
ZOMBIE
ZAPPER

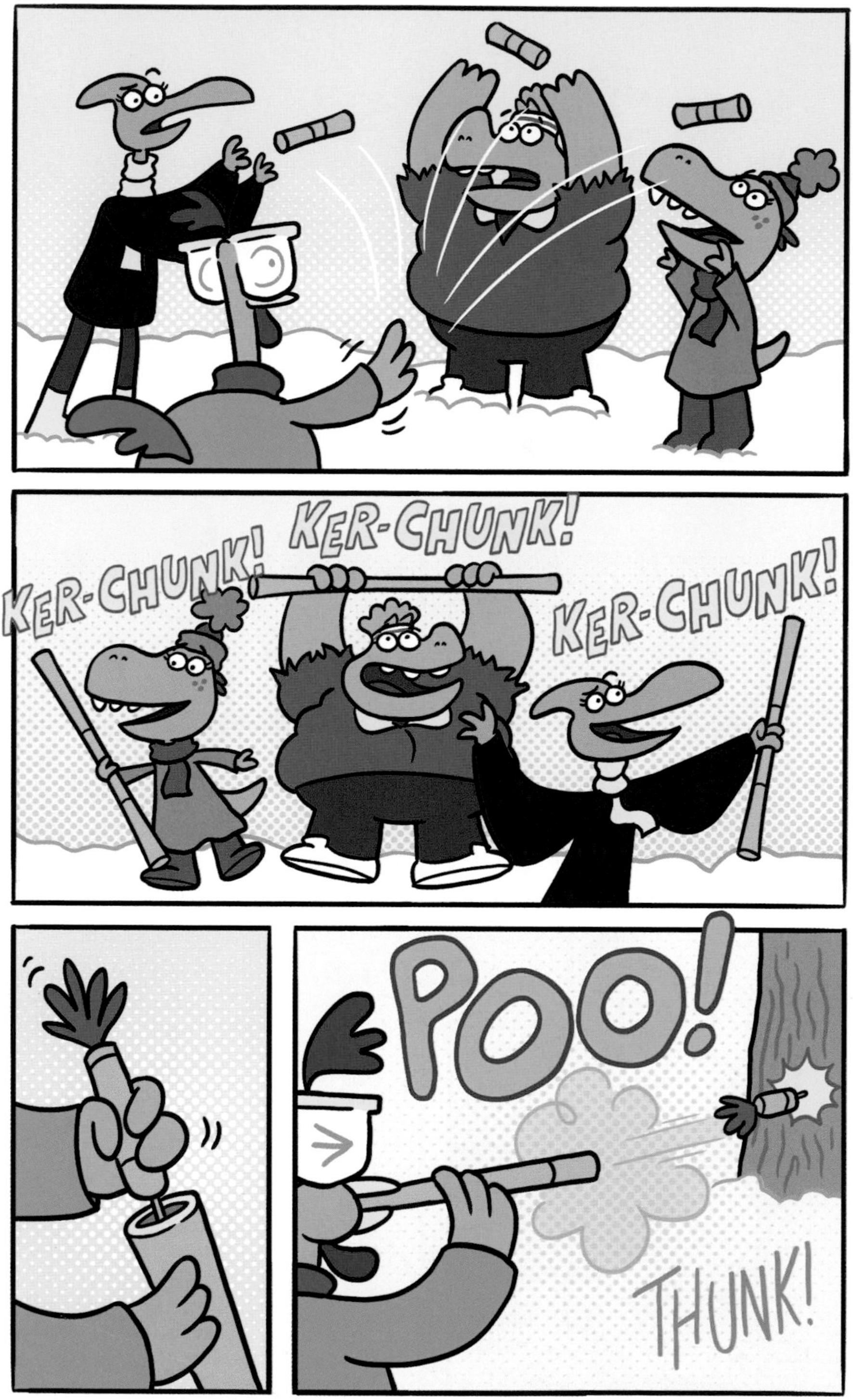
KER-CHUNK!
KER-CHUNK!
KER-CHUNK!
POO!
THUNK!

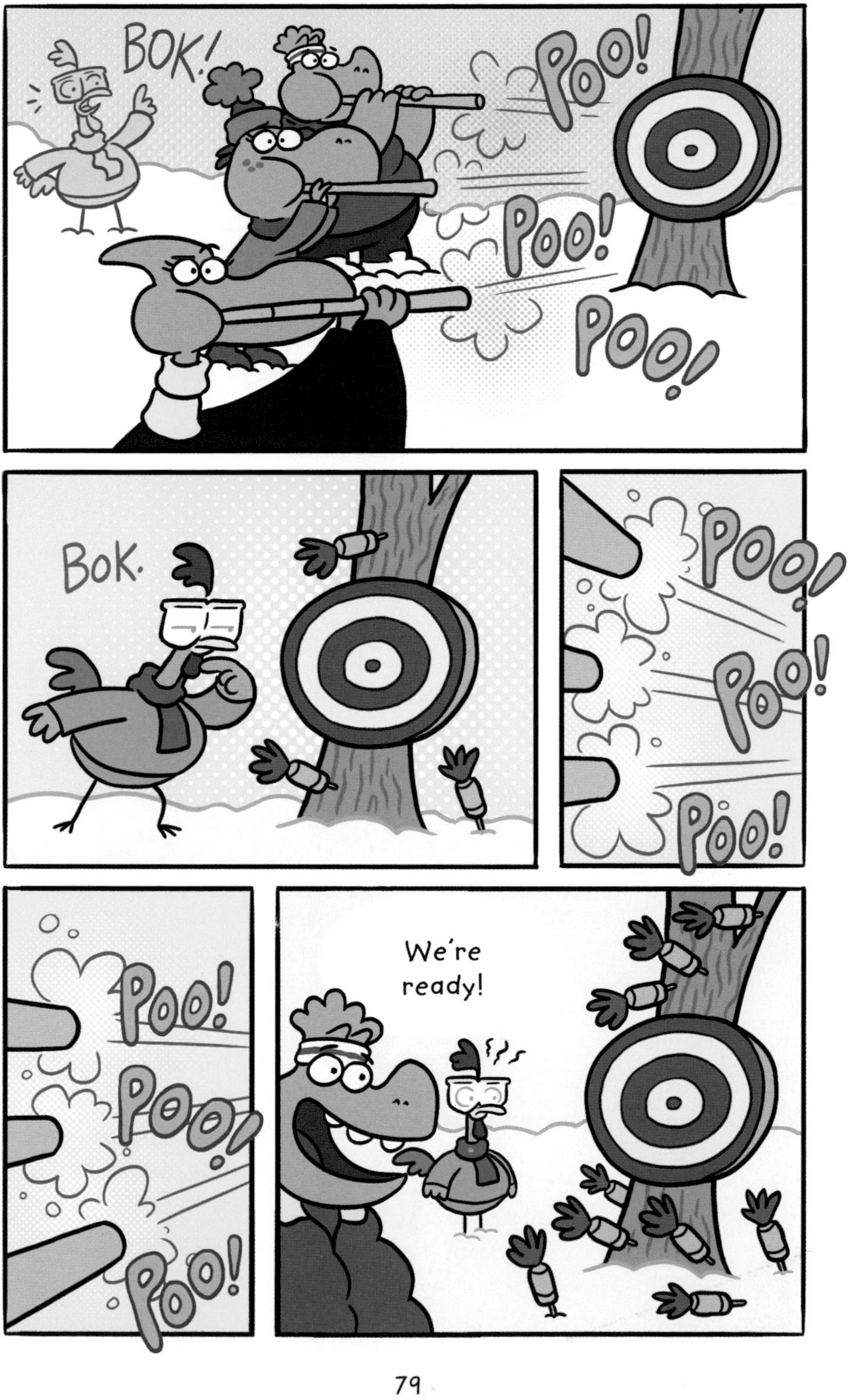
BOK!
POO!
POO!
POO!
BOK.
POO!
POO!
POO!
POO!
POO!
POO!
We're ready!

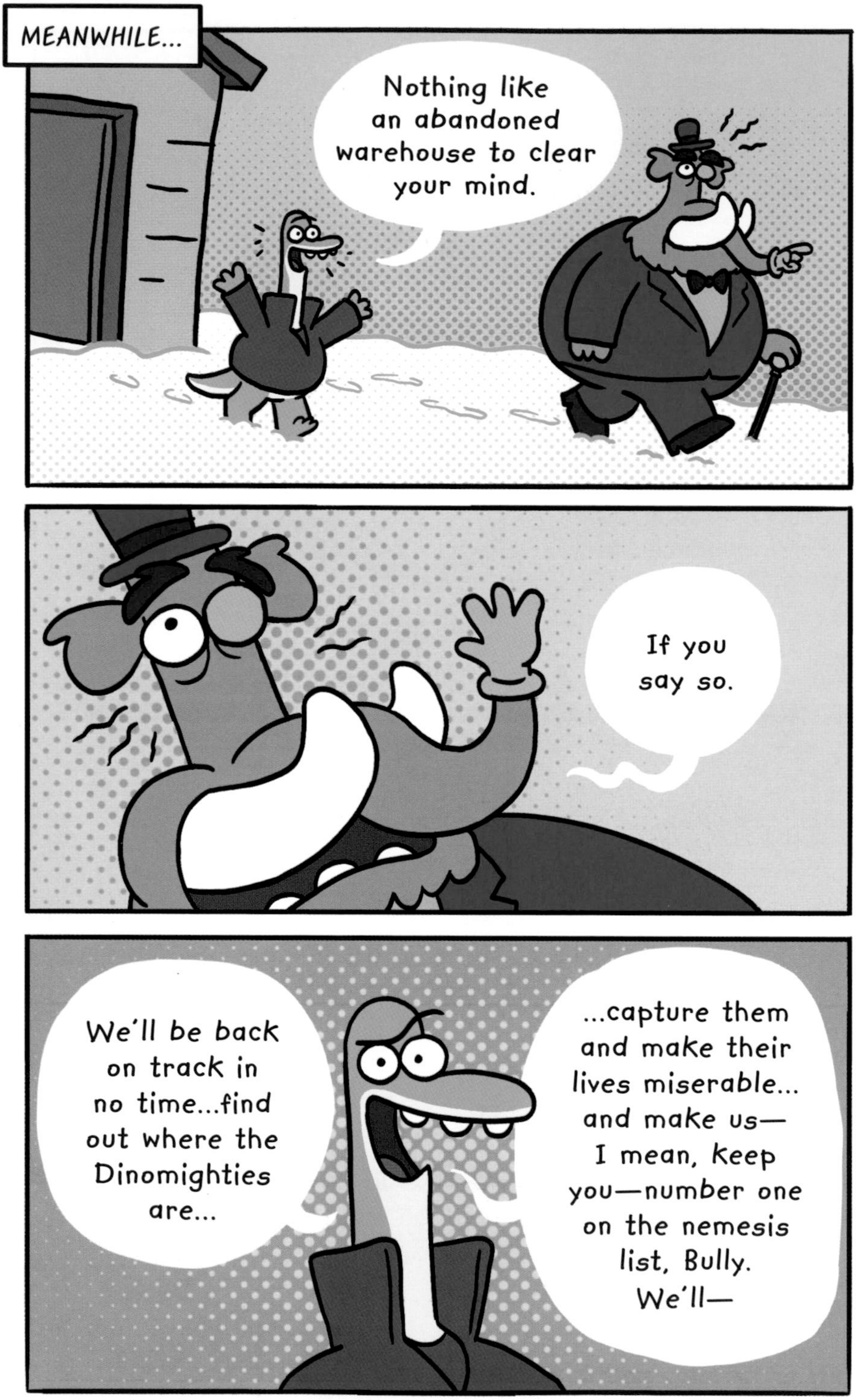
MEANWHILE...
Nothing like an abandoned warehouse to clear your mind.
If you say so.
We'll be back on track in no time...find out where the Dinomighties are...
...capture them and make their lives miserable... and make us— I mean, keep you—number one on the nemesis list, Bully. We'll—

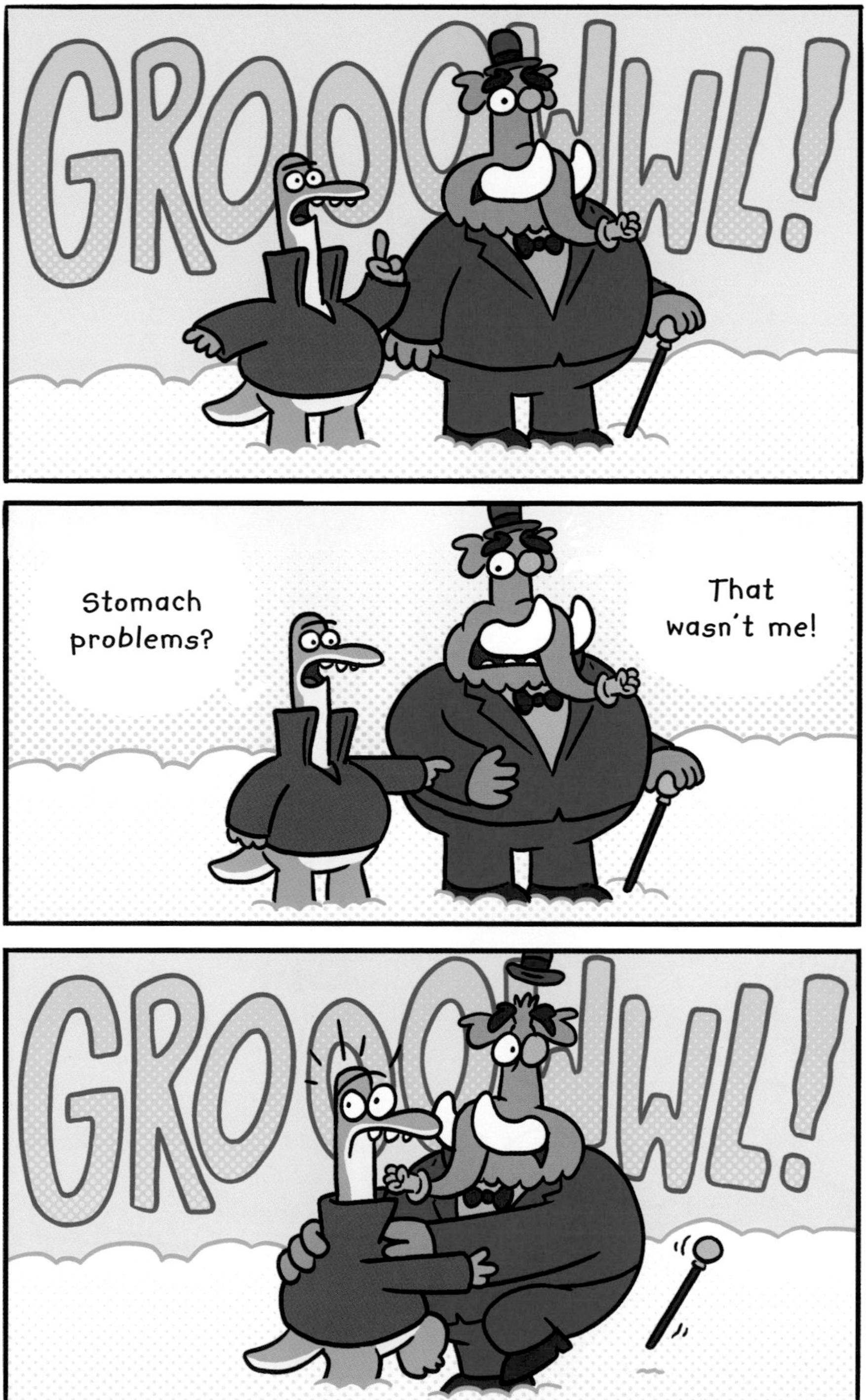
GROOOWL!
Stomach problems?
That wasn't me!
GROOOWL!

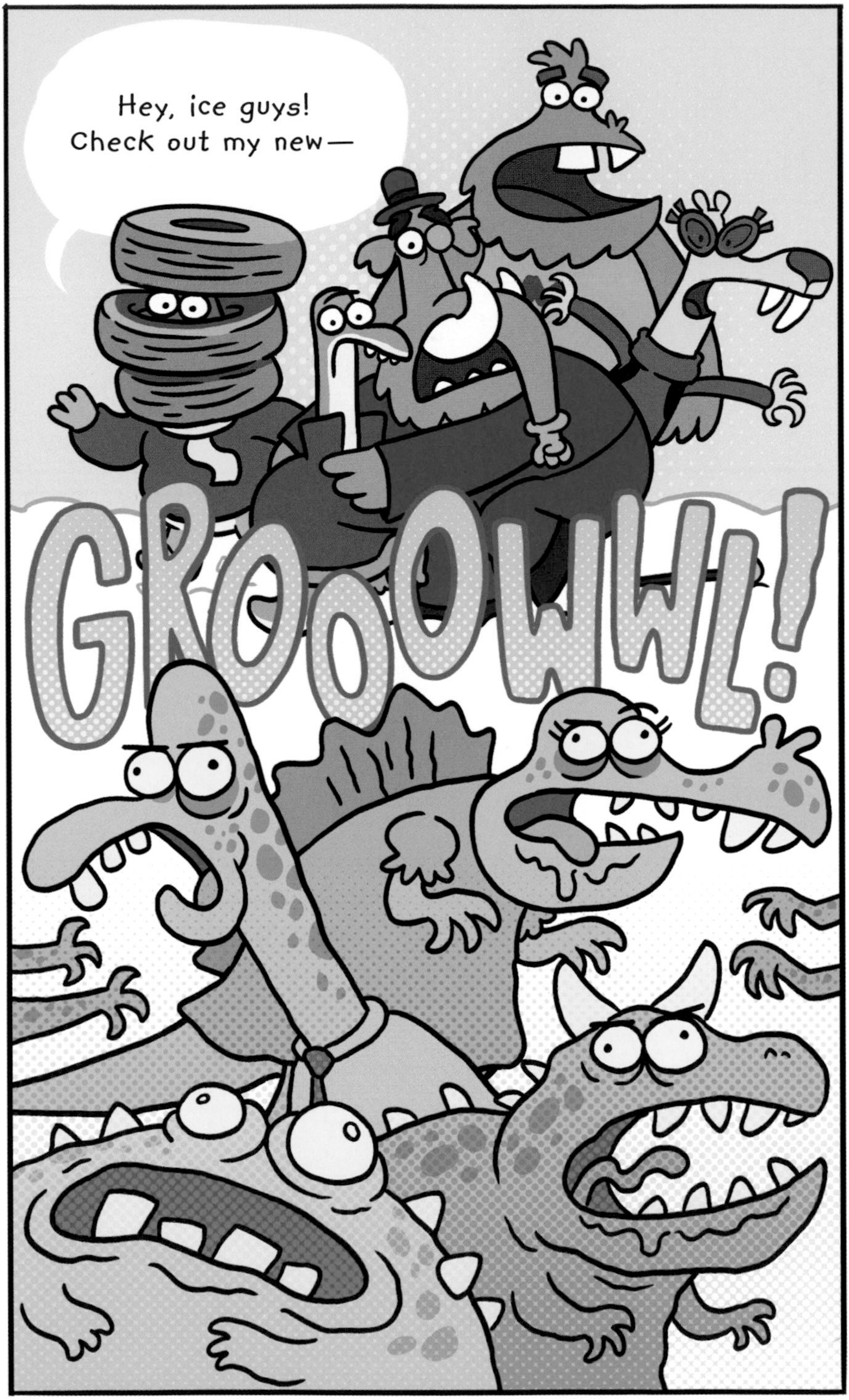
Hey, ice guys!
Check out my new—
GROOOWWL!

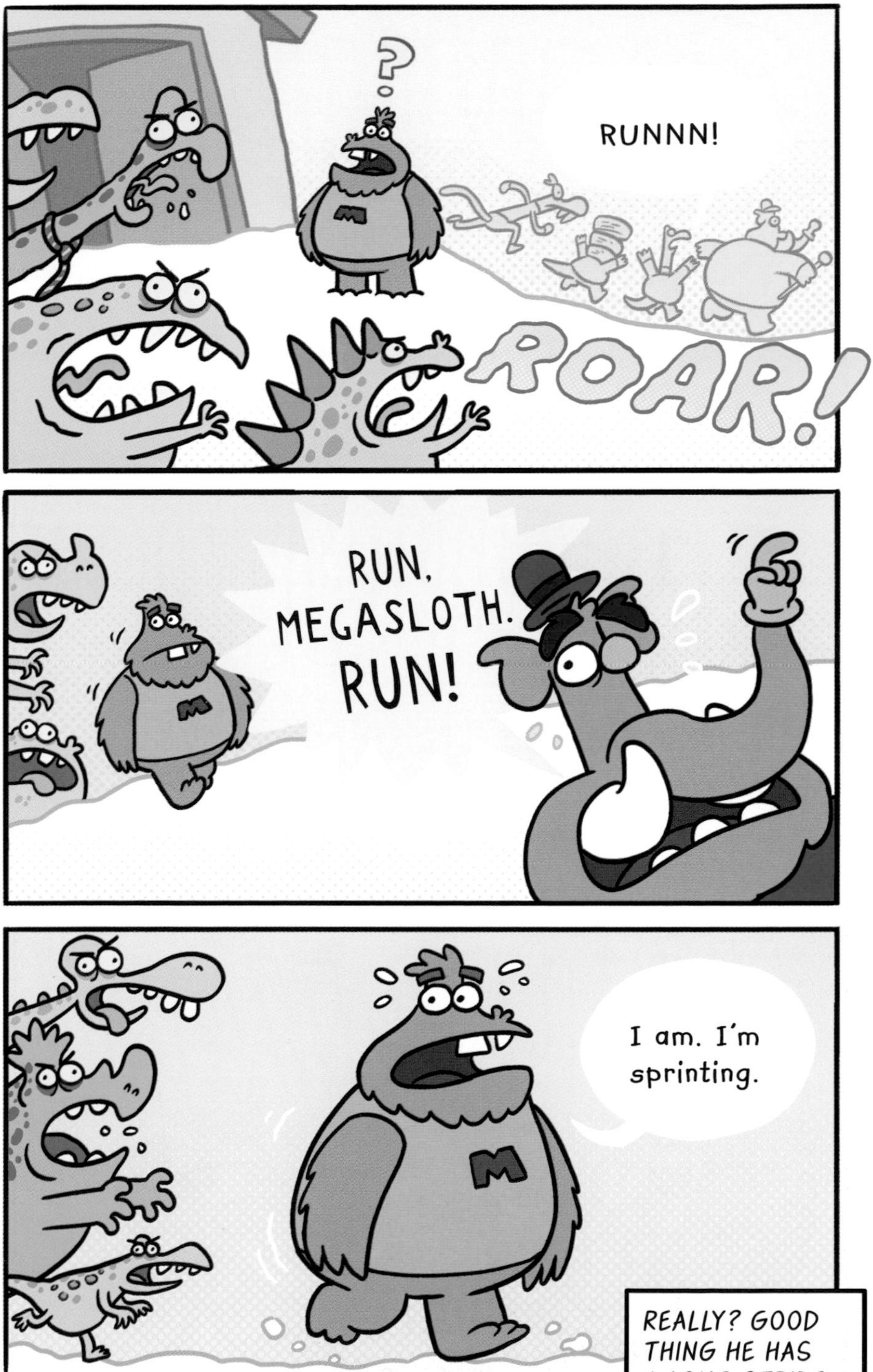
?
RUNNN!
ROAR!
RUN, MEGASLOTH. RUN!
I am. I'm sprinting.
REALLY? GOOD THING HE HAS A LONG STRIDE...

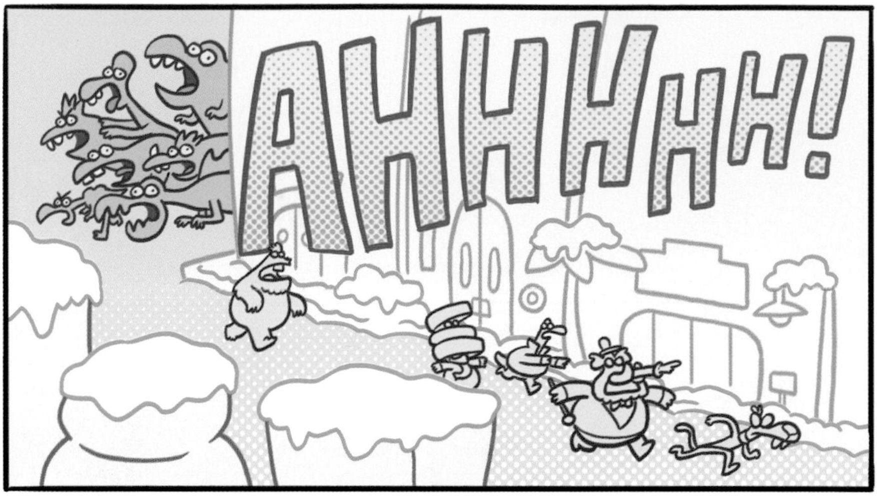
AHHHHHH!

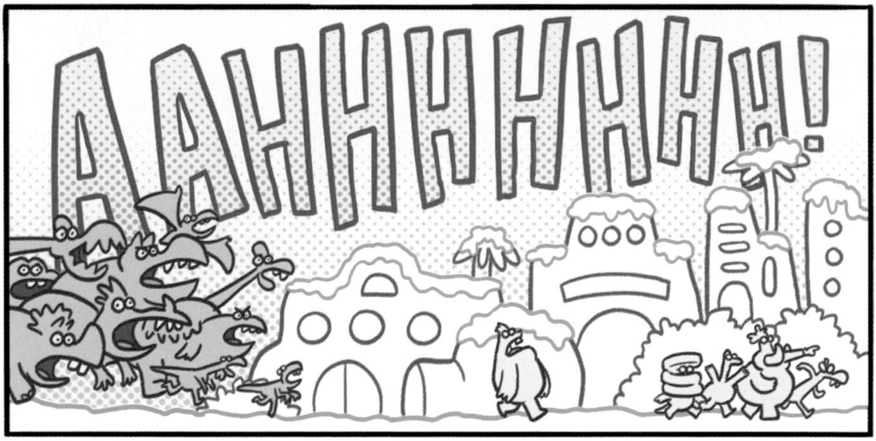
AAHHHHHHHH!

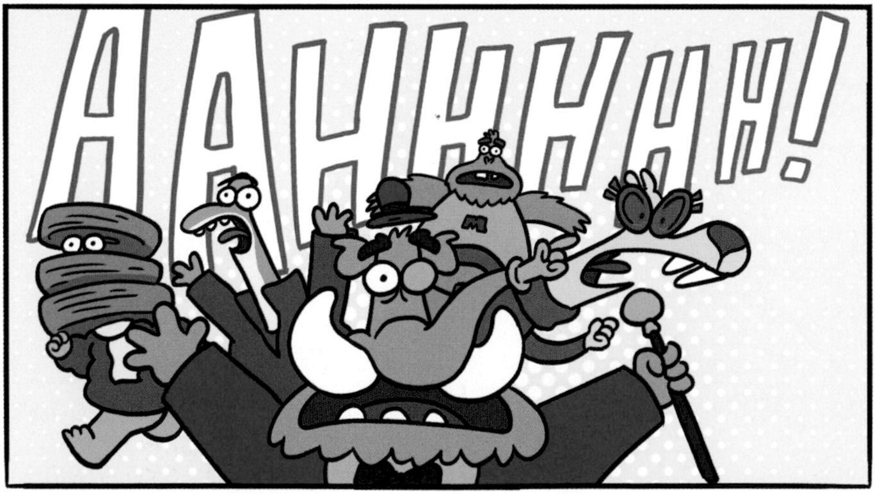
AAHHHHHH!

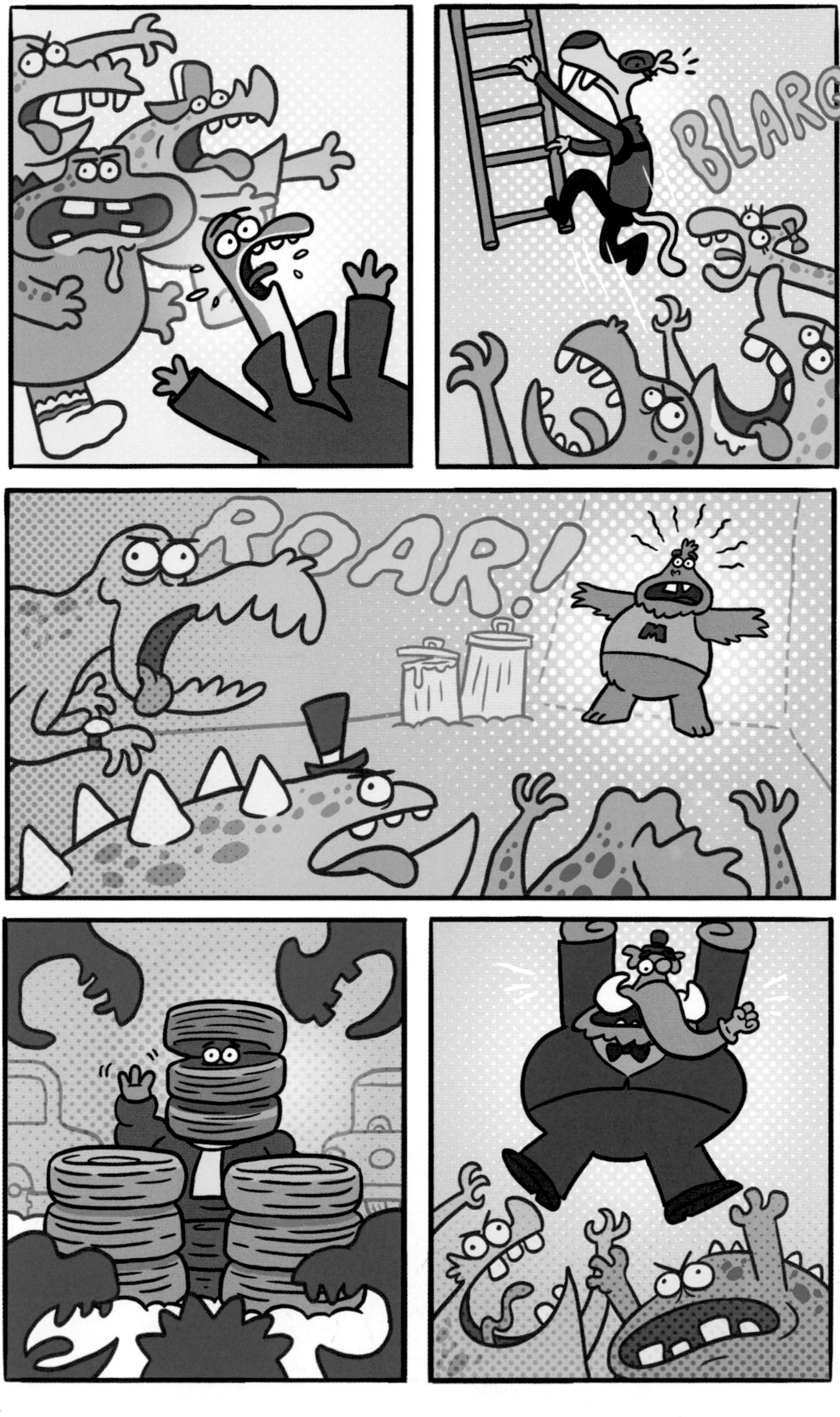
BLARG!
ROAR!

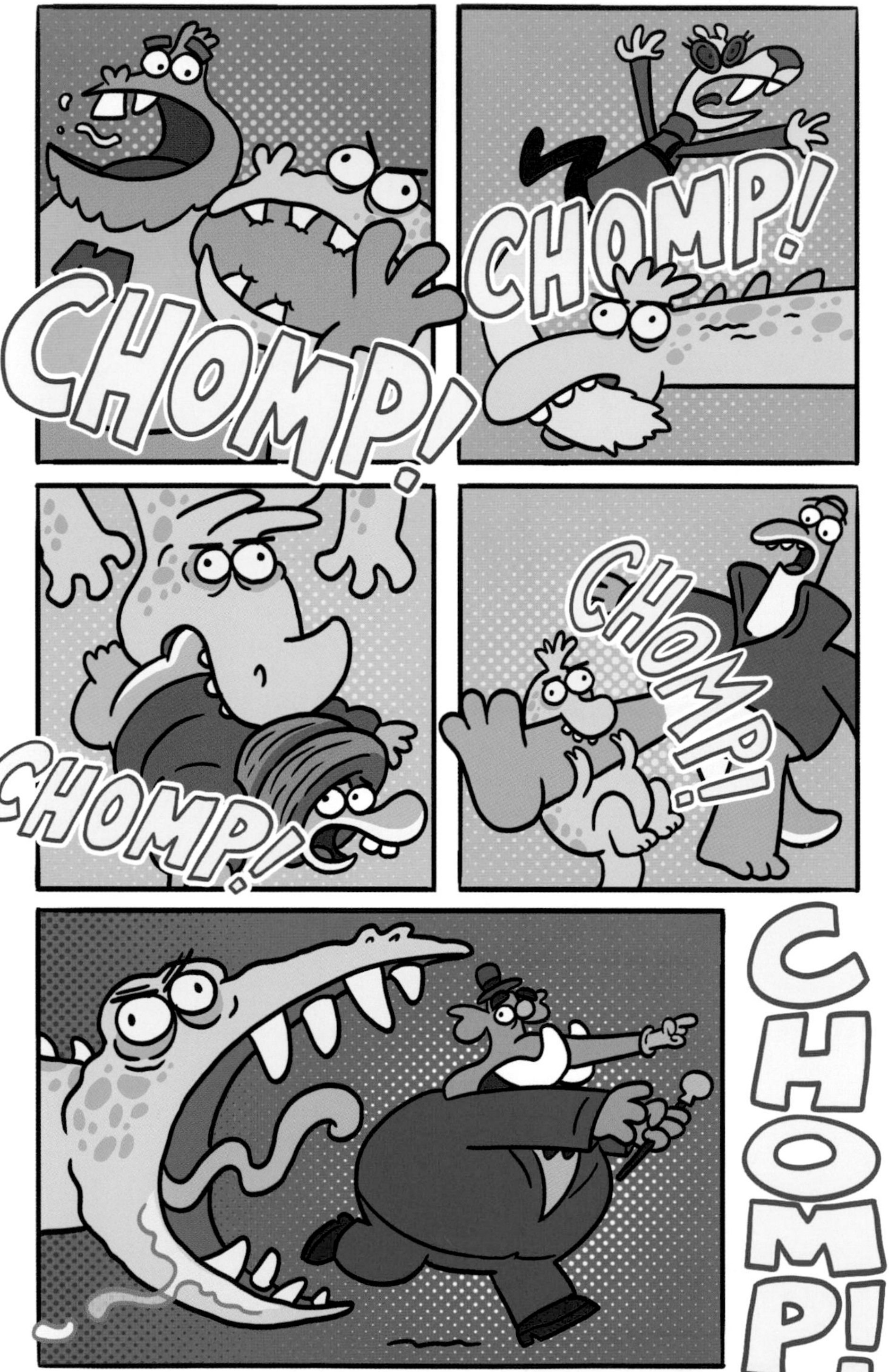
CHOMP!
CHOMP!
CHOMP!
CHOMP!
CHOMP!

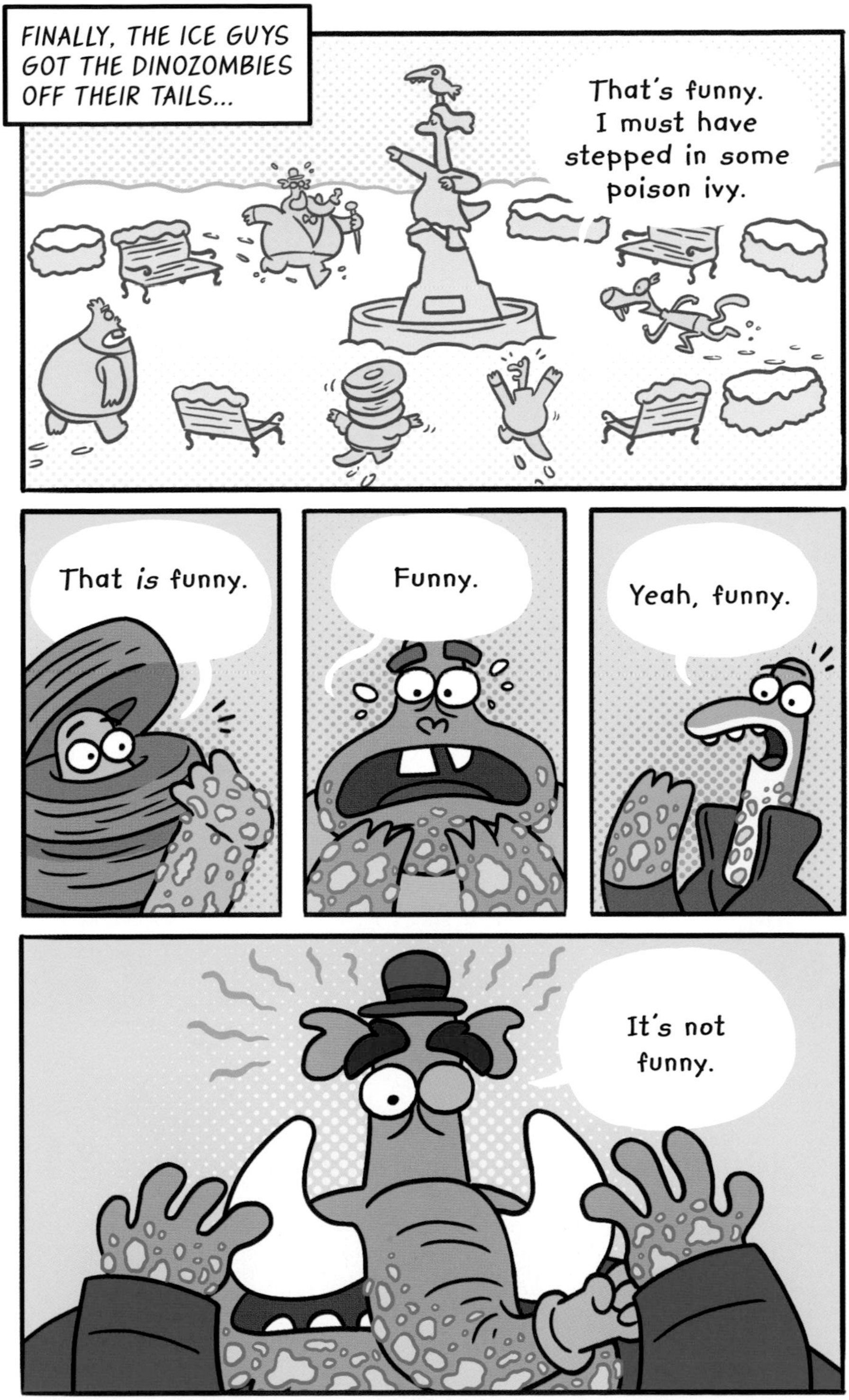
FINALLY, THE ICE GUYS GOT THE DINOZOMBIES OFF THEIR TAILS...
That's funny. I must have stepped in some poison ivy.
That *is* funny.
Funny.
Yeah, funny.
It's not funny.

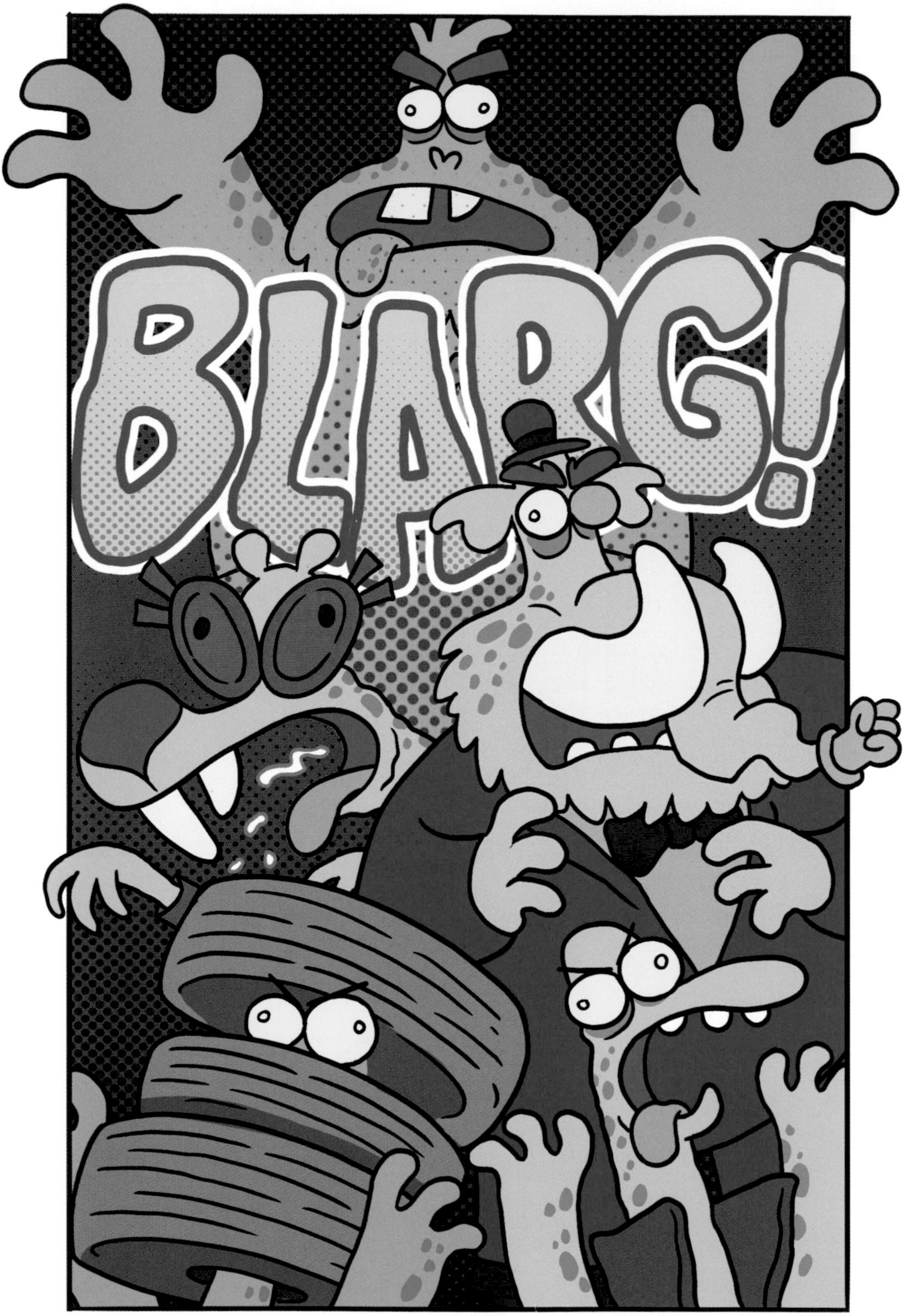
BLARG!

MEANWHILE...EQUIPPED WITH BACH'S BLOWGUN CREATIONS, THE DINOMIGHTIES HEAD TO DINOTOWN.

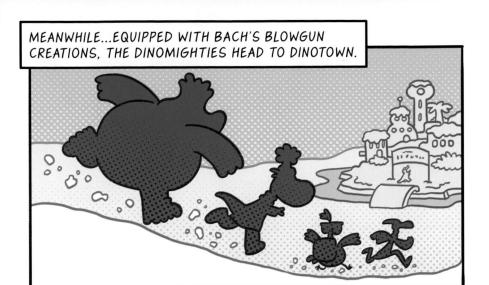

EEK!

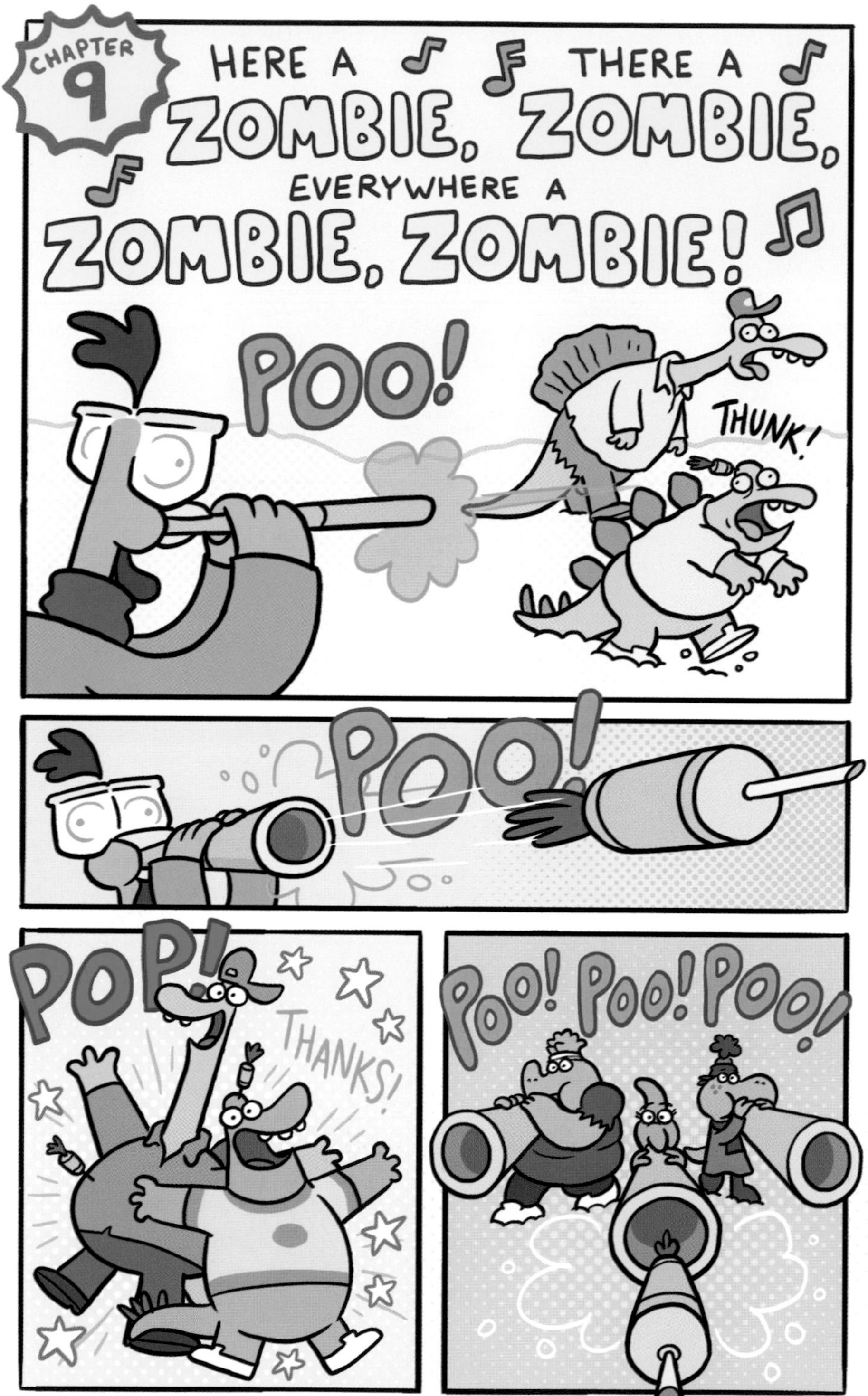
CHAPTER 9
HERE A ♪ ♪ THERE A ♪
ZOMBIE, ZOMBIE,
EVERYWHERE A
ZOMBIE, ZOMBIE!
POO!
THUNK!
POO!
POP!
THANKS!
POO! POO! POO!

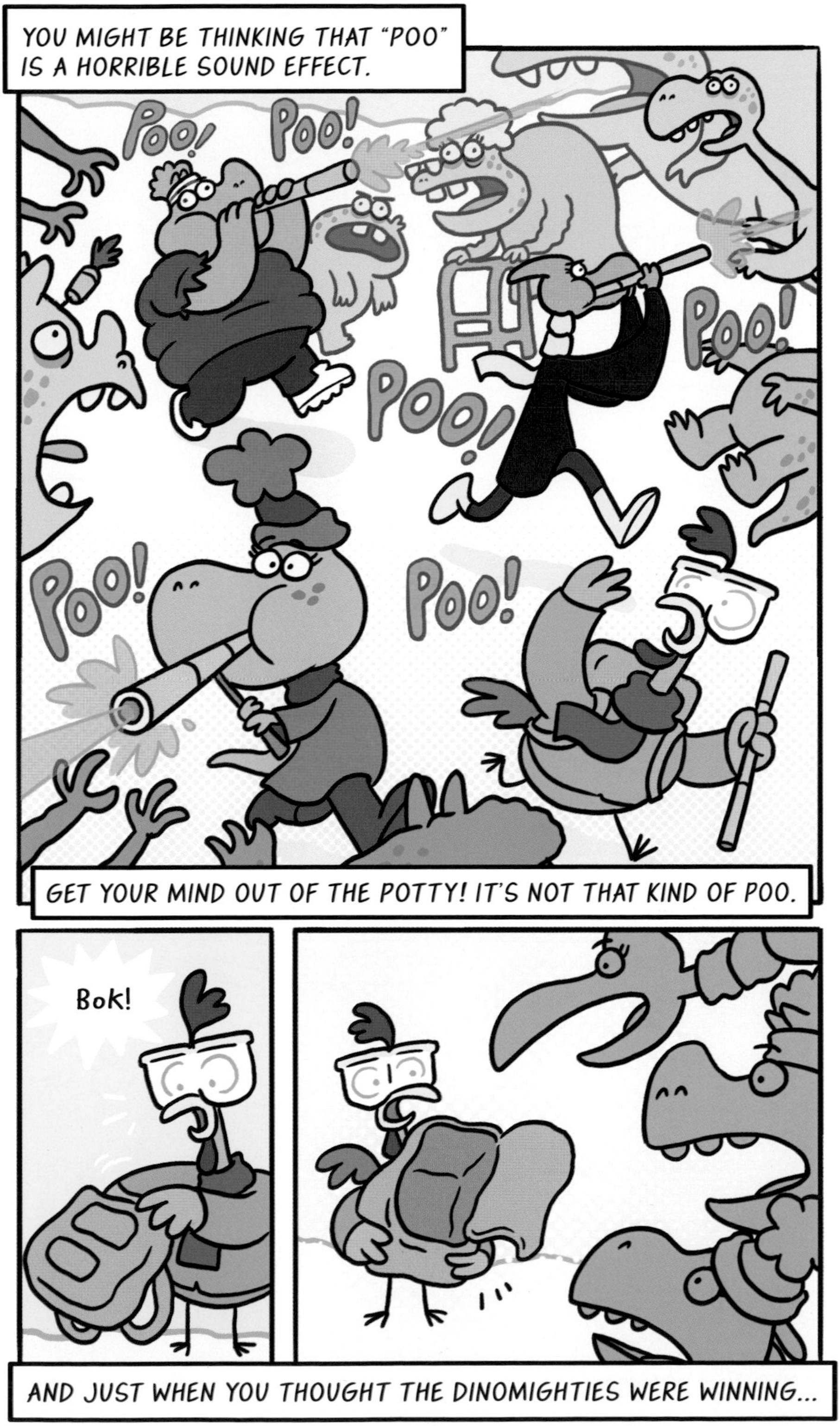
YOU MIGHT BE THINKING THAT "POO" IS A HORRIBLE SOUND EFFECT.
POO!
POO!
POO!
POO!
POO!
POO!
GET YOUR MIND OUT OF THE POTTY! IT'S NOT THAT KIND OF POO.
Bok!
AND JUST WHEN YOU THOUGHT THE DINOMIGHTIES WERE WINNING...

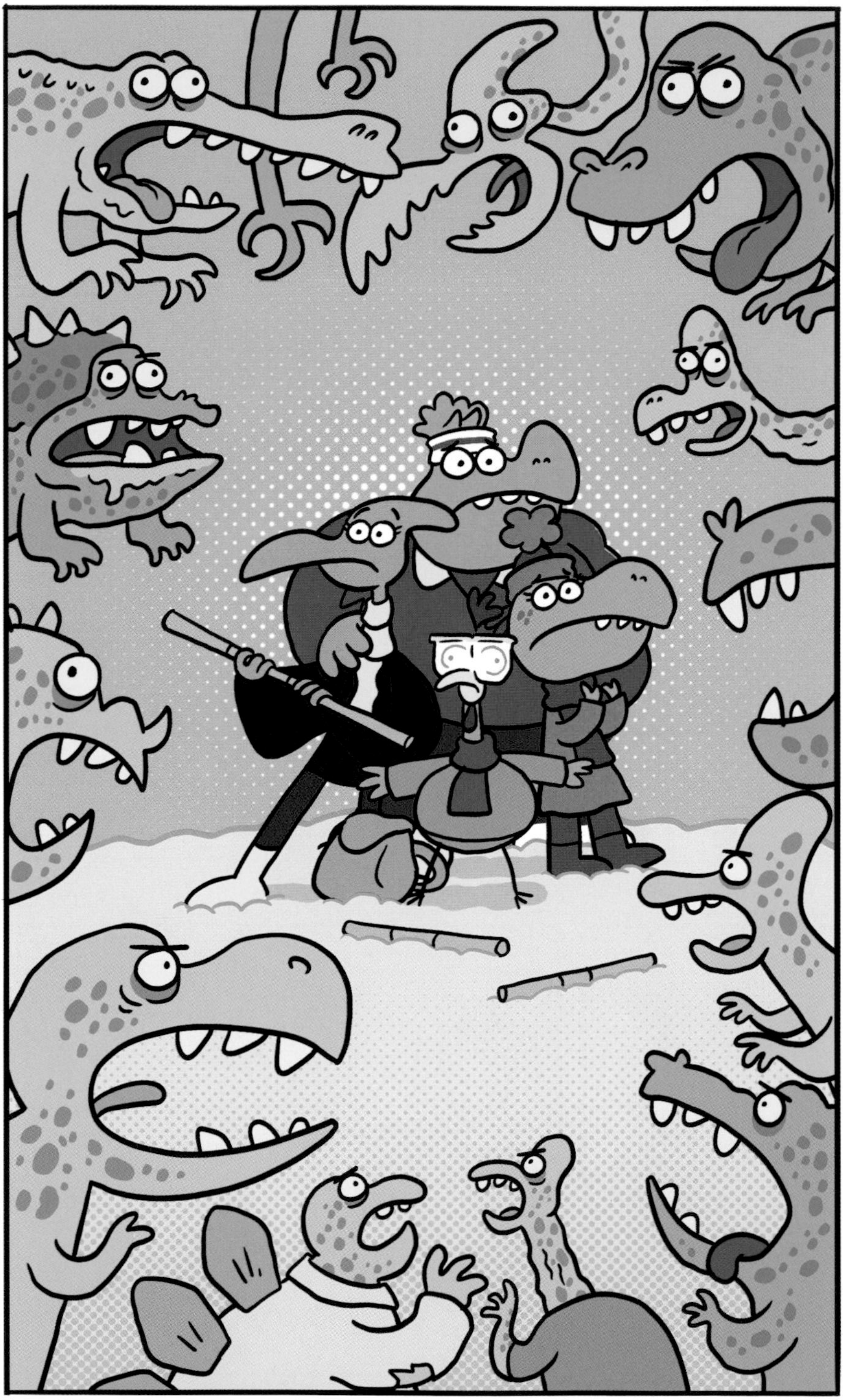

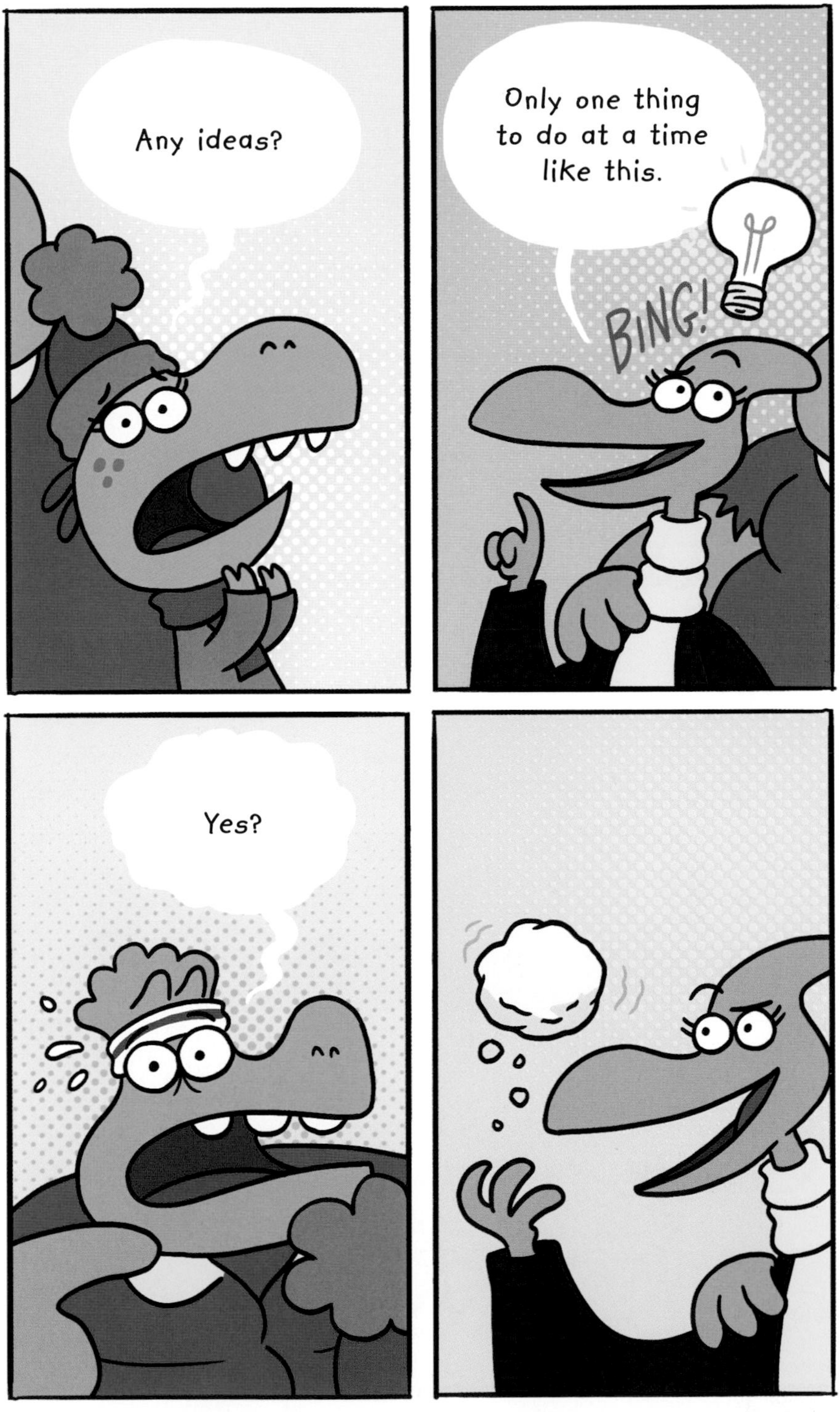
Any ideas?
Only one thing to do at a time like this.
BING!
Yes?

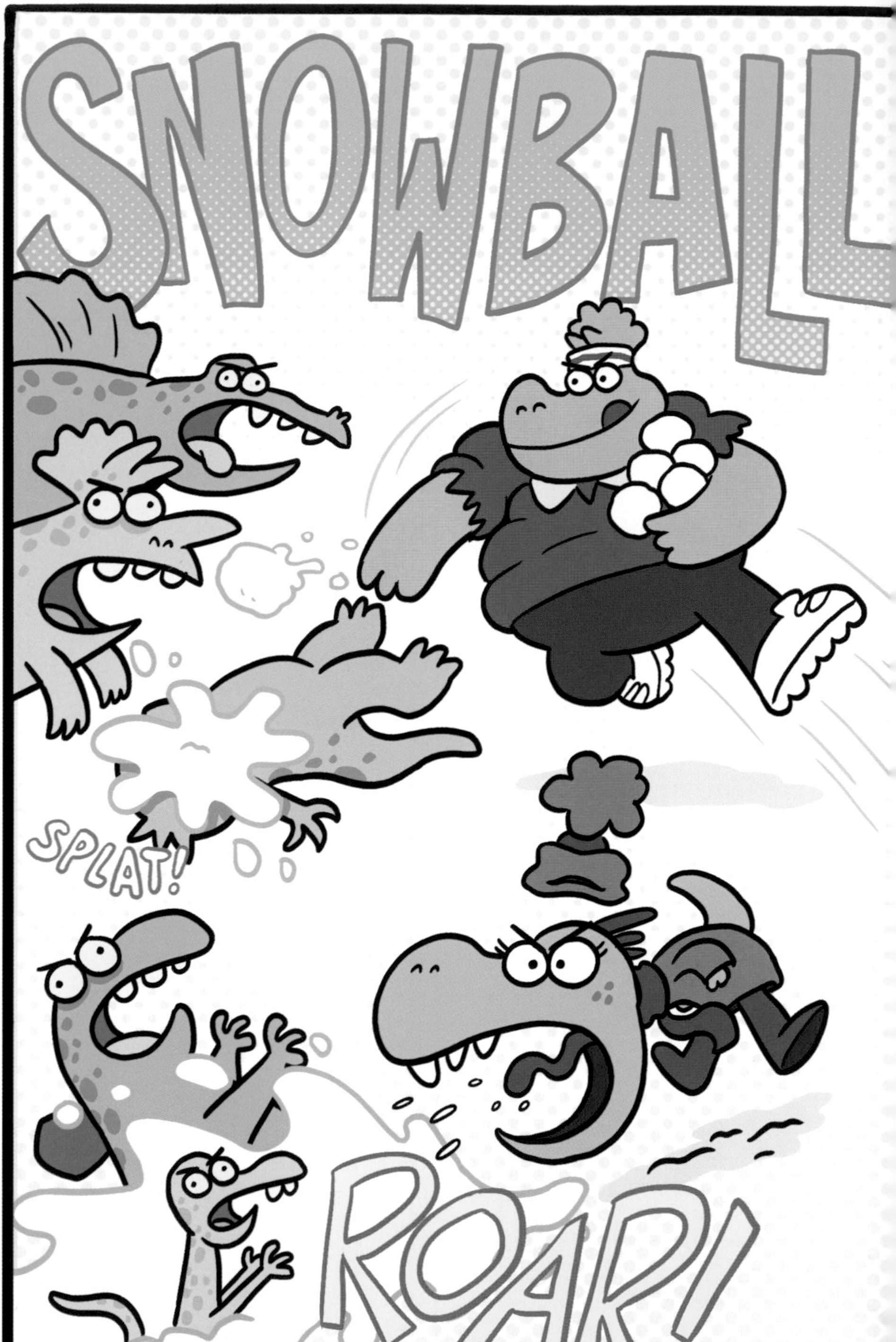
SNOWBALL
SPLAT!
ROAR!

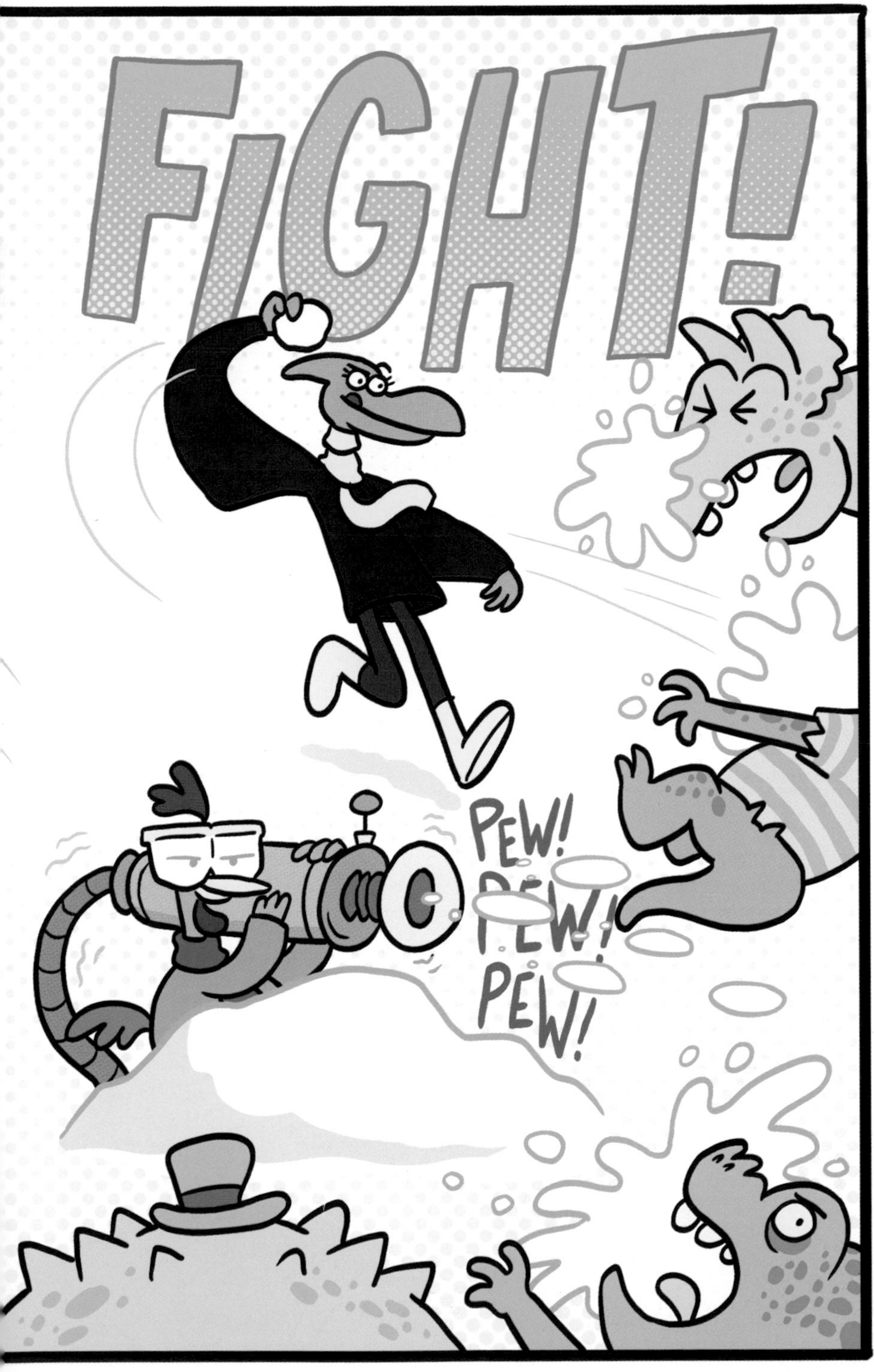
FIGHT!
PEW!
PEW!
PEW!

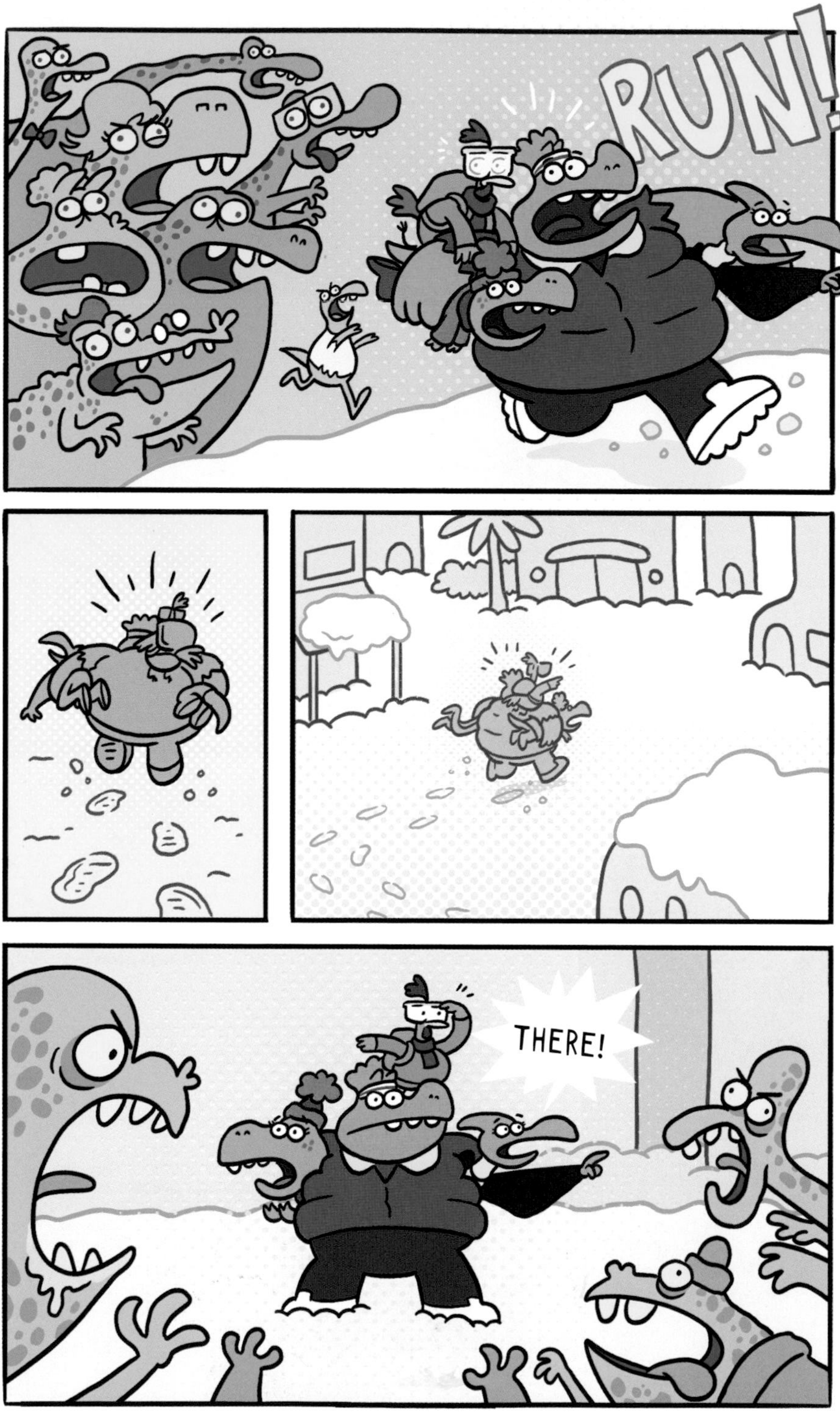
RUN!
THERE!

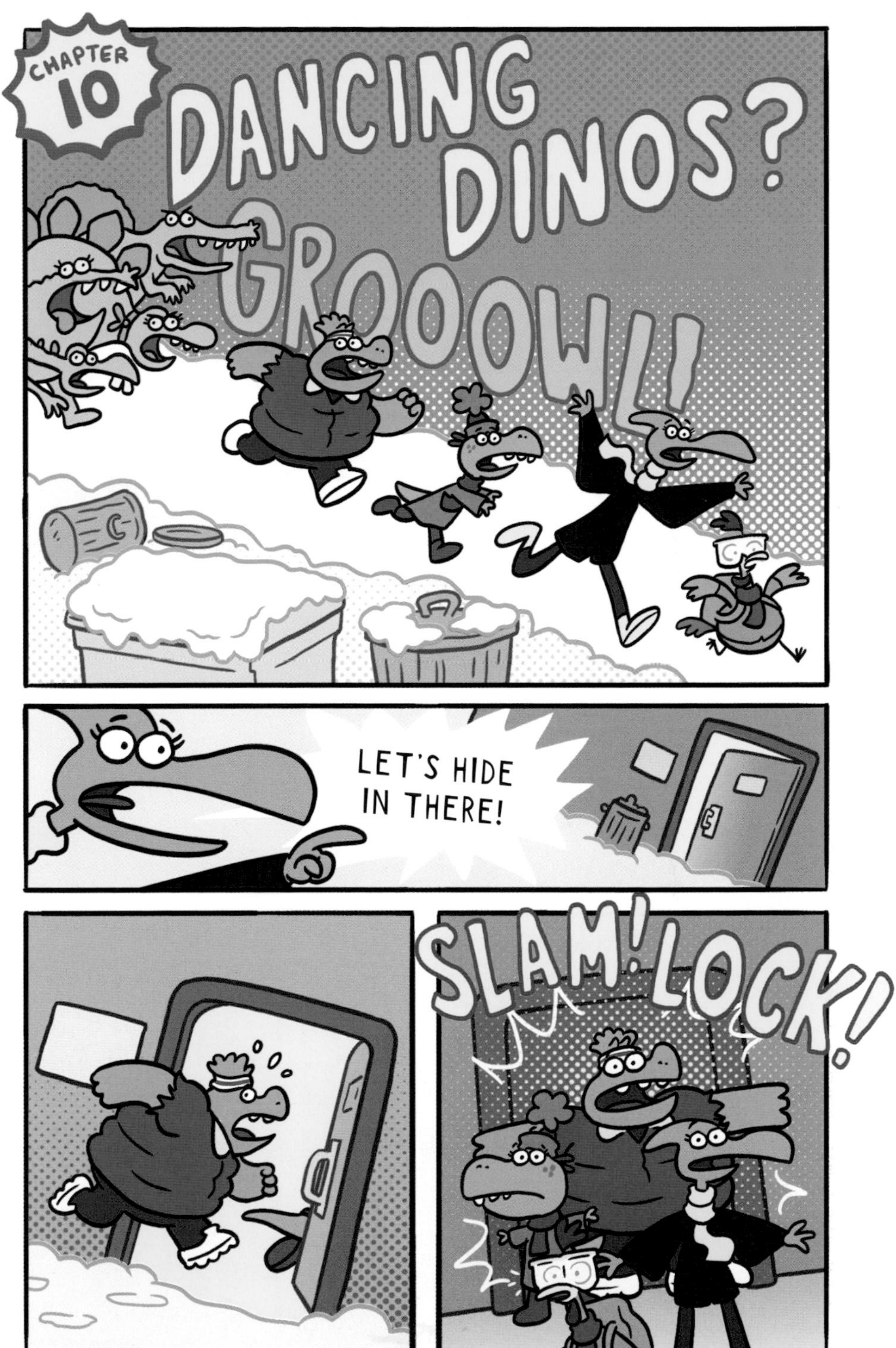
CHAPTER 10
DANCING DINOS?
GROOOWL!
LET'S HIDE IN THERE!
SLAM! LOCK!

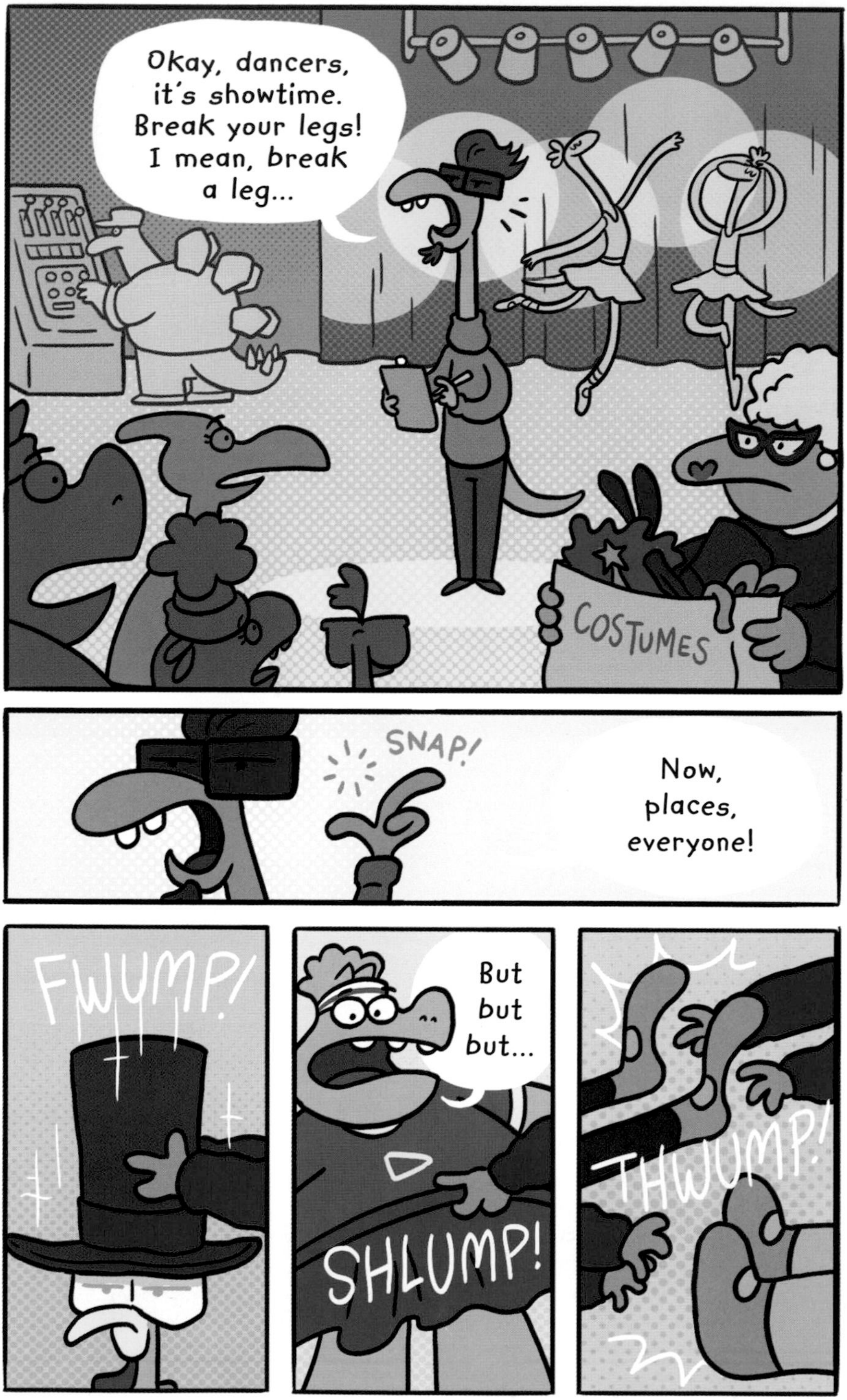
Okay, dancers, it's showtime. Break your legs! I mean, break a leg...
COSTUMES
SNAP!
Now, places, everyone!
FWUMP!
But but but...
SHLUMP!
THWUMP!

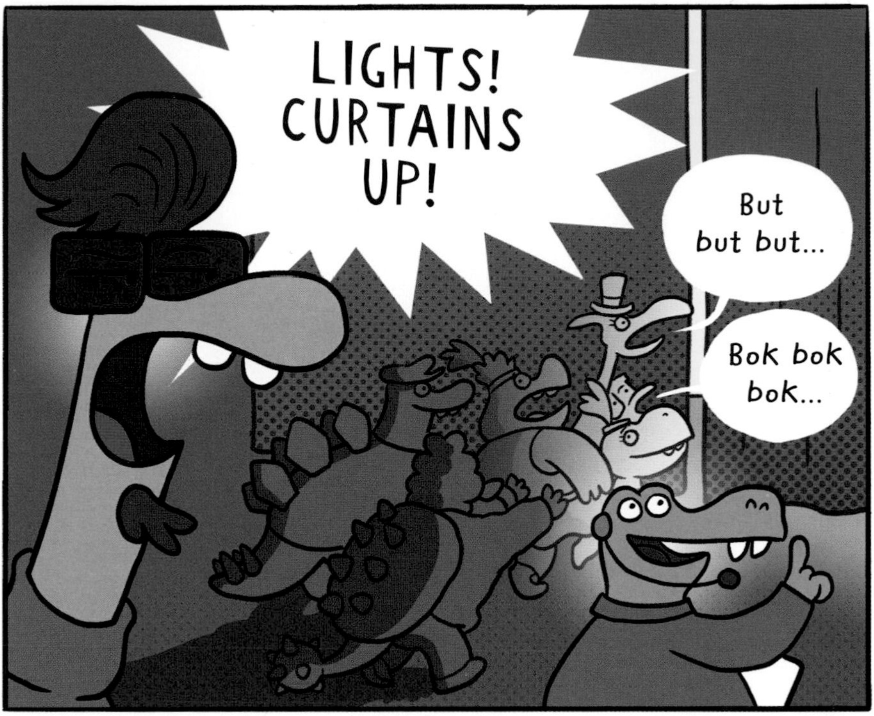
LIGHTS! CURTAINS UP!
But but but...
Bok bok bok...

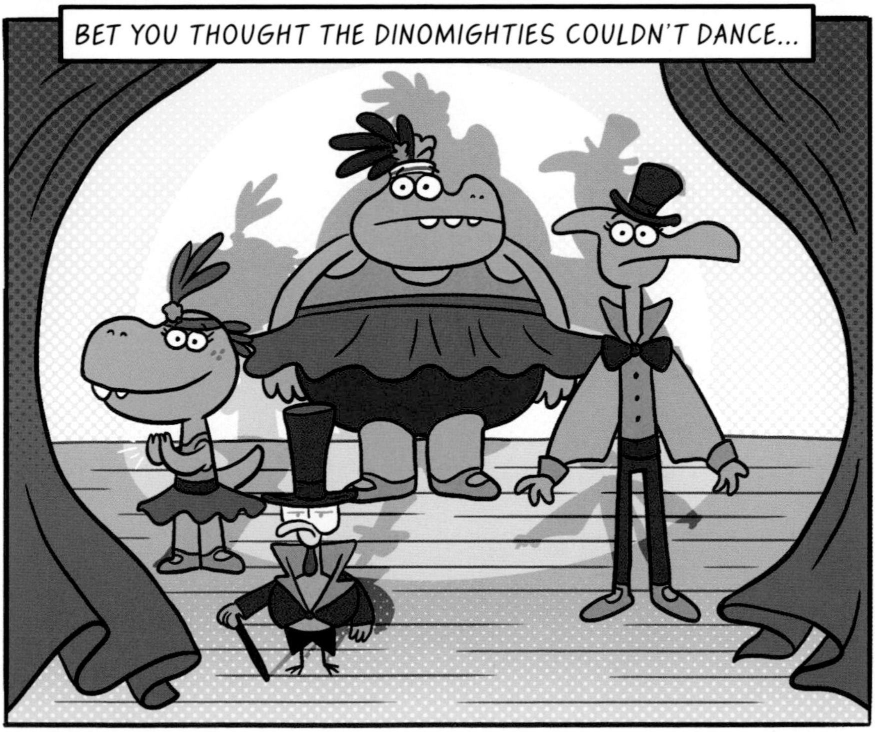
BET YOU THOUGHT THE DINOMIGHTIES COULDN'T DANCE...

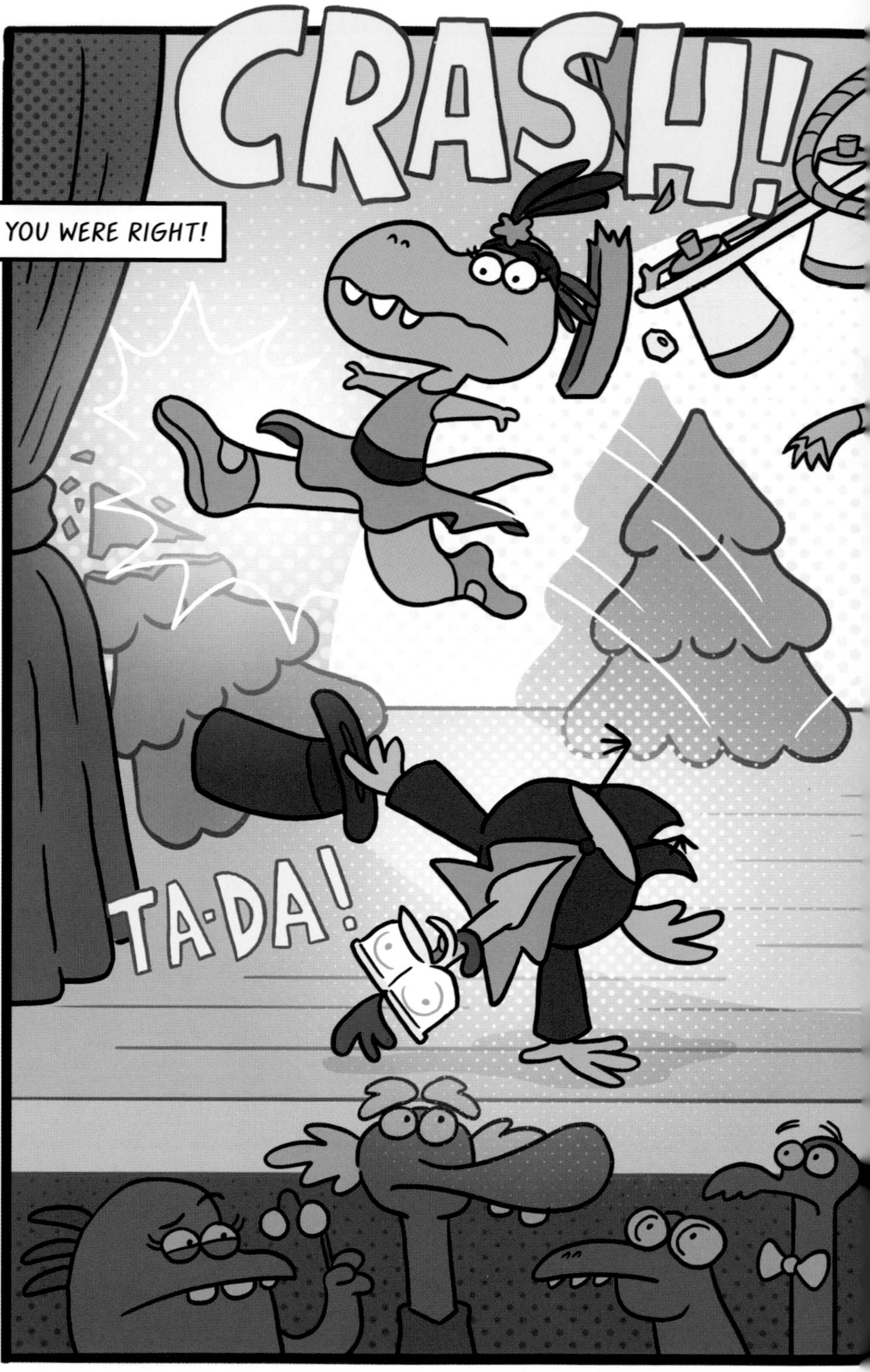
CRASH!
YOU WERE RIGHT!
TA-DA!

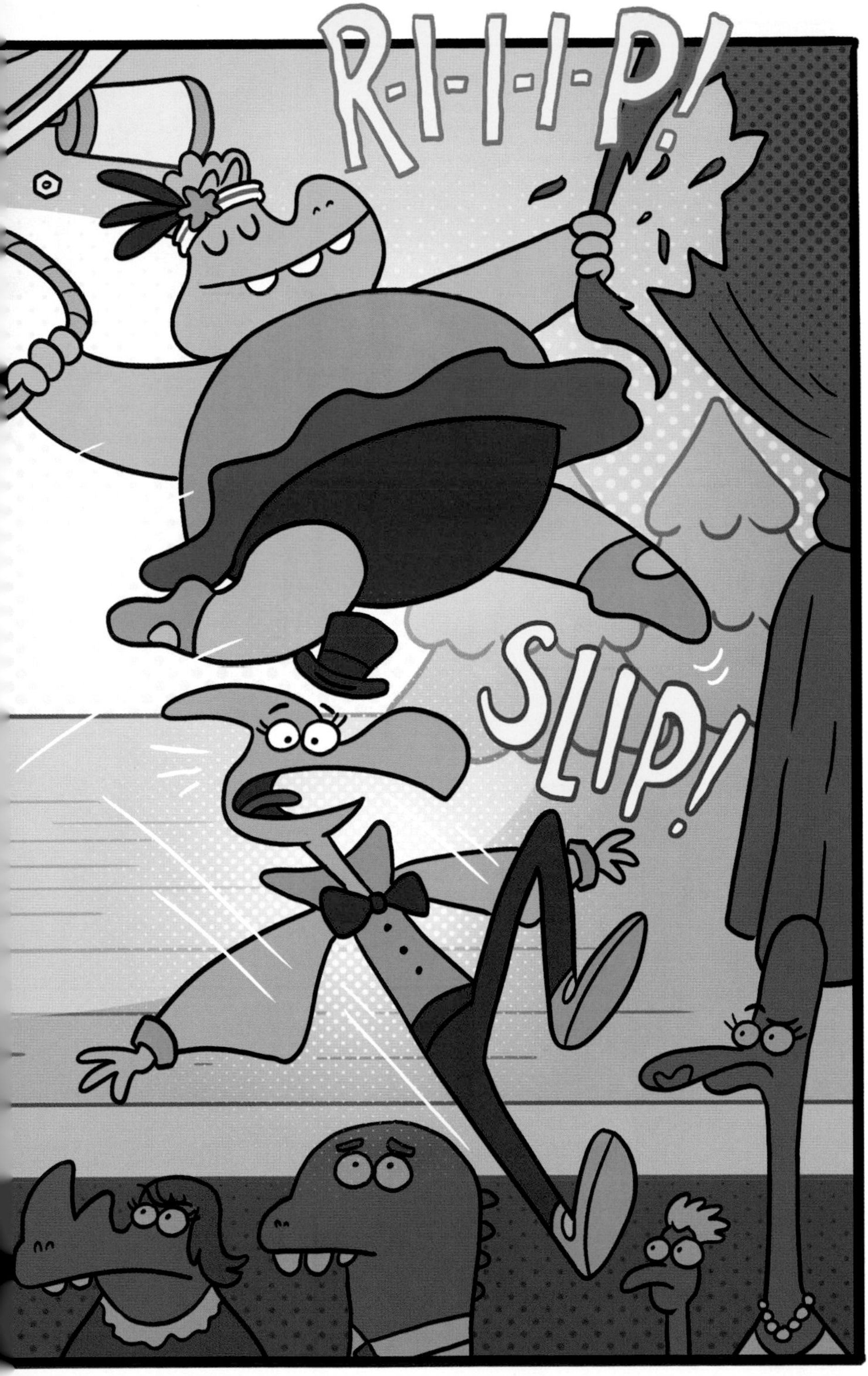
R-I-I-I-P!
SLIP!

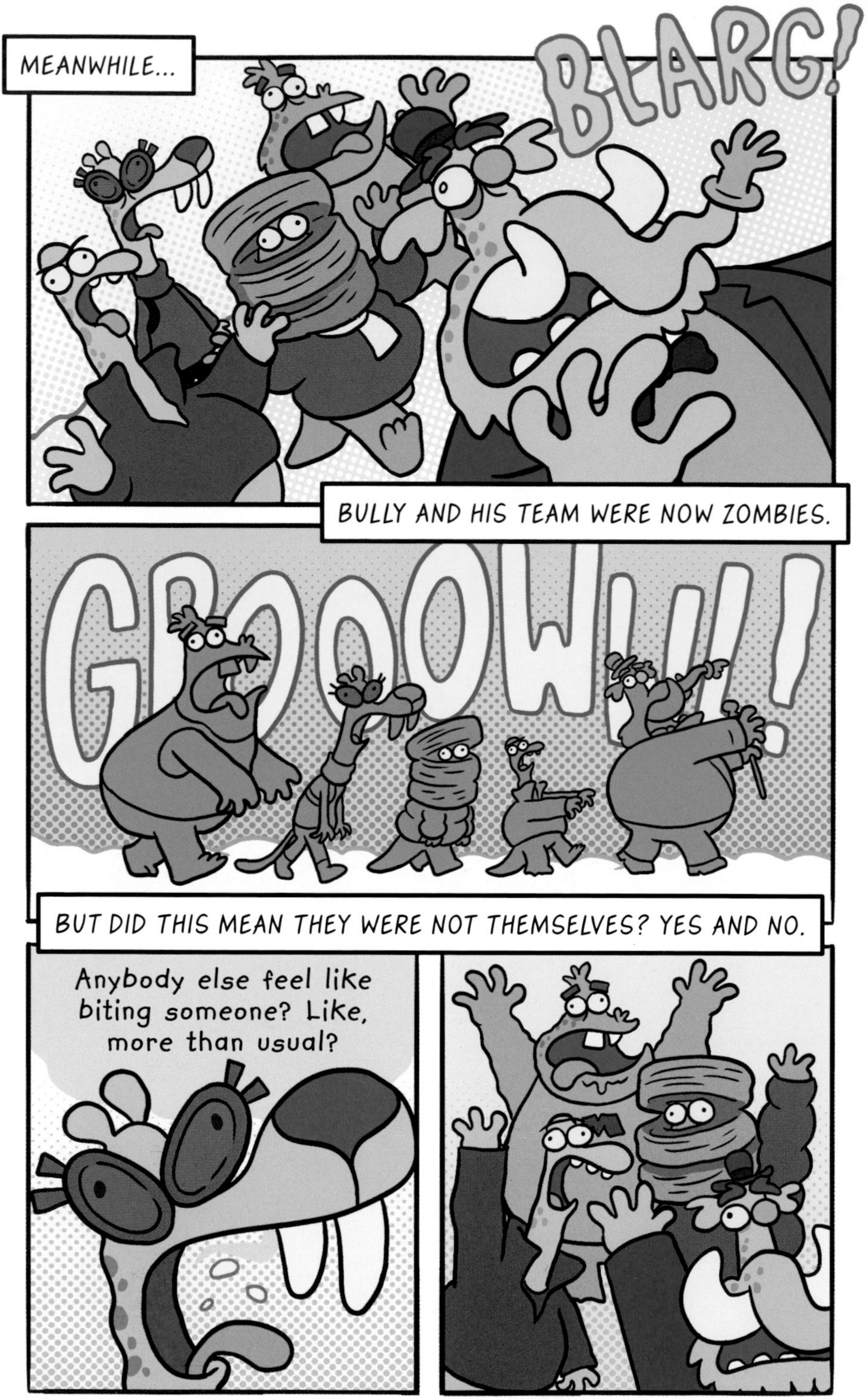
MEANWHILE...
BLARG!
BULLY AND HIS TEAM WERE NOW ZOMBIES.
GROOOWL!!
BUT DID THIS MEAN THEY WERE NOT THEMSELVES? YES AND NO.
Anybody else feel like biting someone? Like, more than usual?

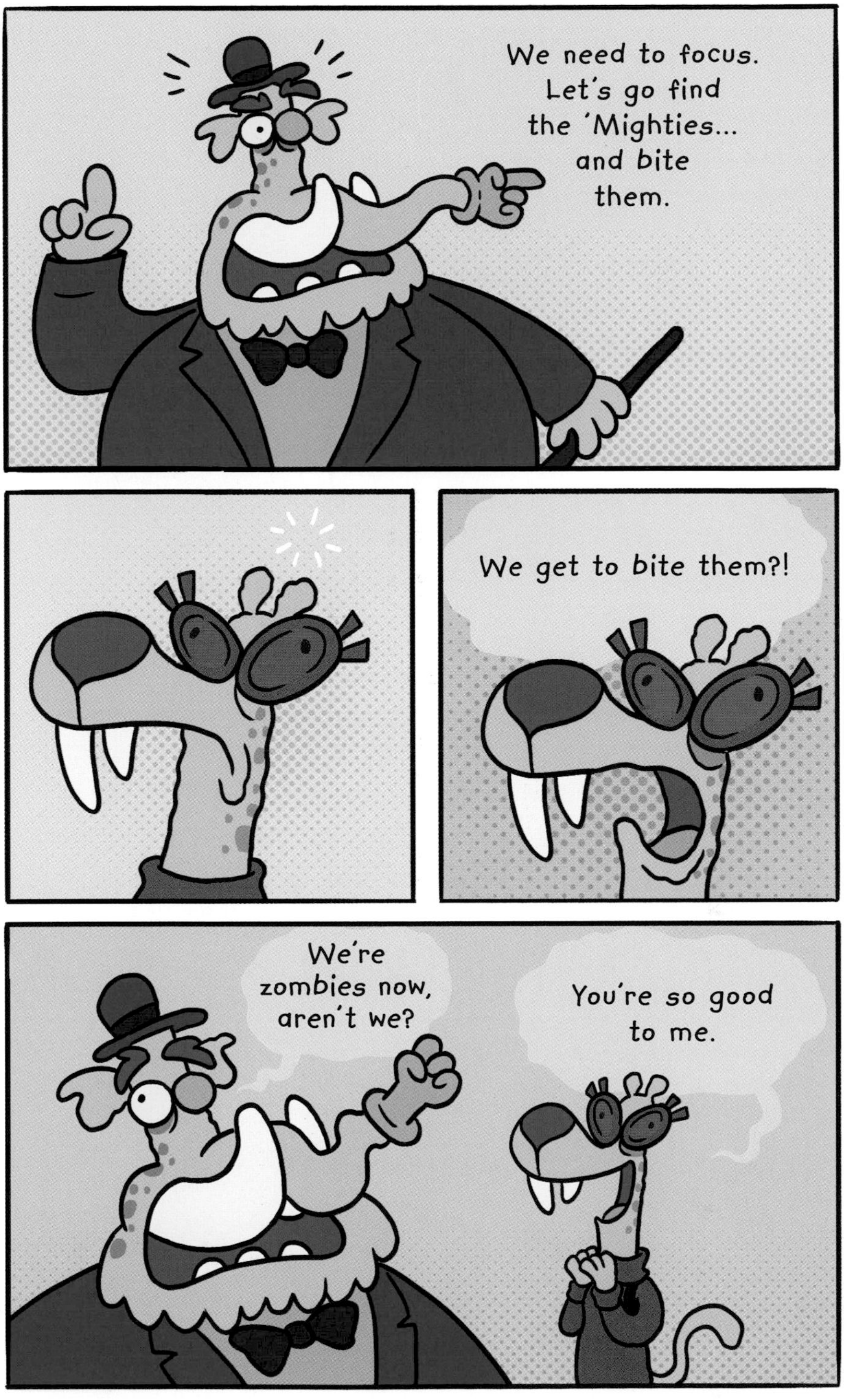
We need to focus. Let's go find the 'Mighties... and bite them.
We get to bite them?!
We're zombies now, aren't we?
You're so good to me.

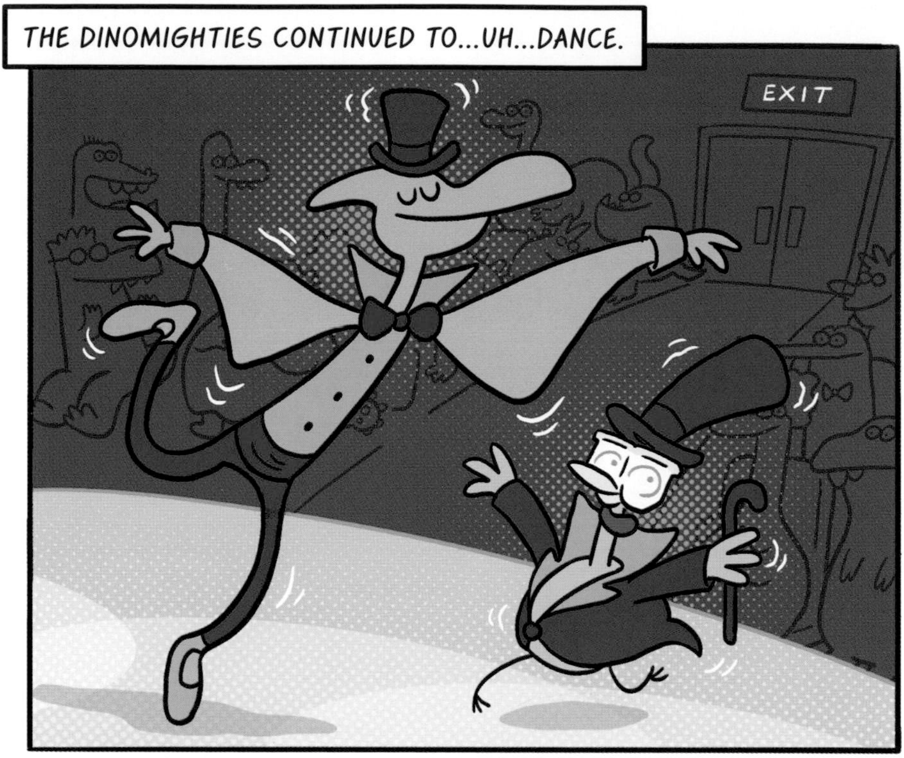
THE DINOMIGHTIES CONTINUED TO...UH...DANCE.
EXIT

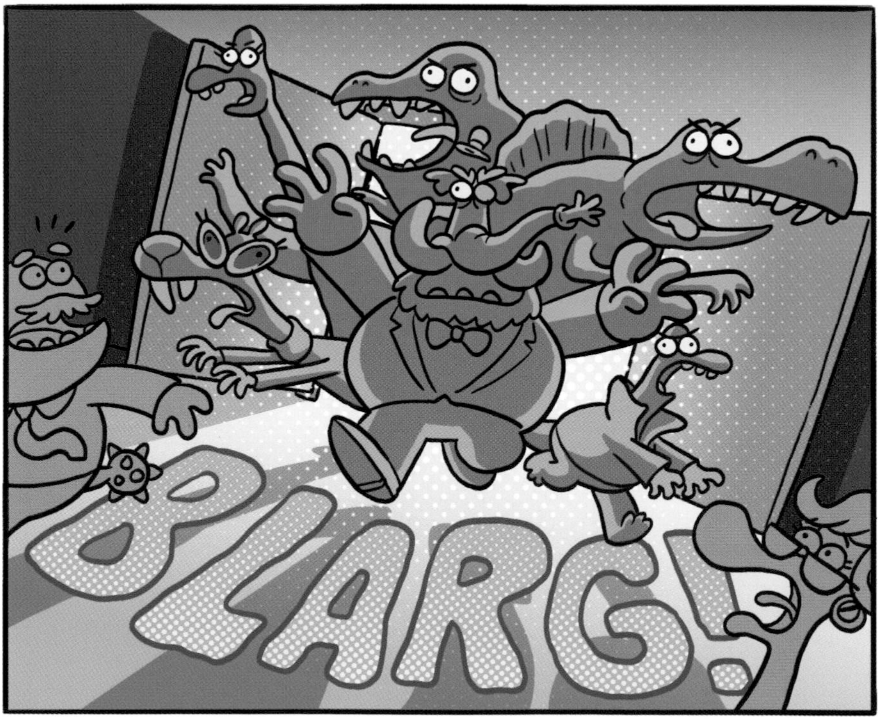
BLARG!

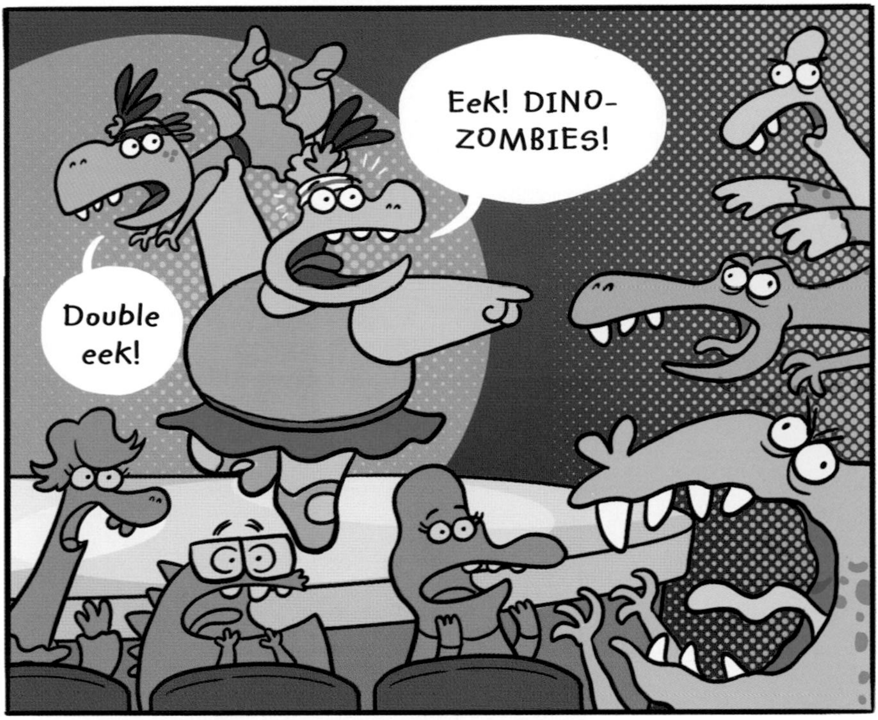
Eek! DINO-
ZOMBIES!
Double
eek!

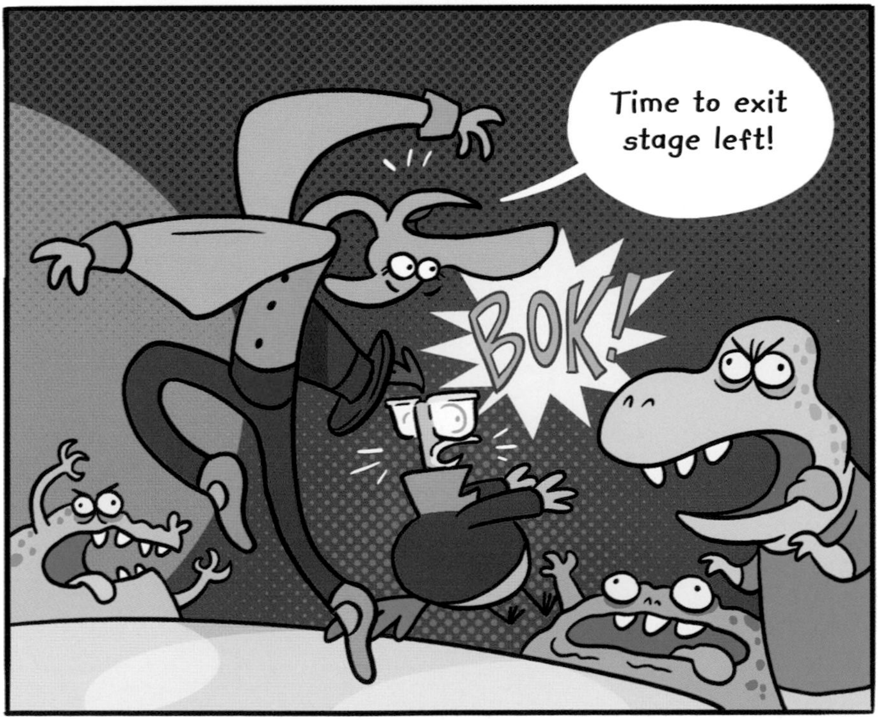
Time to exit
stage left!
BOK!

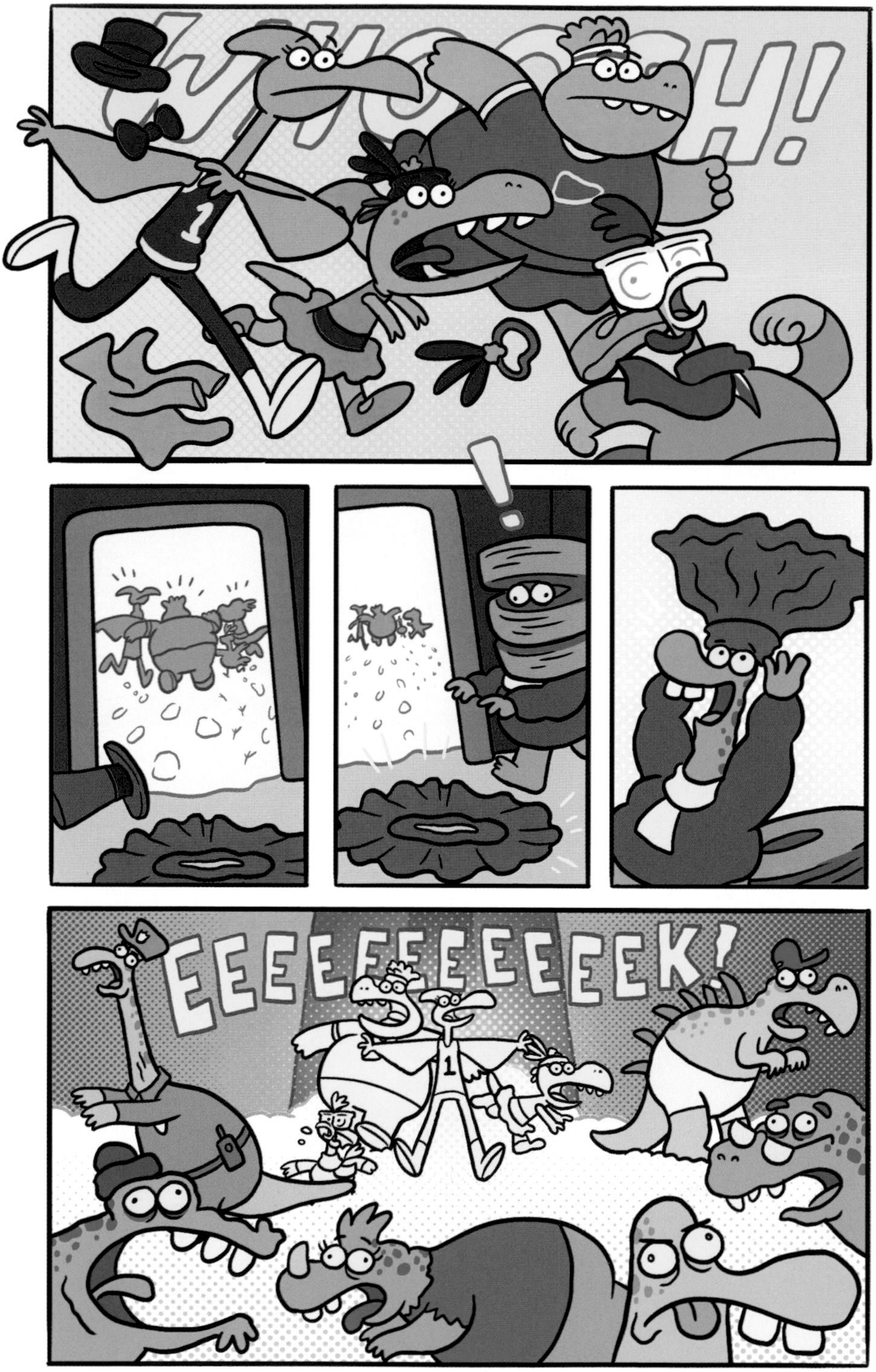
WHOOSH!
!
EEEEEEEEEEEK!

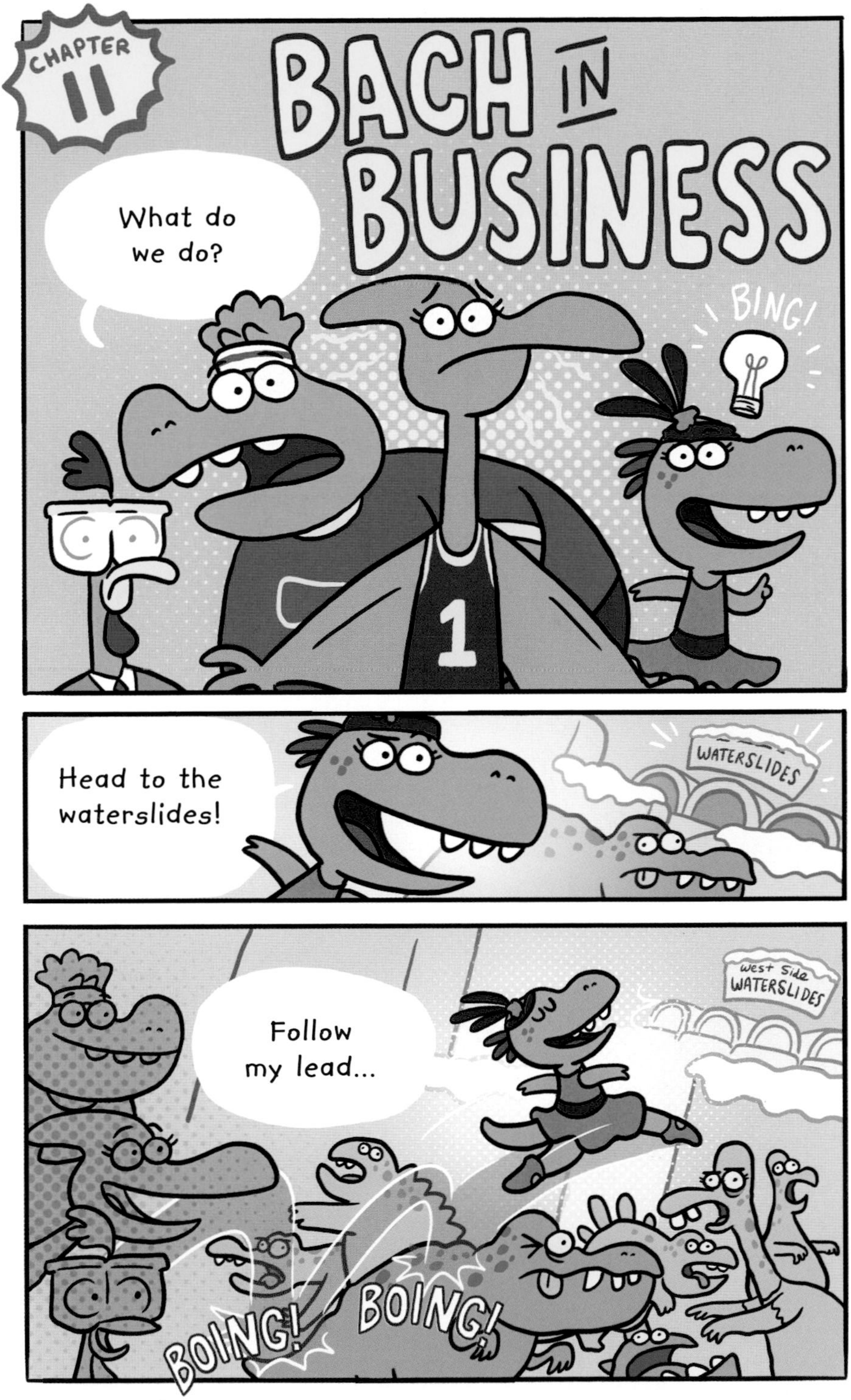
CHAPTER 11
BACH IN BUSINESS
What do we do?
BING!
Head to the waterslides!
WATERSLIDES
Follow my lead...
West Side WATERSLIDES
BOING!
BOING!

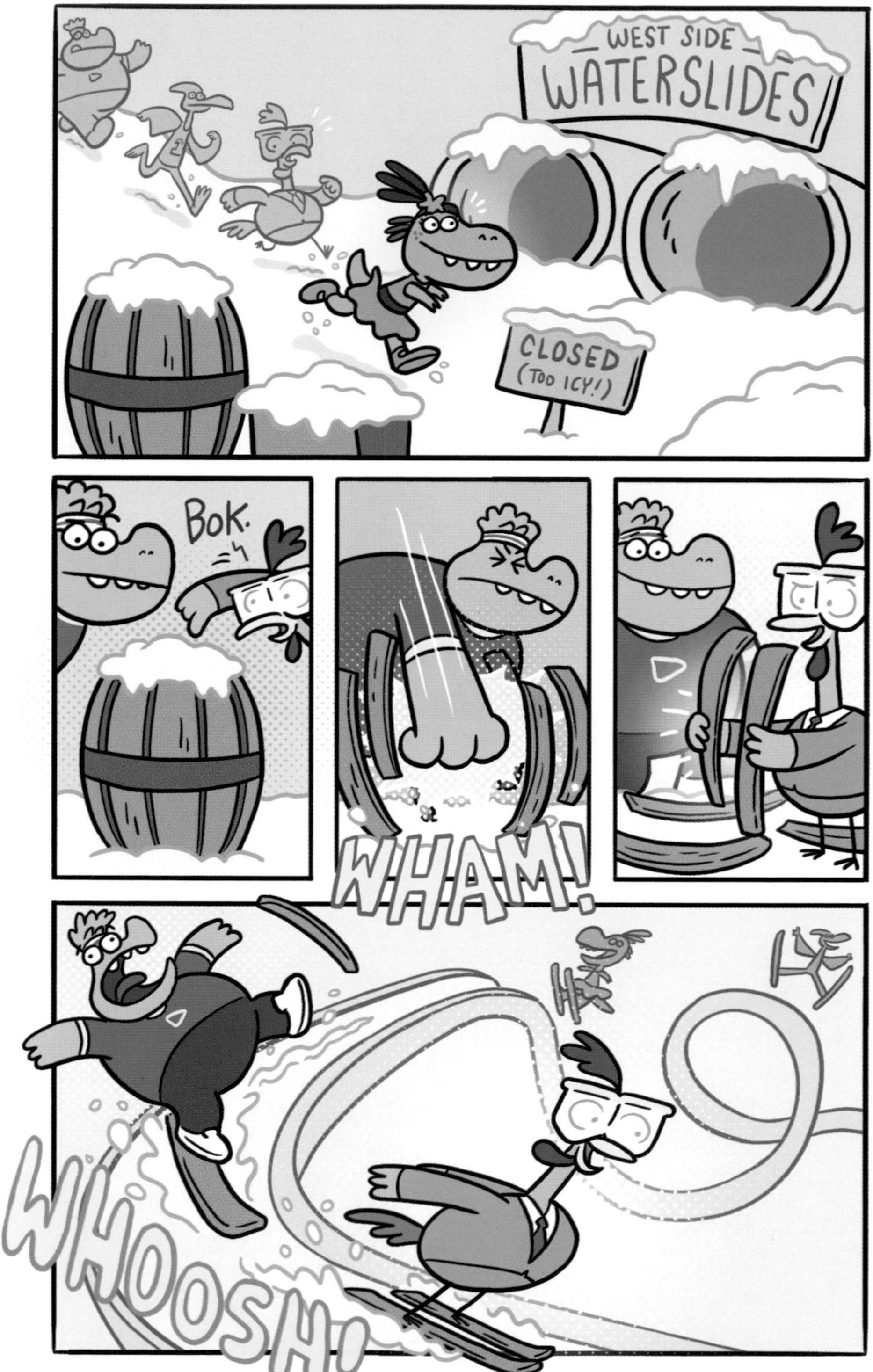
WEST SIDE
WATERSLIDES
CLOSED
(TOO ICY!)
BOK.
WHAM!
WHOOSH!

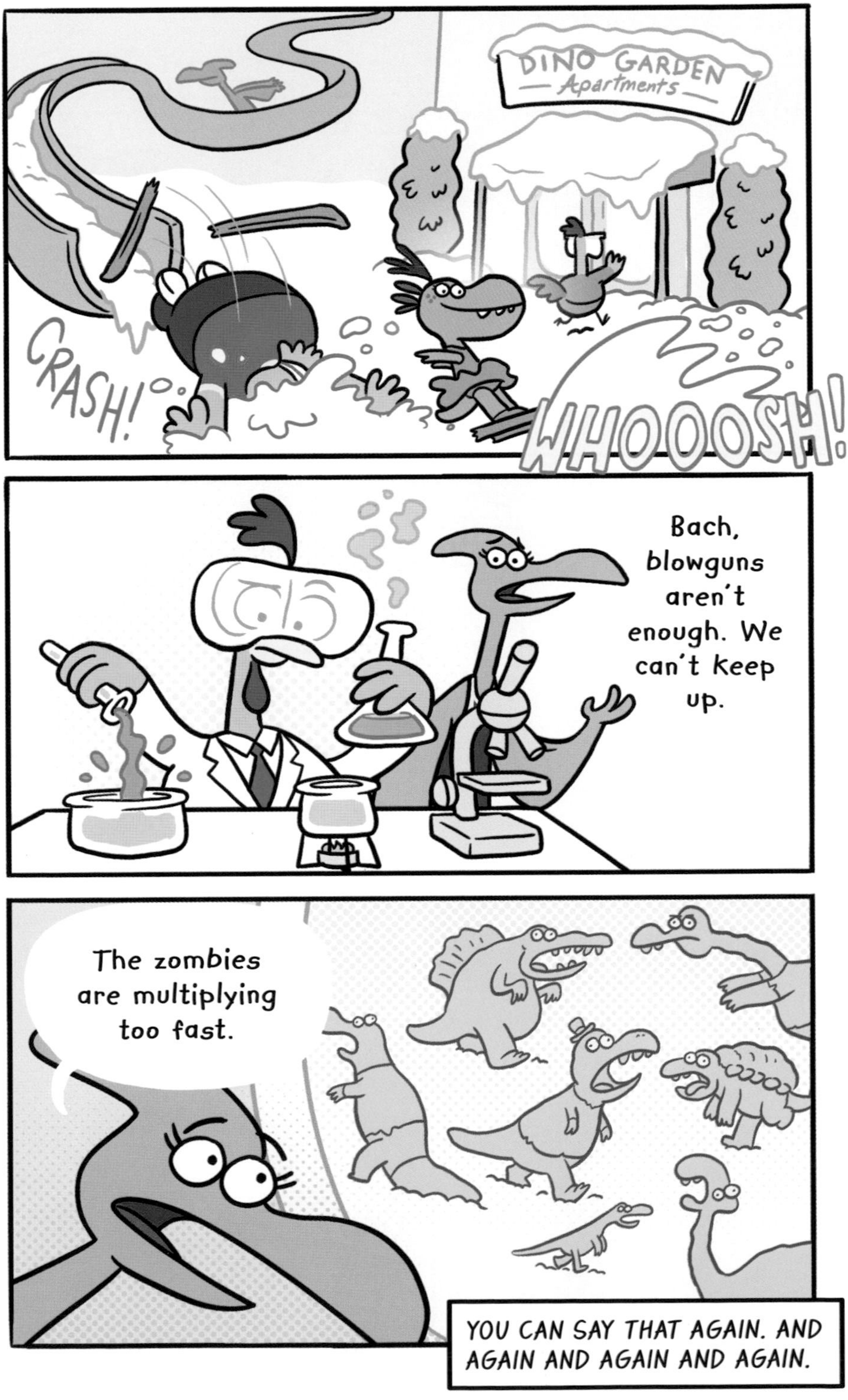
DINO GARDEN
Apartments
CRASH!
WHOOOOSH!
Bach, blowguns aren't enough. We can't keep up.
The zombies are multiplying too fast.
YOU CAN SAY THAT AGAIN. AND AGAIN AND AGAIN AND AGAIN.

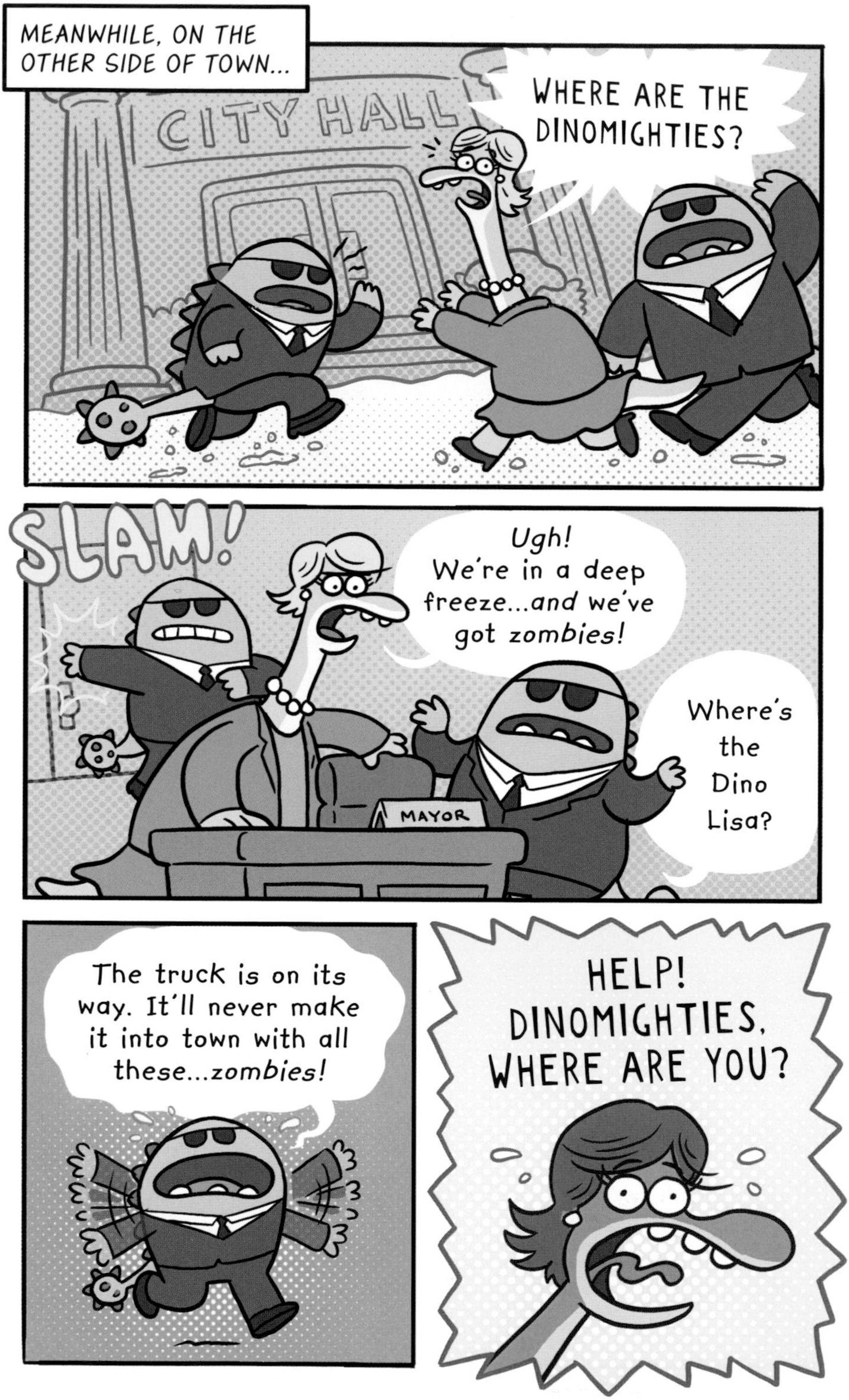
MEANWHILE, ON THE OTHER SIDE OF TOWN...
CITY HALL
WHERE ARE THE DINOMIGHTIES?
SLAM!
Ugh! We're in a deep freeze...and we've got zombies!
MAYOR
Where's the Dino Lisa?
The truck is on its way. It'll never make it into town with all these...zombies!
HELP! DINOMIGHTIES, WHERE ARE YOU?

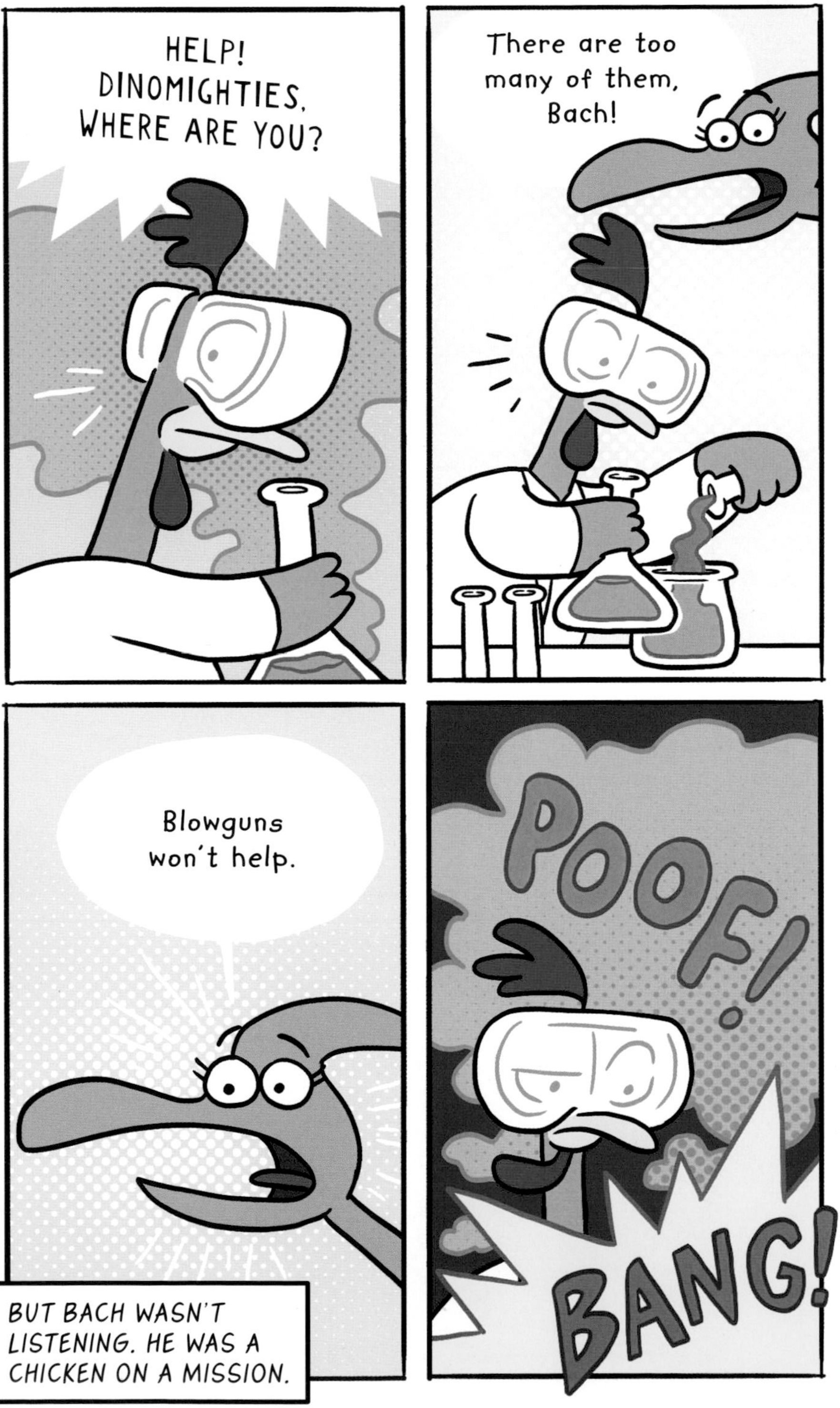
HELP! DINOMIGHTIES, WHERE ARE YOU?
There are too many of them, Bach!
Blowguns won't help.
BUT BACH WASN'T LISTENING. HE WAS A CHICKEN ON A MISSION.
POOF!
BANG!

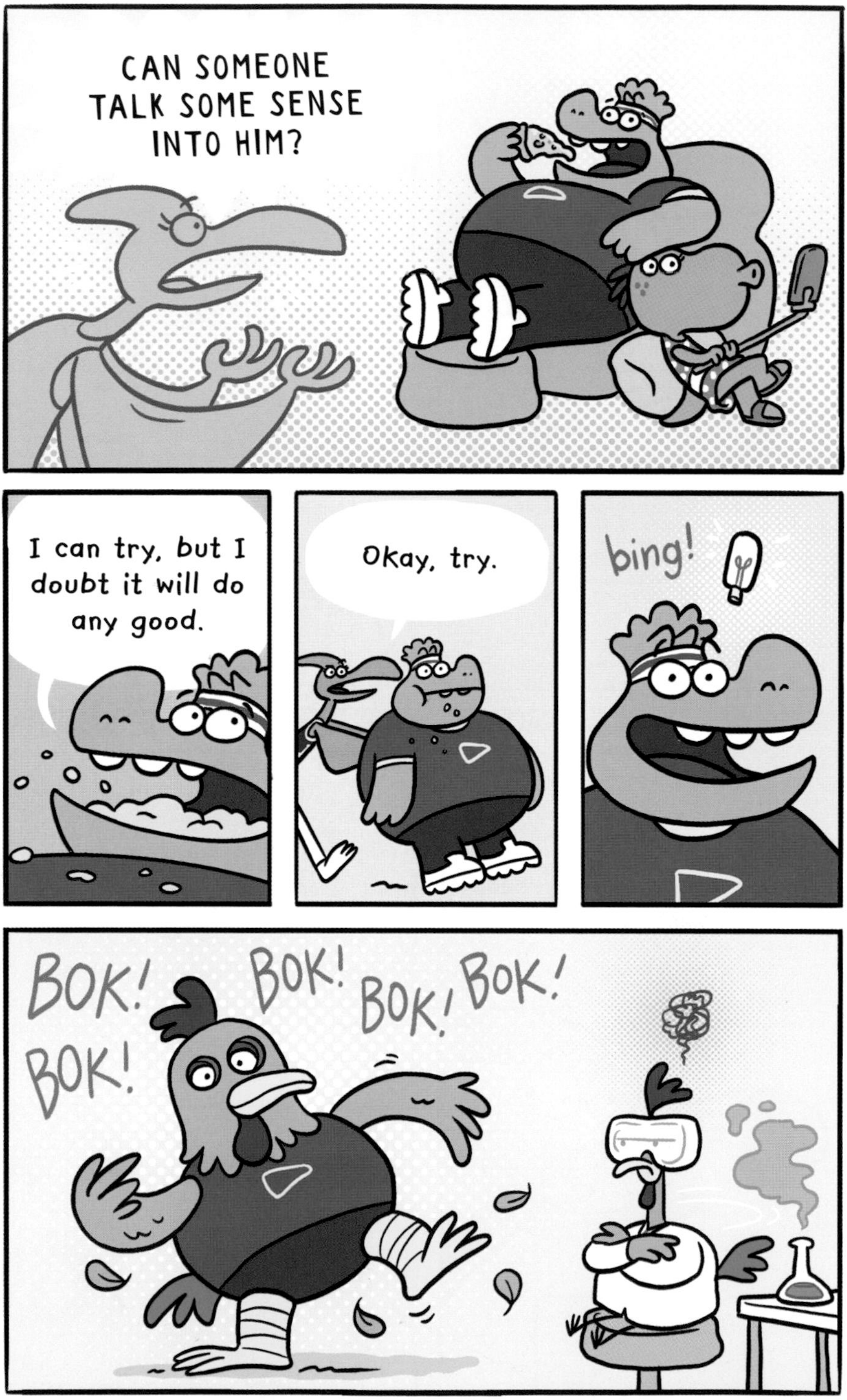
CAN SOMEONE TALK SOME SENSE INTO HIM?
I can try, but I doubt it will do any good.
Okay, try.
bing!
BOK! BOK! BOK! BOK! BOK!

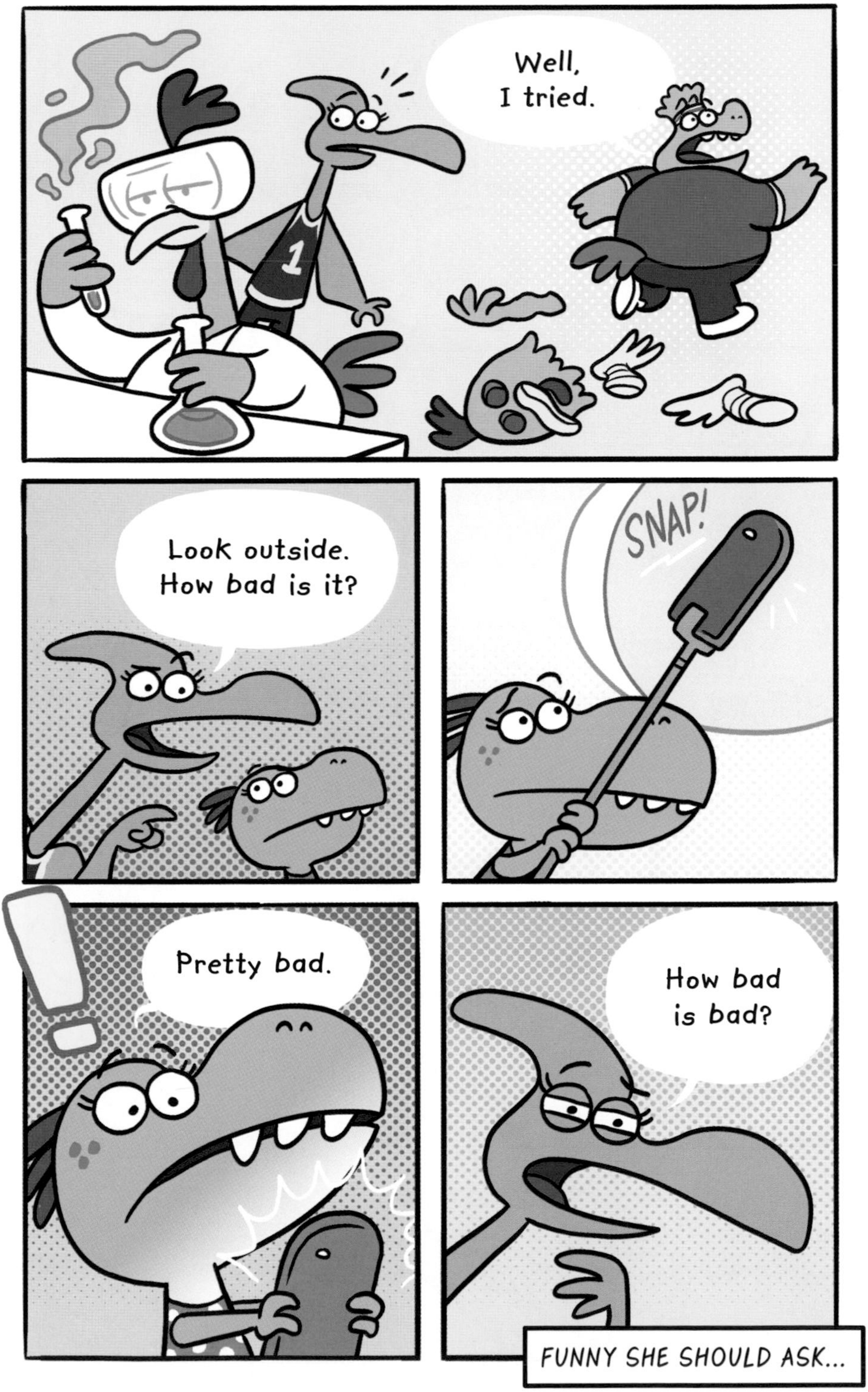
Well,
I tried.
Look outside.
How bad is it?
SNAP!
Pretty bad.
How bad
is bad?
FUNNY SHE SHOULD ASK...

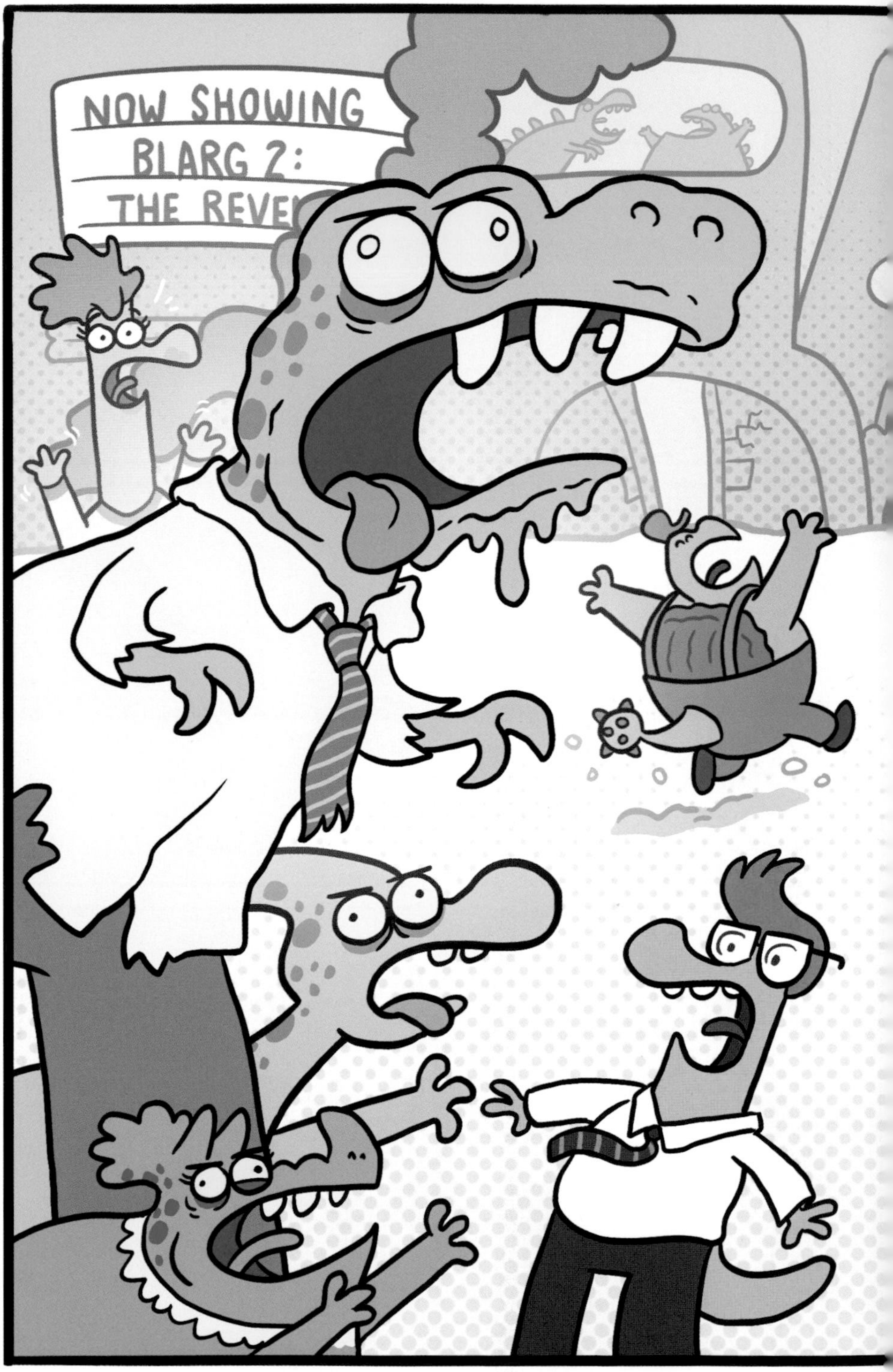
NOW SHOWING
BLARG 2:
THE REVEN

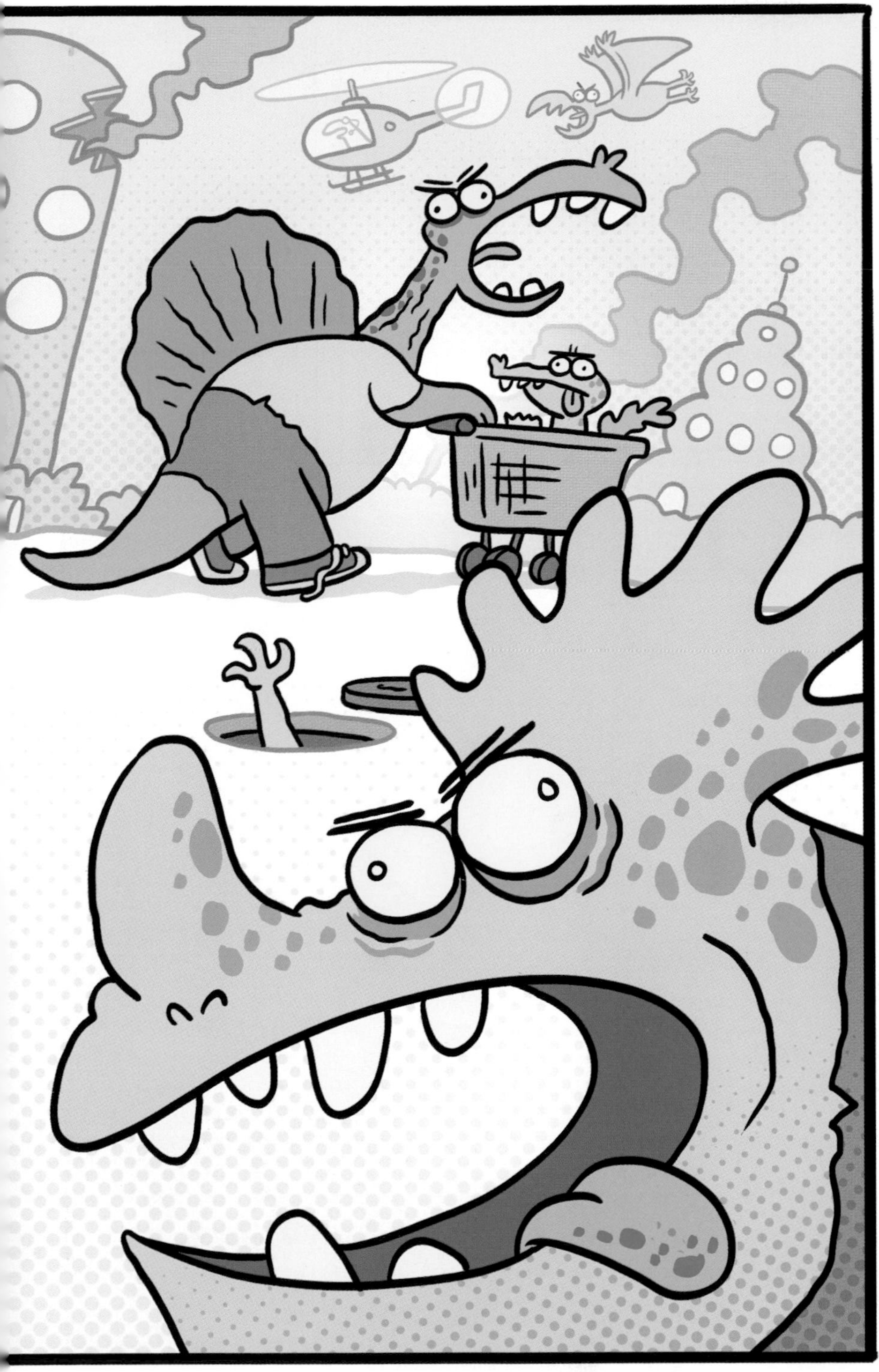

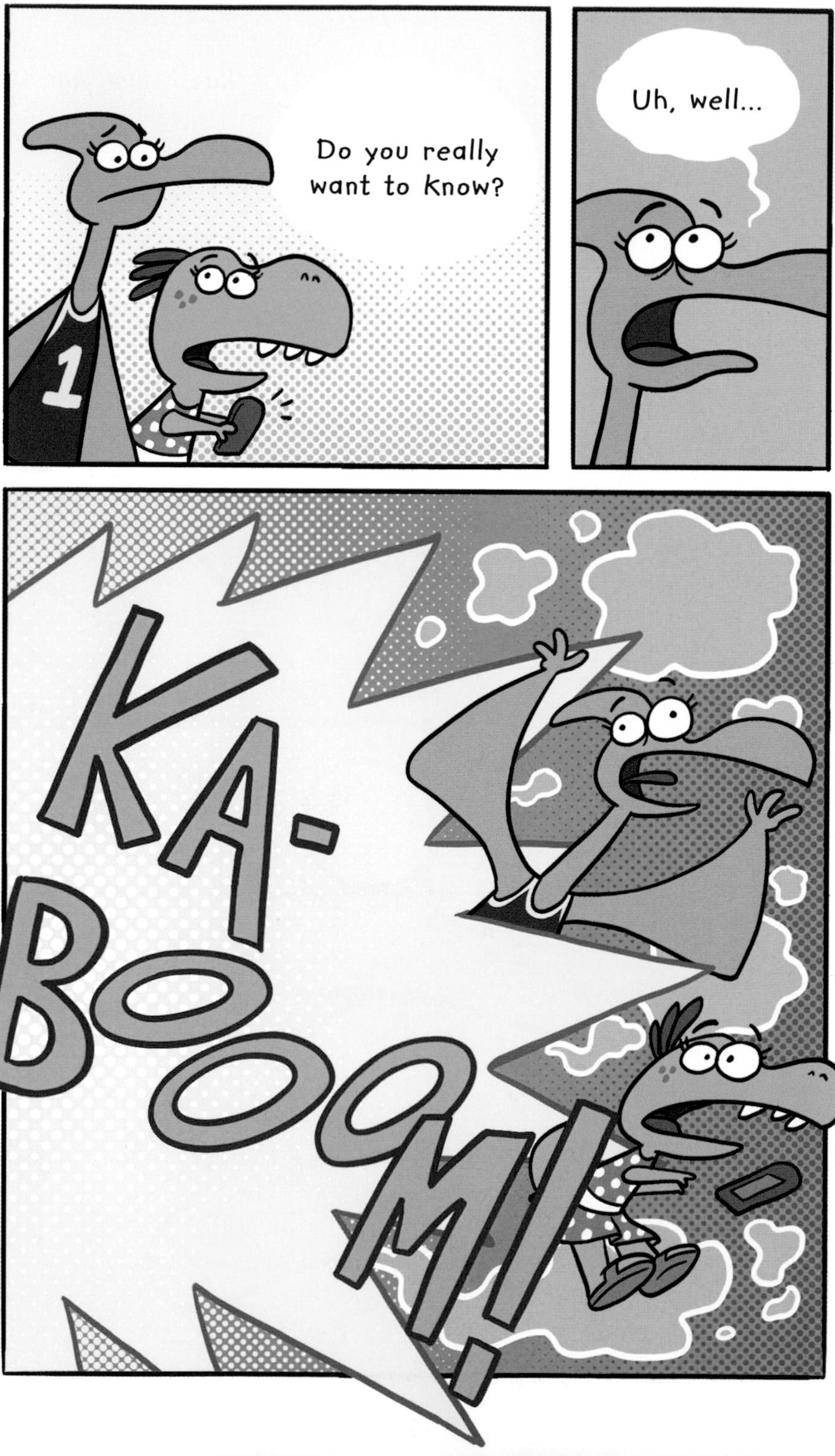
Do you really want to know?
Uh, well...
KA-BOOOM!

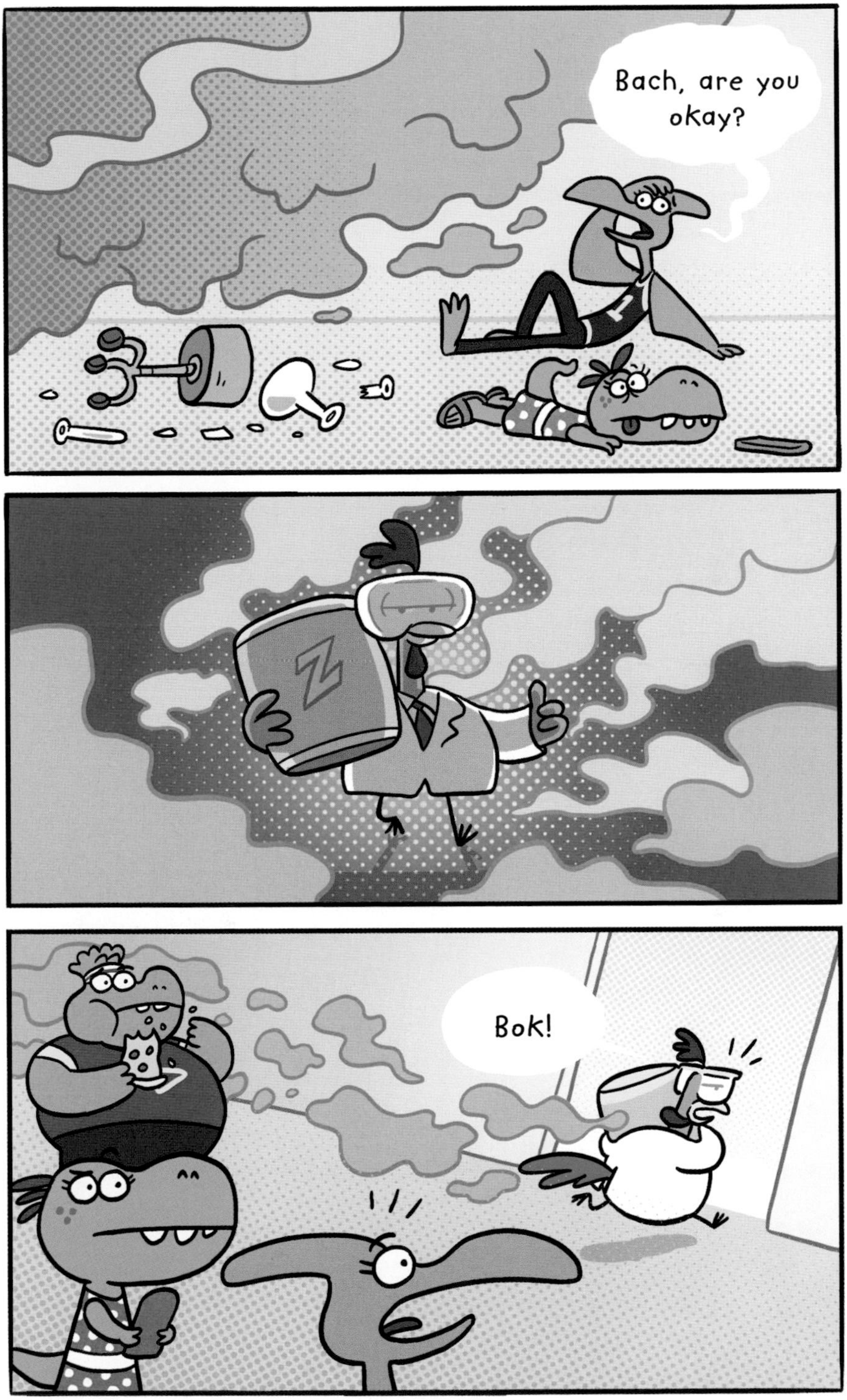
Bach, are you okay?
Bok!

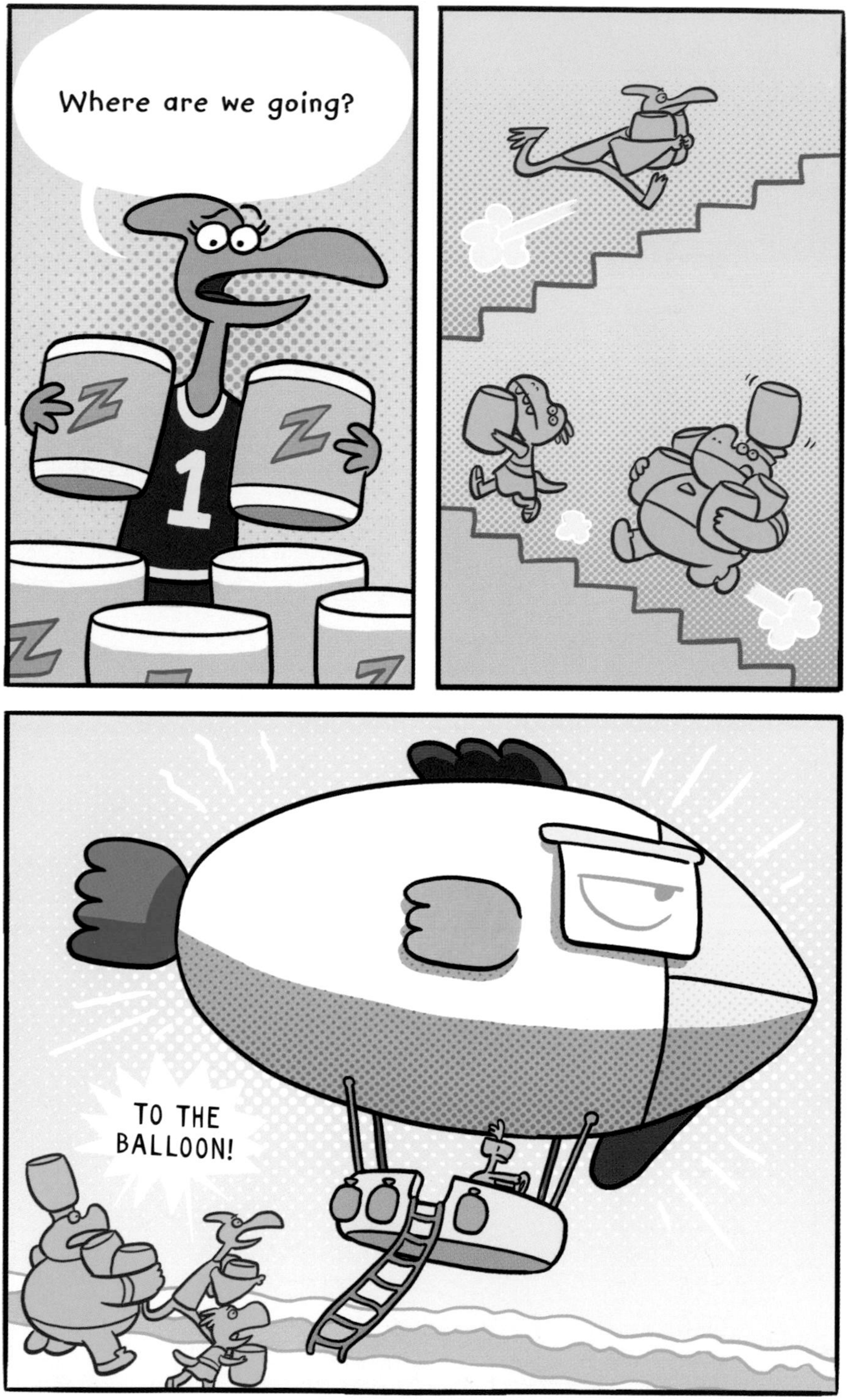
Where are we going?
TO THE BALLOON!

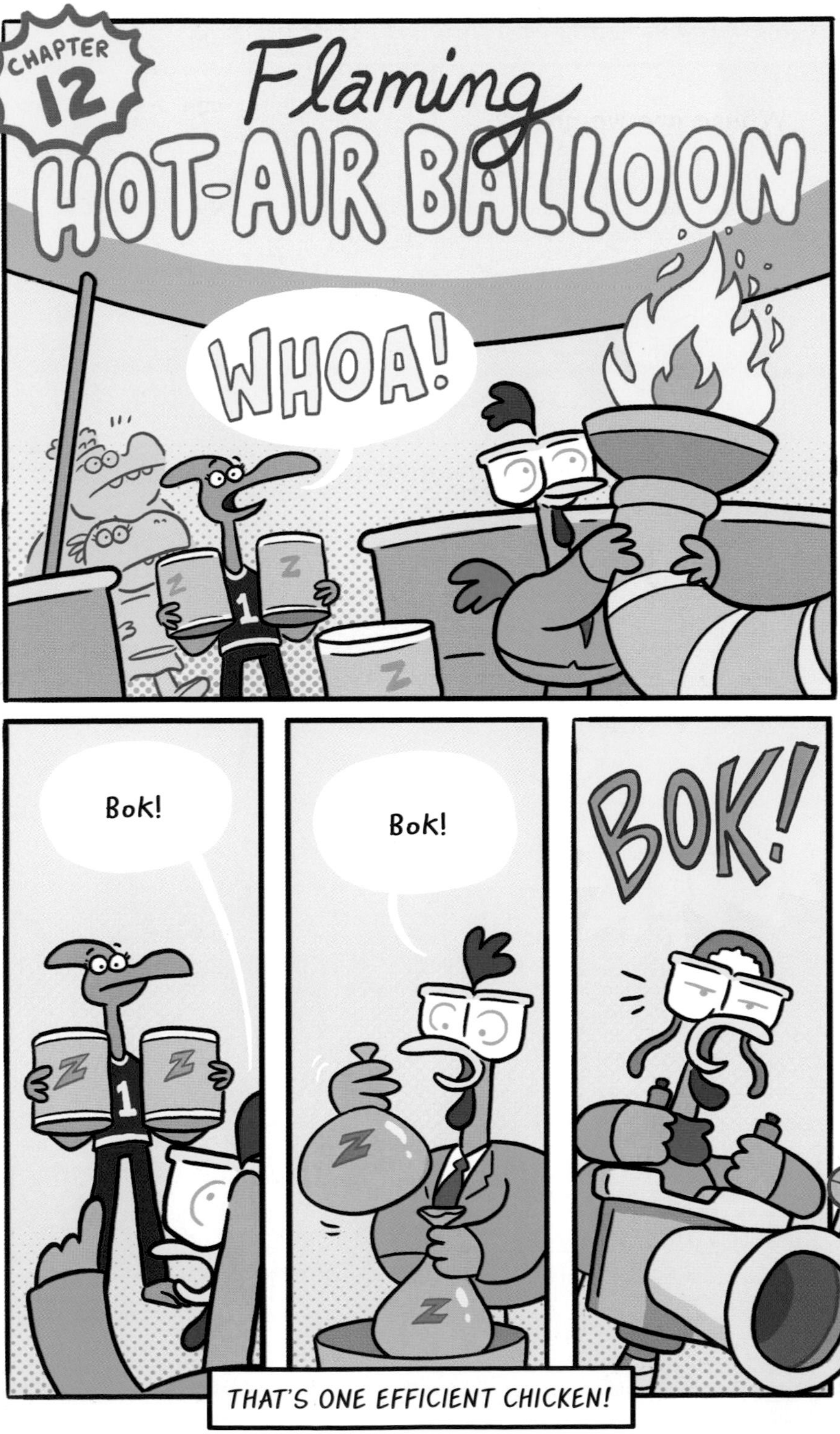
CHAPTER 12
Flaming
HOT-AIR BALLOON
WHOA!
Bok!
Bok!
BOK!
THAT'S ONE EFFICIENT CHICKEN!

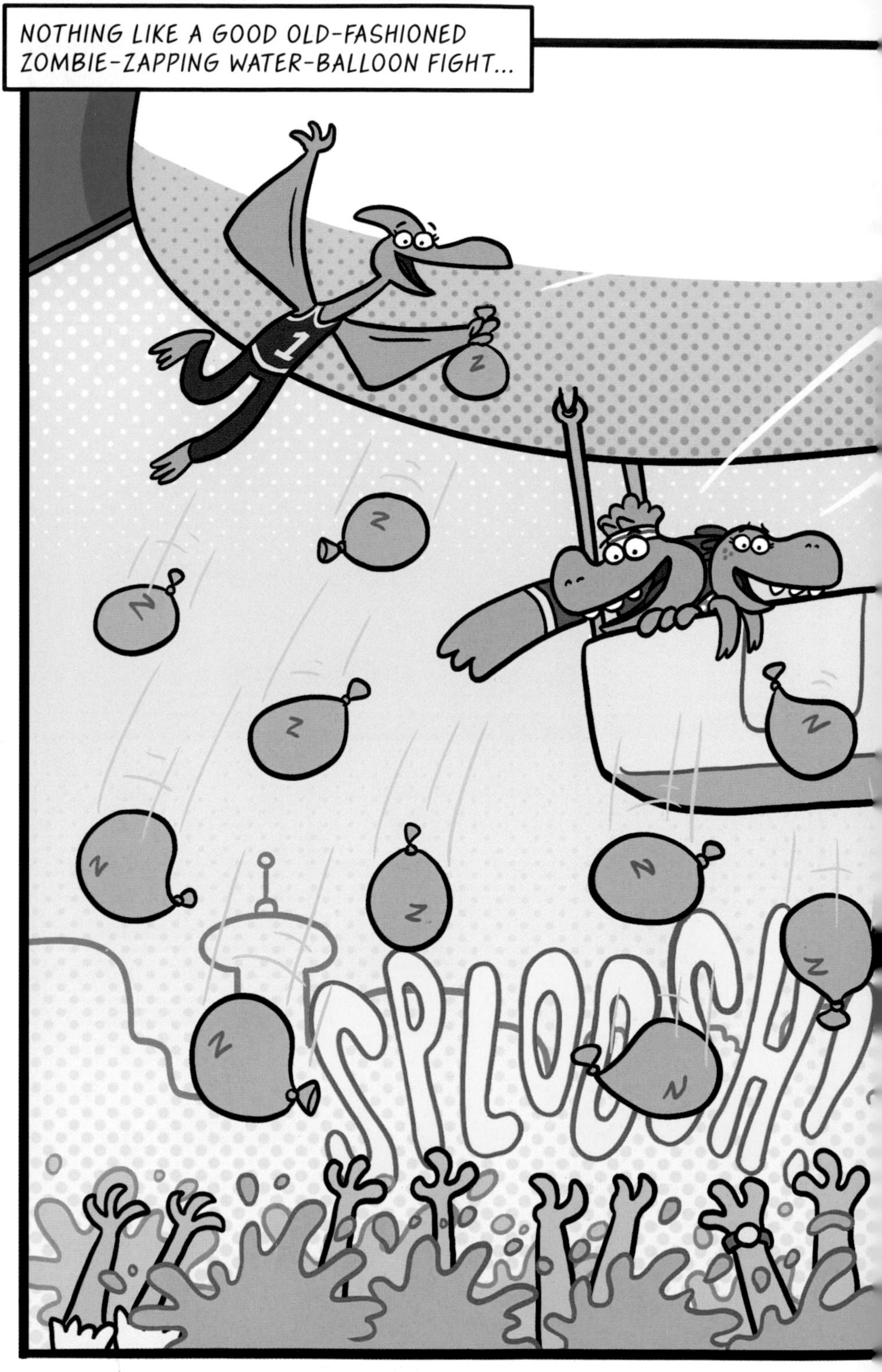
NOTHING LIKE A GOOD OLD-FASHIONED ZOMBIE-ZAPPING WATER-BALLOON FIGHT...
SPLOOSH!

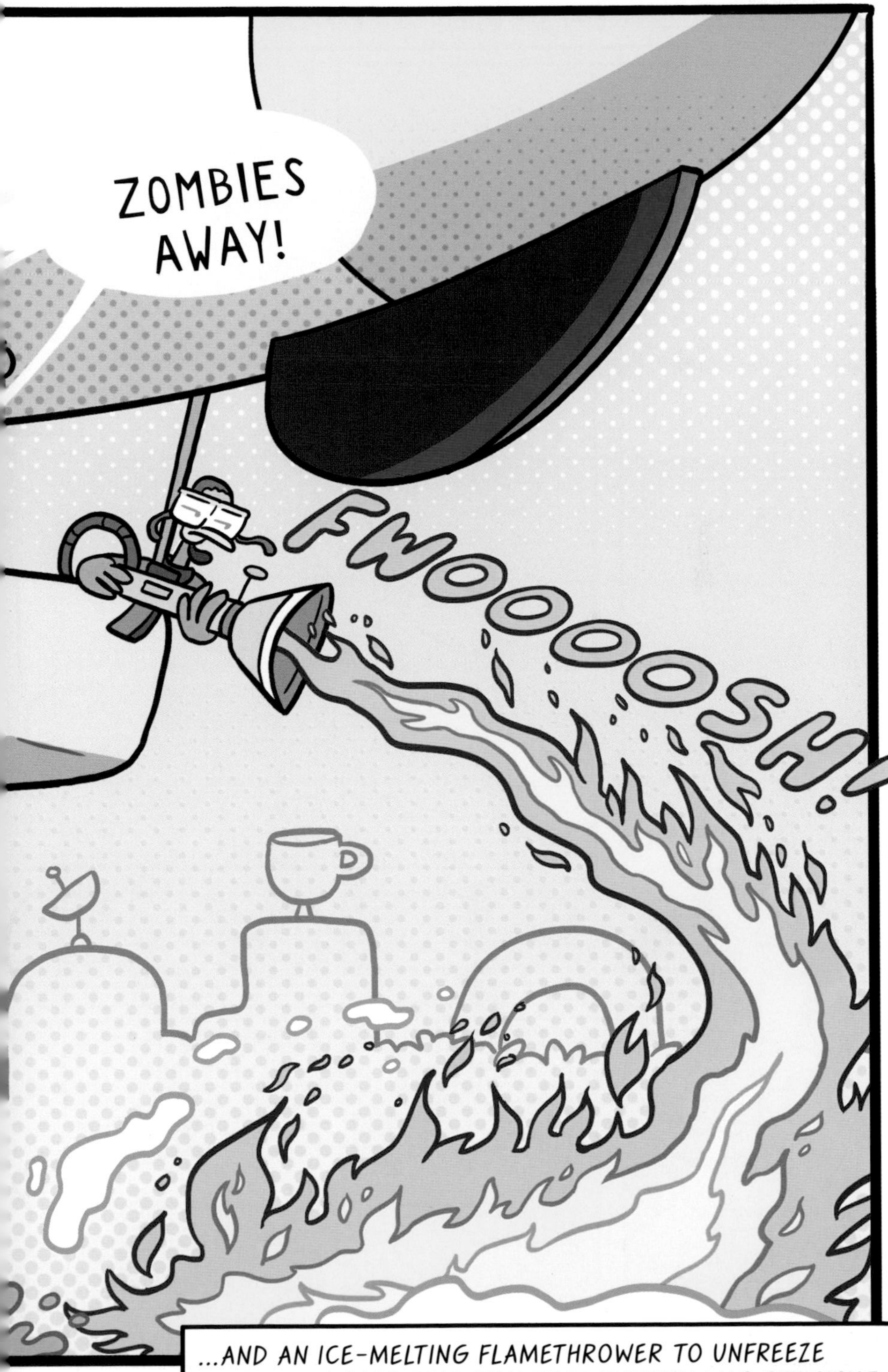
ZOMBIES AWAY!
FWOOOOOSH!
...AND AN ICE-MELTING FLAMETHROWER TO UNFREEZE DINOTOWN! SEE? TOLD YOU THAT CHICKEN WAS EFFICIENT.

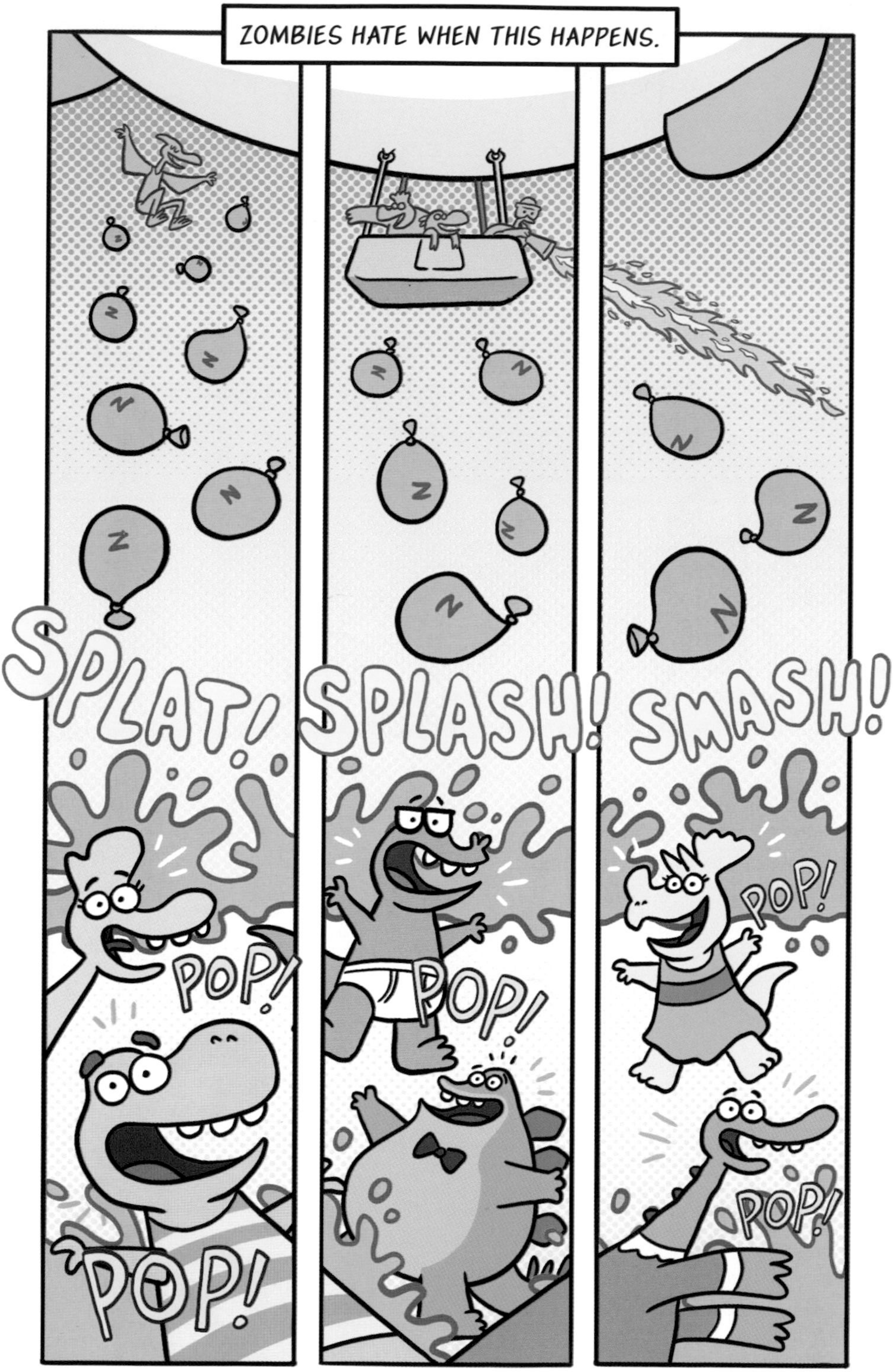
ZOMBIES HATE WHEN THIS HAPPENS.
SPLAT!
POP!
POP!
SPLASH!
POP!
SMASH!
POP!
POP!

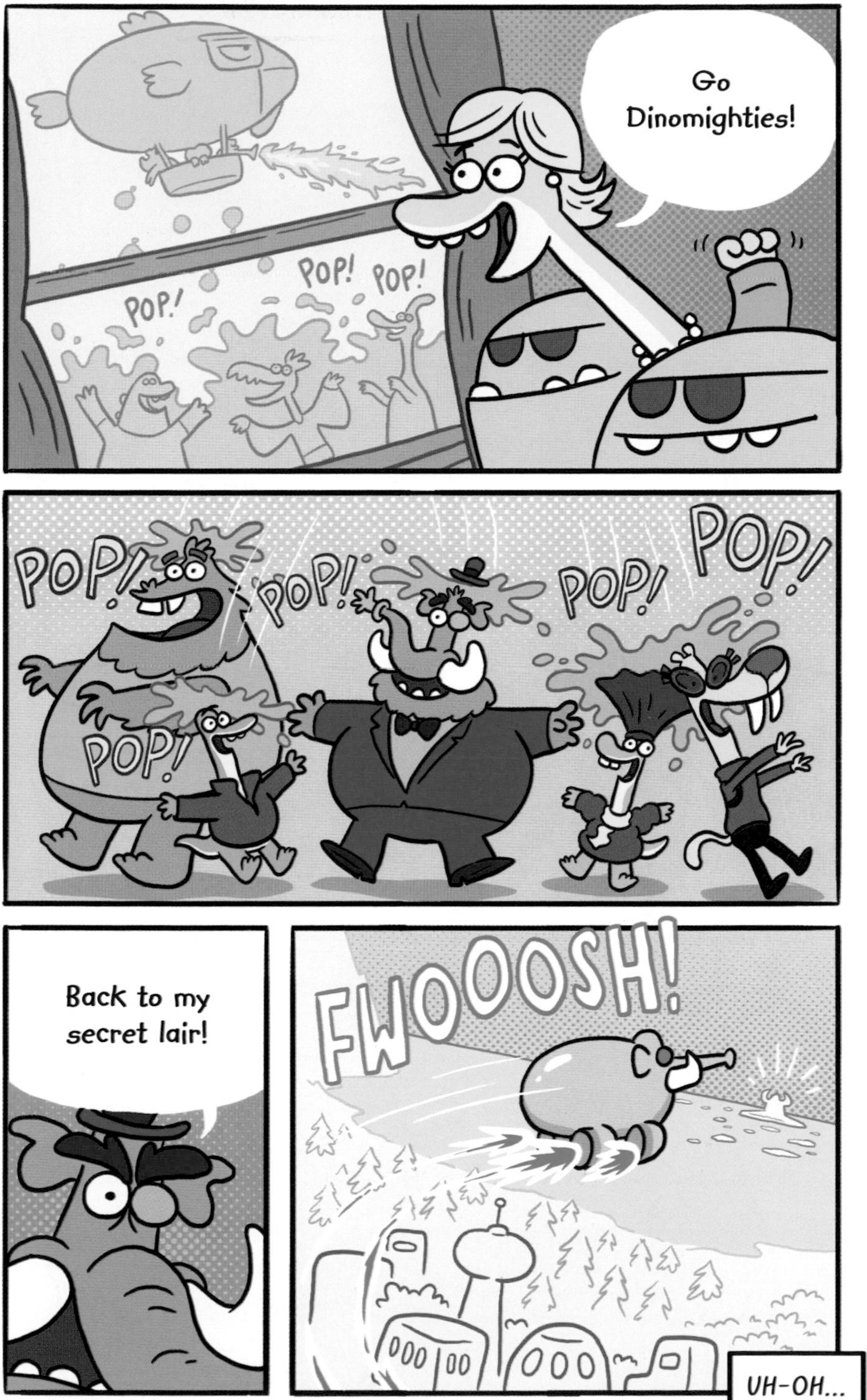
Go Dinomighties!
POP! POP!
POP!
POP!
POP!
POP!
POP!
POP!
Back to my secret lair!
FWOOOSH!
UH-OH...

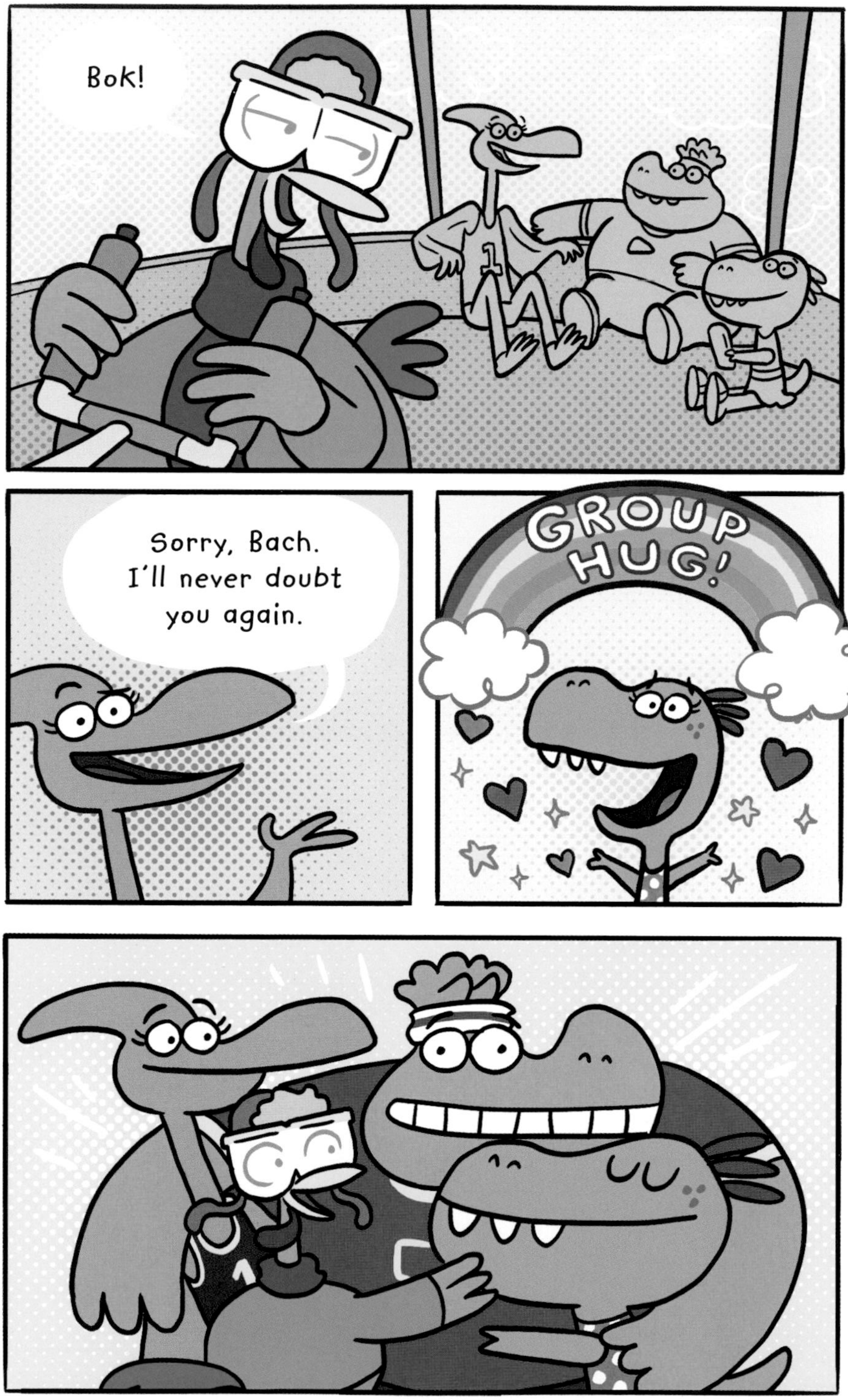
Bok!
Sorry, Bach. I'll never doubt you again.
GROUP HUG!

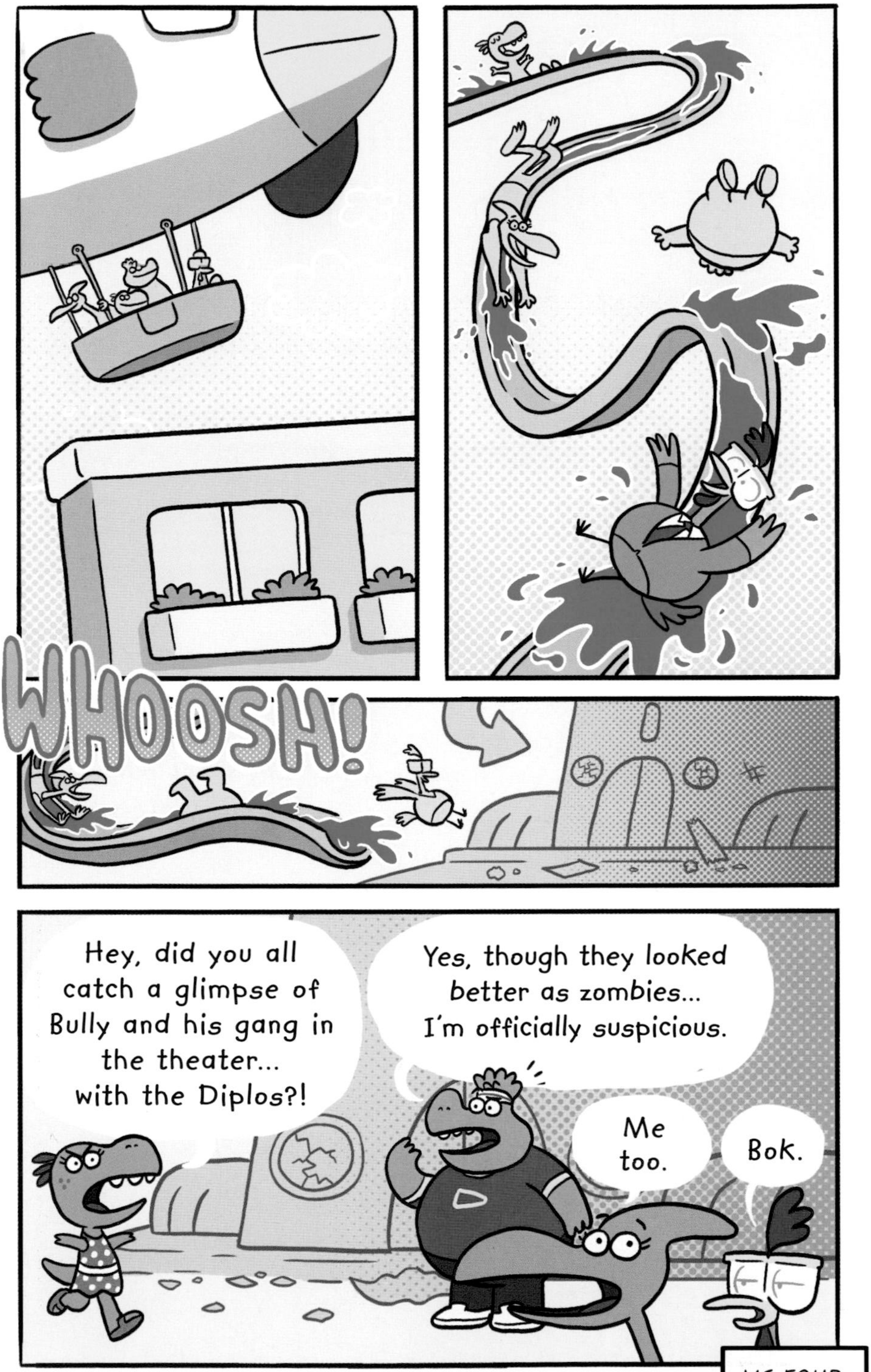
WHOOSH!
Hey, did you all catch a glimpse of Bully and his gang in the theater... with the Diplos?!
Yes, though they looked better as zombies... I'm officially suspicious.
Me too.
Bok.
ME FOUR.

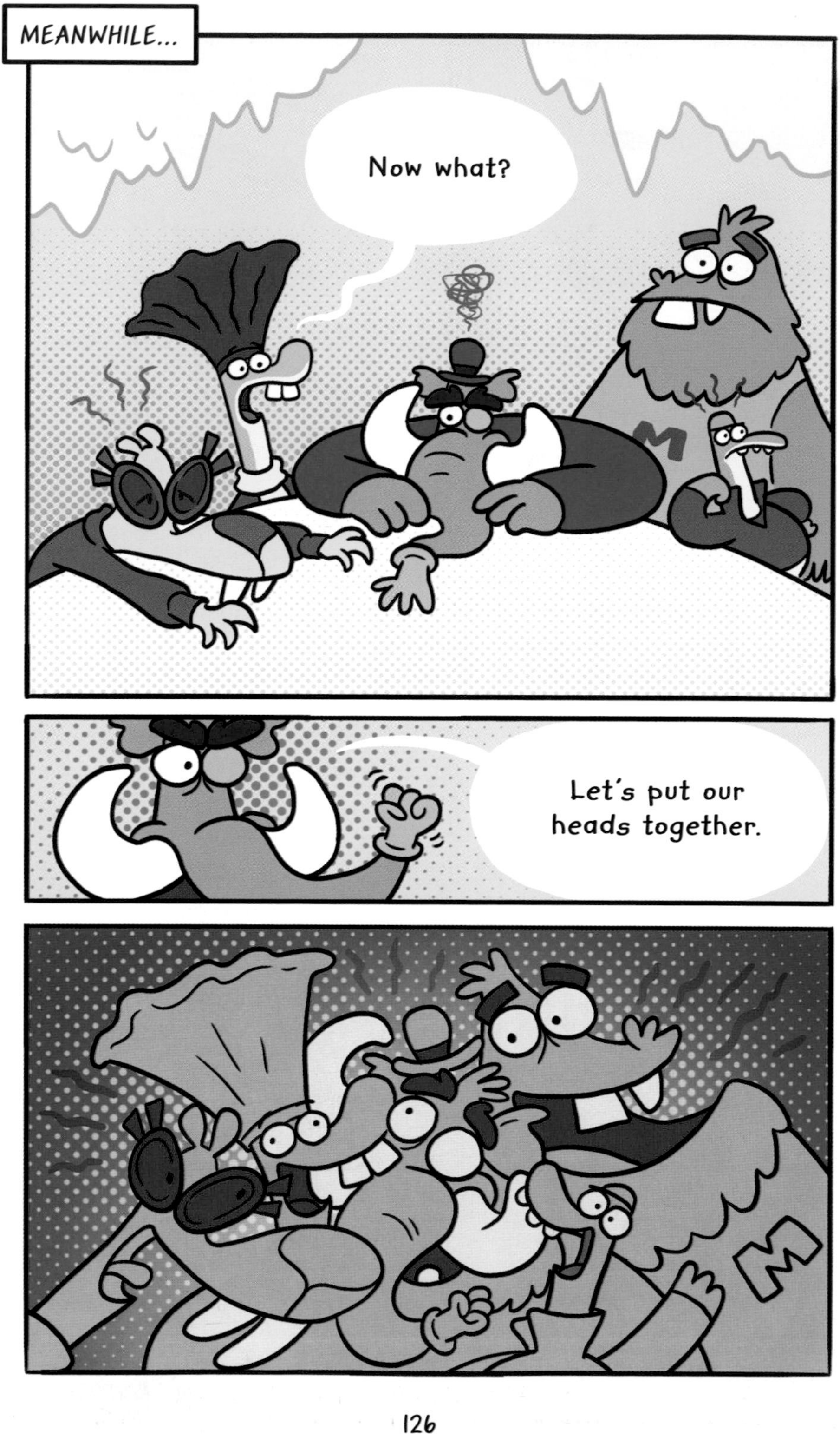
MEANWHILE...
Now what?
Let's put our heads together.

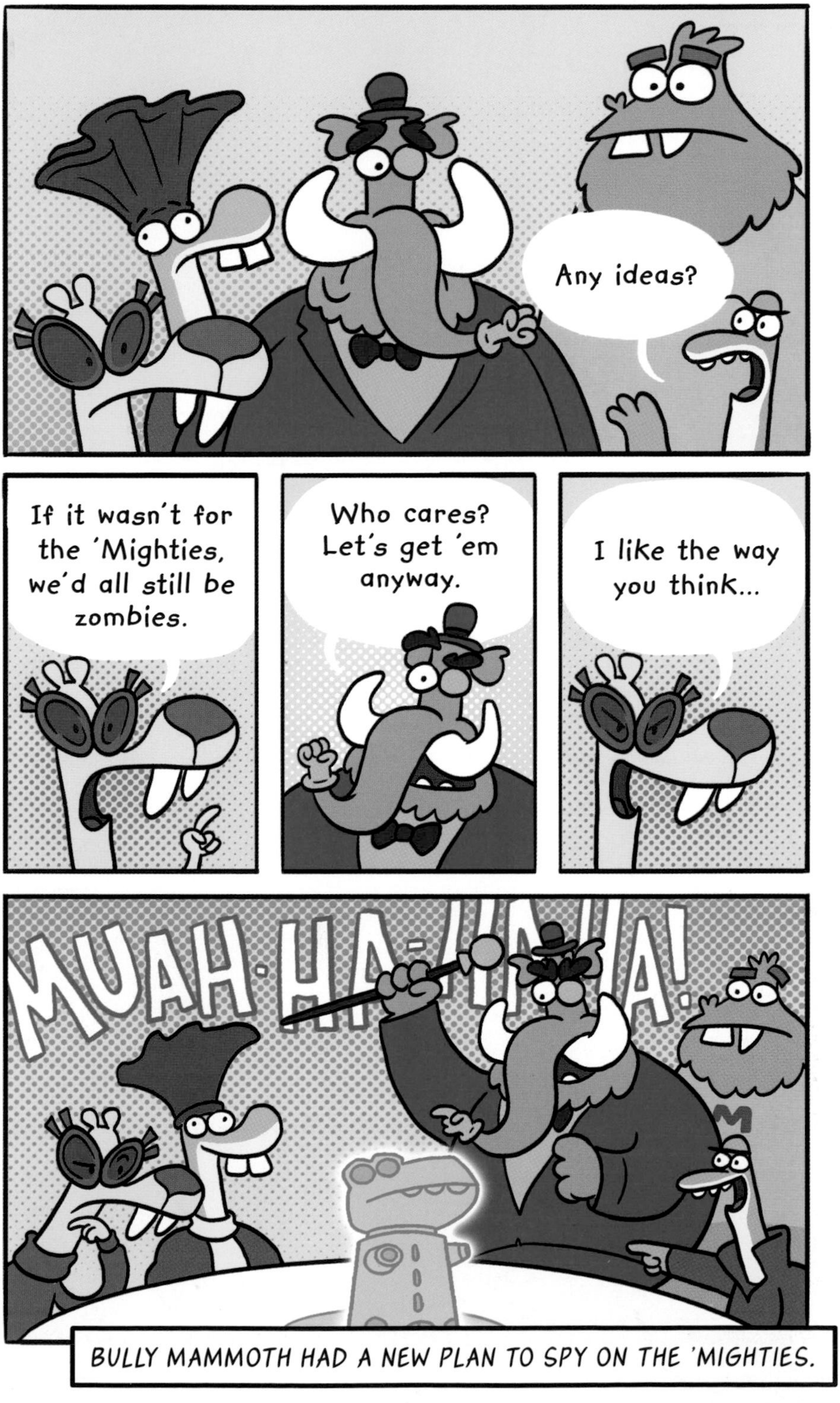

Any ideas?
If it wasn't for the 'Mighties, we'd all still be zombies.
Who cares? Let's get 'em anyway.
I like the way you think...
MUAH-HA-HA-HA!
BULLY MAMMOTH HAD A NEW PLAN TO SPY ON THE 'MIGHTIES.

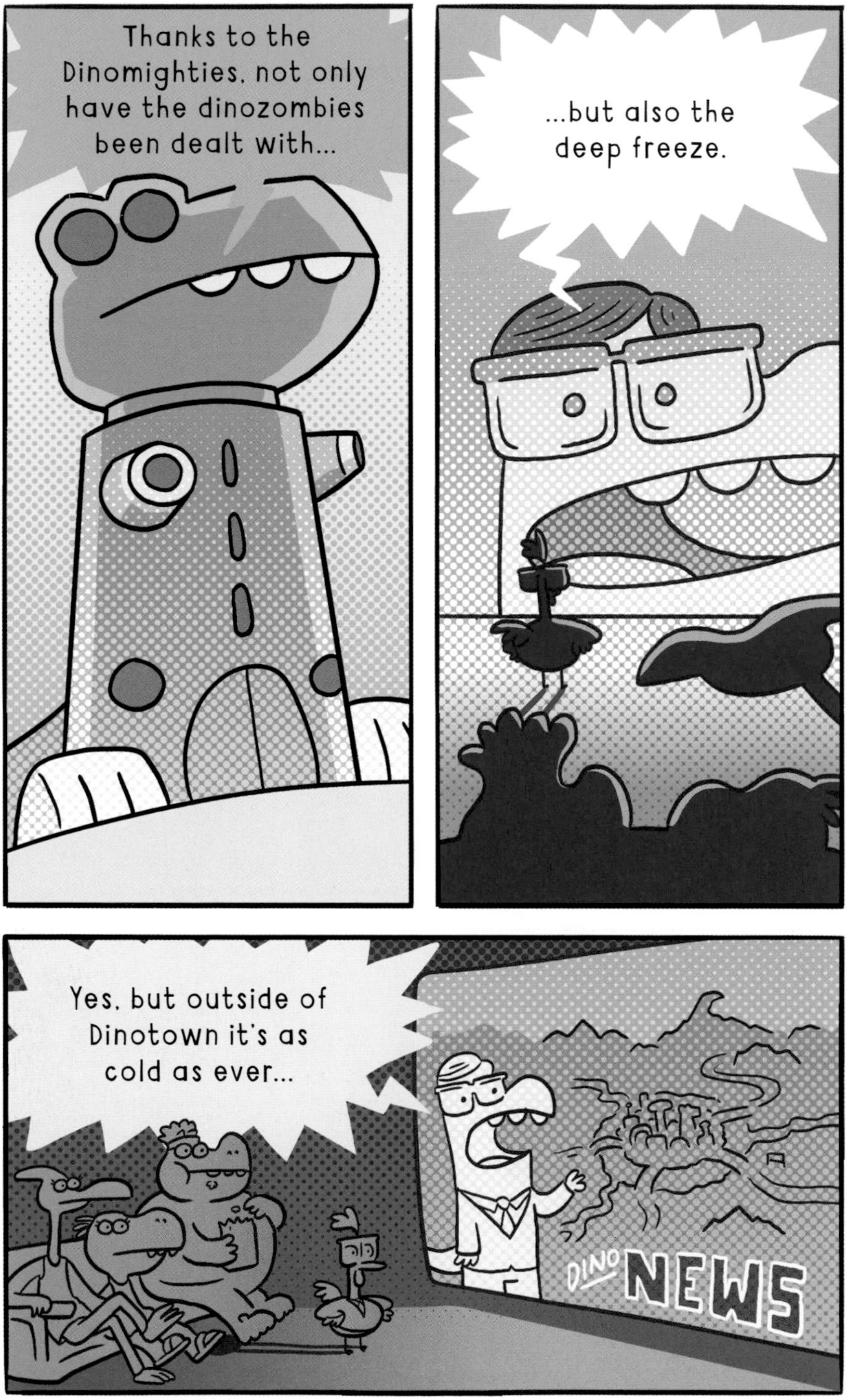
Thanks to the Dinomighties, not only have the dinozombies been dealt with...
...but also the deep freeze.
Yes, but outside of Dinotown it's as cold as ever...
DINO NEWS

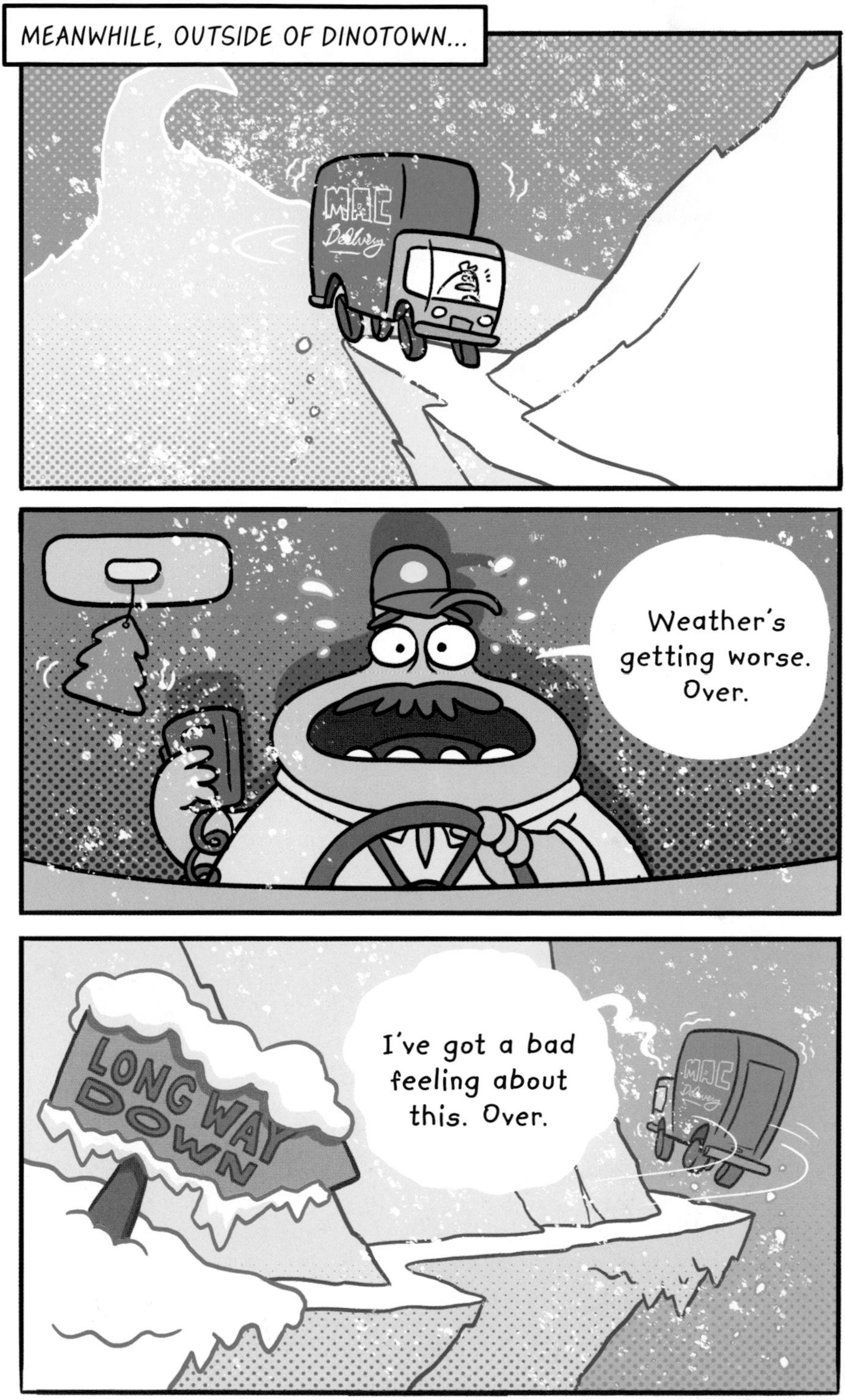
MEANWHILE, OUTSIDE OF DINOTOWN...
MAC Delivery
Weather's getting worse. Over.
LONG WAY DOWN
I've got a bad feeling about this. Over.
MAC Delivery

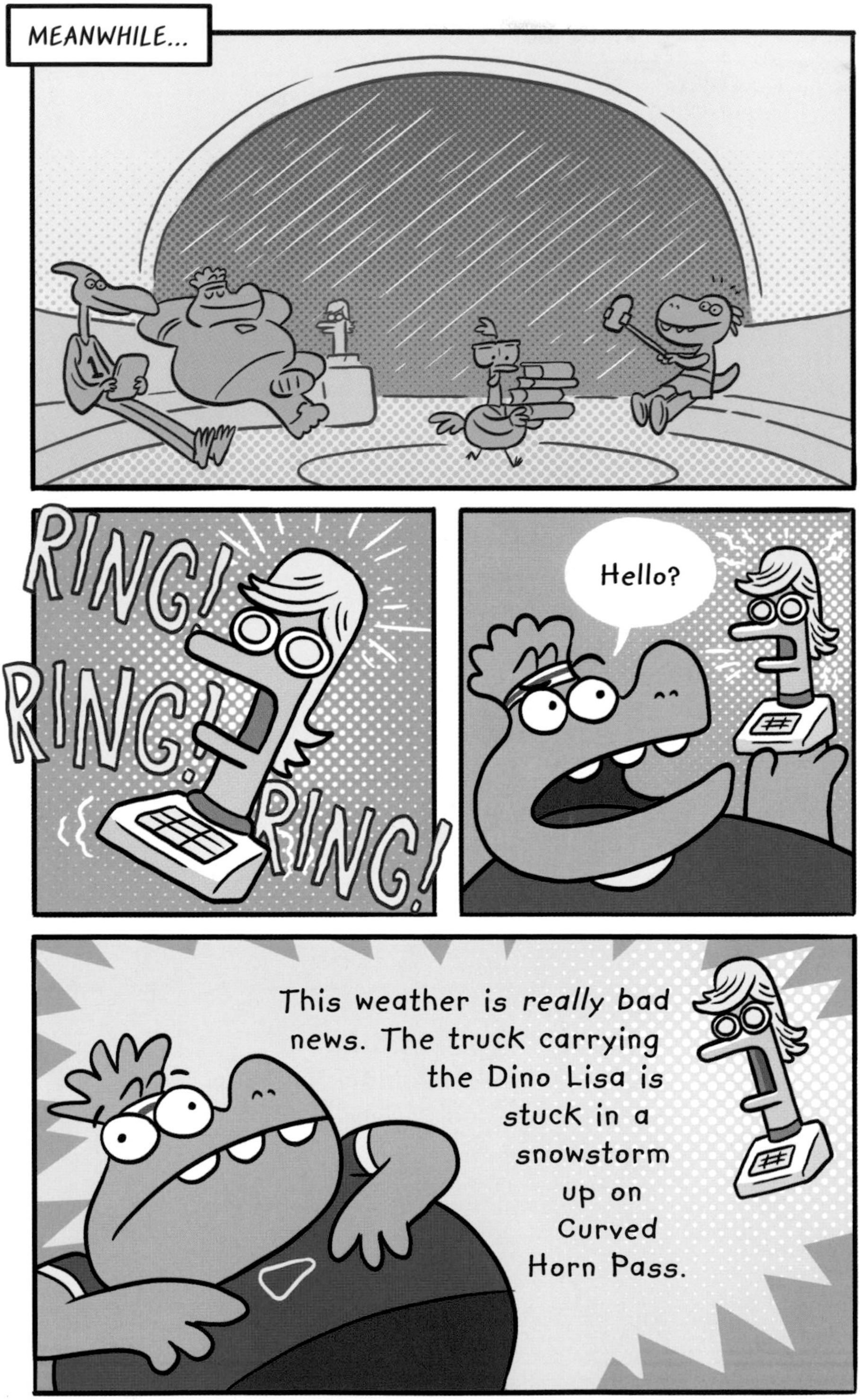
MEANWHILE...
RING! RING! RING!
Hello?
This weather is *really* bad news. The truck carrying the Dino Lisa is stuck in a snowstorm up on Curved Horn Pass.

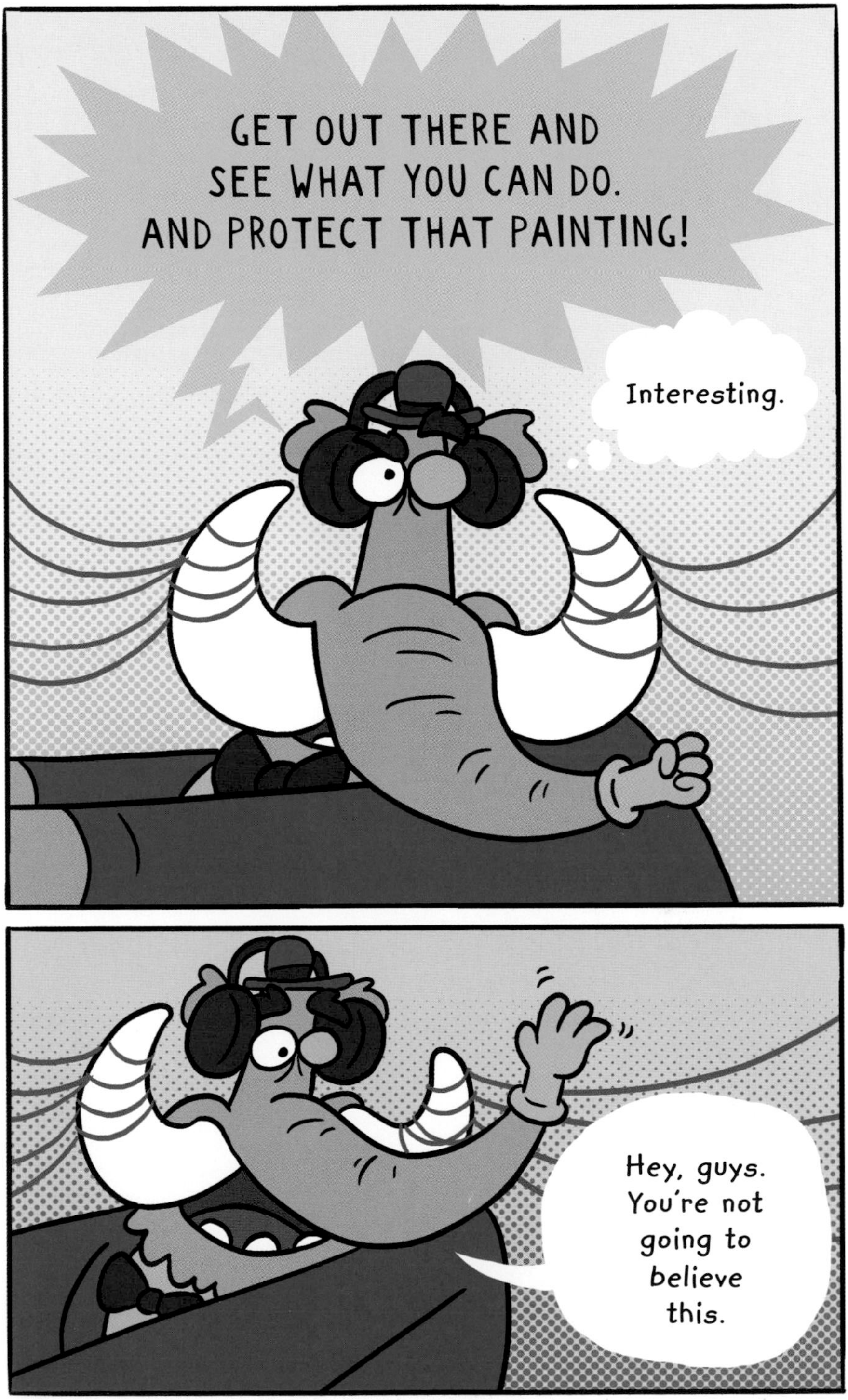

GET OUT THERE AND SEE WHAT YOU CAN DO. AND PROTECT THAT PAINTING!
Interesting.
Hey, guys. You're not going to believe this.

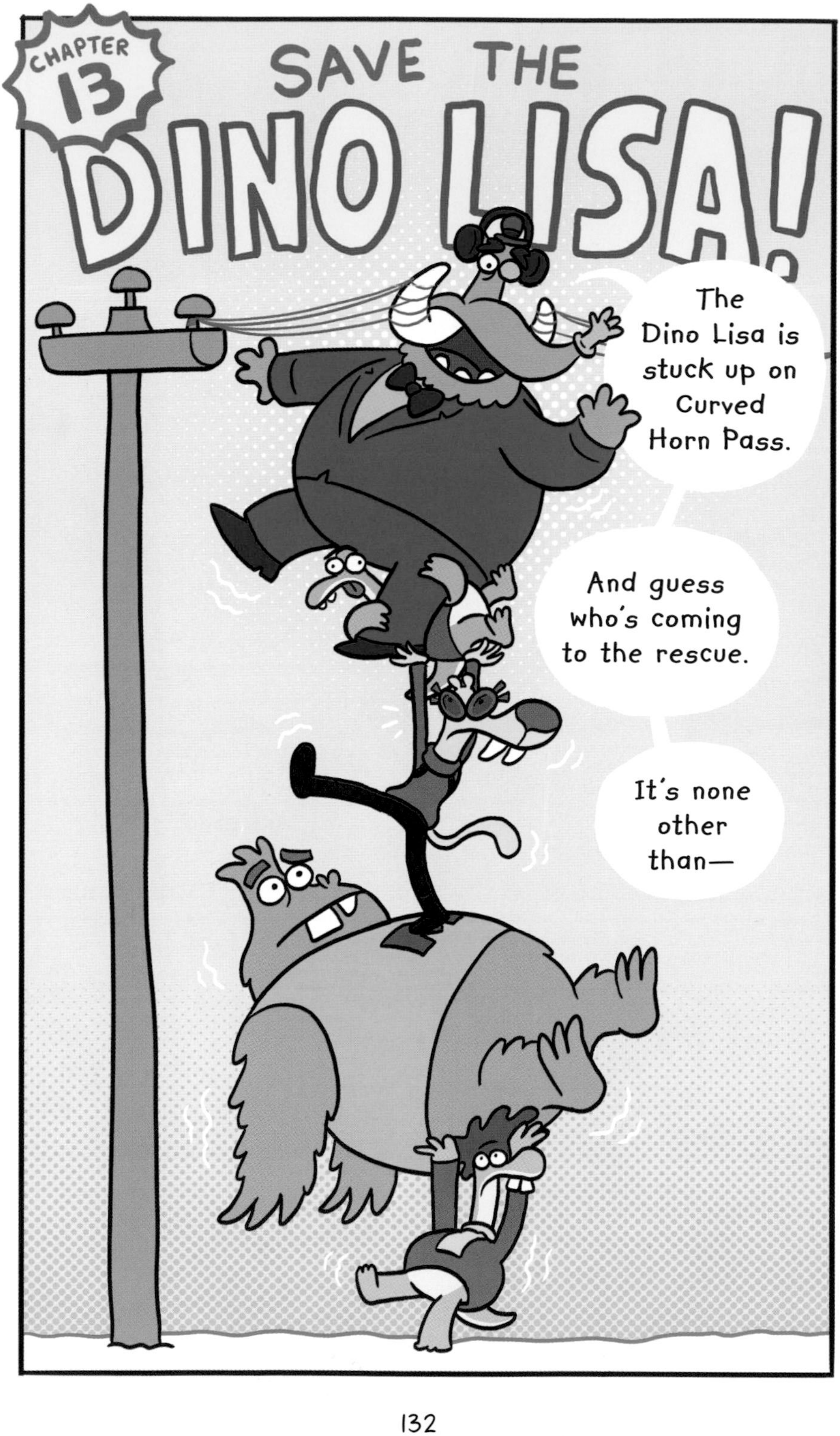
CHAPTER 13
SAVE THE DINO LISA!
The Dino Lisa is stuck up on Curved Horn Pass.
And guess who's coming to the rescue.
It's none other than—

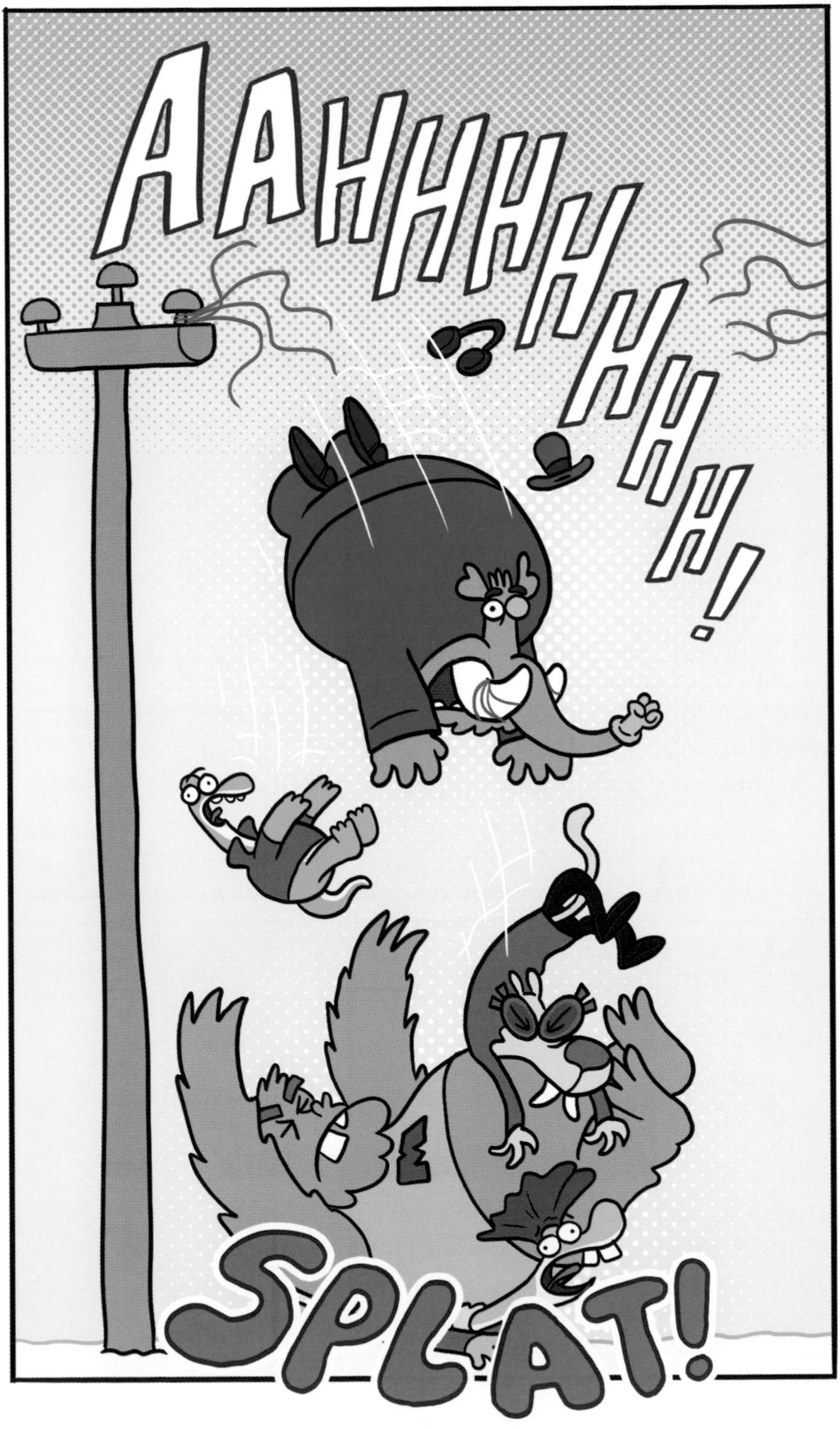
AAHHHHHHHHHHH!
SPLAT!

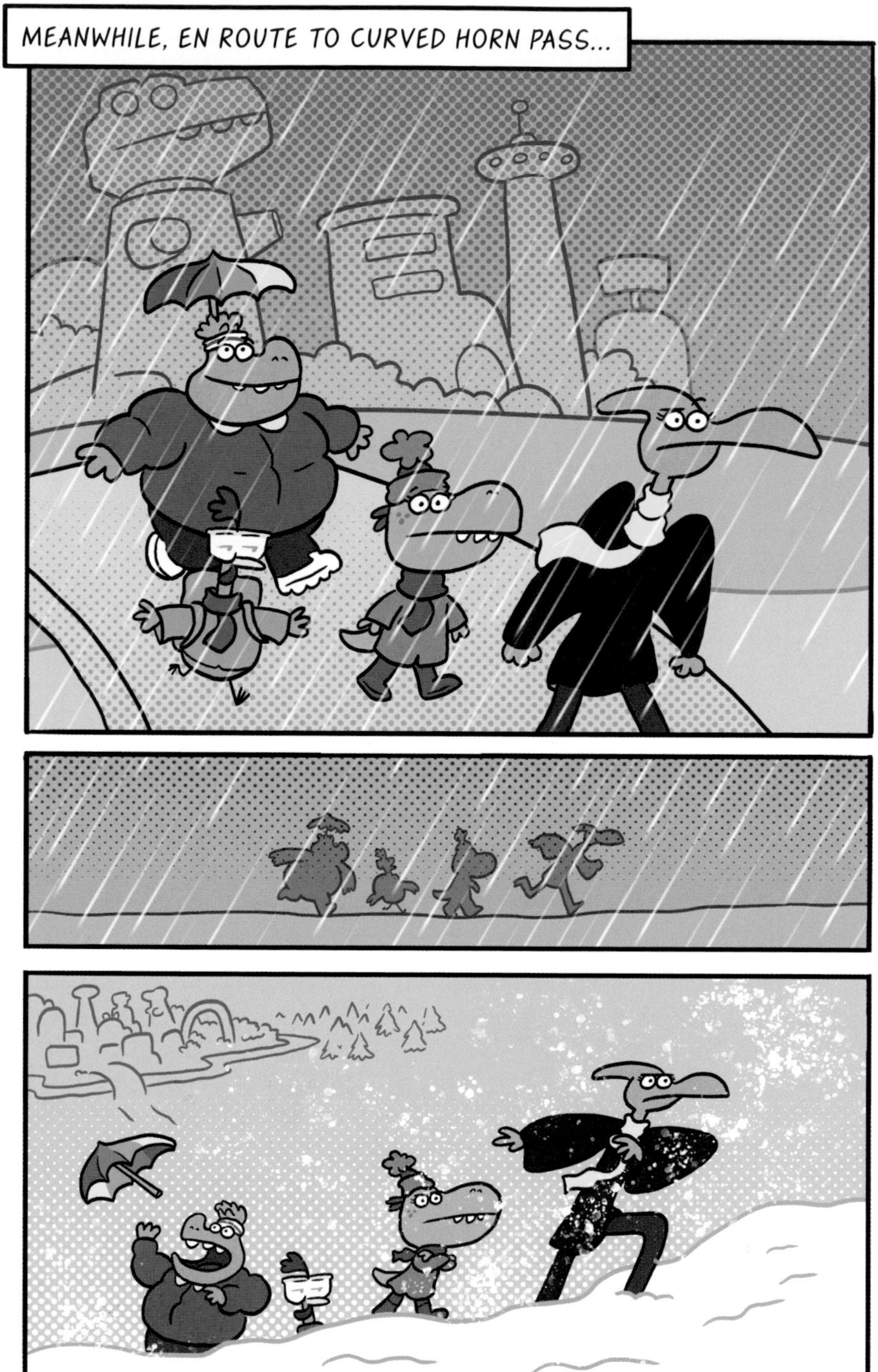
MEANWHILE, EN ROUTE TO CURVED HORN PASS...

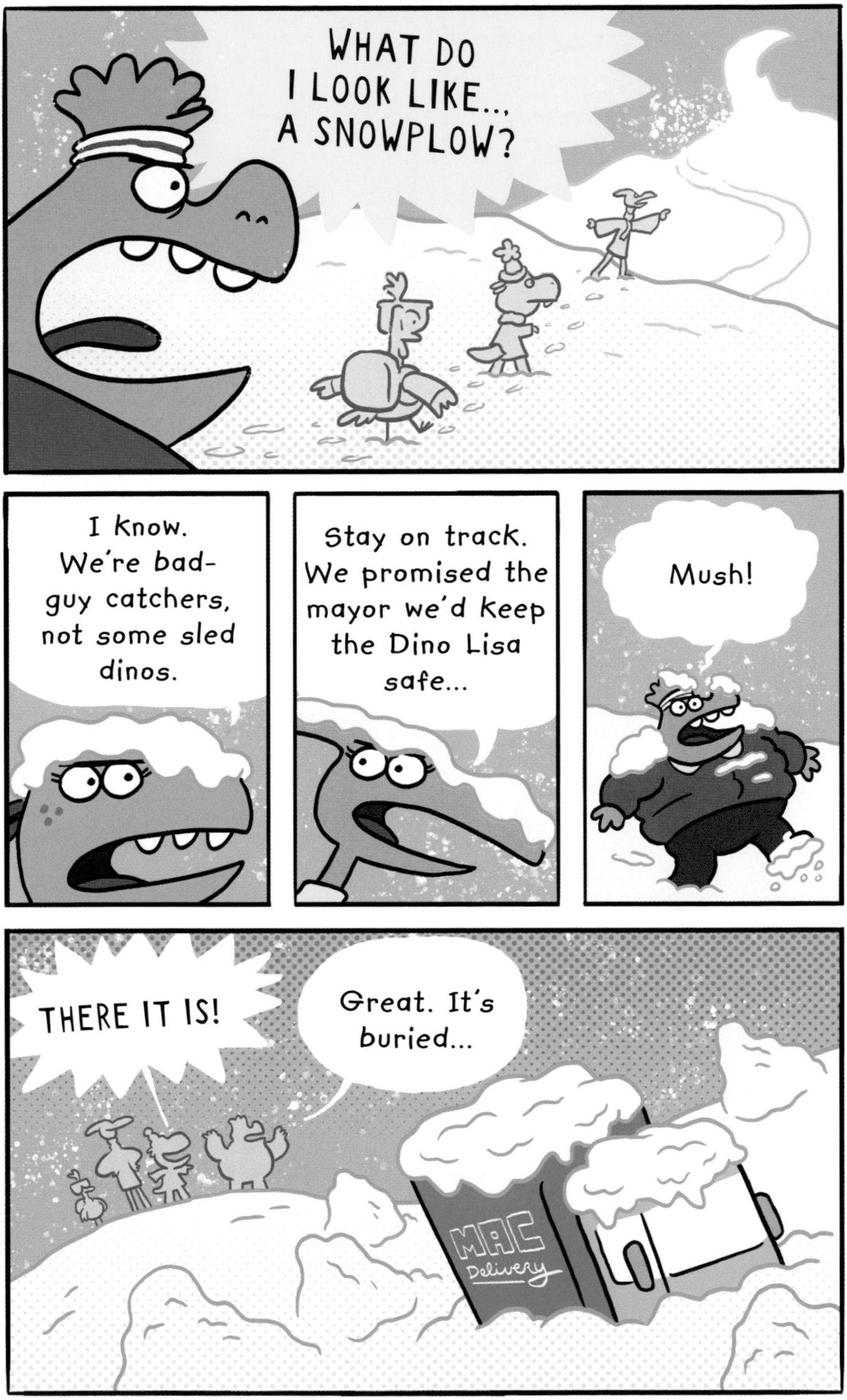
WHAT DO I LOOK LIKE... A SNOWPLOW?
I know. We're bad-guy catchers, not some sled dinos.
Stay on track. We promised the mayor we'd keep the Dino Lisa safe...
Mush!
THERE IT IS!
Great. It's buried...
MAC Delivery

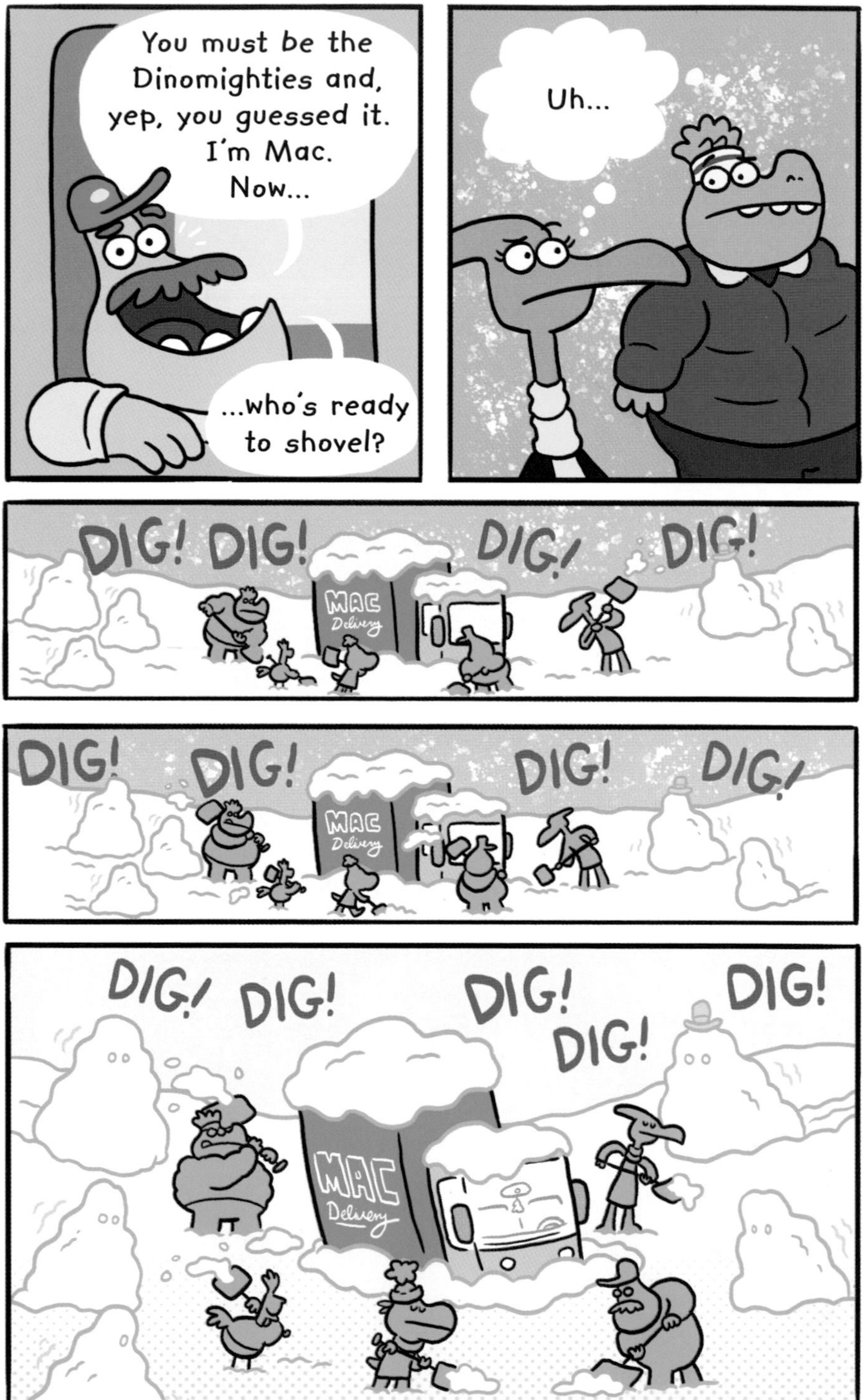
You must be the Dinomighties and, yep, you guessed it. I'm Mac. Now...
...who's ready to shovel?
Uh...
DIG! DIG! DIG! DIG!
DIG! DIG! DIG! DIG!
MAC Delivery
DIG! DIG! DIG! DIG! DIG!
MAC Delivery

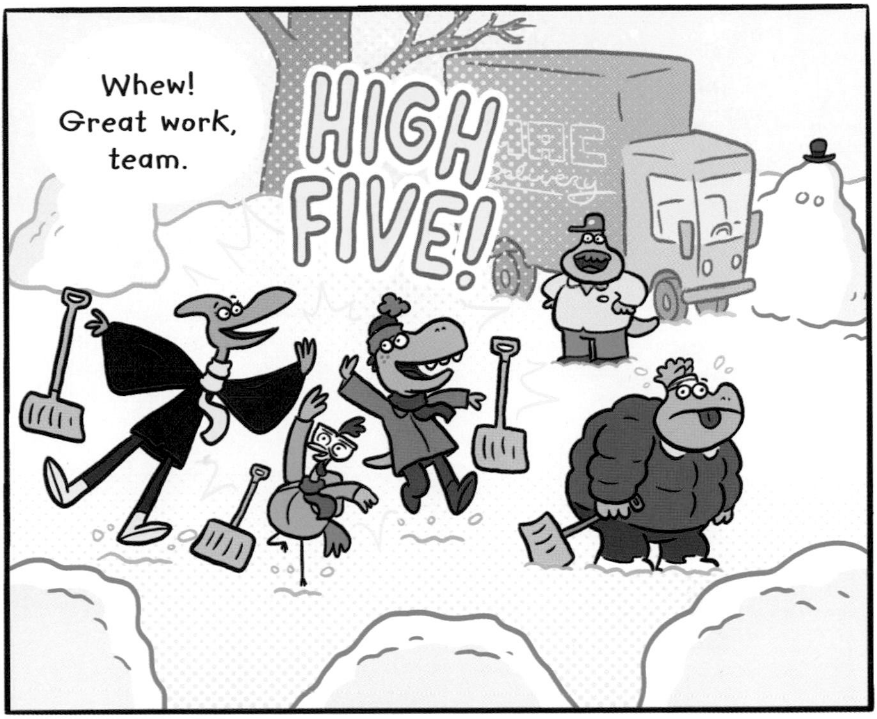
Whew! Great work, team.
HIGH FIVE!
MAC Delivery

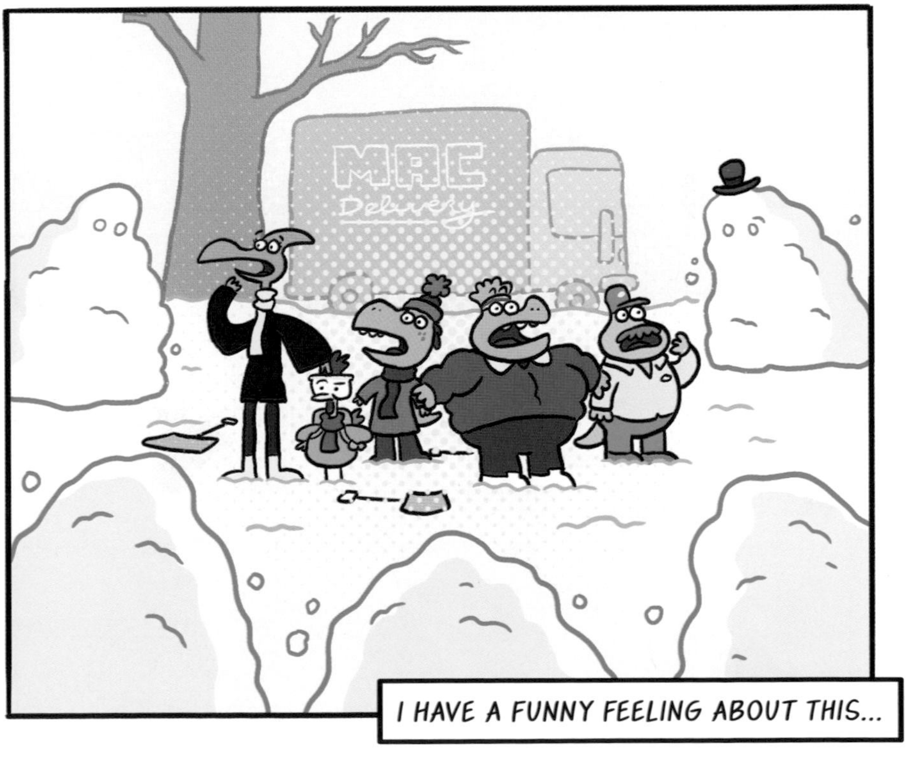
MAC Delivery
I HAVE A FUNNY FEELING ABOUT THIS...

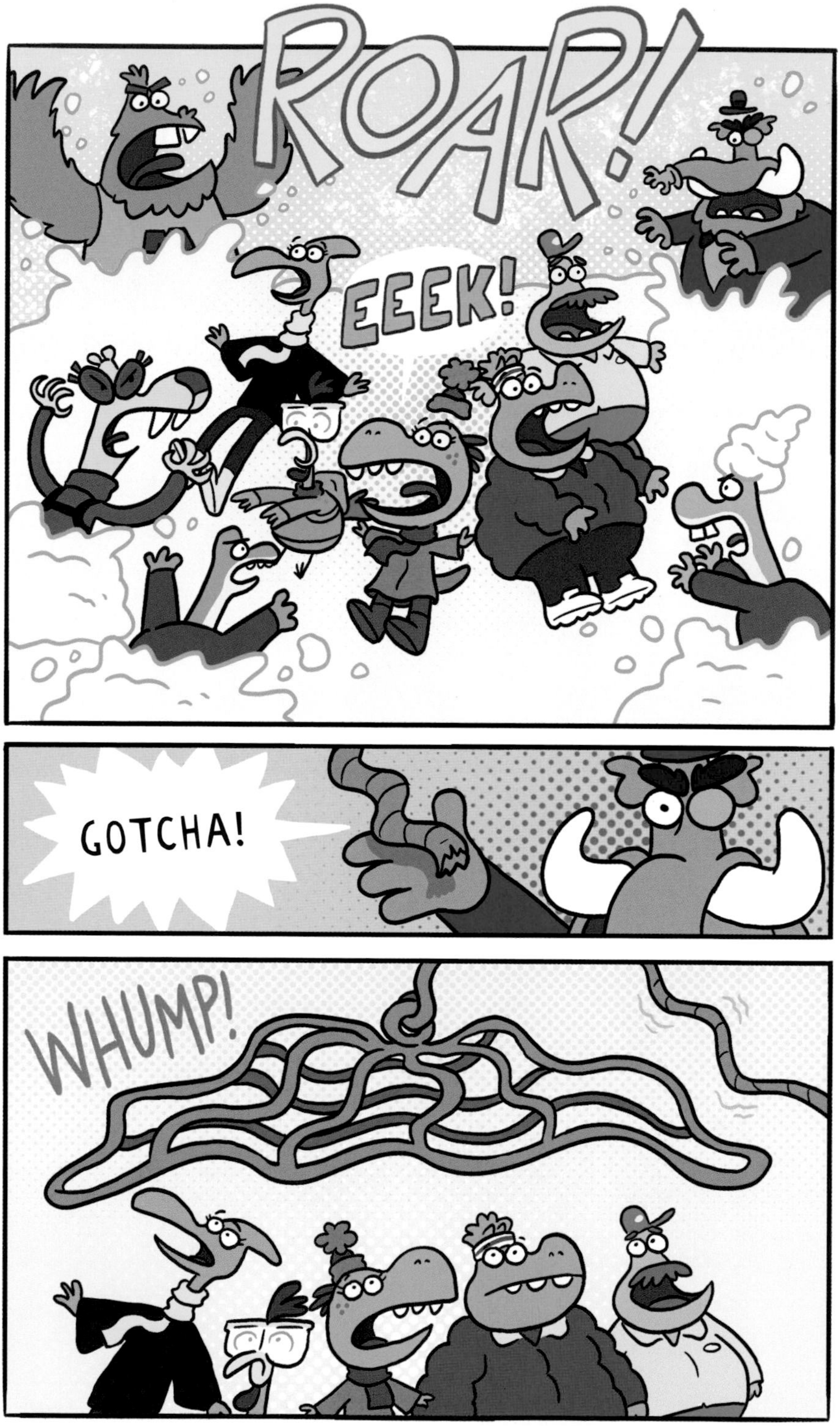
ROAR!
EEEK!
GOTCHA!
WHUMP!

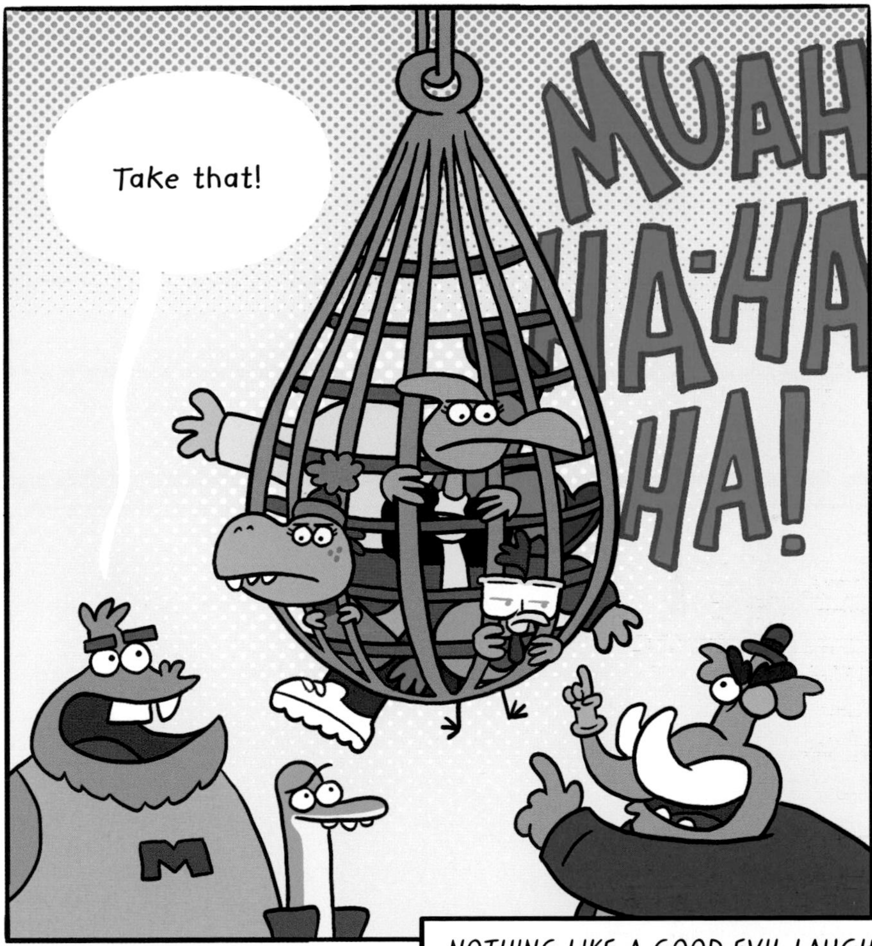
Take that!
MUAH HA-HA HA!

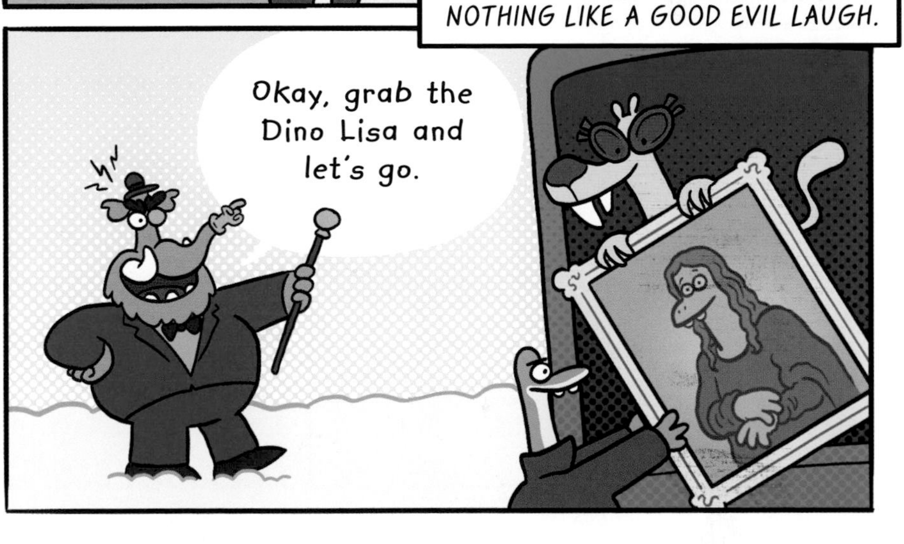
NOTHING LIKE A GOOD EVIL LAUGH.
Okay, grab the Dino Lisa and let's go.

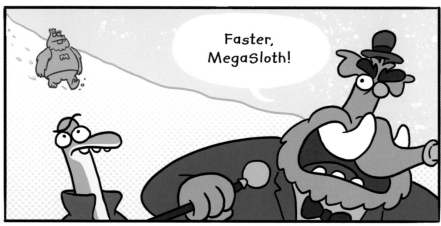

Faster, MegaSloth!

I'll get there when I get there.

TRUDGE.
TRUDGE.
TRUDGE.

Uh, okay?

WHAT, BULLY? HE'S GOING AT A SLOTH'S PACE.

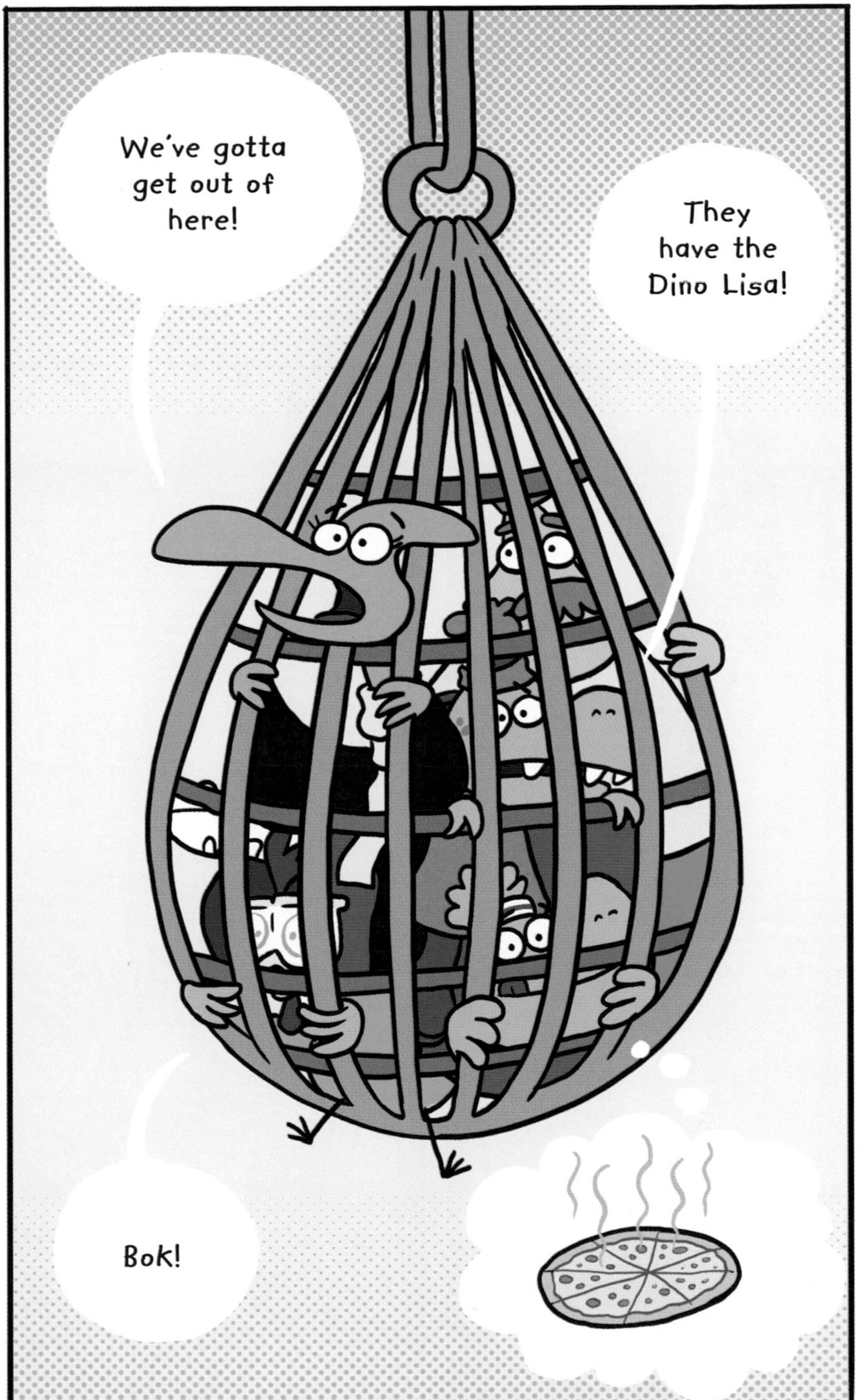
We've gotta get out of here!
They have the Dino Lisa!
Bok!

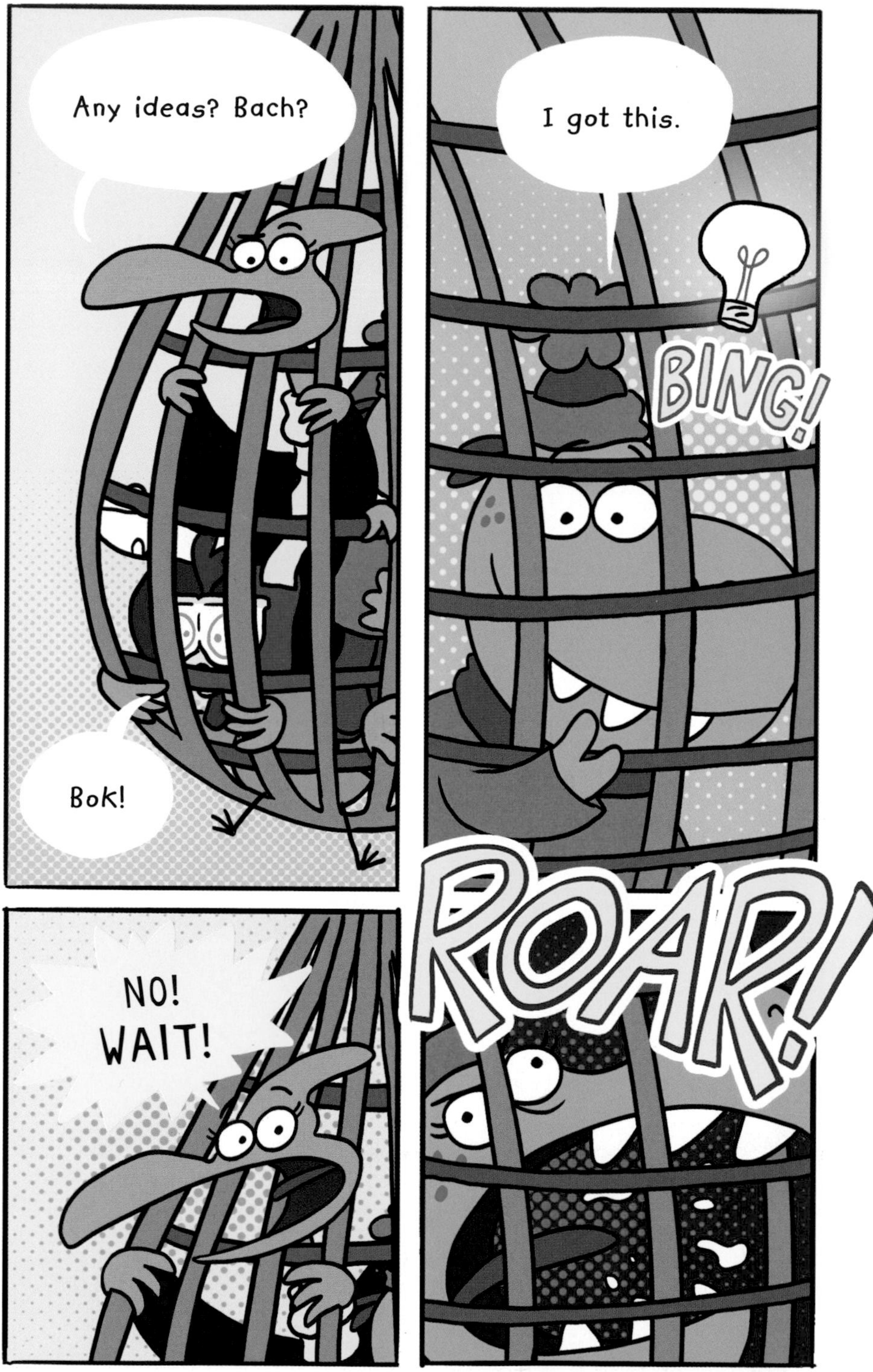
Any ideas? Bach?
Bok!
I got this.
BING!
NO! WAIT!
ROAR!

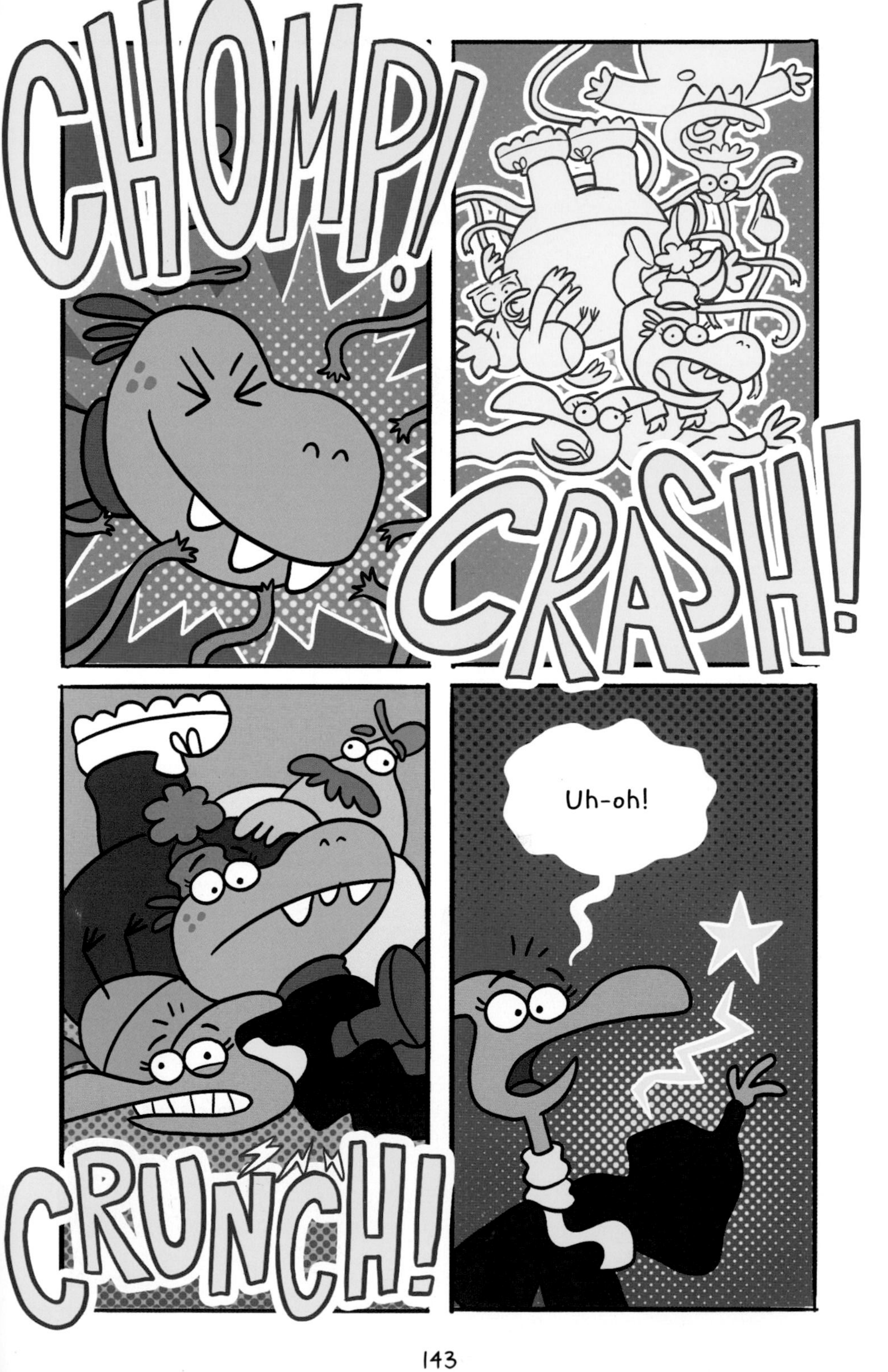
CHOMP!
CRASH!
CRUNCH!
Uh-oh!

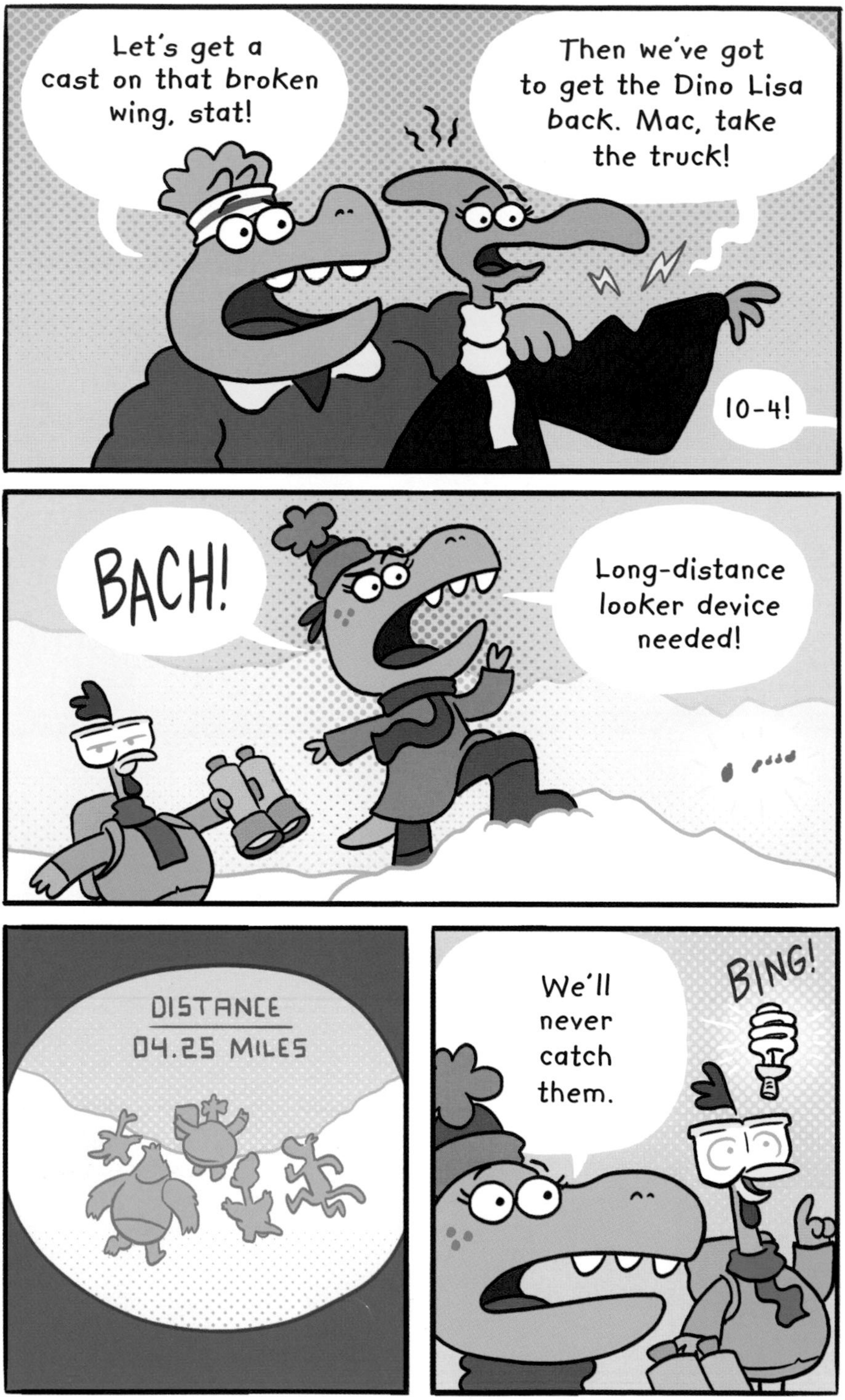
Let's get a cast on that broken wing, stat!
Then we've got to get the Dino Lisa back. Mac, take the truck!
10-4!
BACH!
Long-distance looker device needed!
DISTANCE
04.25 MILES
We'll never catch them.
BING!

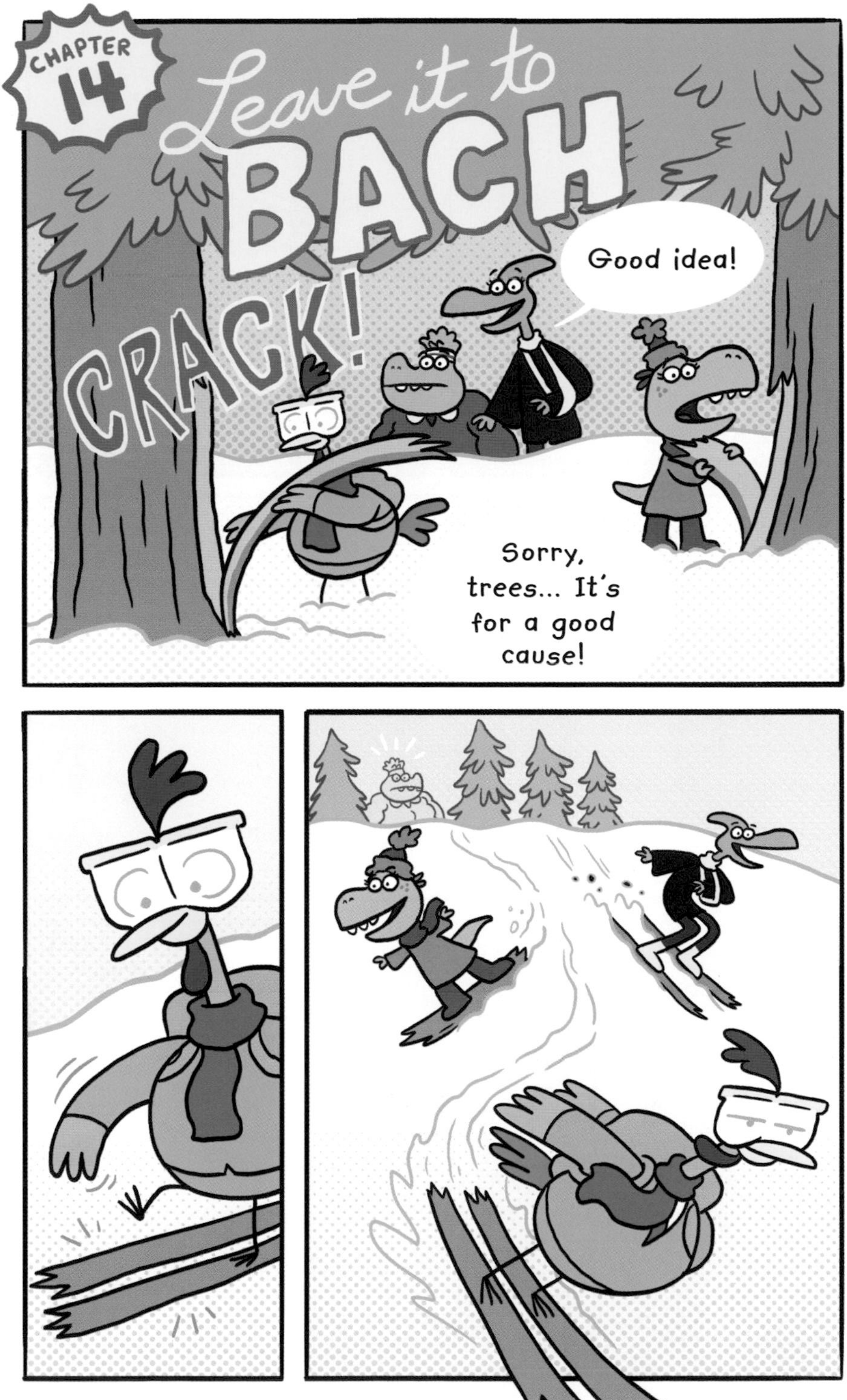
CHAPTER 14
Leave it to BACH
CRACK!
Good idea!
Sorry, trees... It's for a good cause!

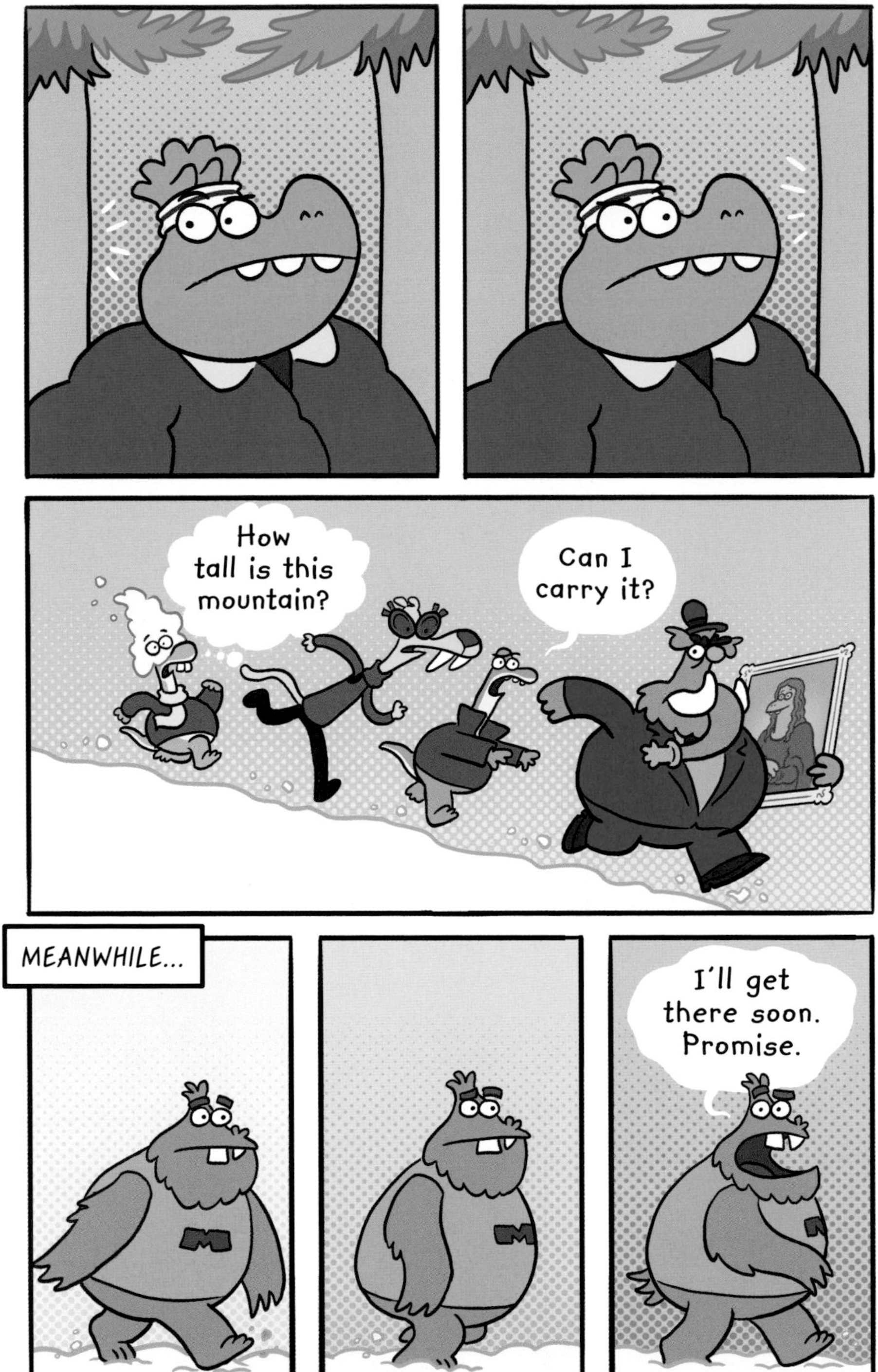
How tall is this mountain?
Can I carry it?
MEANWHILE...
I'll get there soon. Promise.

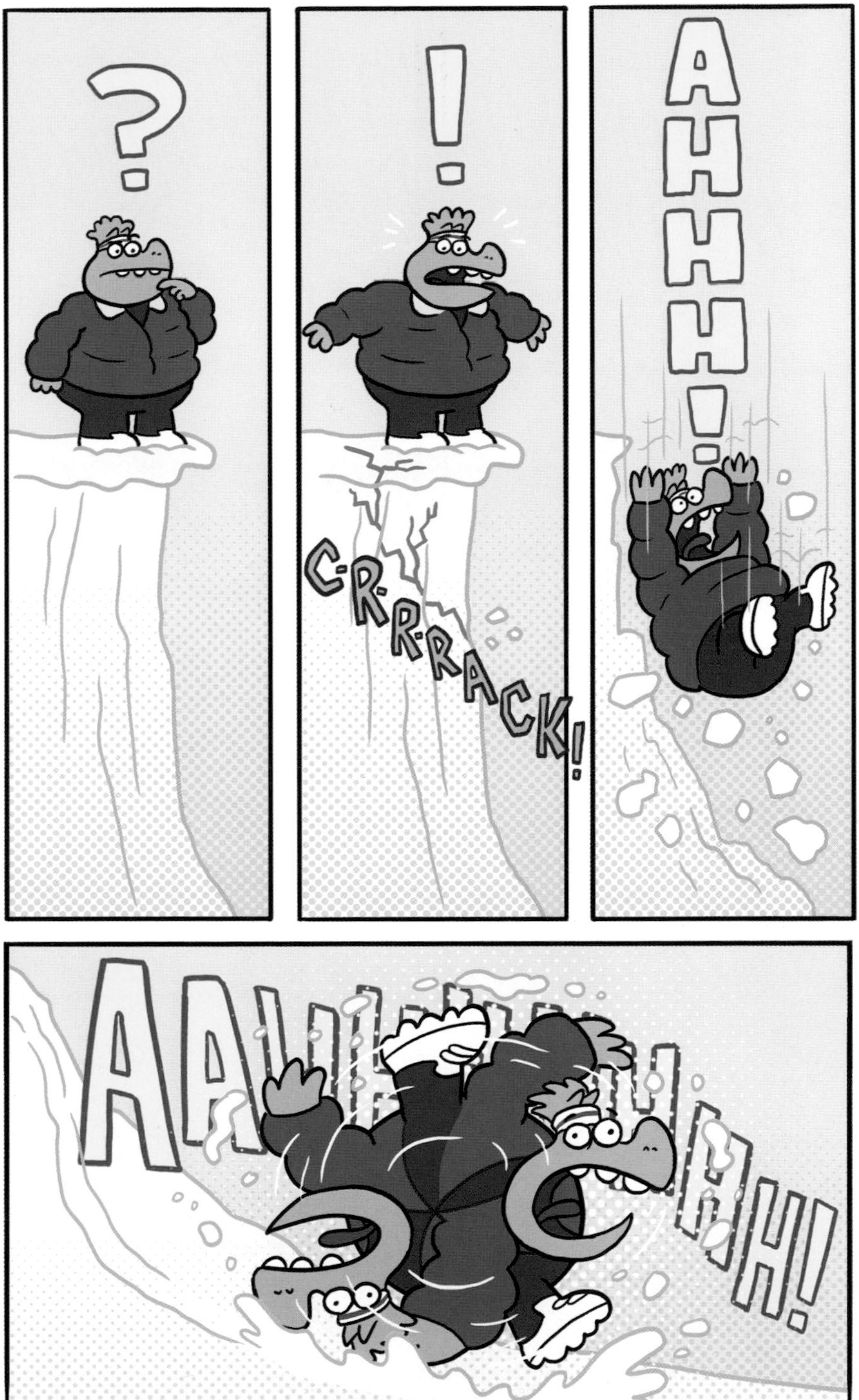
?
!
C-R-R-R-RACK!
AHHHH!
AAHHHHHHHH!

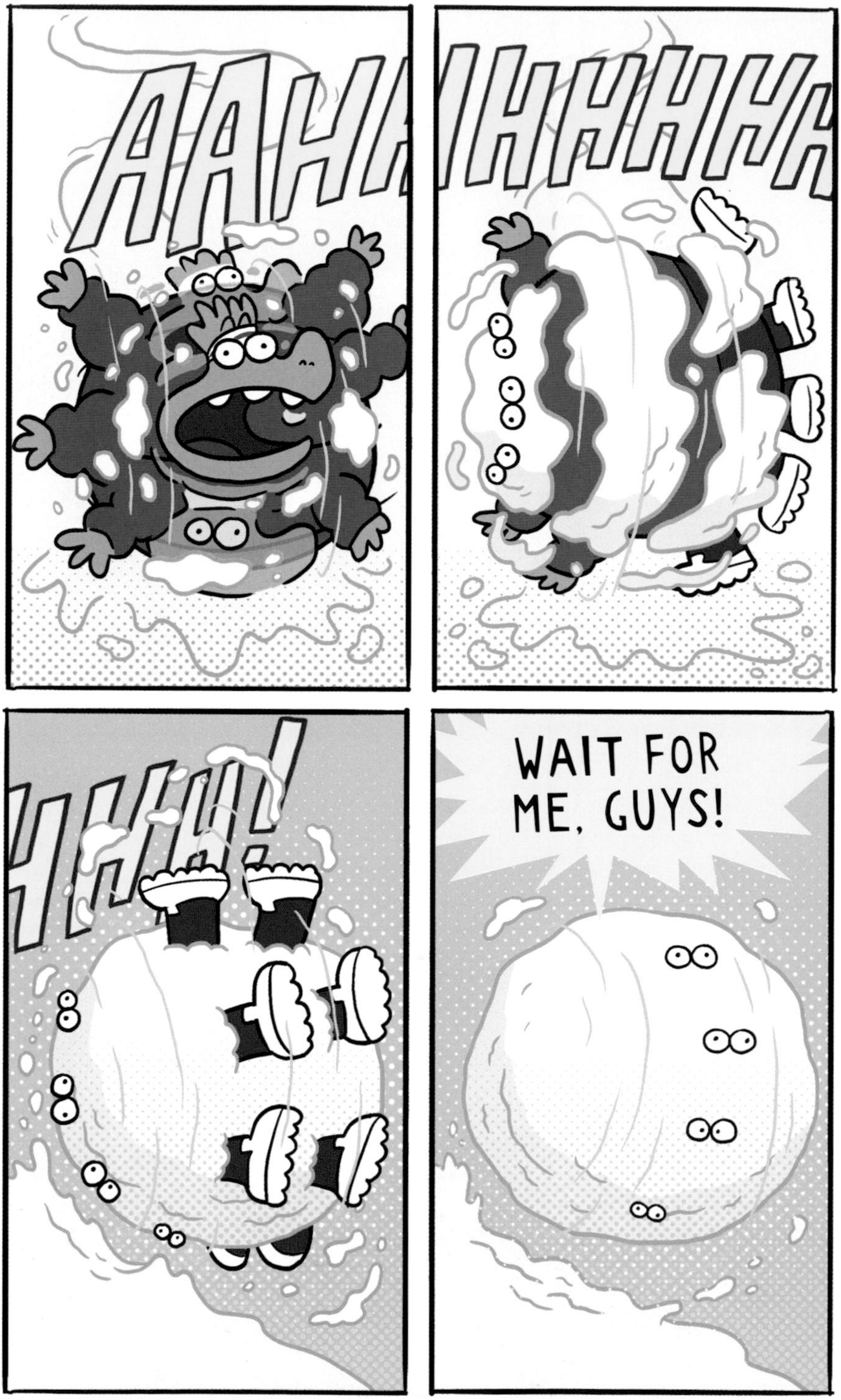
AAHHHHHHHHHHHH!
WAIT FOR ME, GUYS!

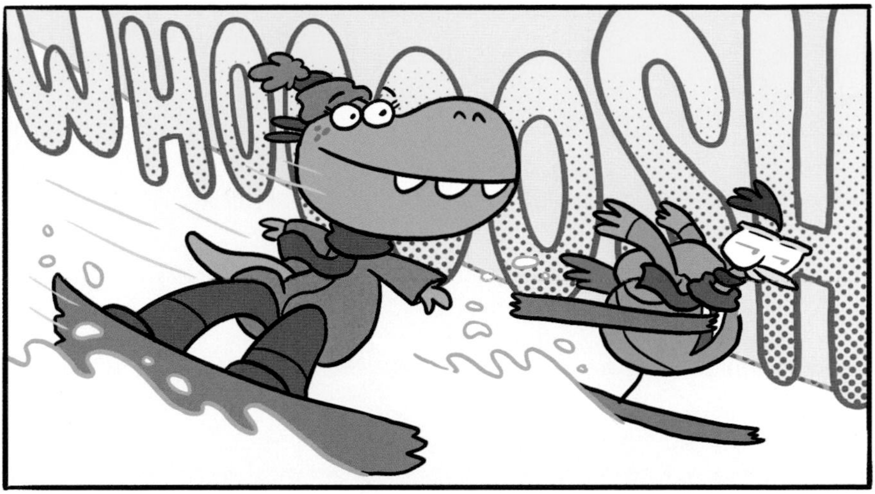
WHOOOOSH!

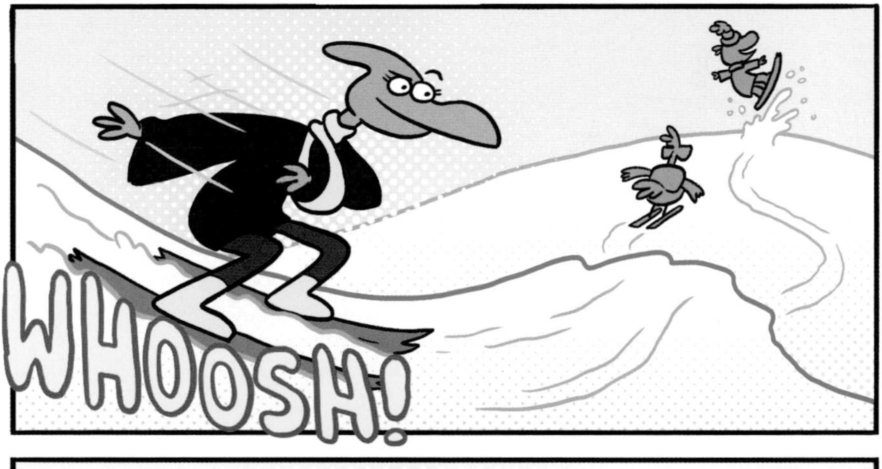
WHOOSH!

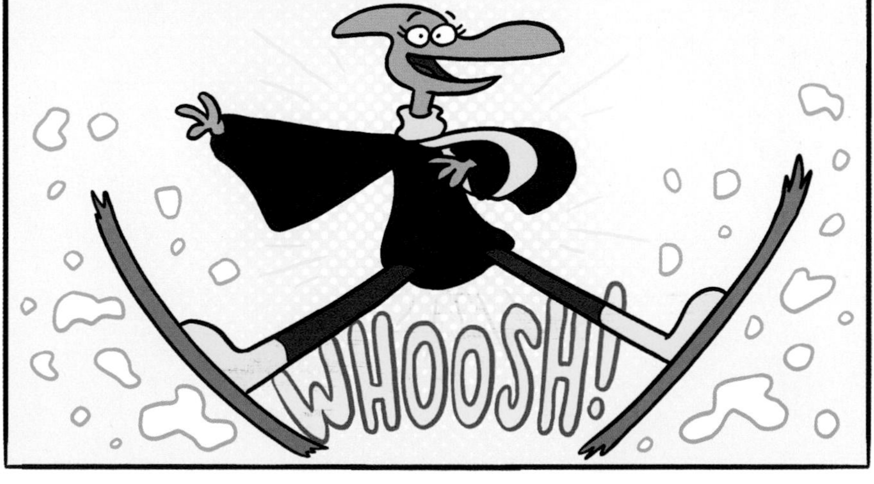
WHOOSH!

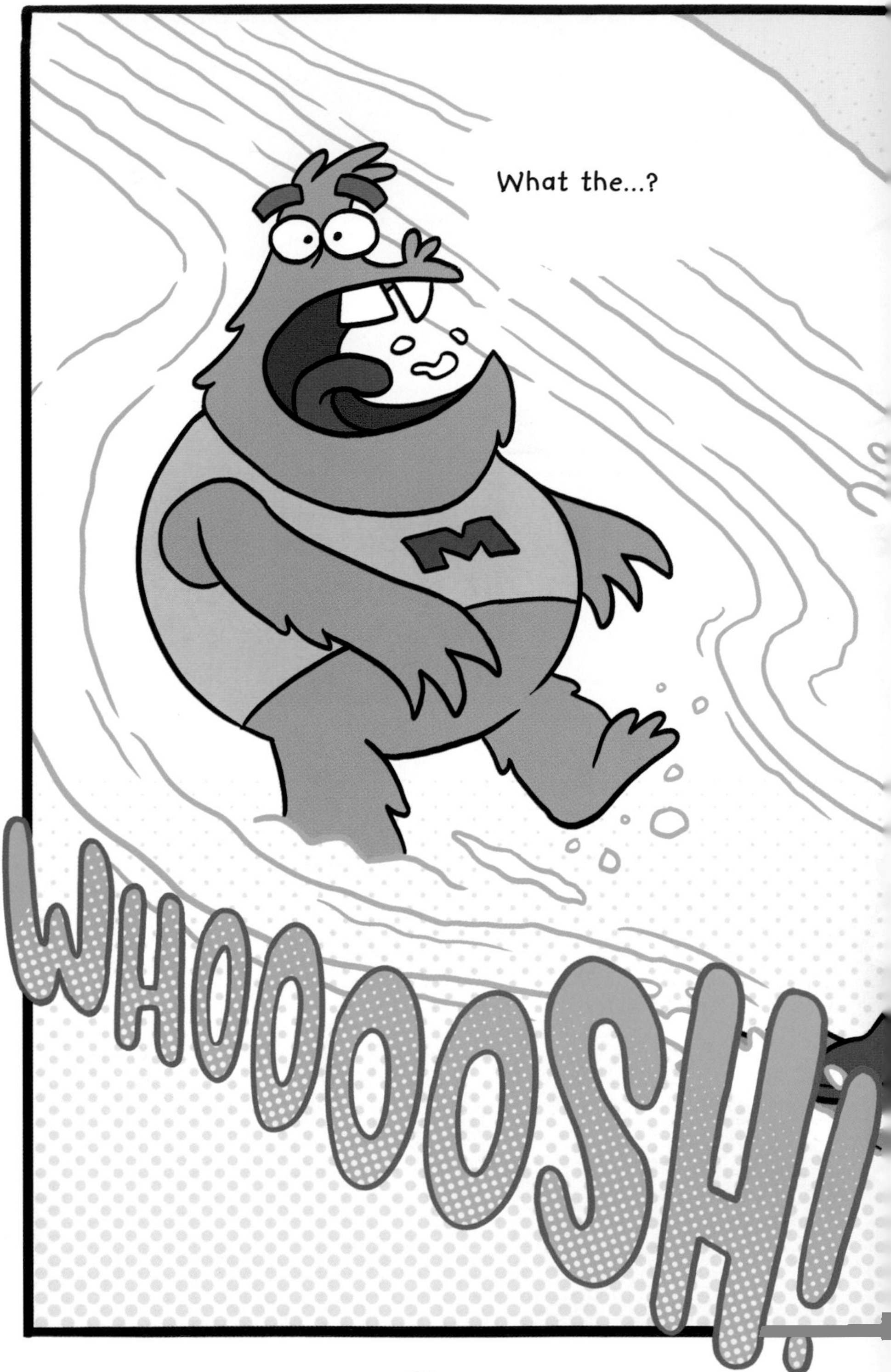
What the...?
WHOOOOSH!

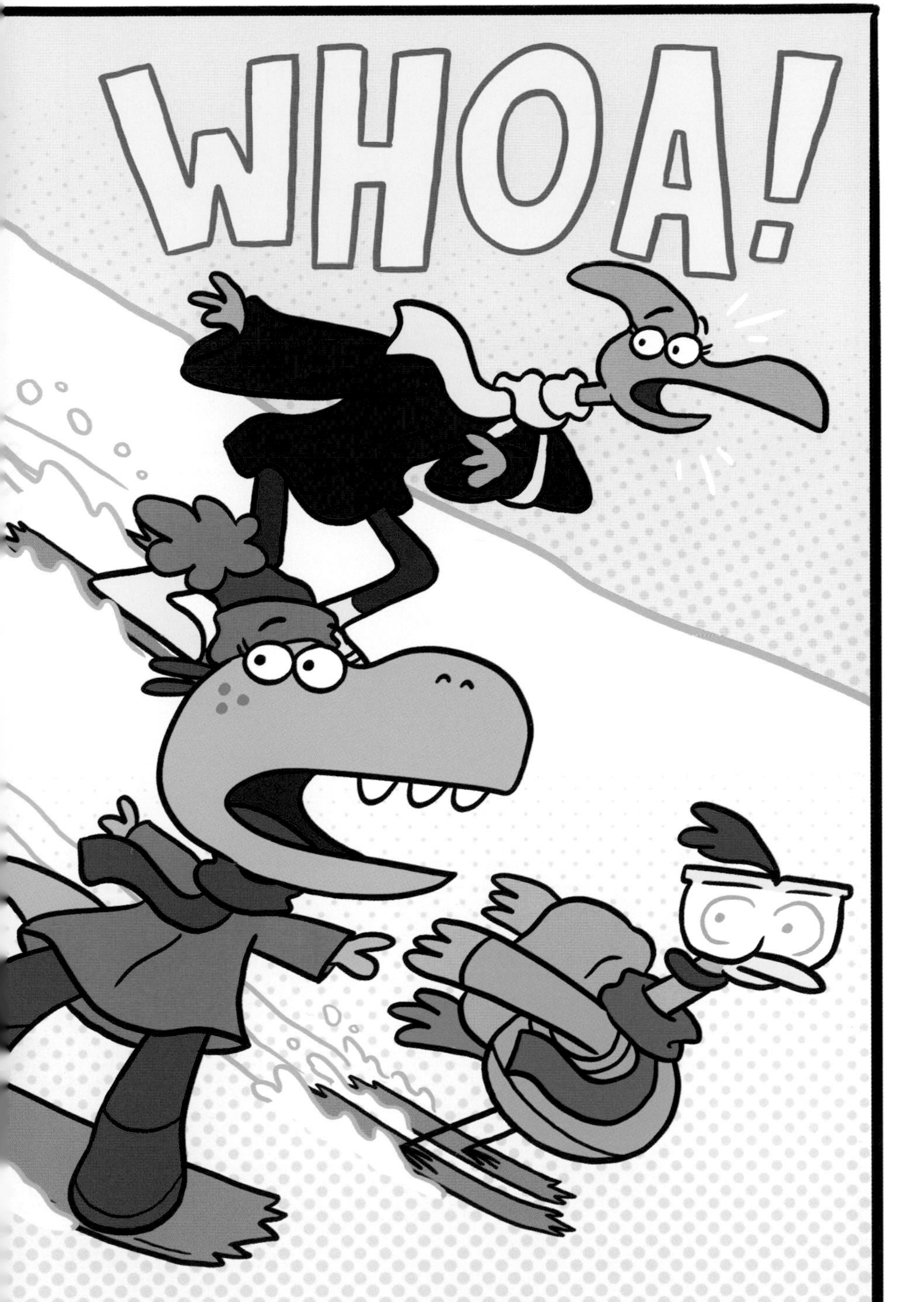
WHOA!

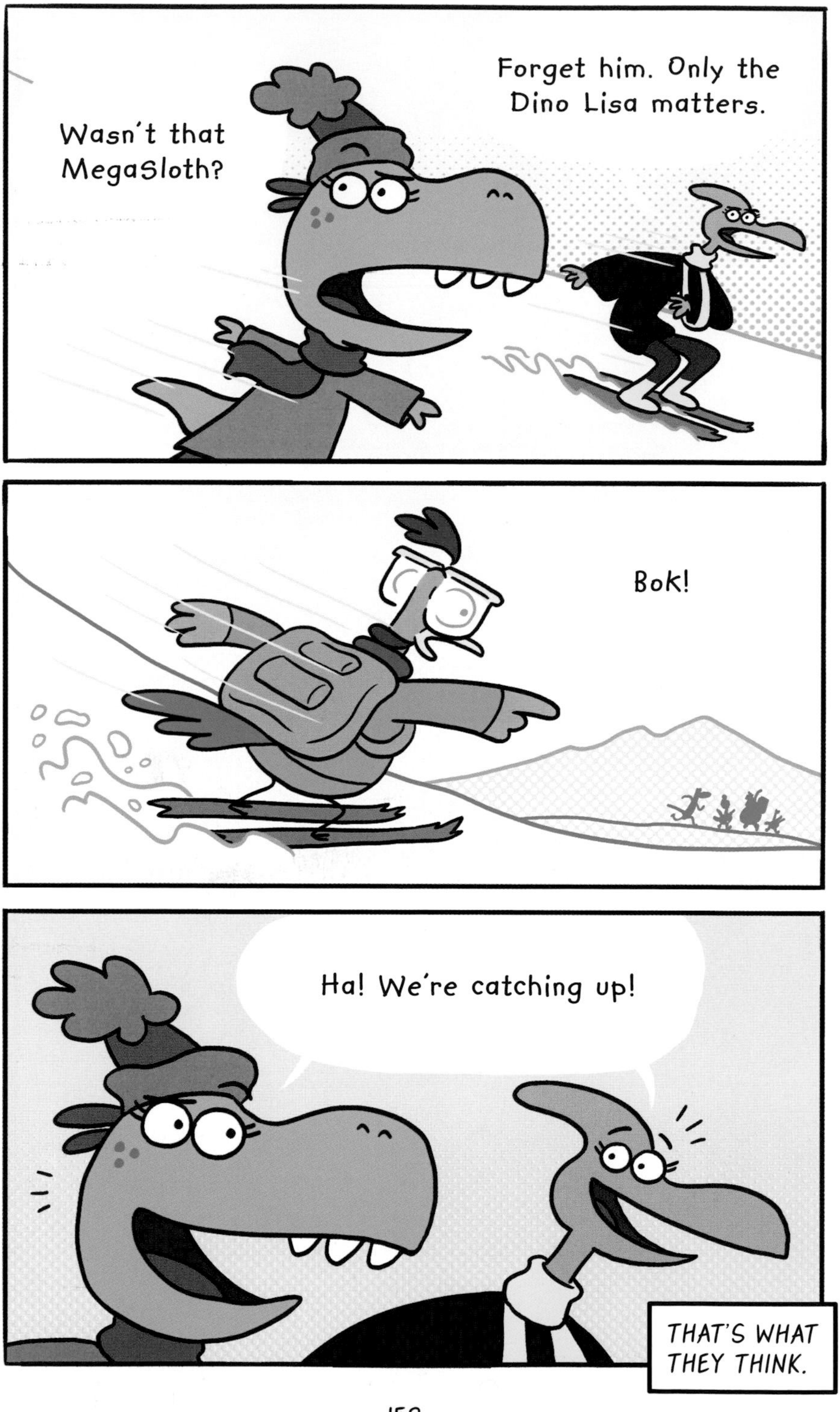
Wasn't that MegaSloth?
Forget him. Only the Dino Lisa matters.
Bok!
Ha! We're catching up!
THAT'S WHAT THEY THINK.

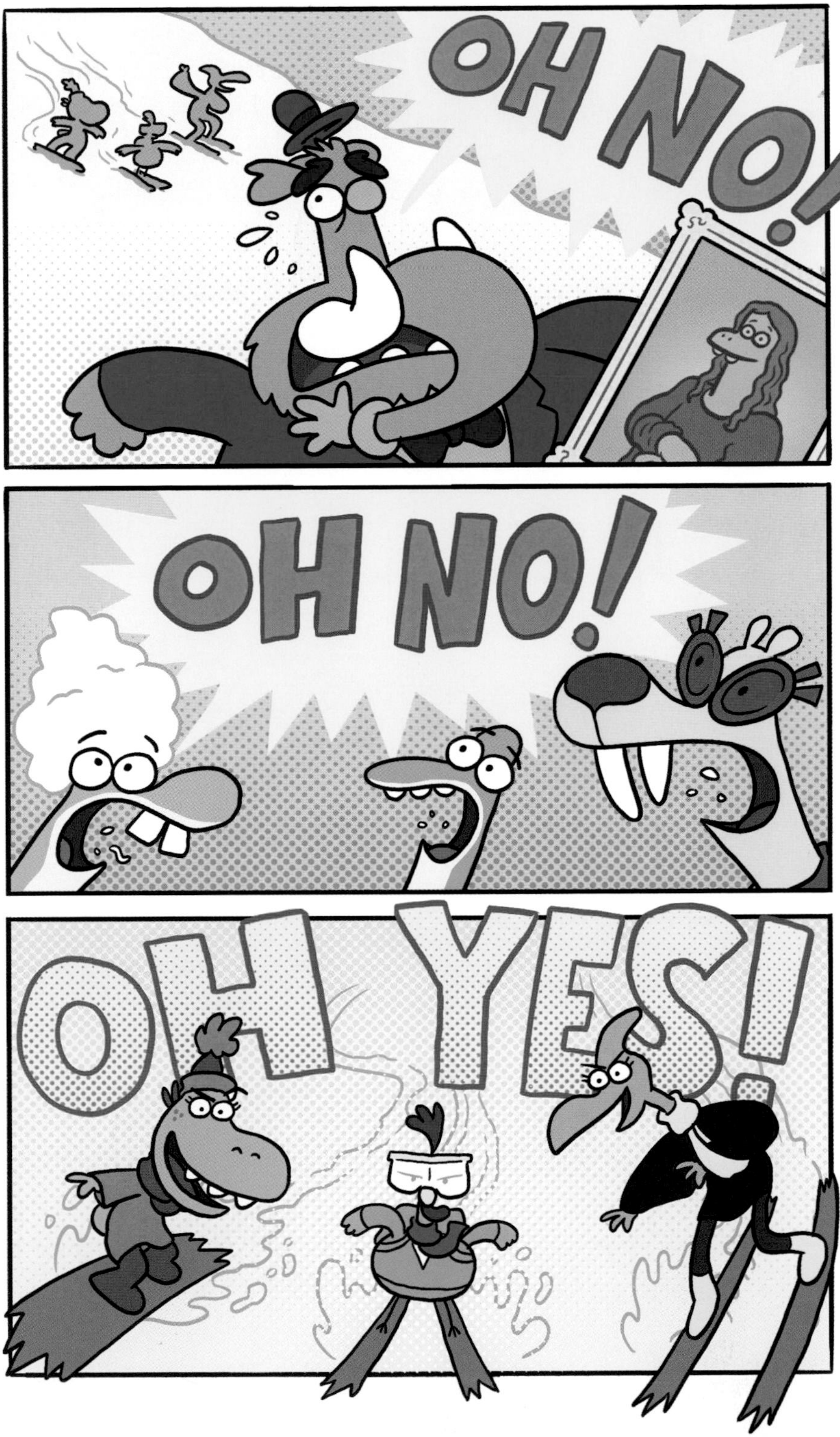
OH NO!
OH NO!
OH YES!

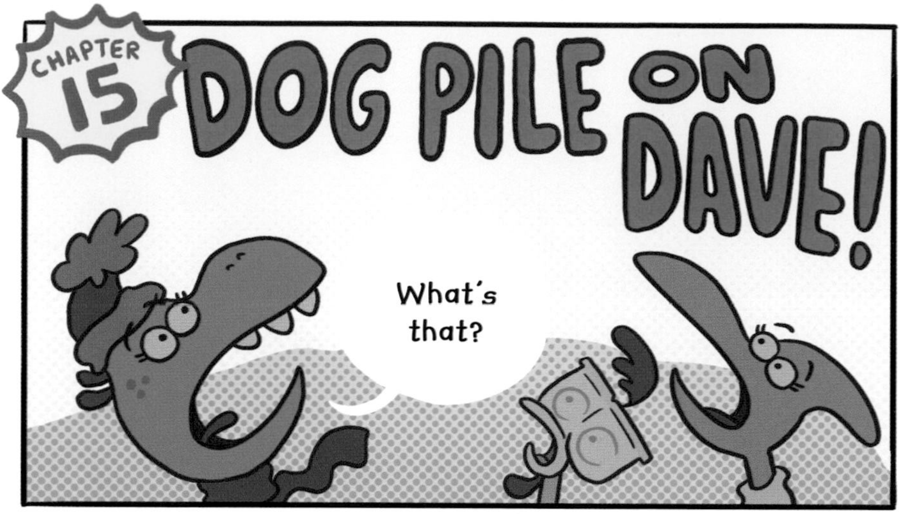
CHAPTER 15
DOG PILE ON DAVE!
What's that?

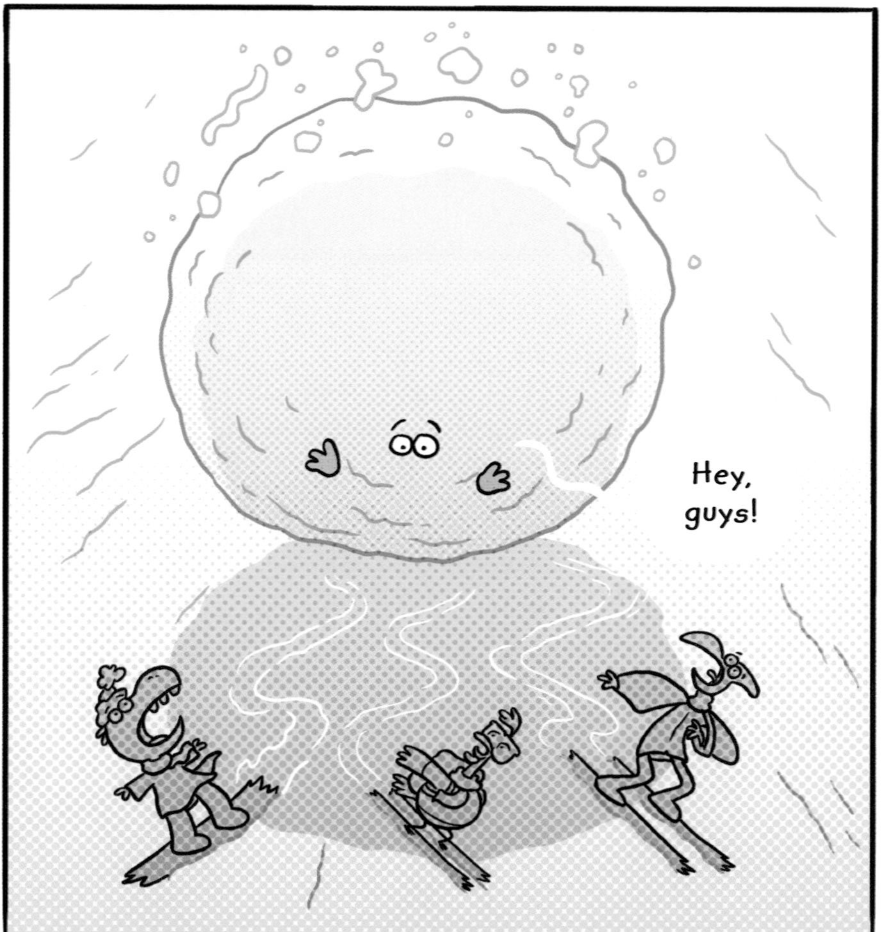
Hey, guys!

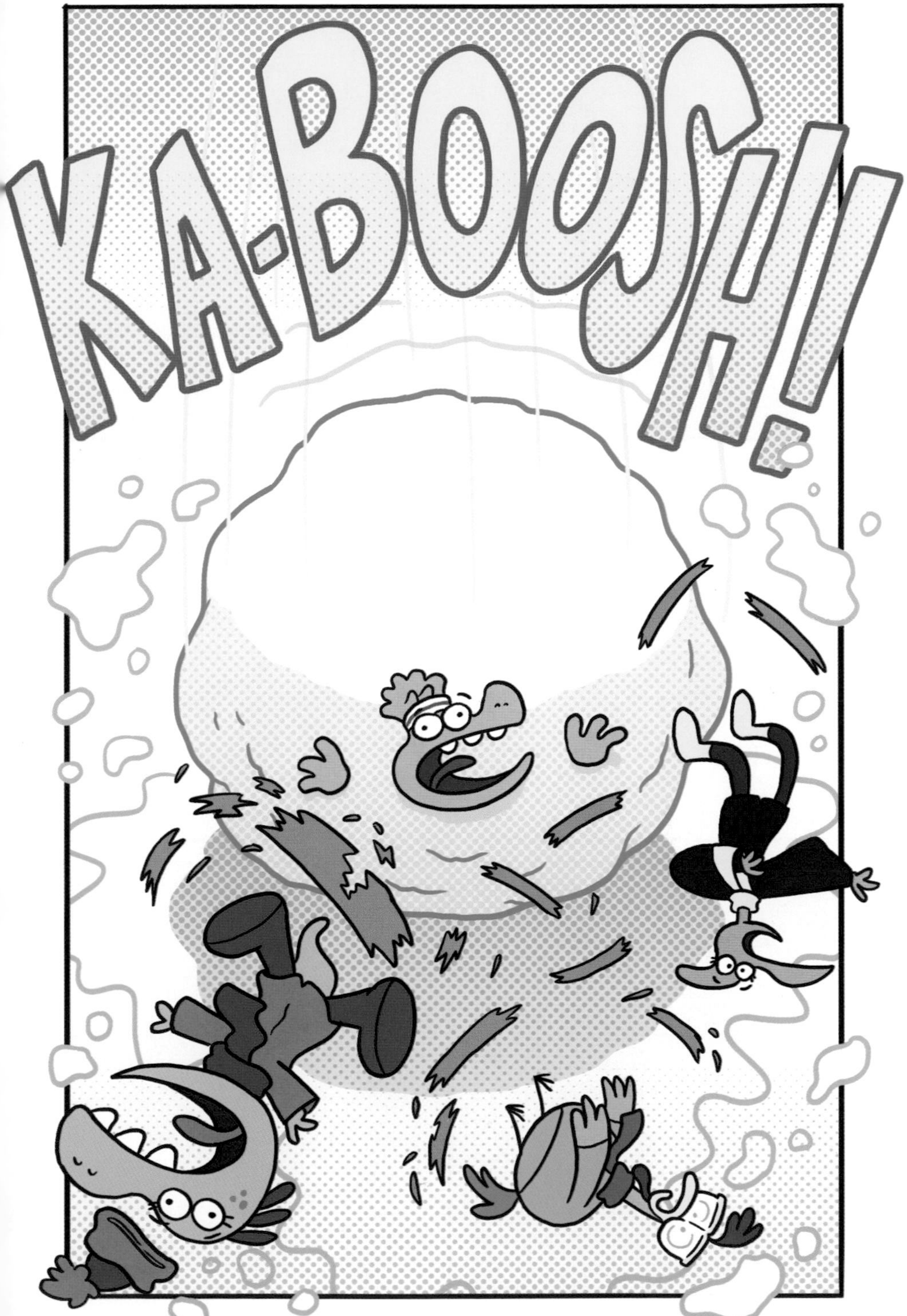
KA-BOOSH!!

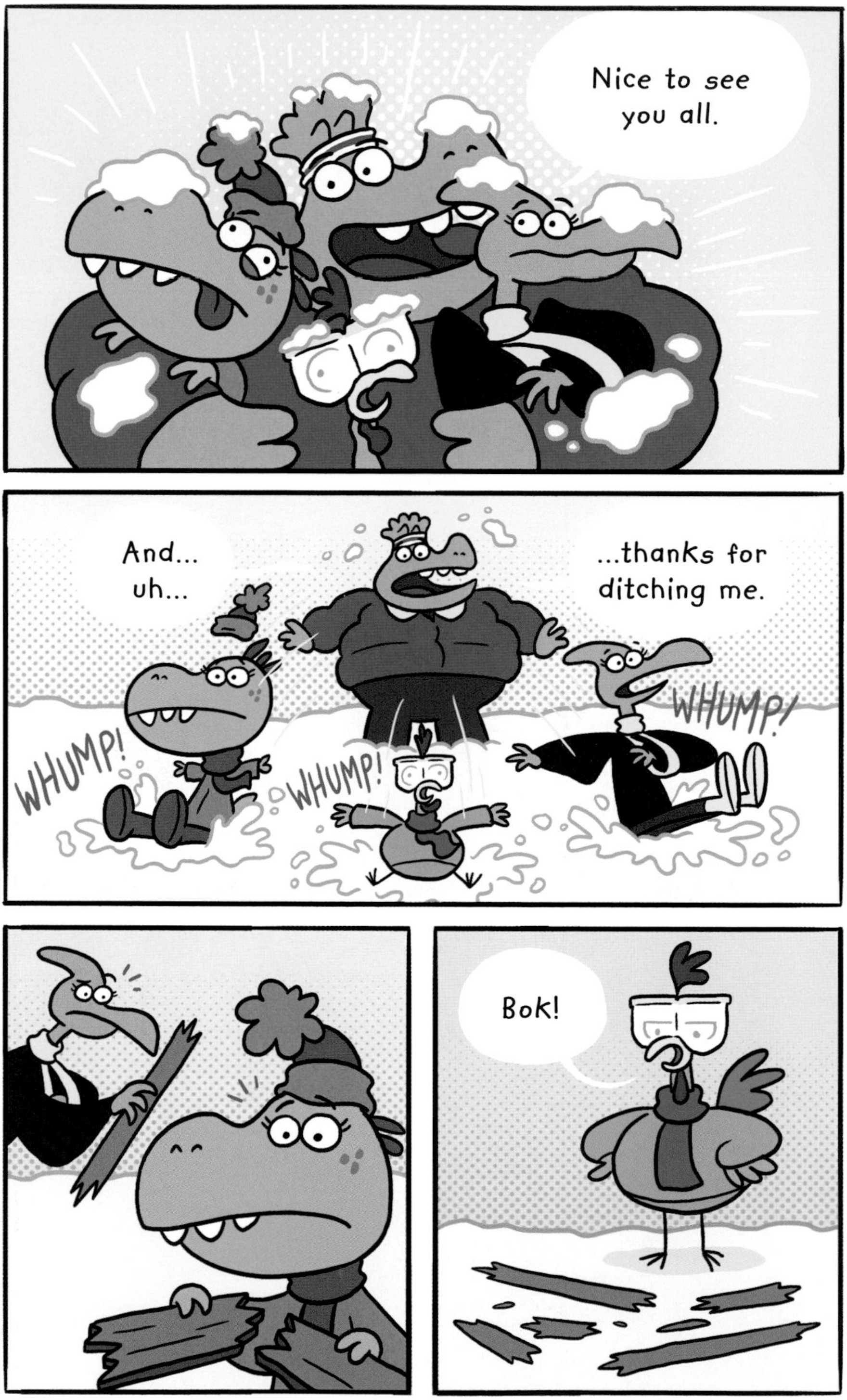
Nice to see you all.
And... uh...
...thanks for ditching me.
WHUMP!
WHUMP!
WHUMP!
Bok!

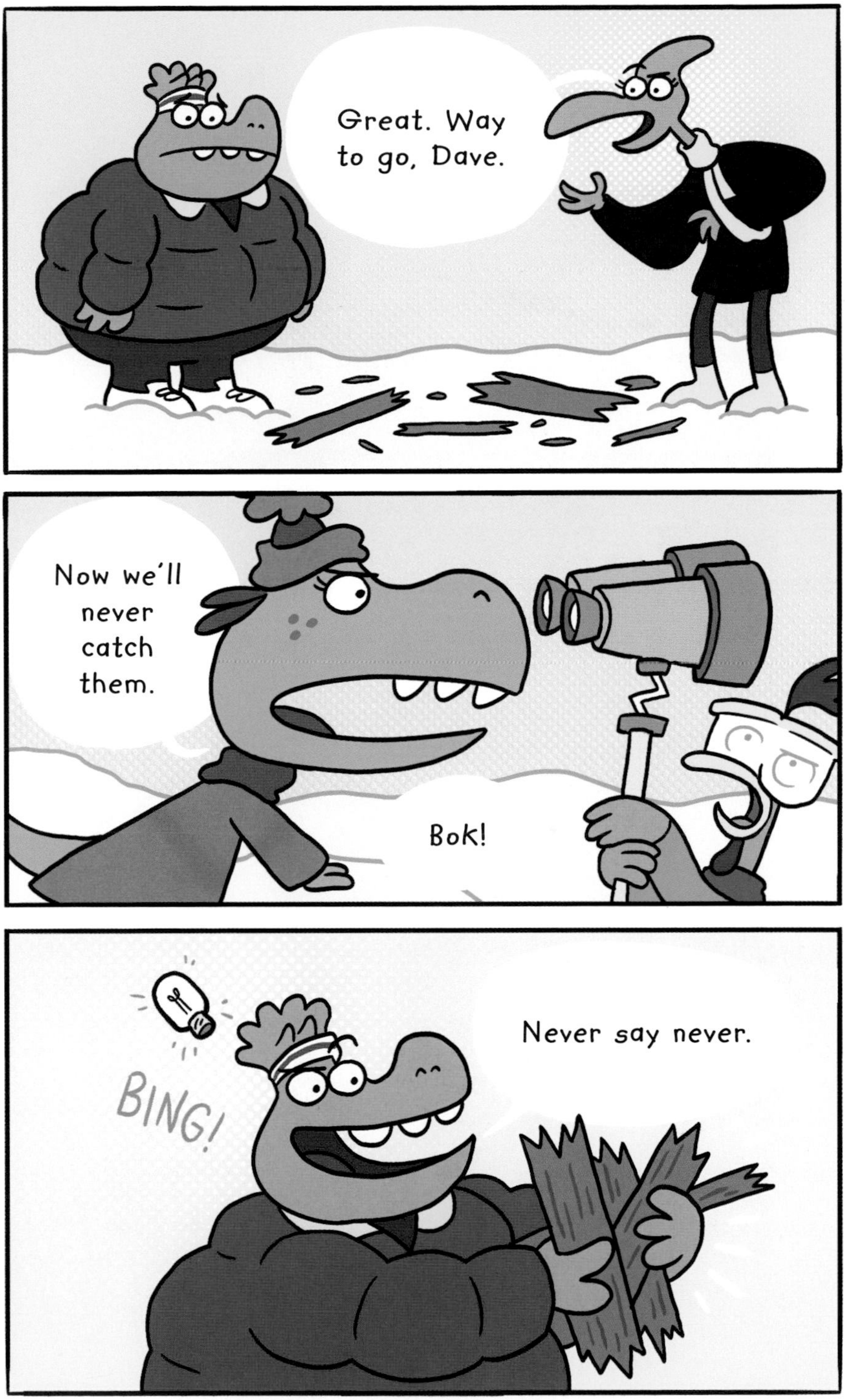
Great. Way to go, Dave.
Now we'll never catch them.
Bok!
BING!
Never say never.

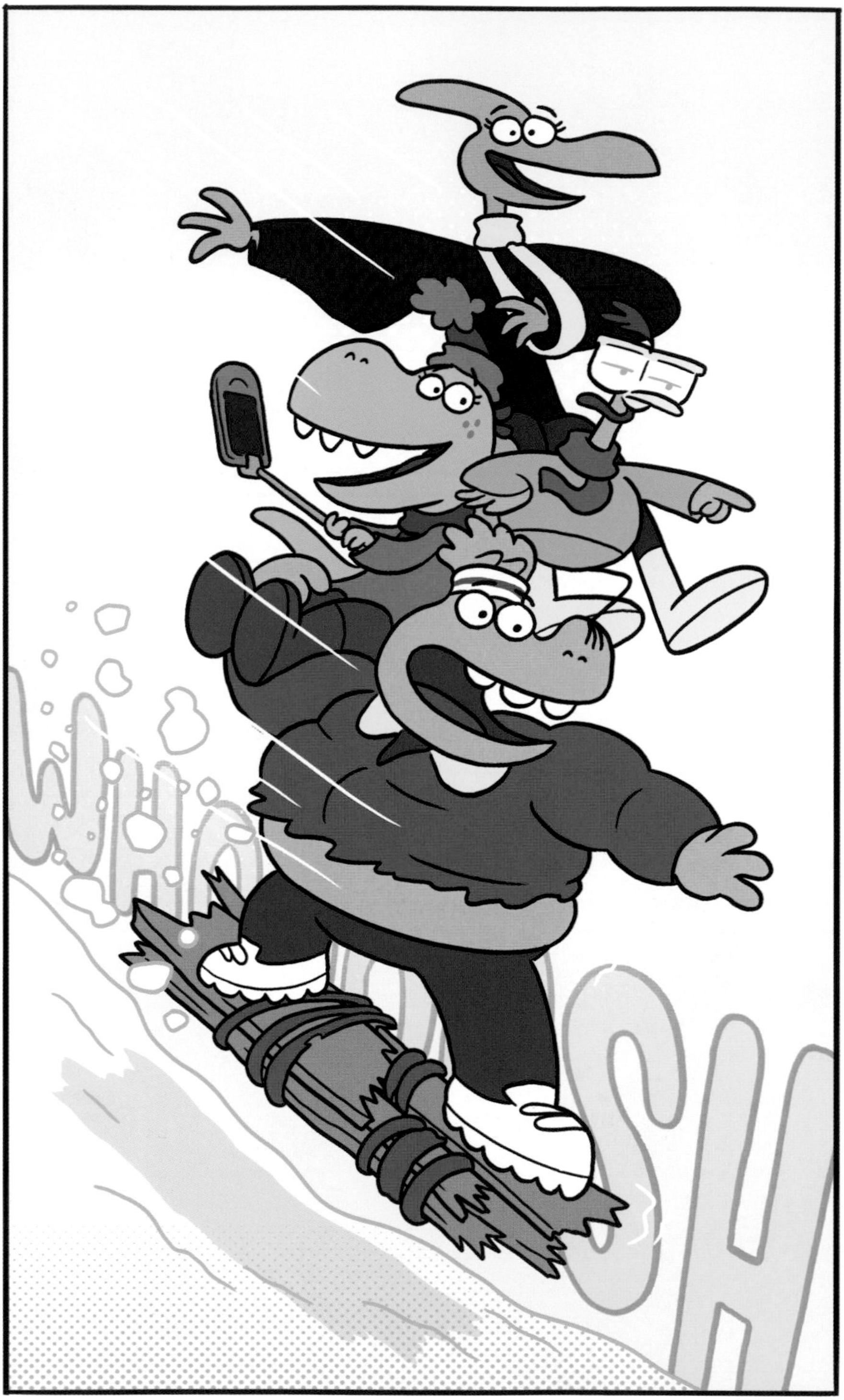
WHOOOSH

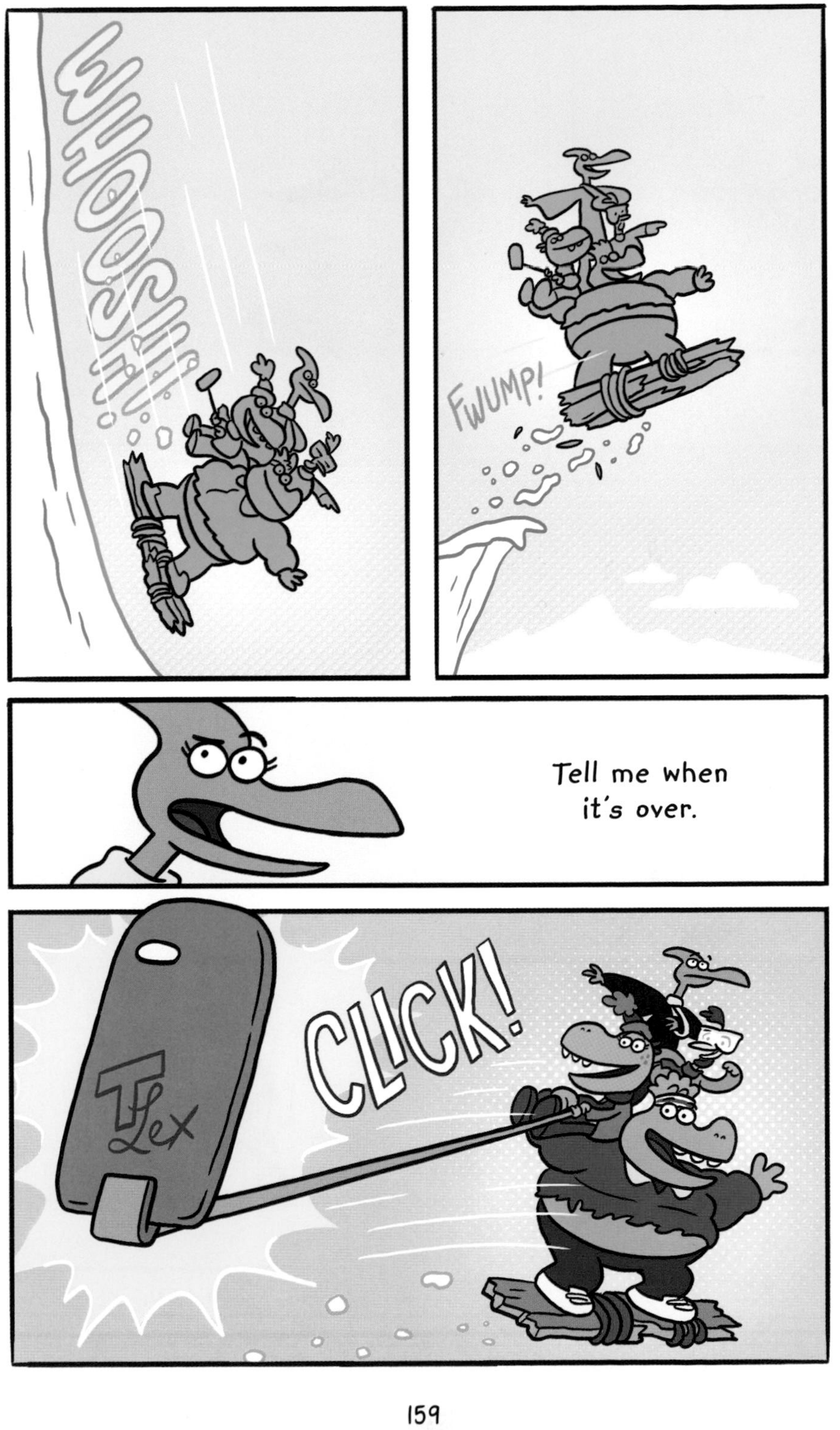
WHOOOSH!!
FWUMP!
Tell me when
it's over.
CLICK!
T-Lex

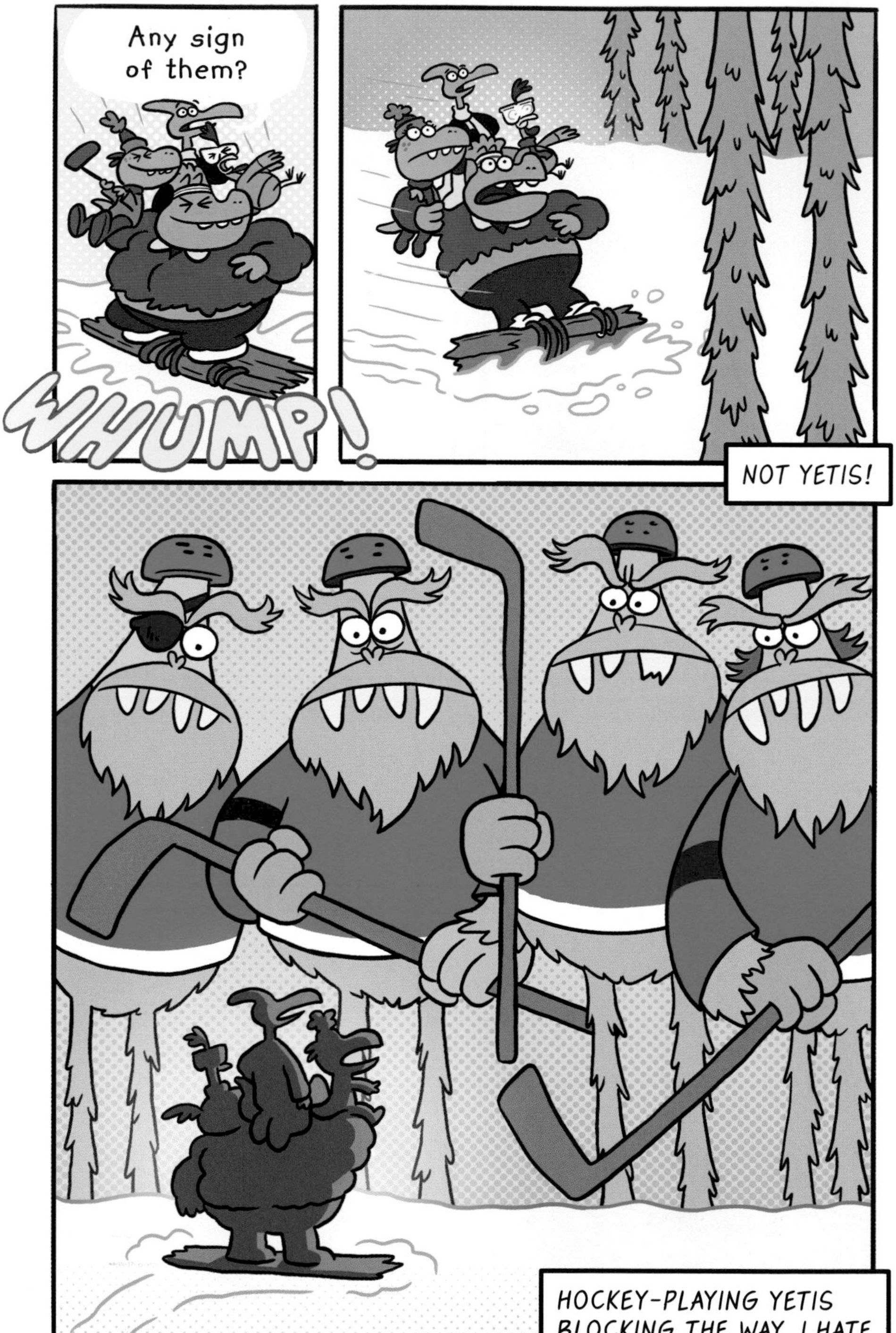
Any sign of them?
WHUMP!
NOT YETIS!
HOCKEY-PLAYING YETIS BLOCKING THE WAY. I HATE WHEN THAT HAPPENS!

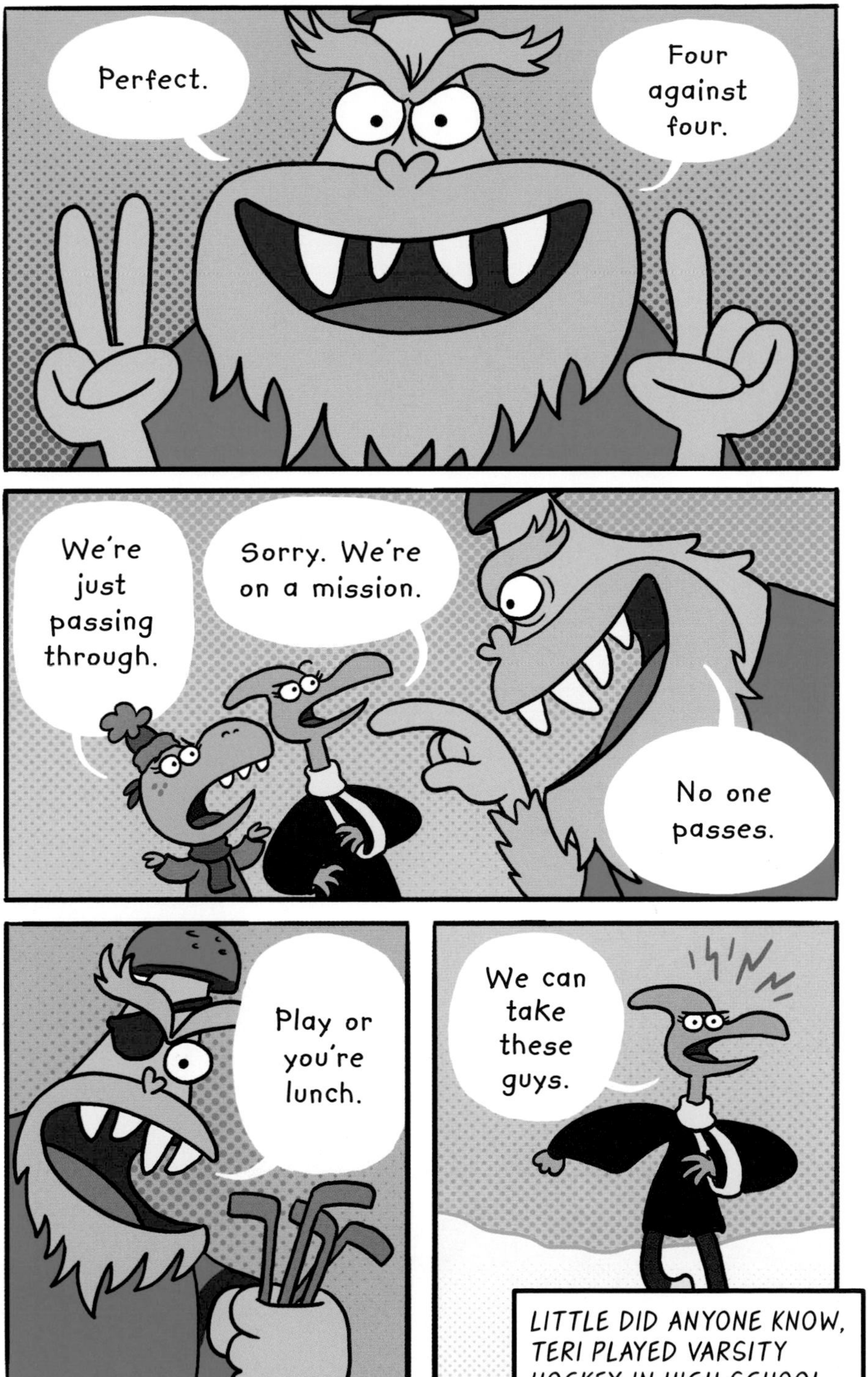
Perfect.
Four against four.
We're just passing through.
Sorry. We're on a mission.
No one passes.
Play or you're lunch.
We can take these guys.
LITTLE DID ANYONE KNOW, TERI PLAYED VARSITY HOCKEY IN HIGH SCHOOL.

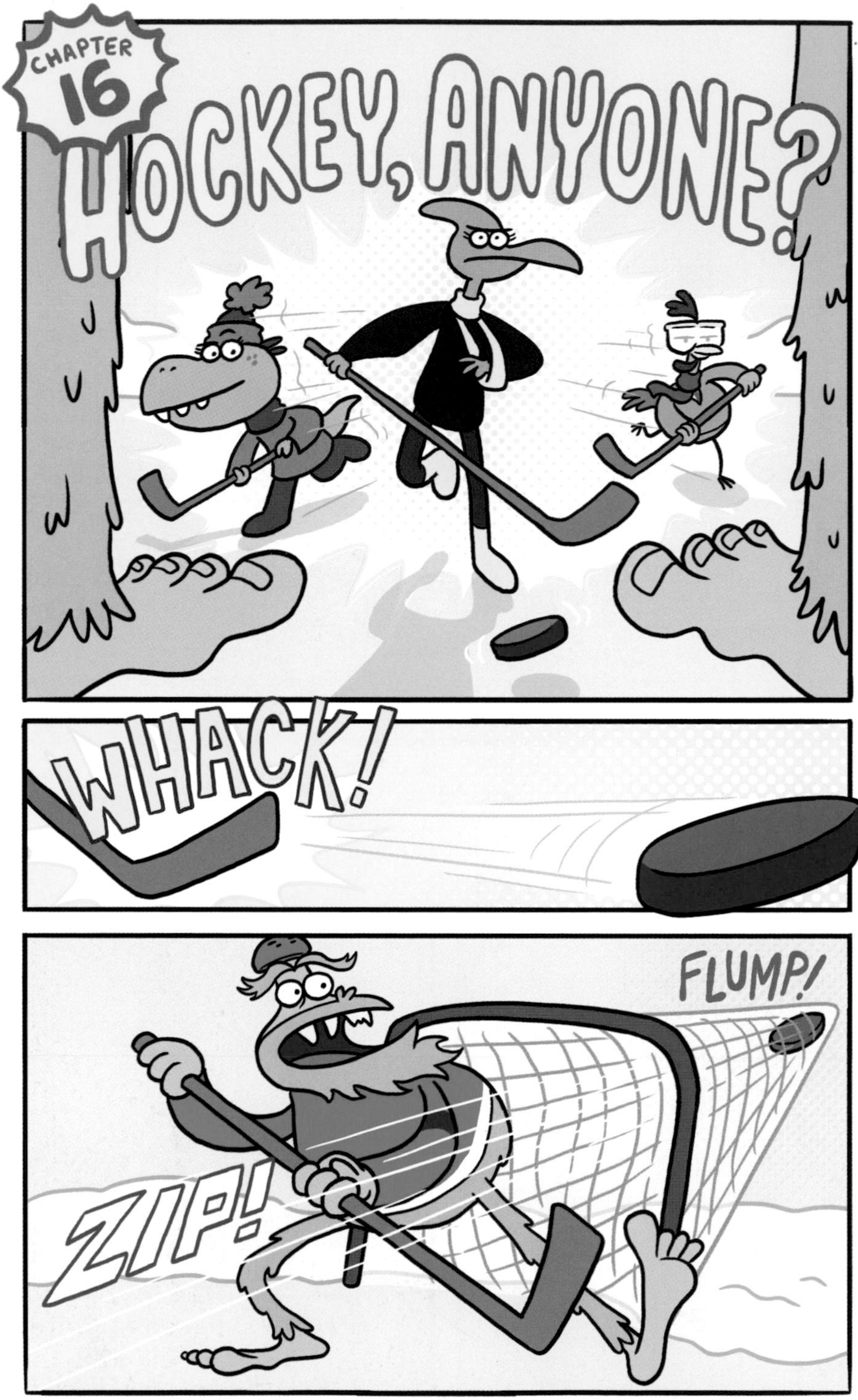
CHAPTER 16
HOCKEY, ANYONE?
WHACK!
FLUMP!
ZIP!

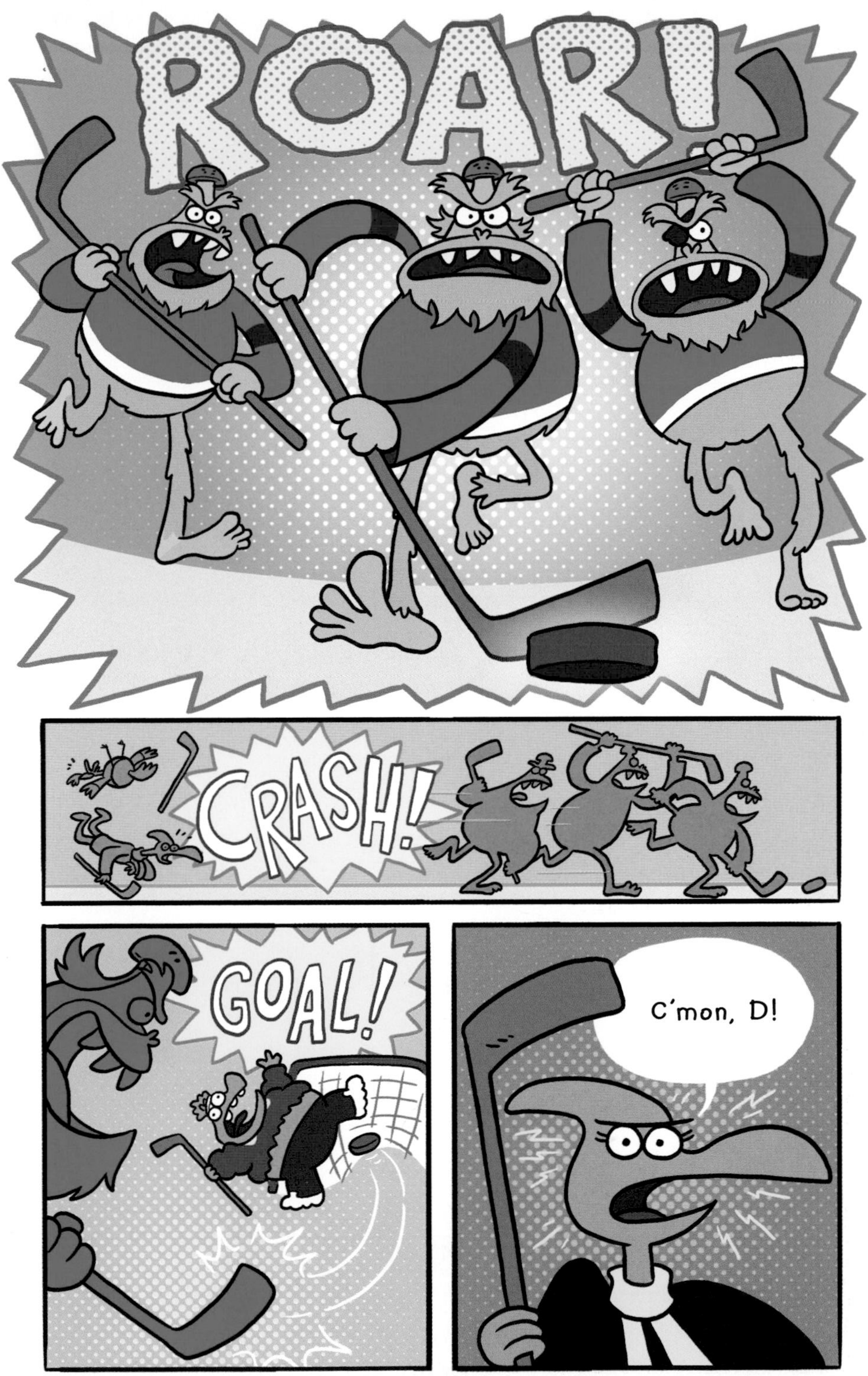
ROAR!
CRASH!
GOAL!
C'mon, D!

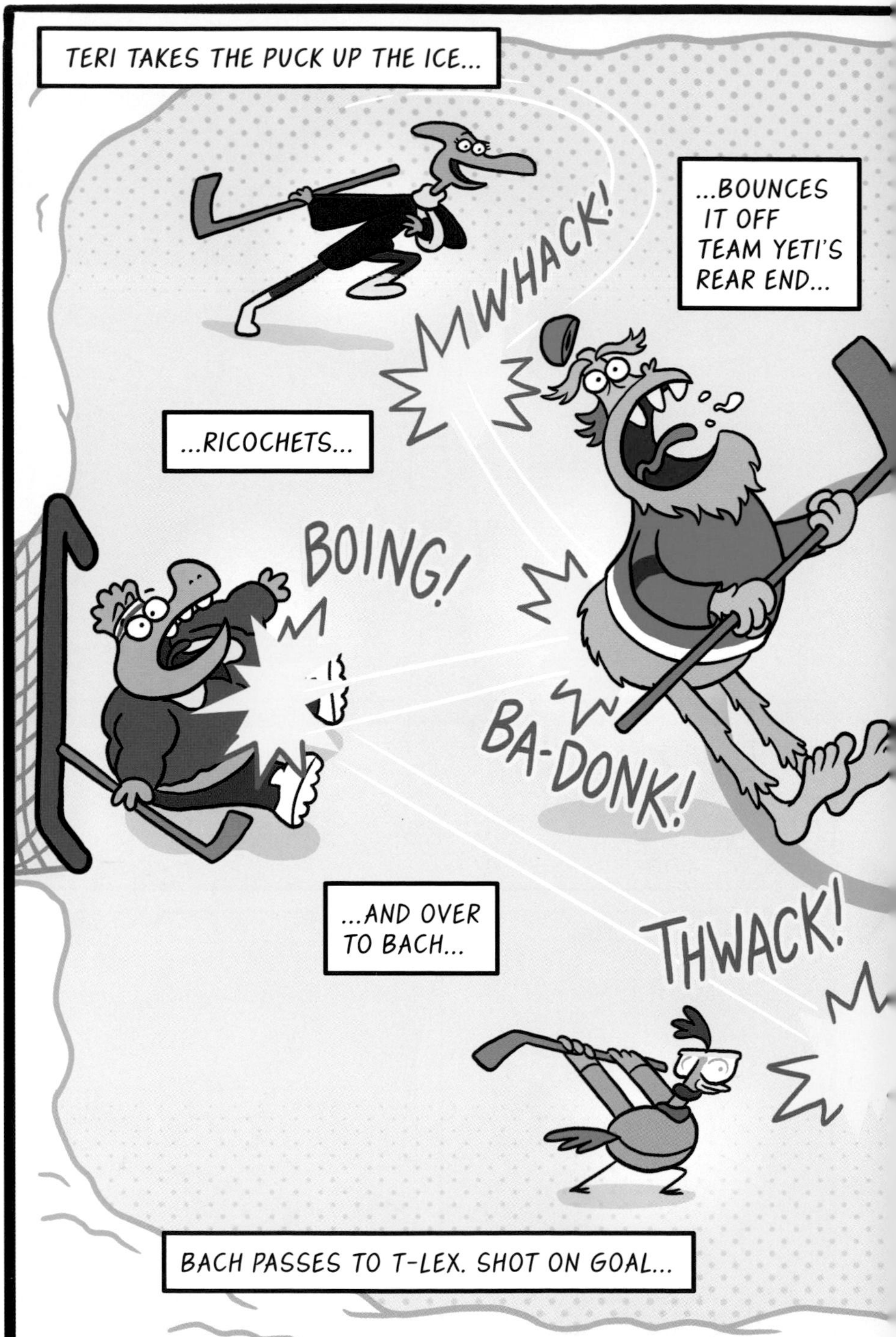
TERI TAKES THE PUCK UP THE ICE...
...BOUNCES IT OFF TEAM YETI'S REAR END...
WHACK!
...RICOCHETS...
BOING!
BA-DONK!
...AND OVER TO BACH...
THWACK!
BACH PASSES TO T-LEX. SHOT ON GOAL...

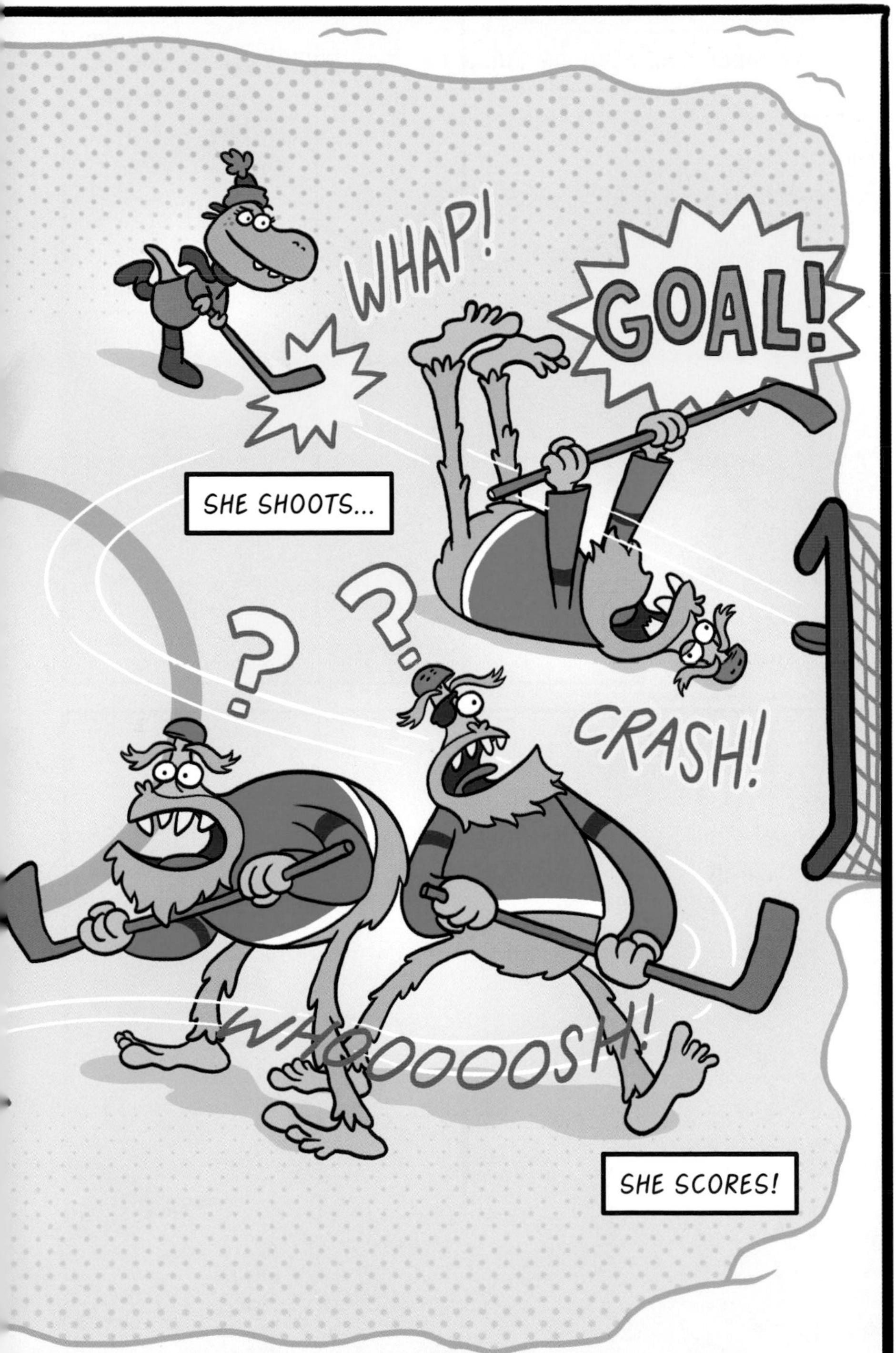
SHE SHOOTS...
WHAP!
GOAL!
CRASH!
WHOOOOOOSH!
SHE SCORES!

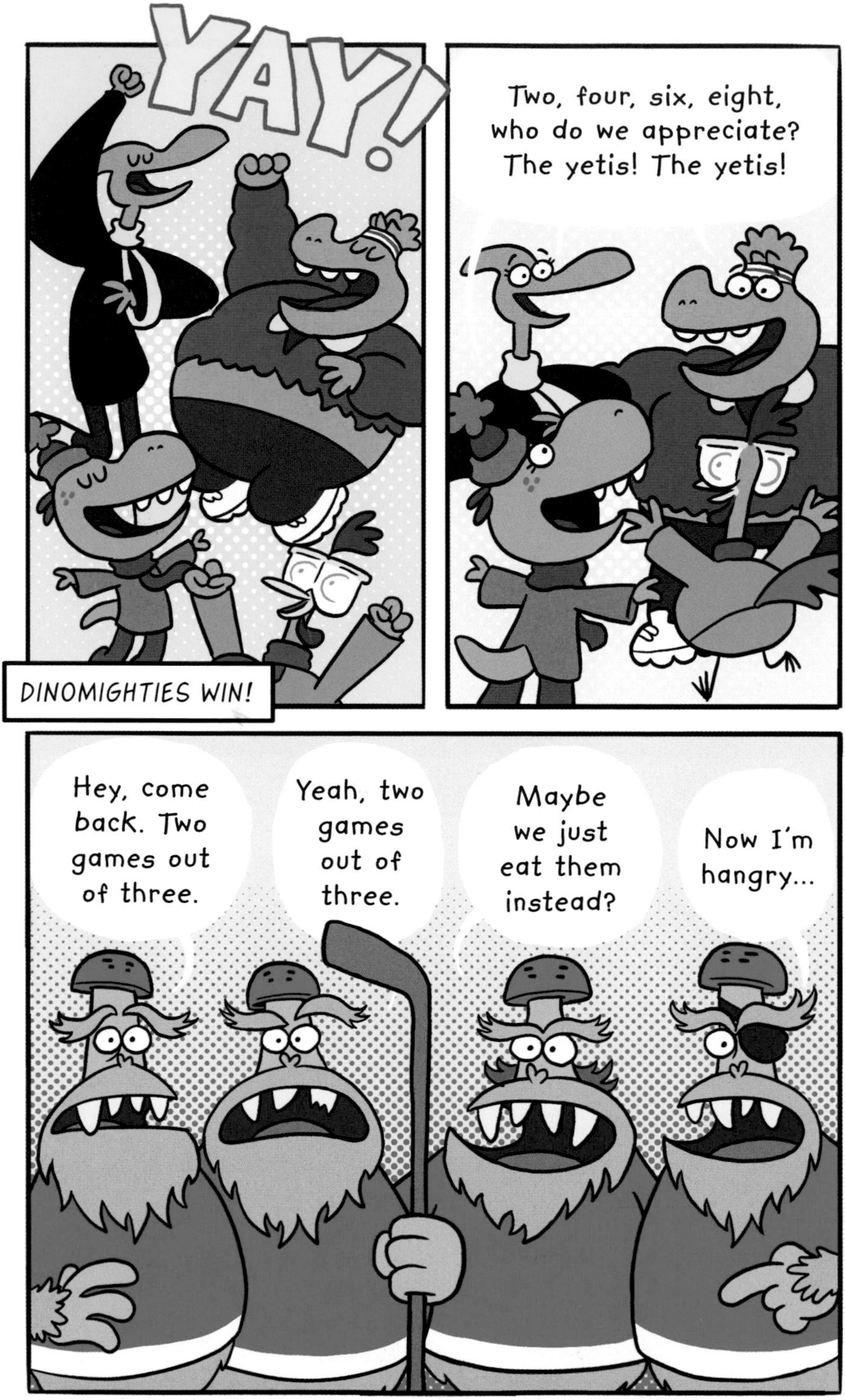
YAY!
DINOMIGHTIES WIN!
Two, four, six, eight, who do we appreciate? The yetis! The yetis!
Hey, come back. Two games out of three.
Yeah, two games out of three.
Maybe we just eat them instead?
Now I'm hangry...

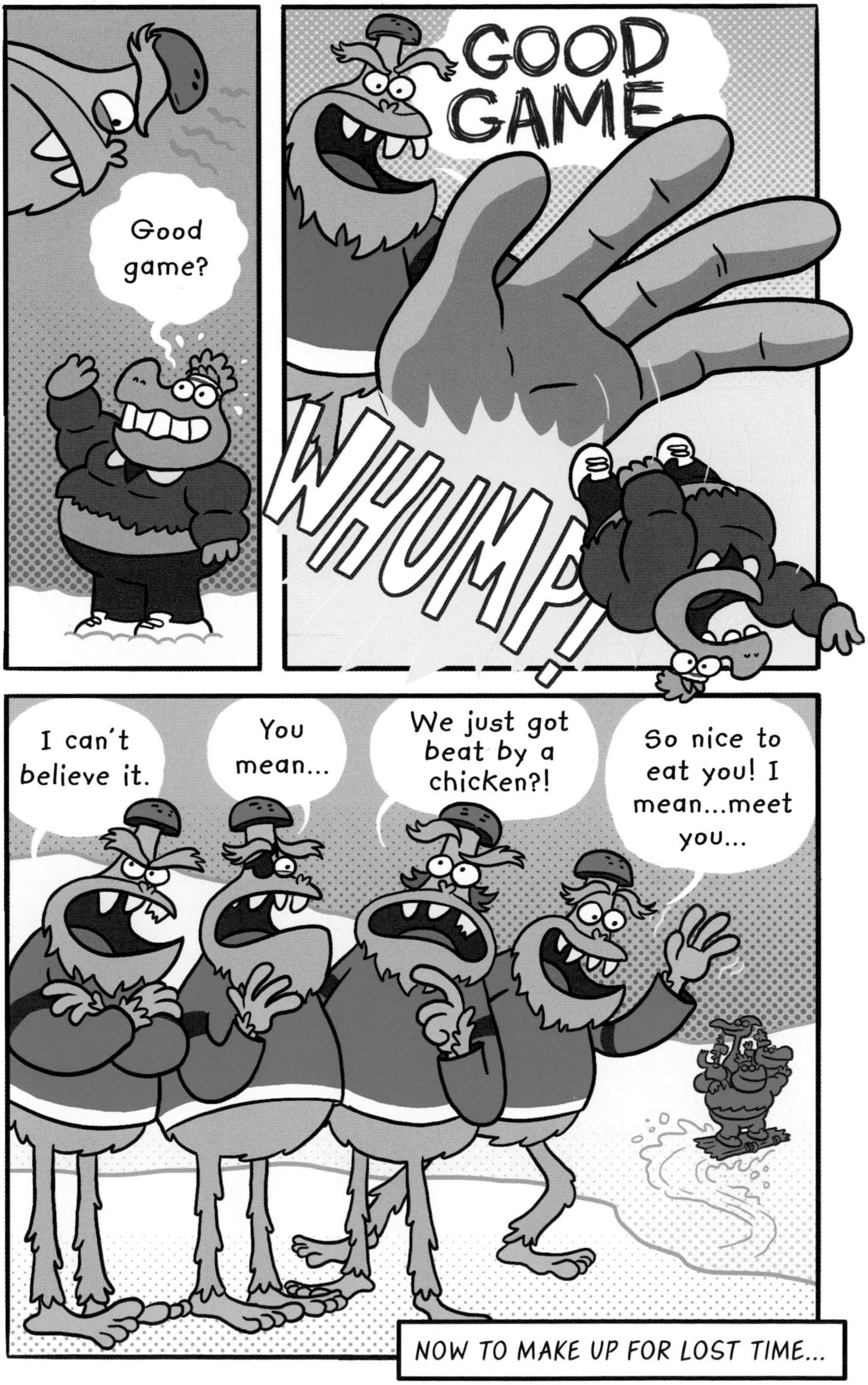
Good game?
GOOD GAME.
WHUMP!
I can't believe it.
You mean...
We just got beat by a chicken?!
So nice to eat you! I mean...meet you...
NOW TO MAKE UP FOR LOST TIME...

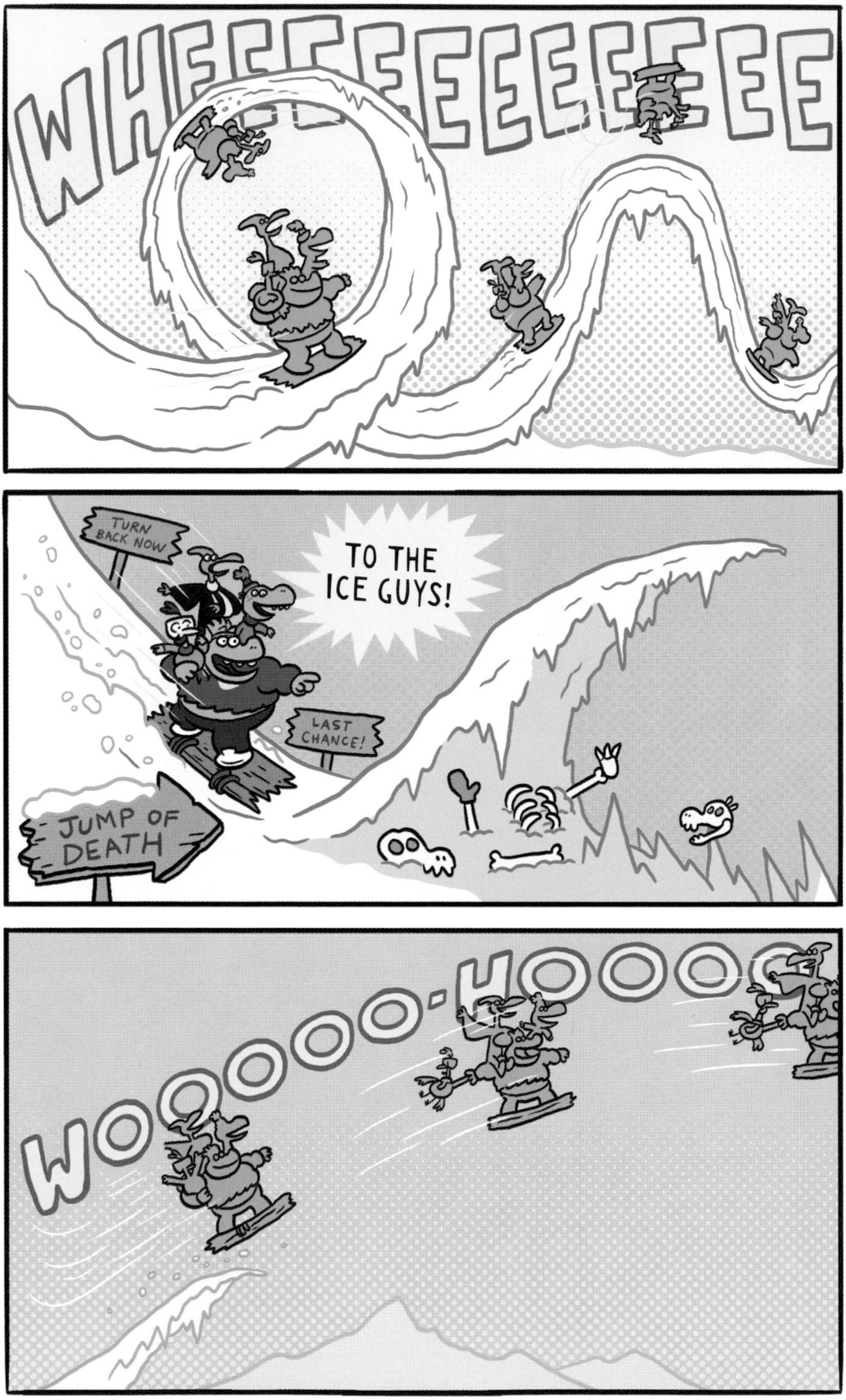
WHEEEEEEEEEEEEE
TURN BACK NOW
TO THE ICE GUYS!
LAST CHANCE!
JUMP OF DEATH
WOOOOOO-HOOOO

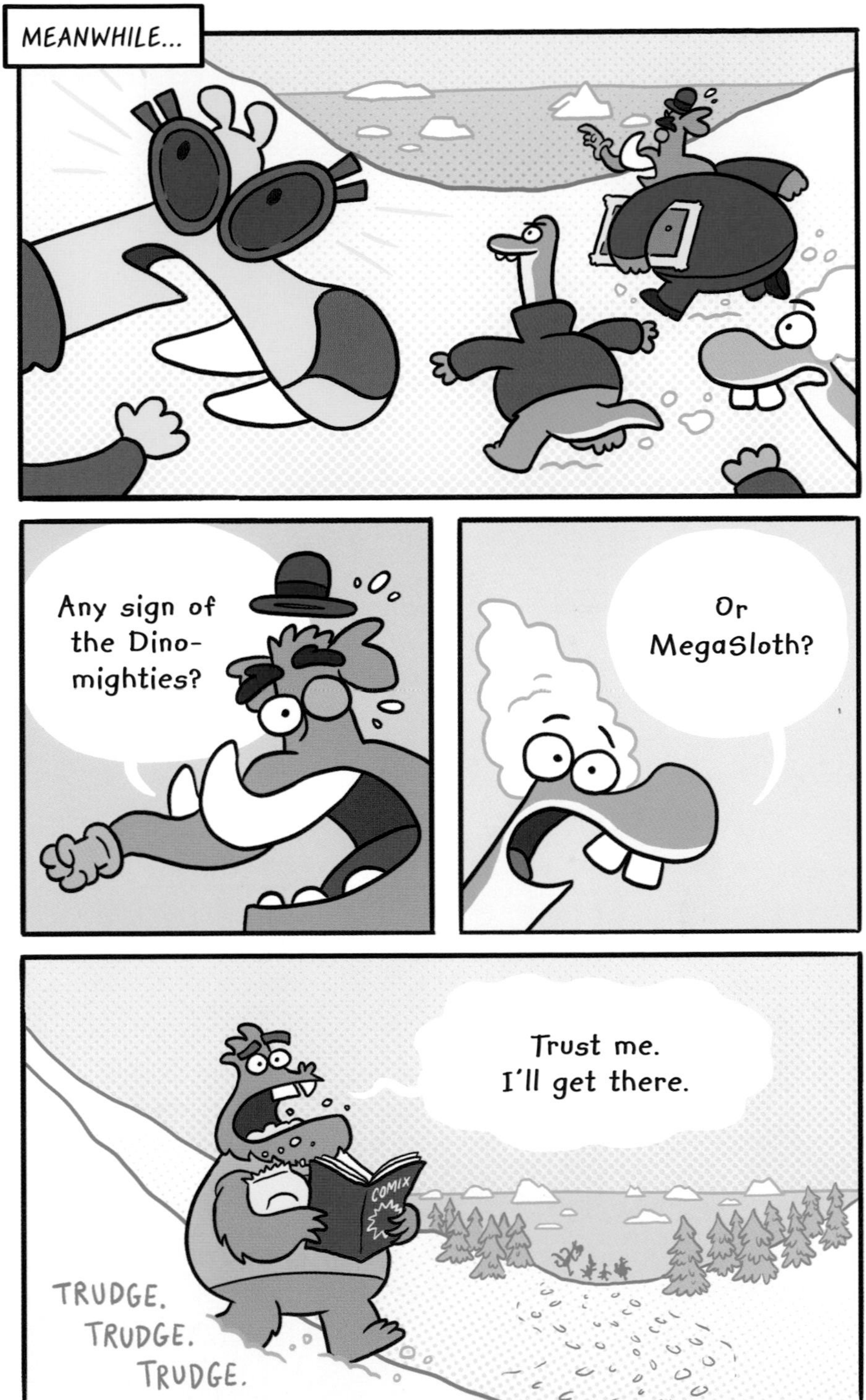
MEANWHILE...
Any sign of the Dino-mighties?
Or MegaSloth?
Trust me. I'll get there.
TRUDGE.
TRUDGE.
TRUDGE.
COMIX

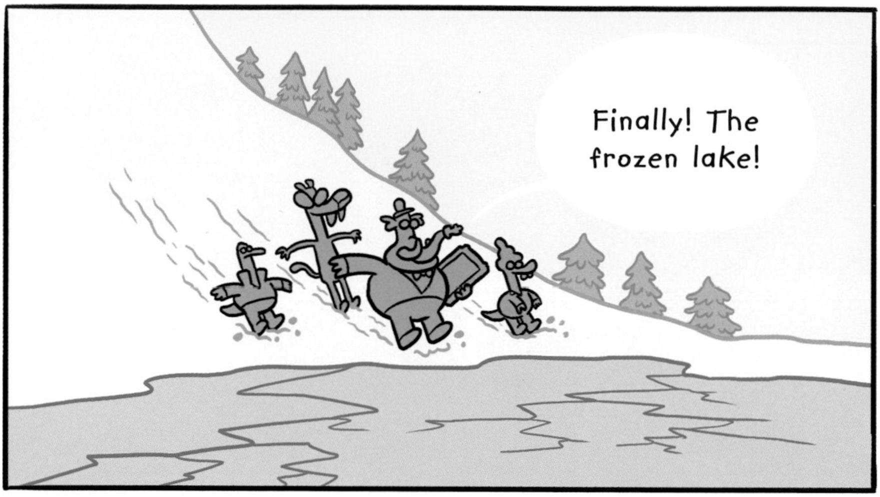
Finally! The frozen lake!

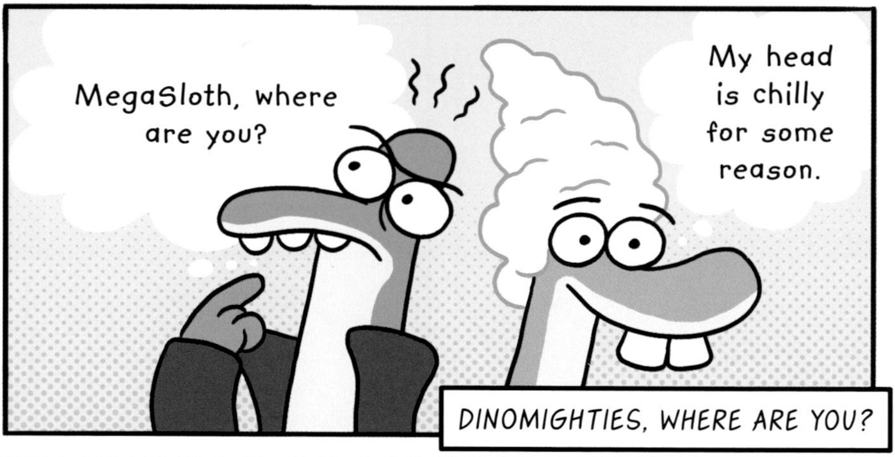
MegaSloth, where are you?
My head is chilly for some reason.
DINOMIGHTIES, WHERE ARE YOU?

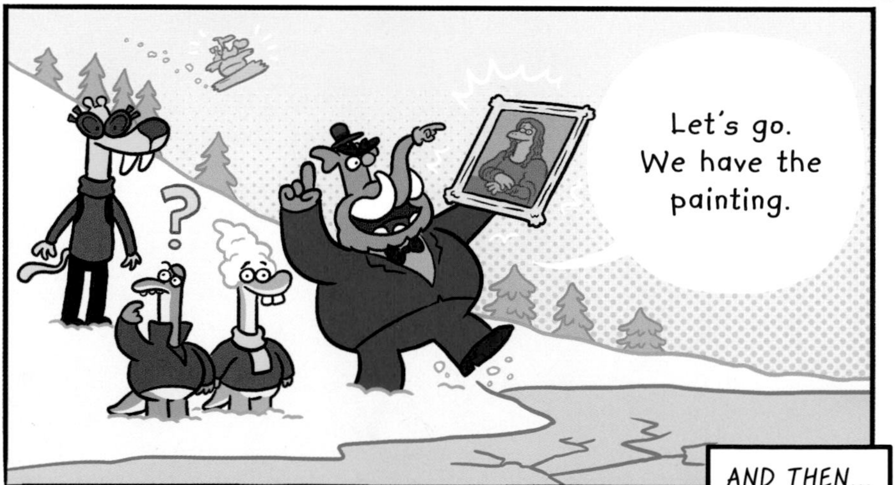
Let's go. We have the painting.
AND THEN...

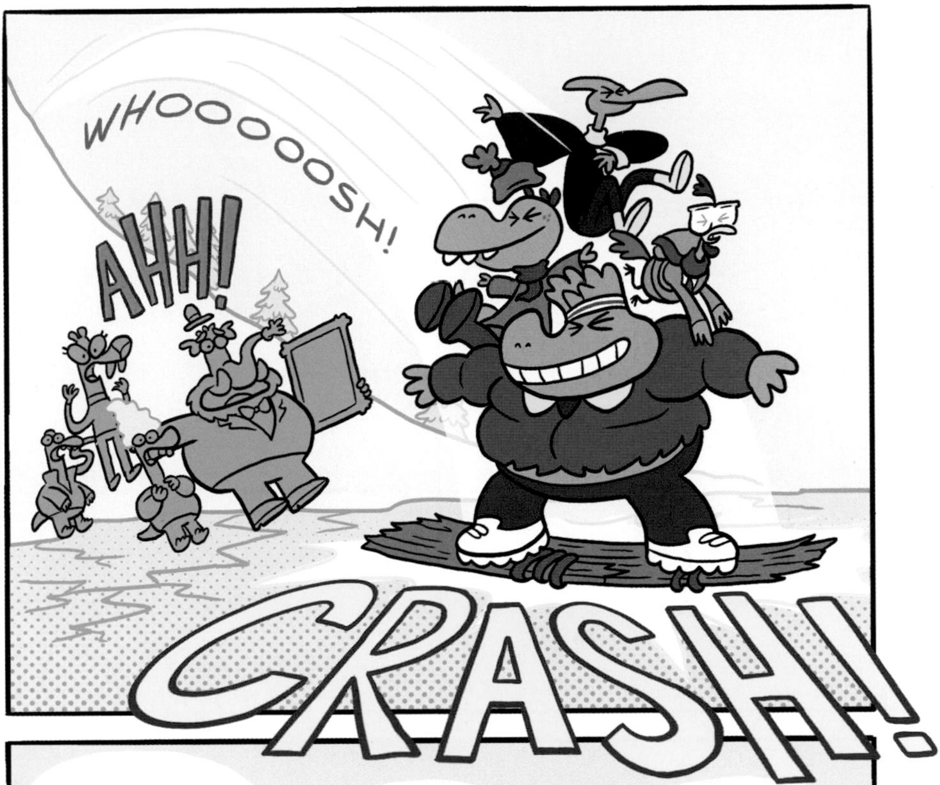
WHOOOOOOSH!
AHH!
CRASH!!

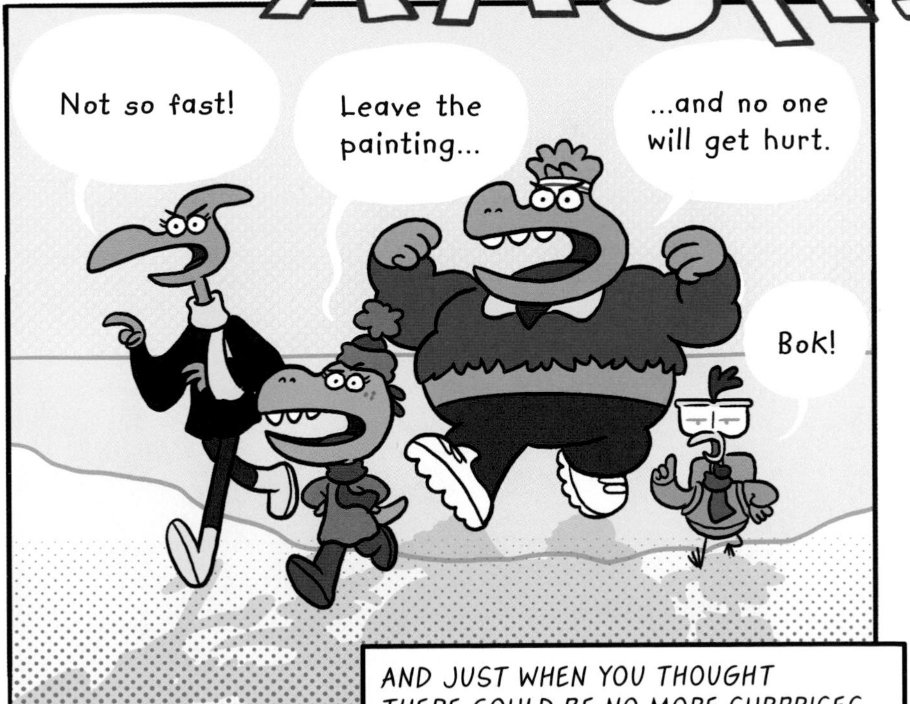
Not so fast!
Leave the painting...
...and no one will get hurt.
Bok!
AND JUST WHEN YOU THOUGHT THERE COULD BE NO MORE SURPRISES...

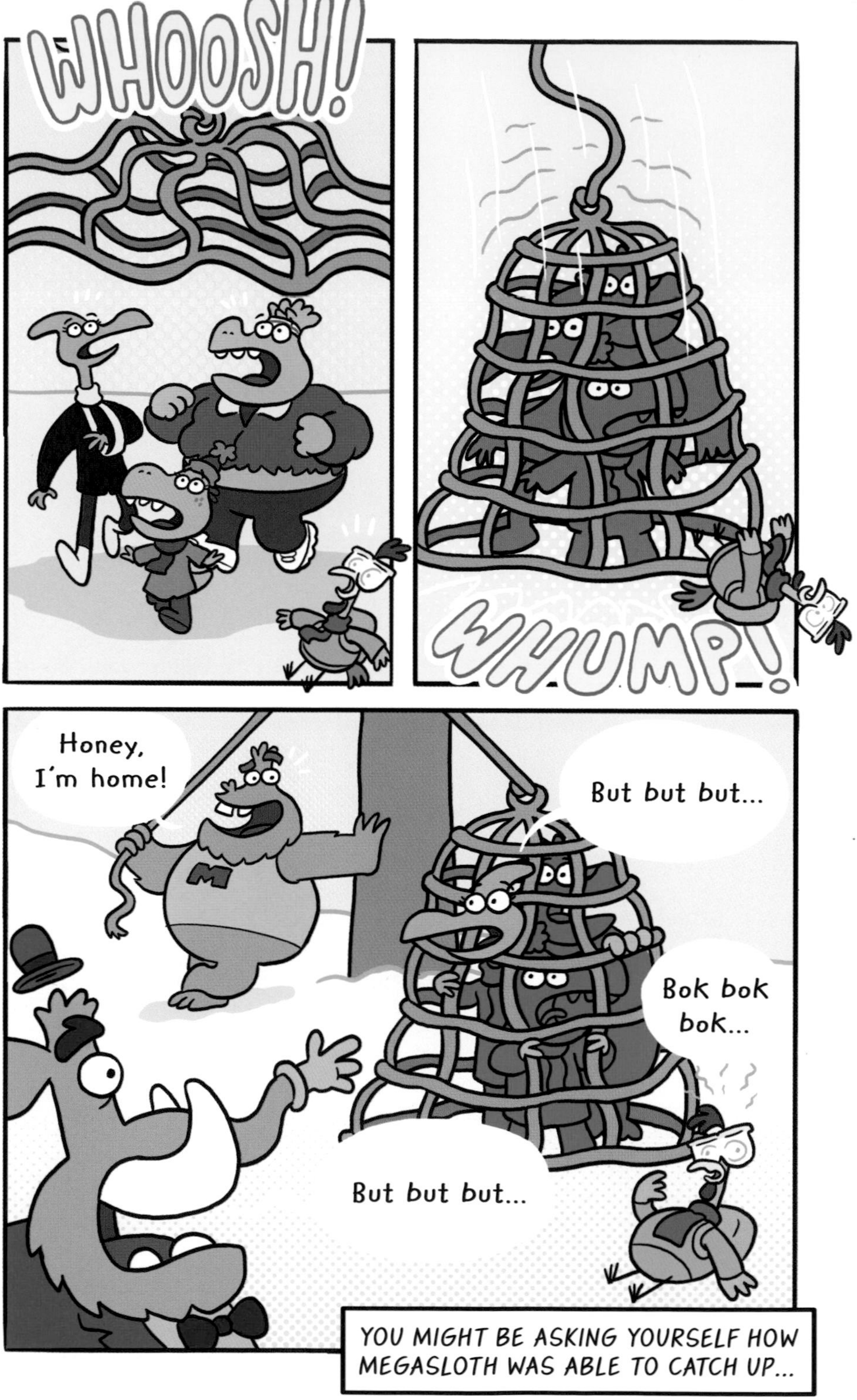
WHOOSH!
WHUMP!
Honey, I'm home!
But but but...
Bok bok bok...
But but but...
YOU MIGHT BE ASKING YOURSELF HOW MEGASLOTH WAS ABLE TO CATCH UP...

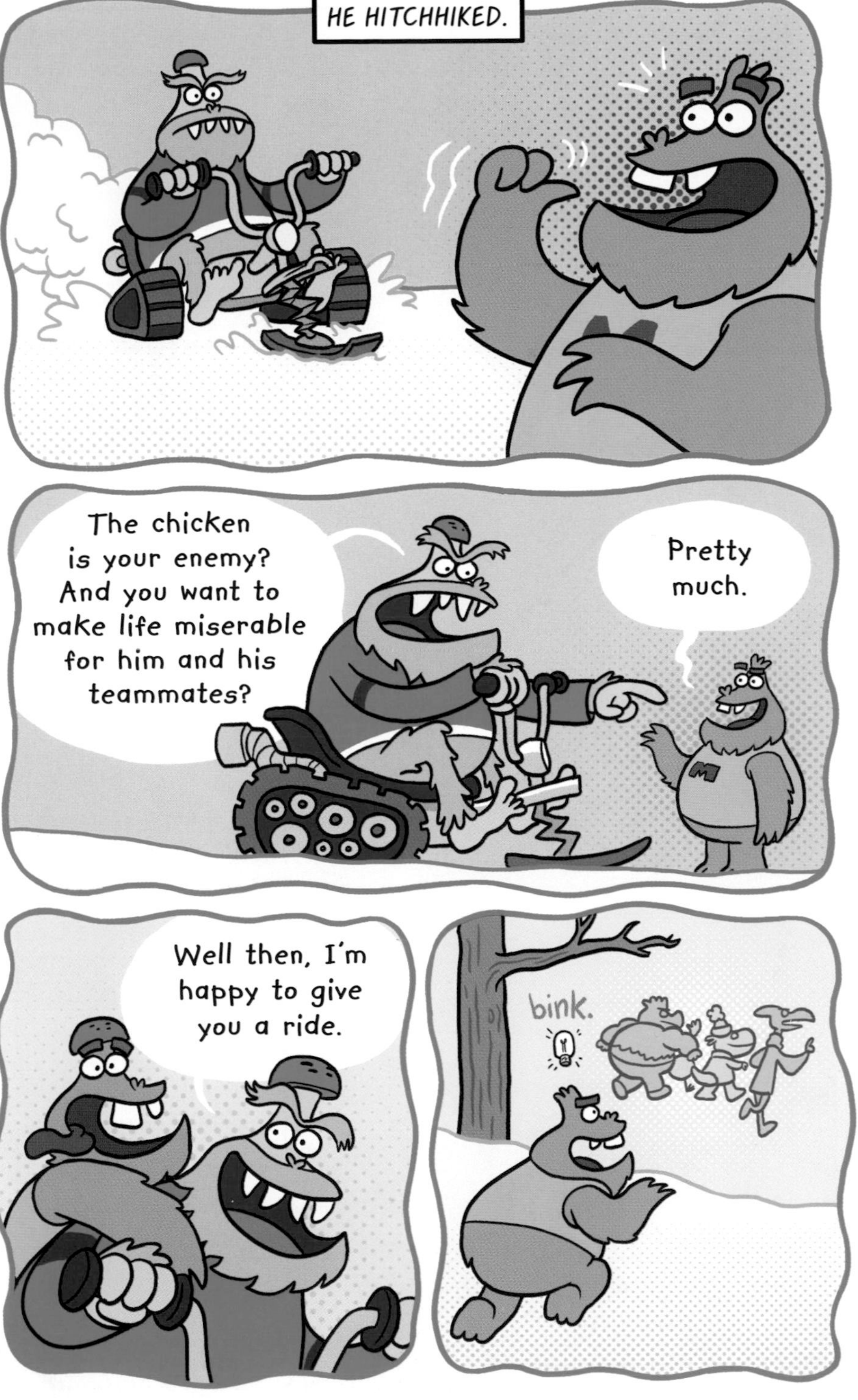
HE HITCHHIKED.
The chicken is your enemy? And you want to make life miserable for him and his teammates?
Pretty much.
Well then, I'm happy to give you a ride.
bink.

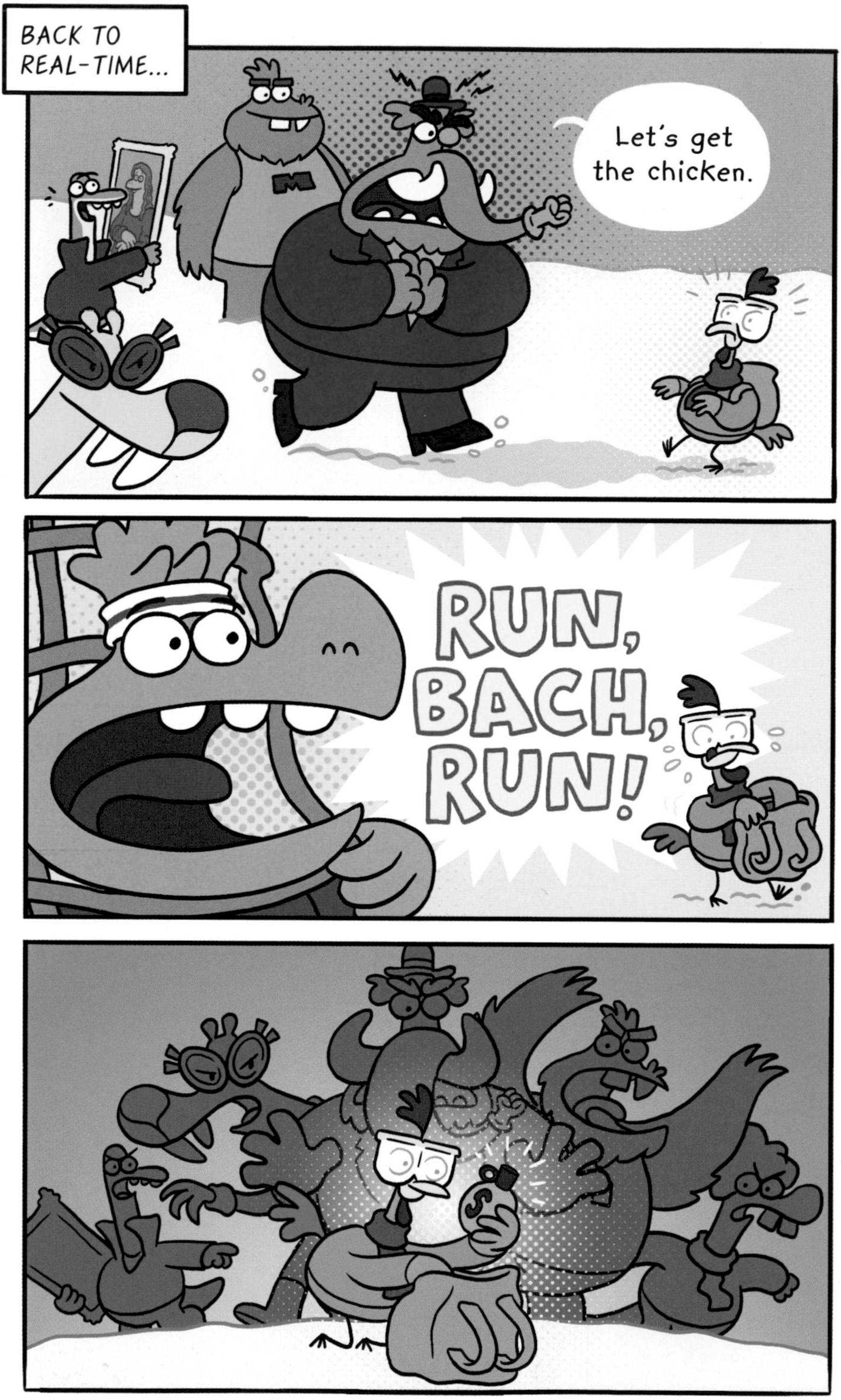
BACK TO REAL-TIME...
Let's get the chicken.
RUN, BACH, RUN!

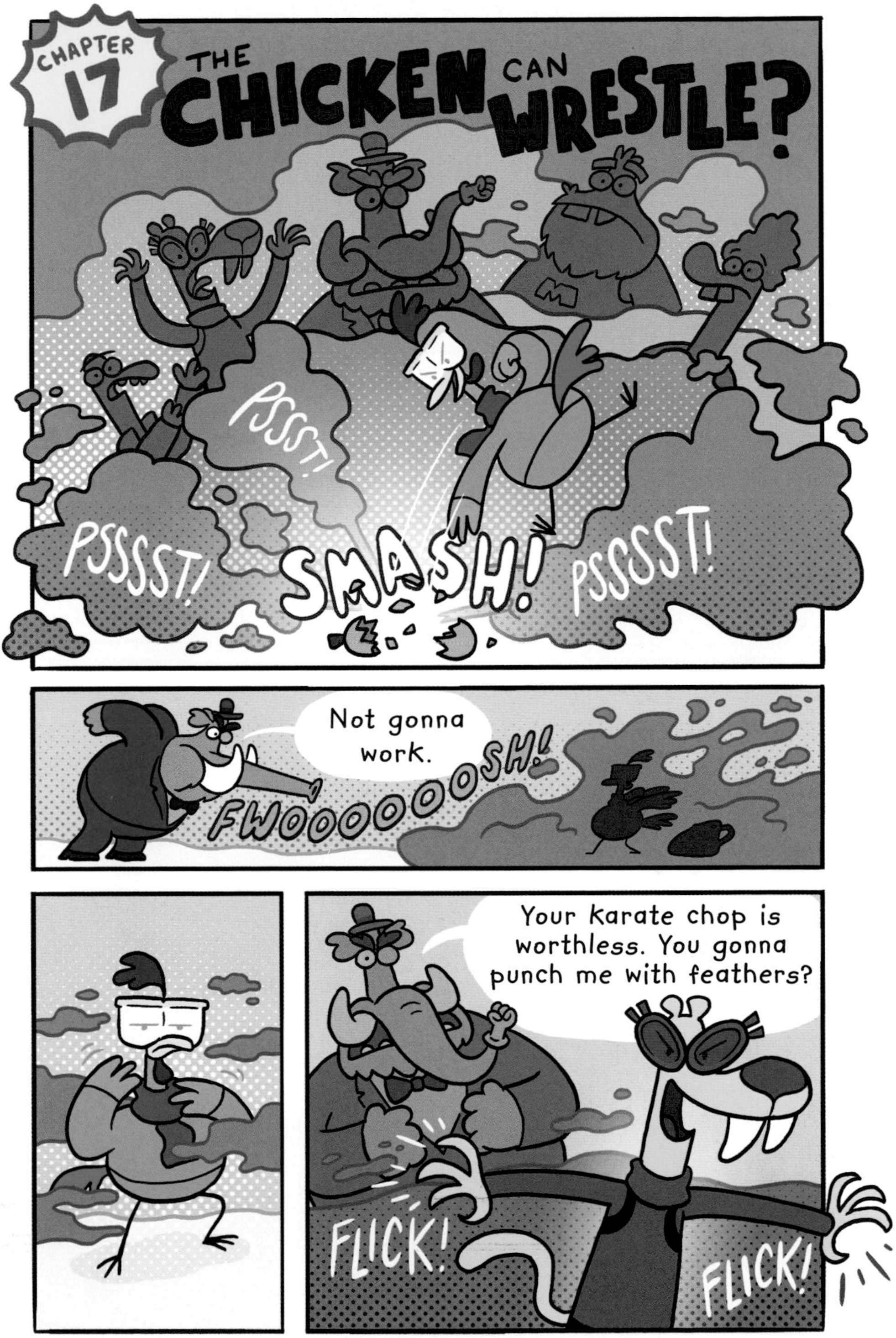
CHAPTER 17
THE CHICKEN CAN WRESTLE?
PSSST!
PSSSST!
SMASH!
PSSSST!
Not gonna work.
FWOOOOOOOSH!
Your karate chop is worthless. You gonna punch me with feathers?
FLICK!
FLICK!

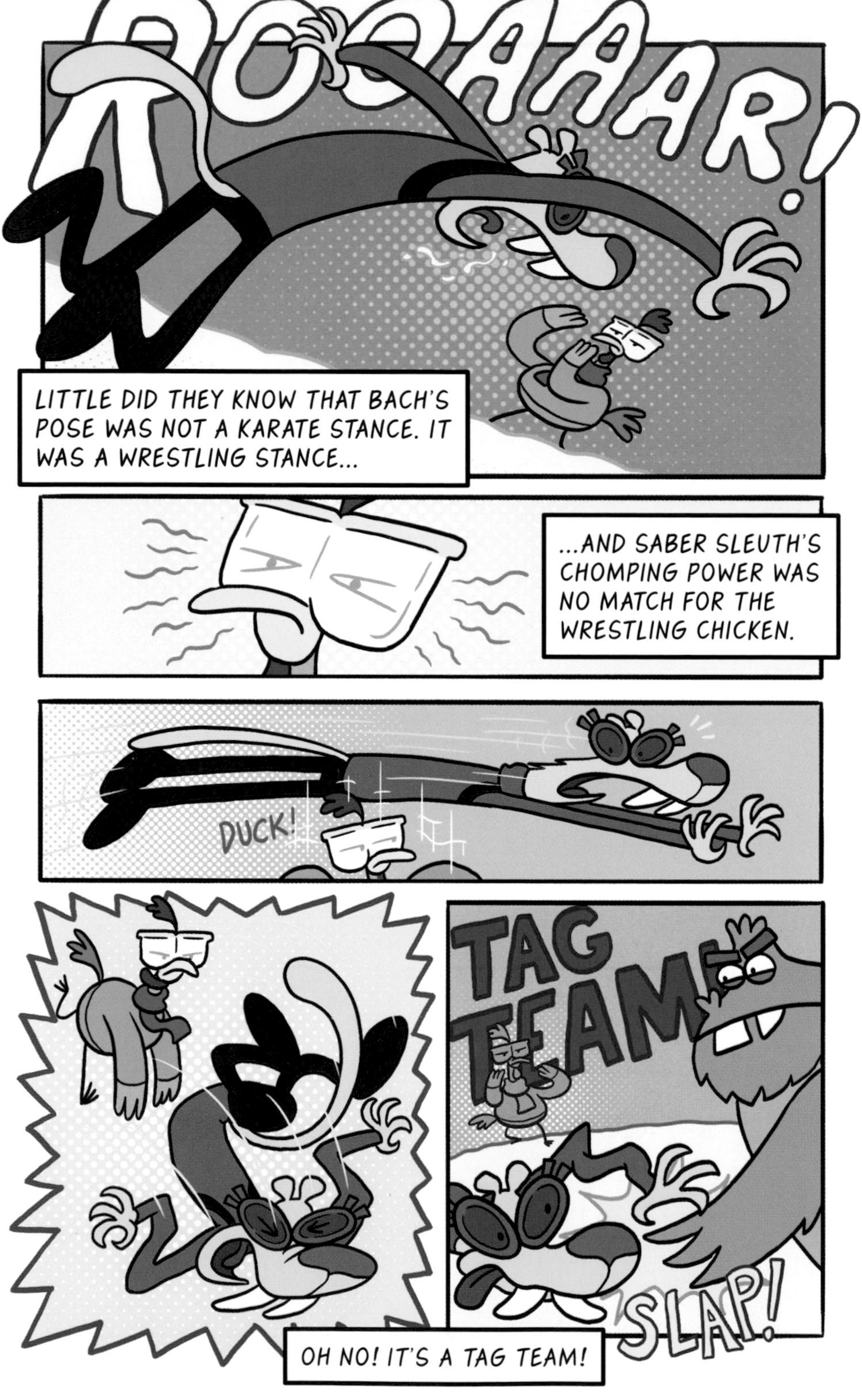

DOOOAAAAR!
LITTLE DID THEY KNOW THAT BACH'S POSE WAS NOT A KARATE STANCE. IT WAS A WRESTLING STANCE...
...AND SABER SLEUTH'S CHOMPING POWER WAS NO MATCH FOR THE WRESTLING CHICKEN.
DUCK!
TAG TEAM!
SLAP!
OH NO! IT'S A TAG TEAM!

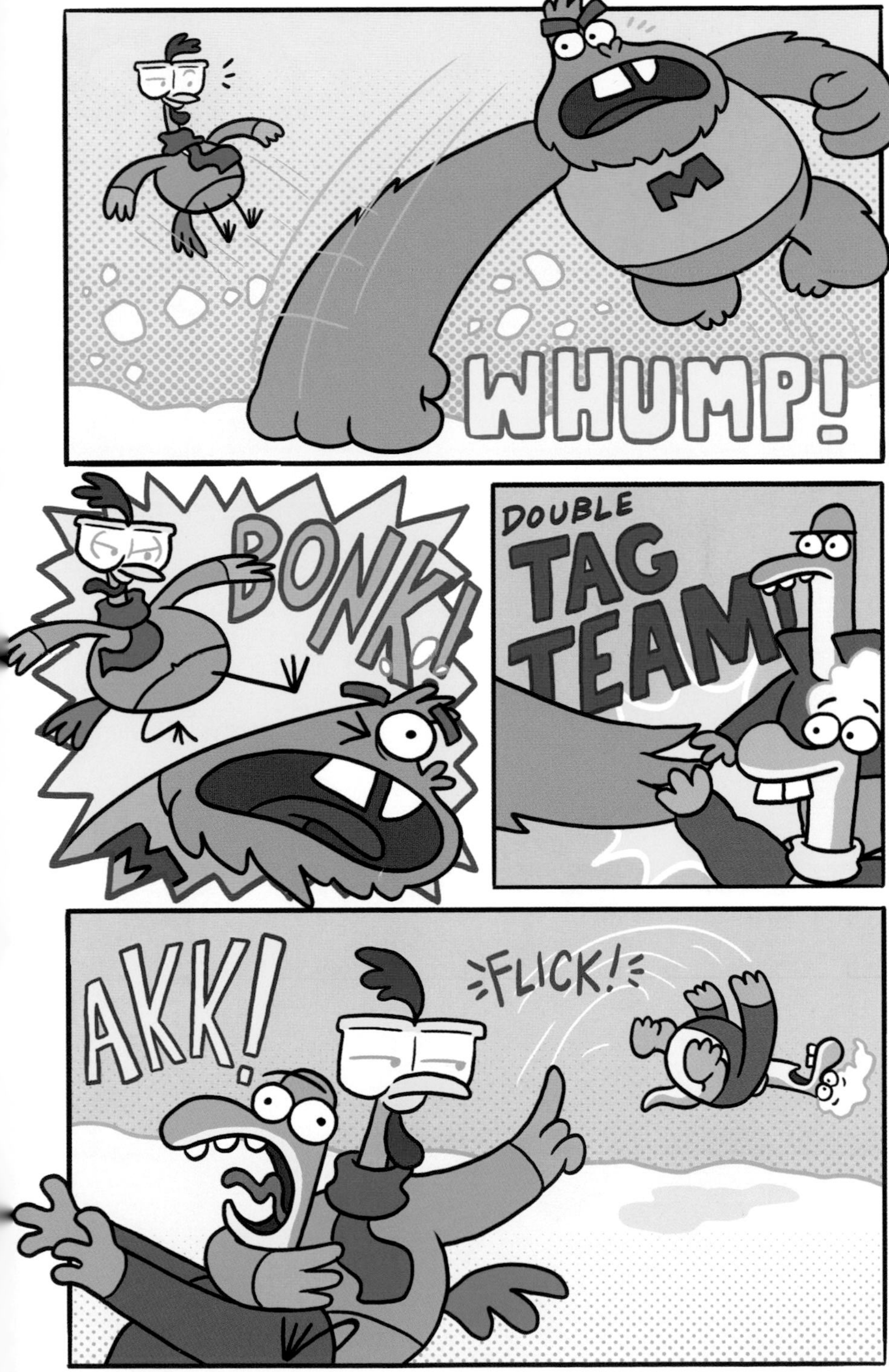
WHUMP!
BONK!
DOUBLE TAG TEAM!
AKK!
FLICK!

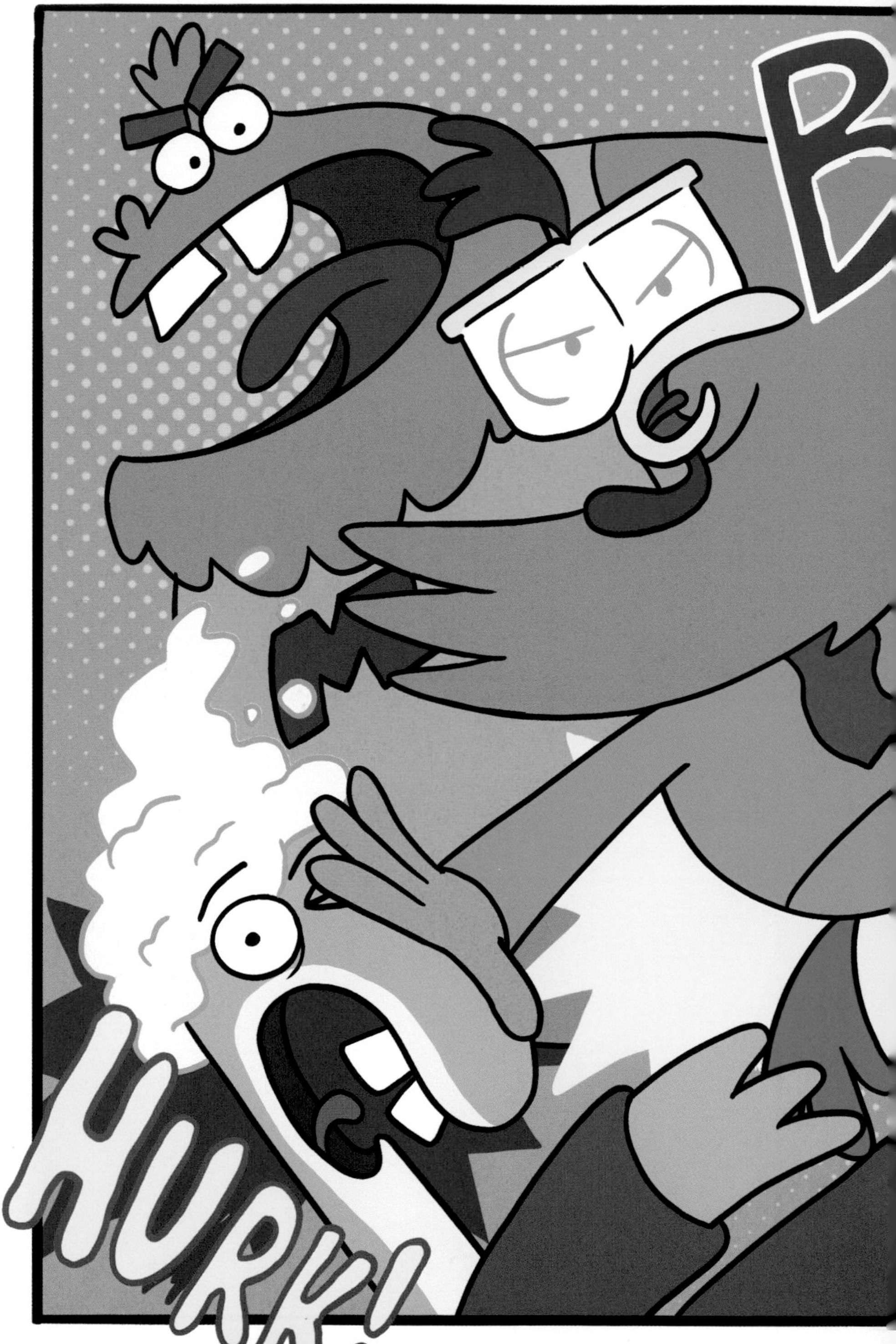
HURK!

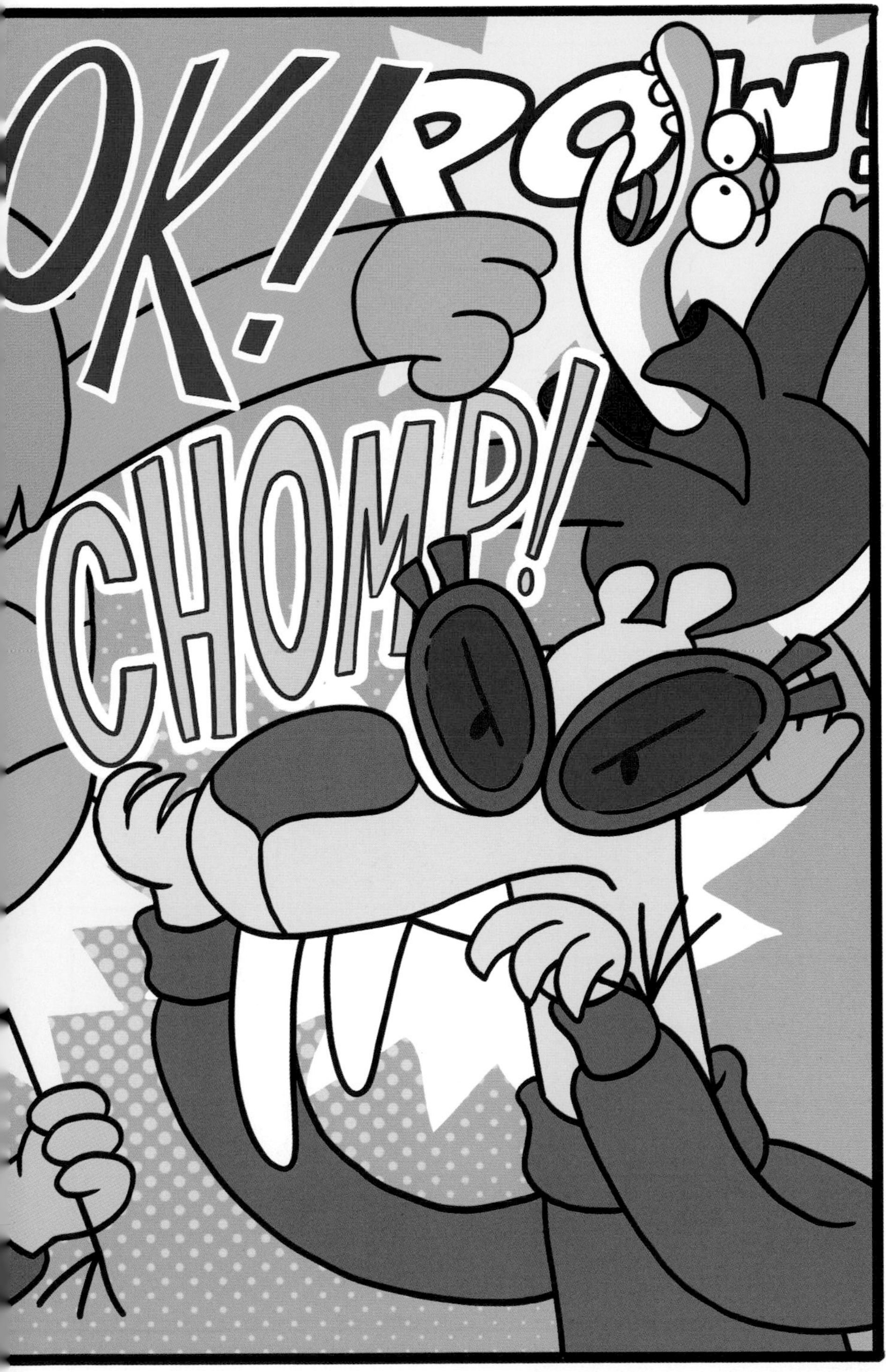
OK!
POW!
CHOMP!

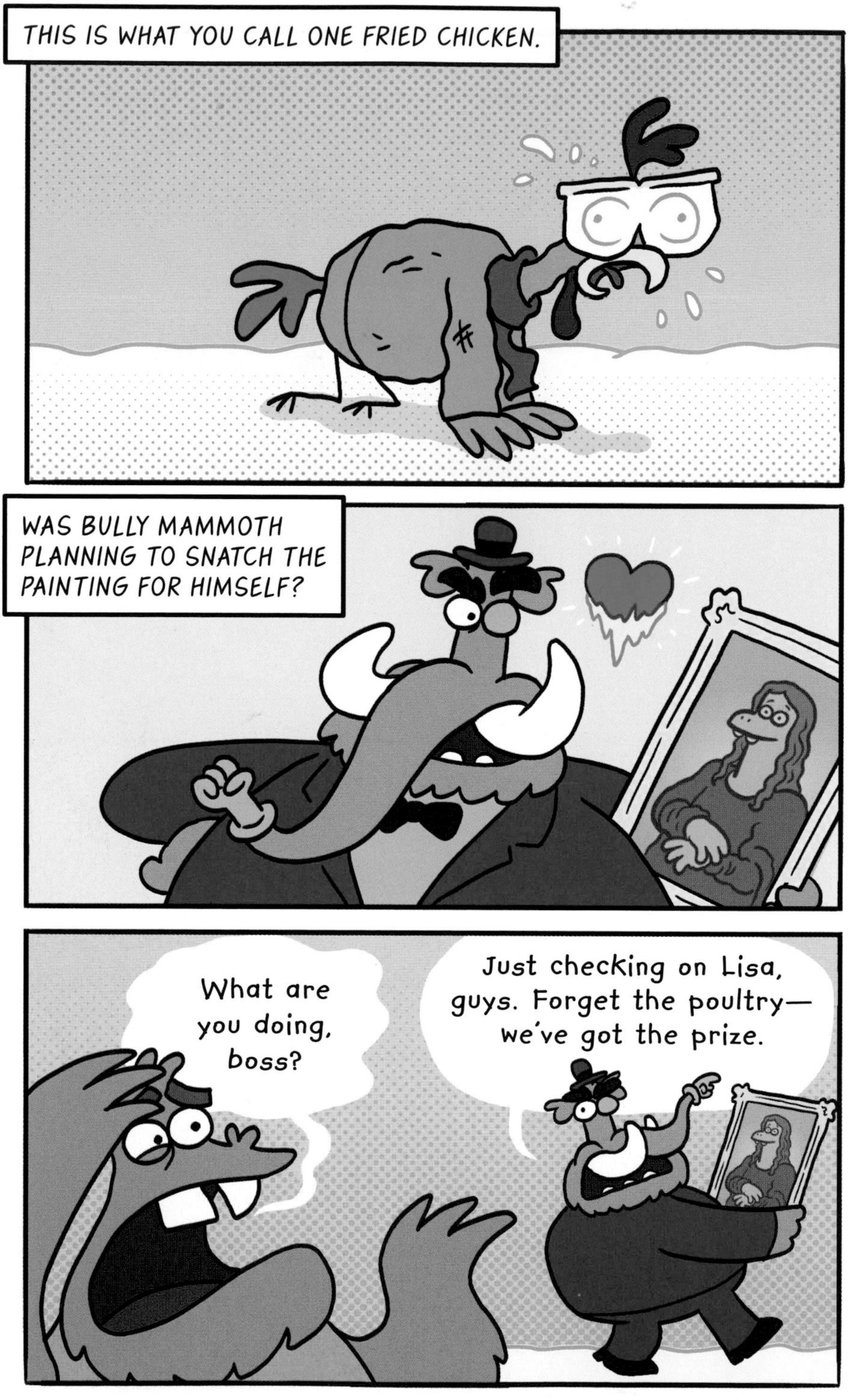
THIS IS WHAT YOU CALL ONE FRIED CHICKEN.
WAS BULLY MAMMOTH PLANNING TO SNATCH THE PAINTING FOR HIMSELF?
What are you doing, boss?
Just checking on Lisa, guys. Forget the poultry—we've got the prize.

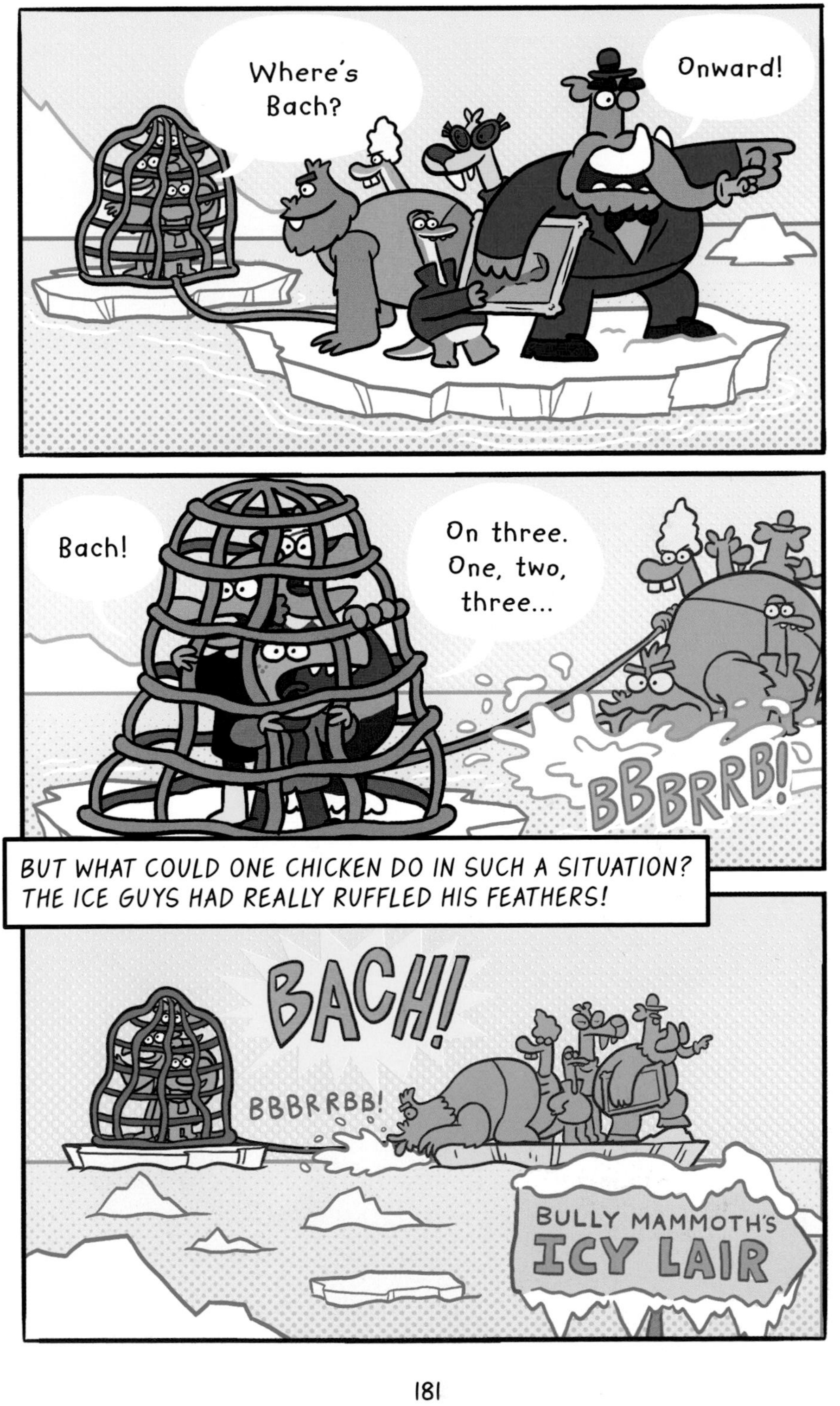
Where's Bach?
Onward!
Bach!
On three. One, two, three...
BBBRRB!
BUT WHAT COULD ONE CHICKEN DO IN SUCH A SITUATION? THE ICE GUYS HAD REALLY RUFFLED HIS FEATHERS!
BACH!
BBBRRBB!
BULLY MAMMOTH'S ICY LAIR

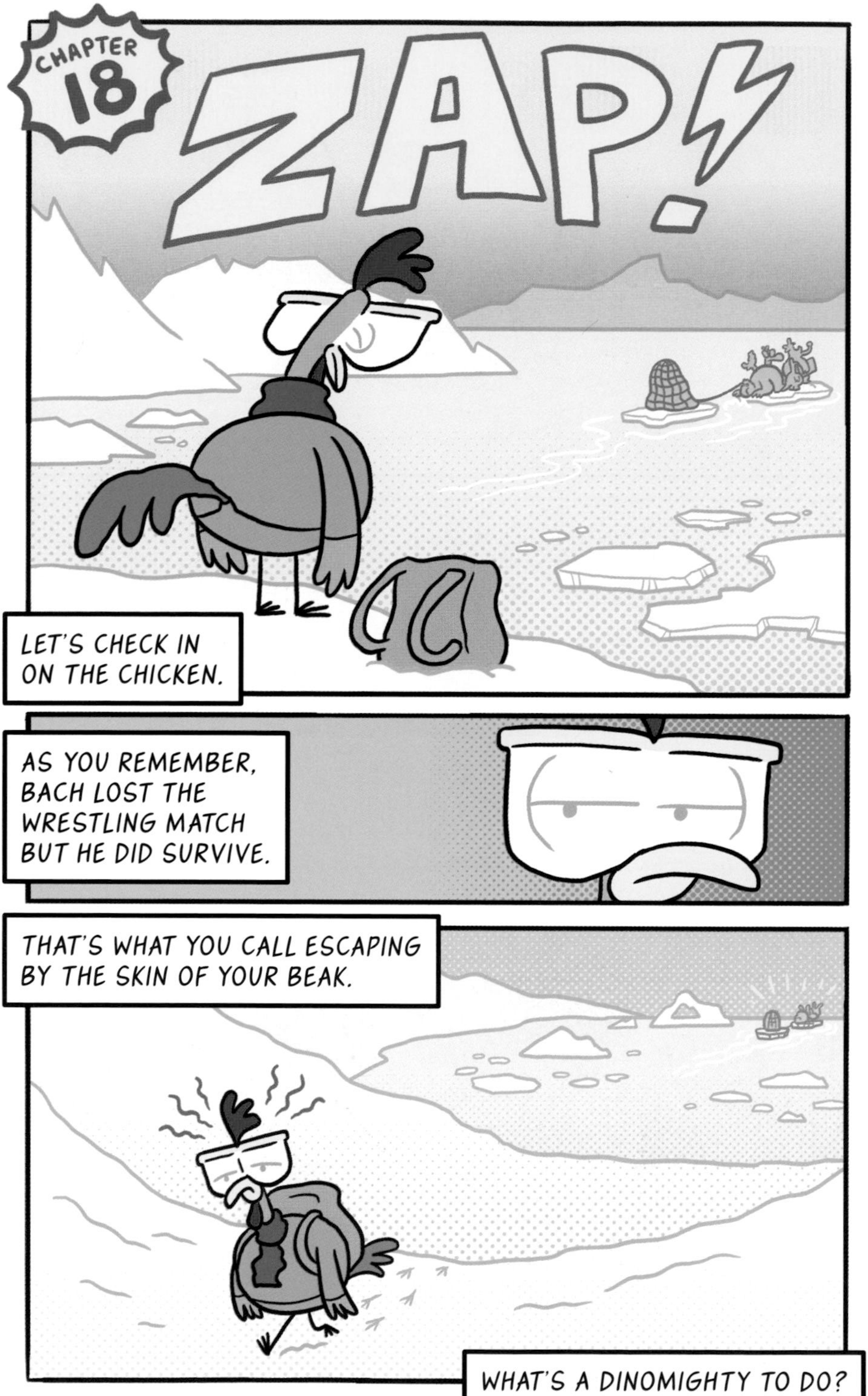
CHAPTER 18
ZAP!
LET'S CHECK IN ON THE CHICKEN.
AS YOU REMEMBER, BACH LOST THE WRESTLING MATCH BUT HE DID SURVIVE.
THAT'S WHAT YOU CALL ESCAPING BY THE SKIN OF YOUR BEAK.
WHAT'S A DINOMIGHTY TO DO?

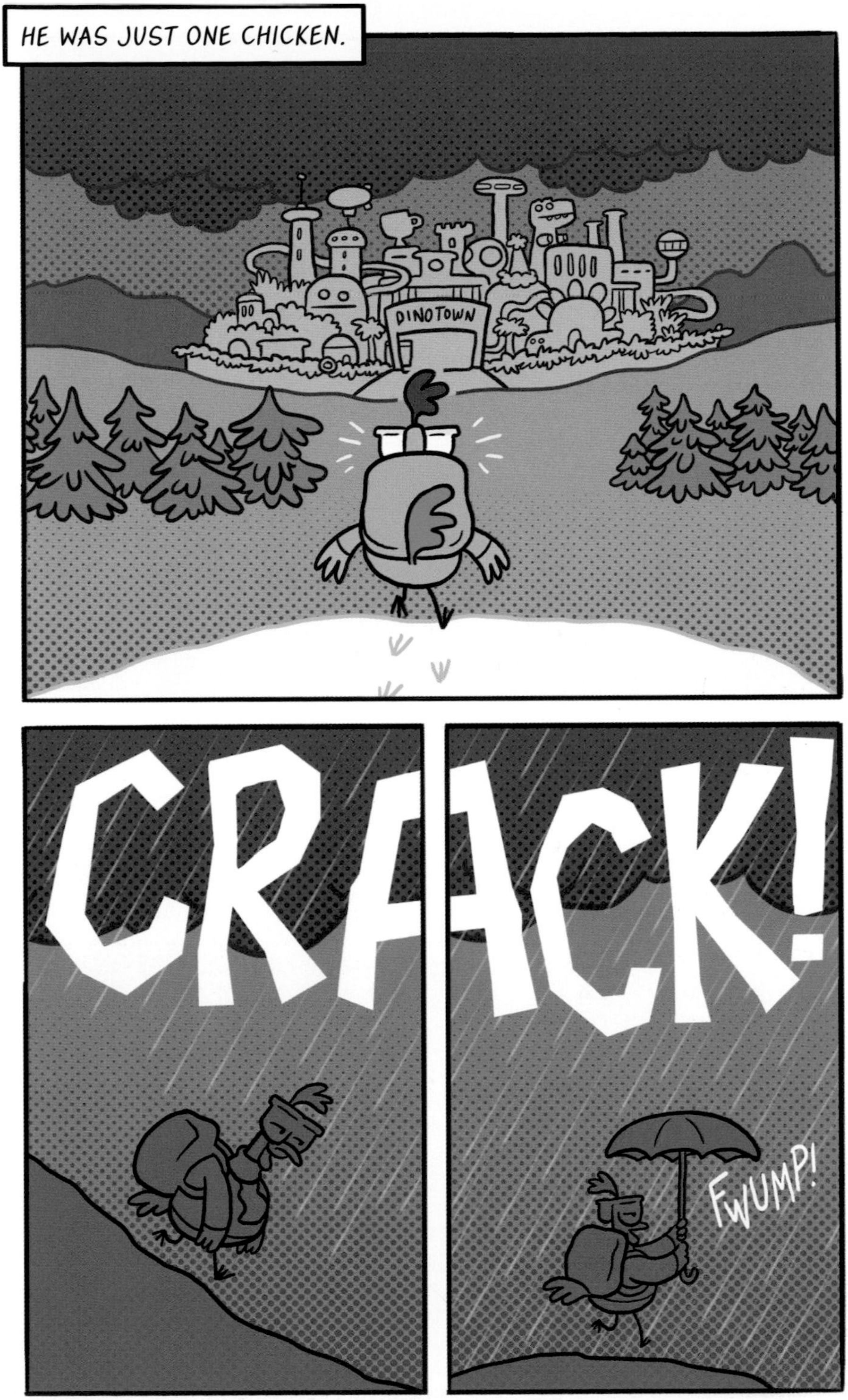
HE WAS JUST ONE CHICKEN.
DINOTOWN
CRACK!
FWUMP!

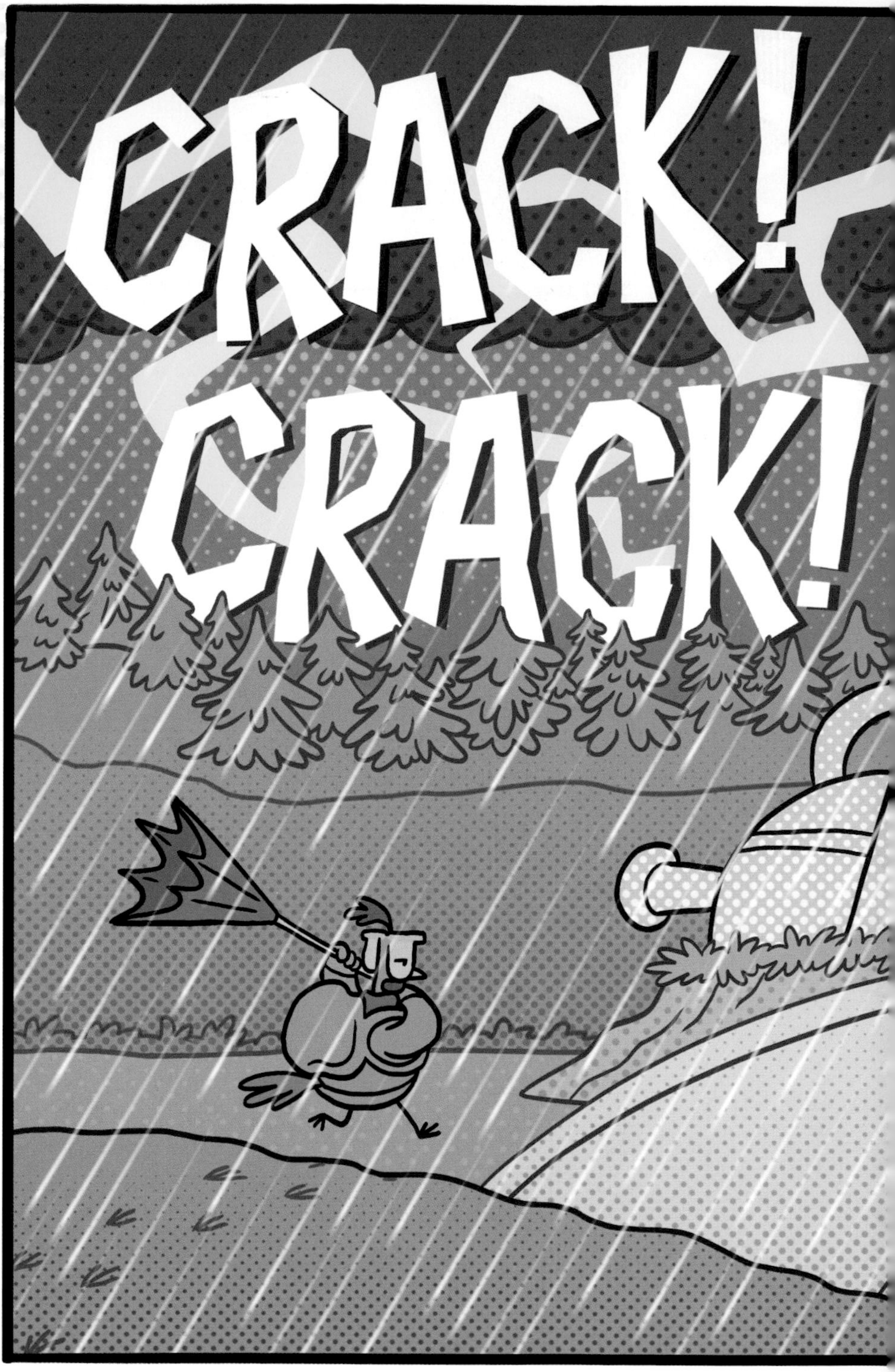
CRACK!
CRACK!

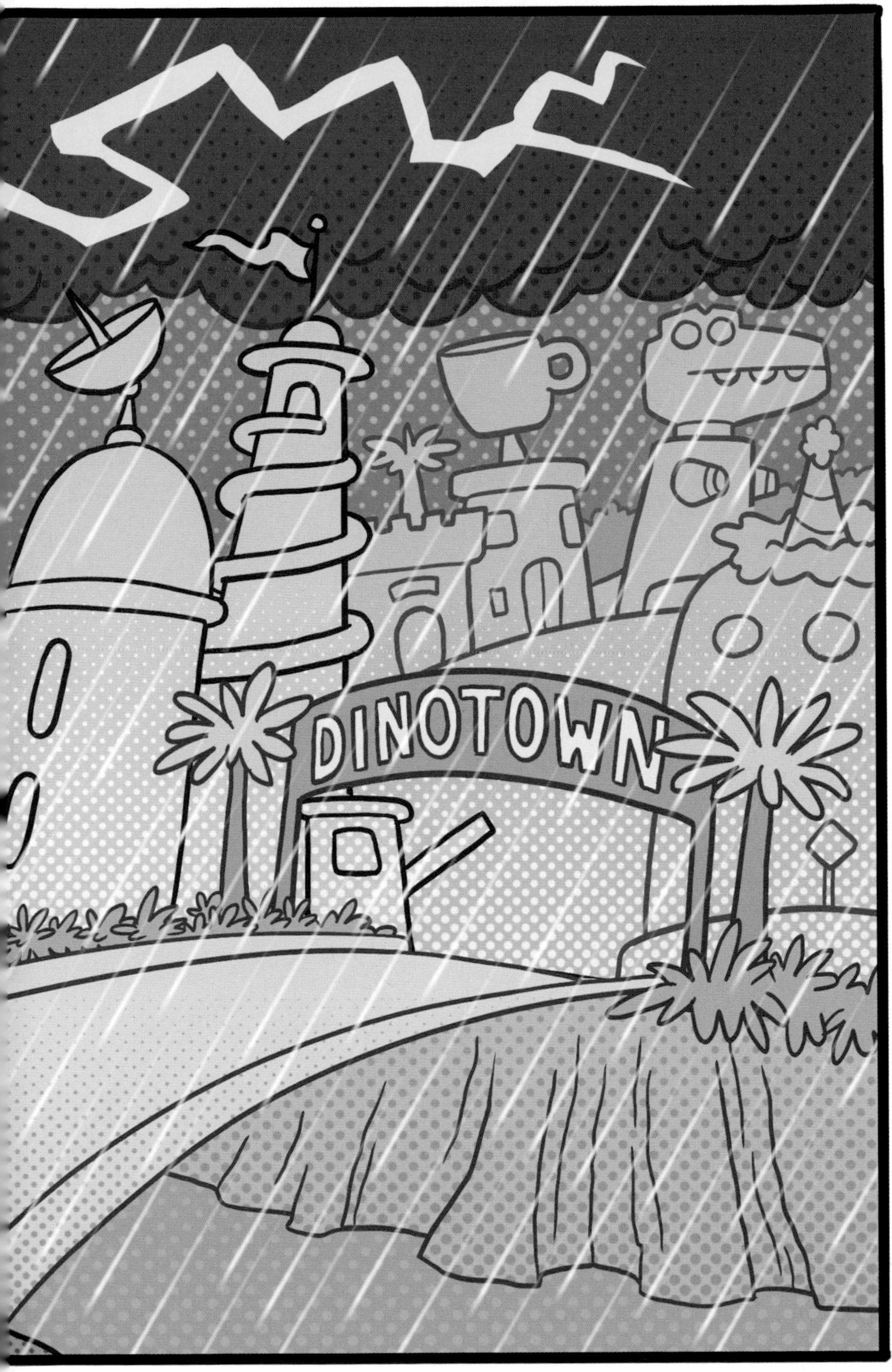
DINOTOWN

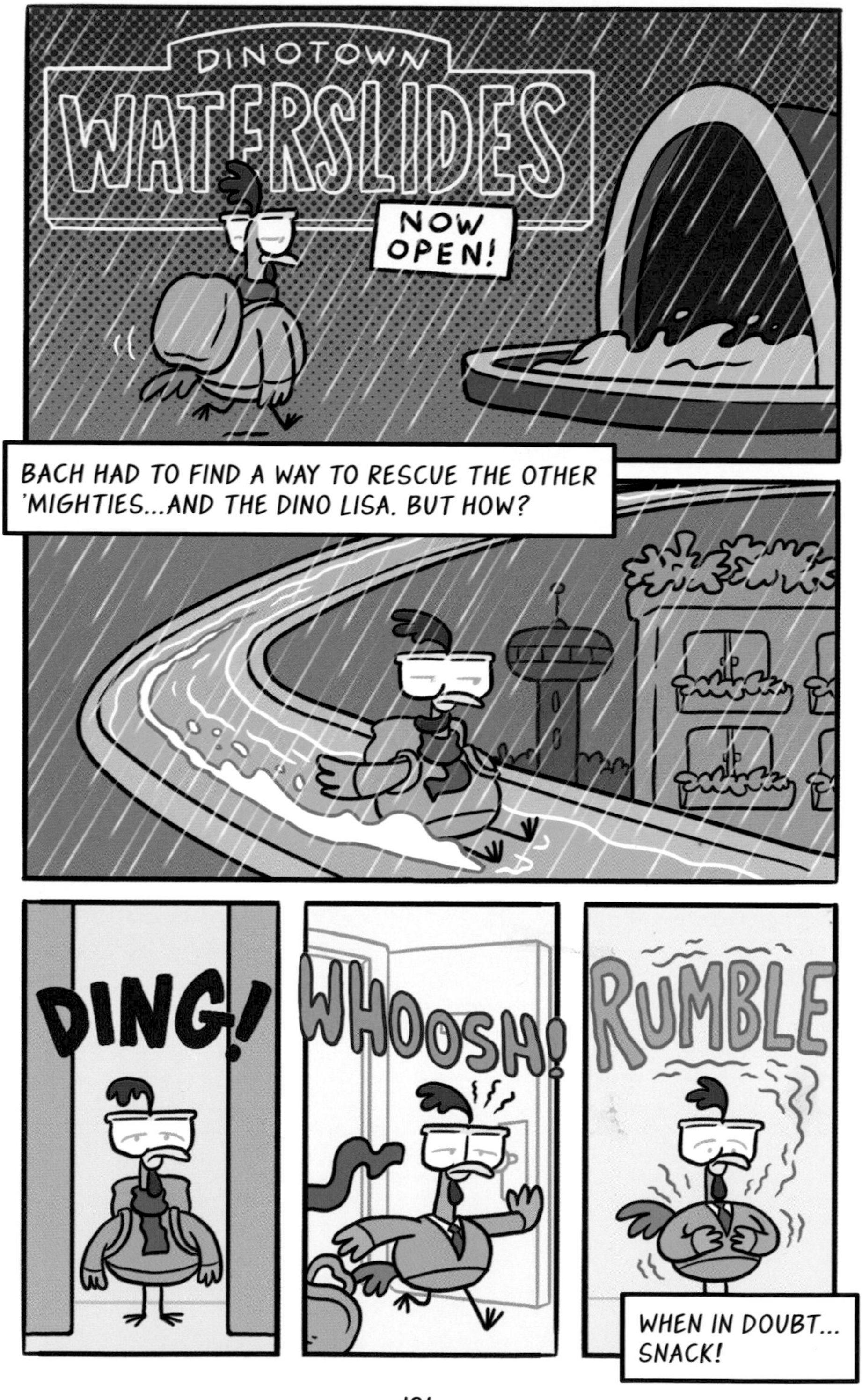
DINOTOWN WATERSLIDES
NOW OPEN!
BACH HAD TO FIND A WAY TO RESCUE THE OTHER 'MIGHTIES...AND THE DINO LISA. BUT HOW?
DING!
WHOOSH!
RUMBLE
WHEN IN DOUBT... SNACK!

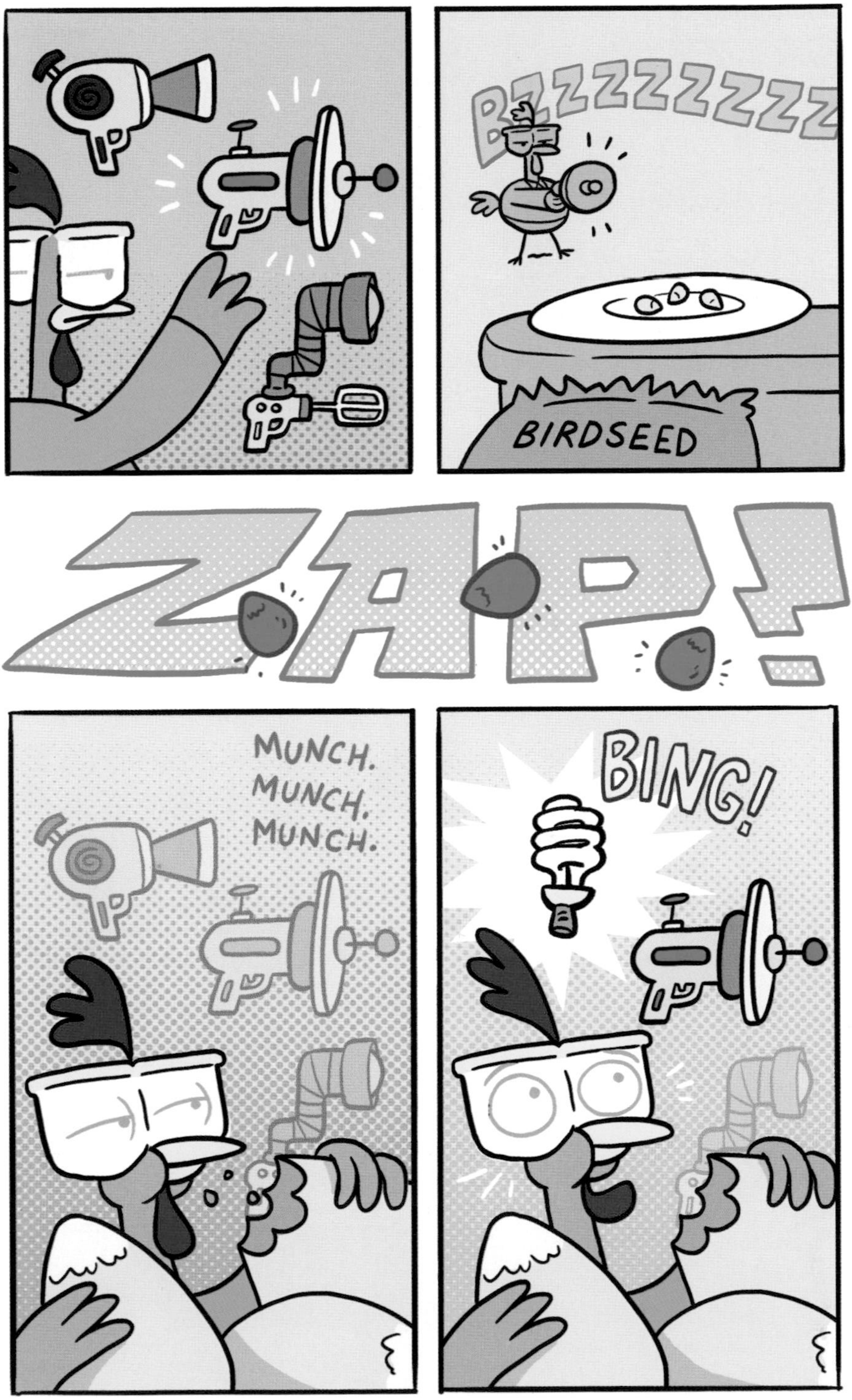
BZZZZZZZZZ
BIRDSEED
ZAP!
MUNCH.
MUNCH.
MUNCH.
BING!

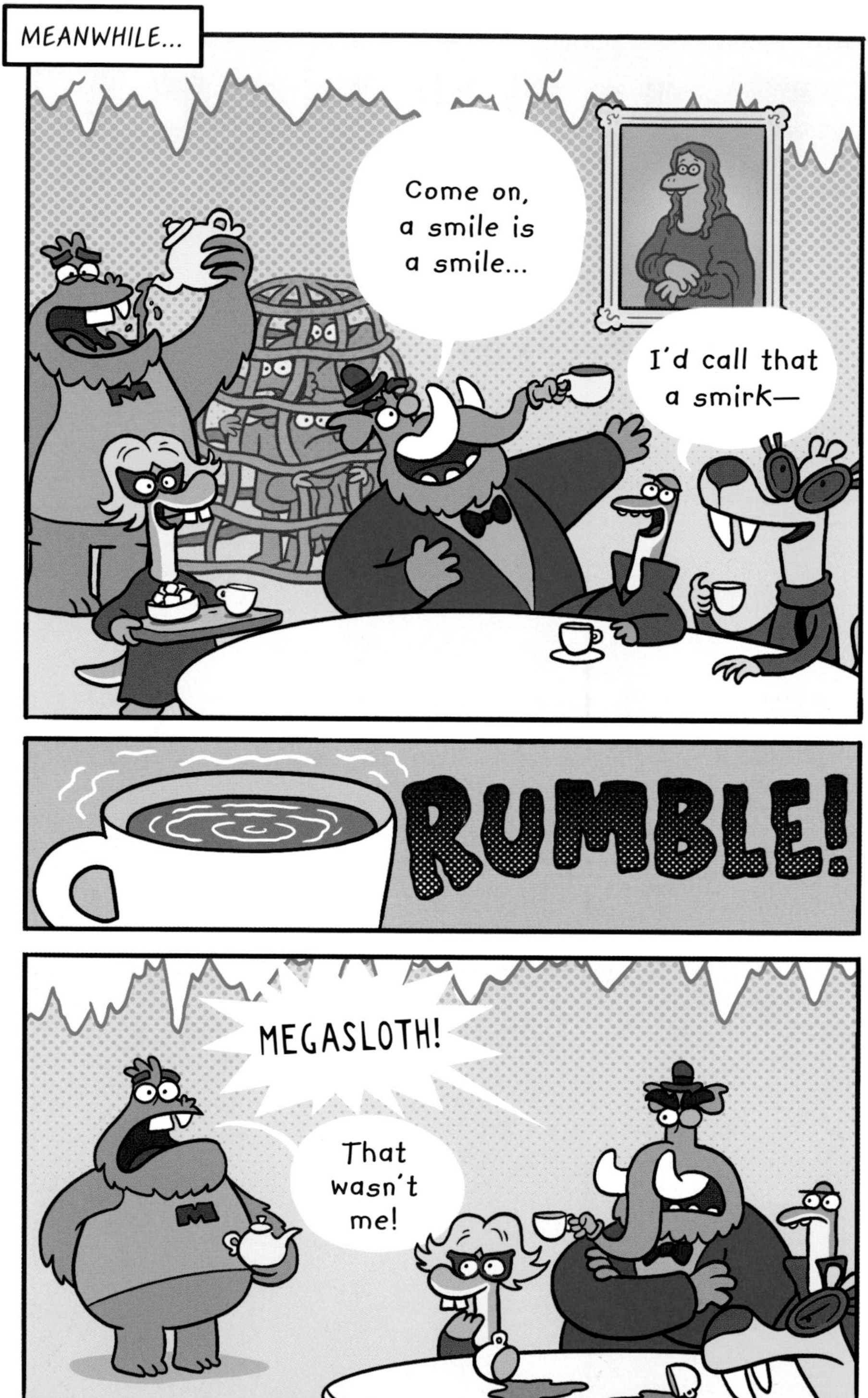
MEANWHILE...
Come on, a smile is a smile...
I'd call that a smirk—
RUMBLE!
MEGASLOTH!
That wasn't me!

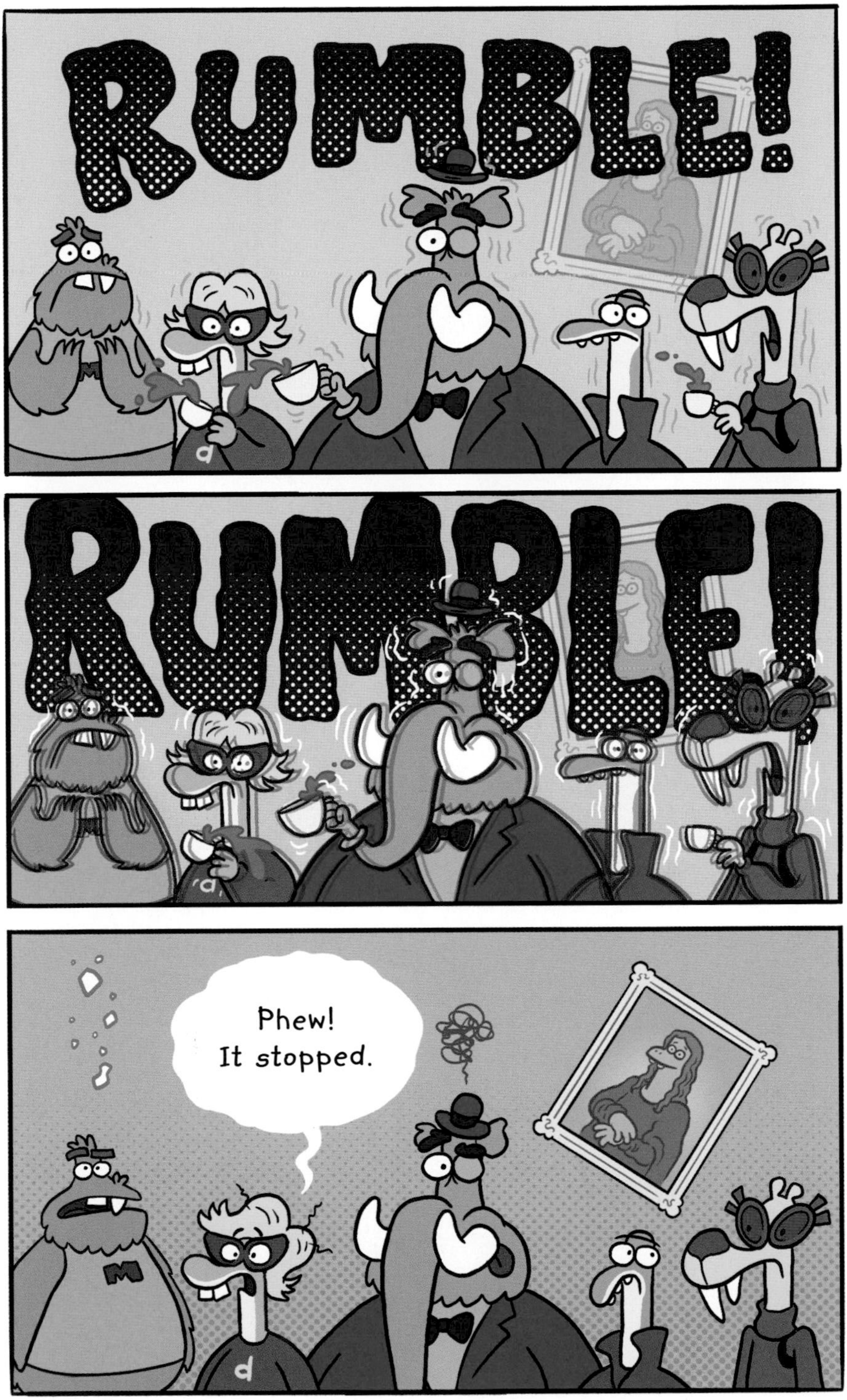
RUMBLE!
RUMBLE!
Phew!
It stopped.

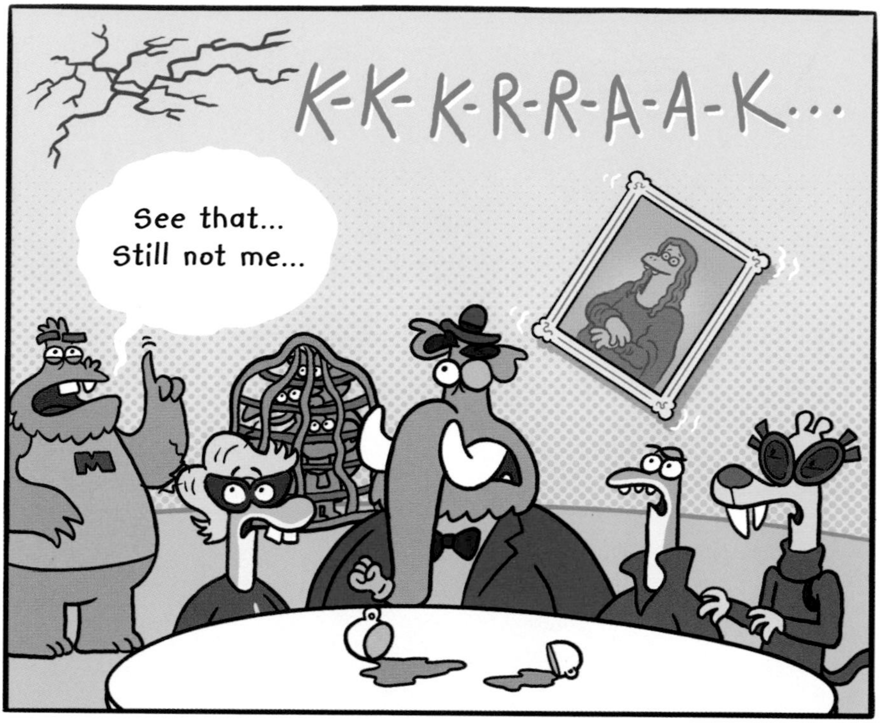
K-K-K-R-R-A-A-K...
See that... Still not me...

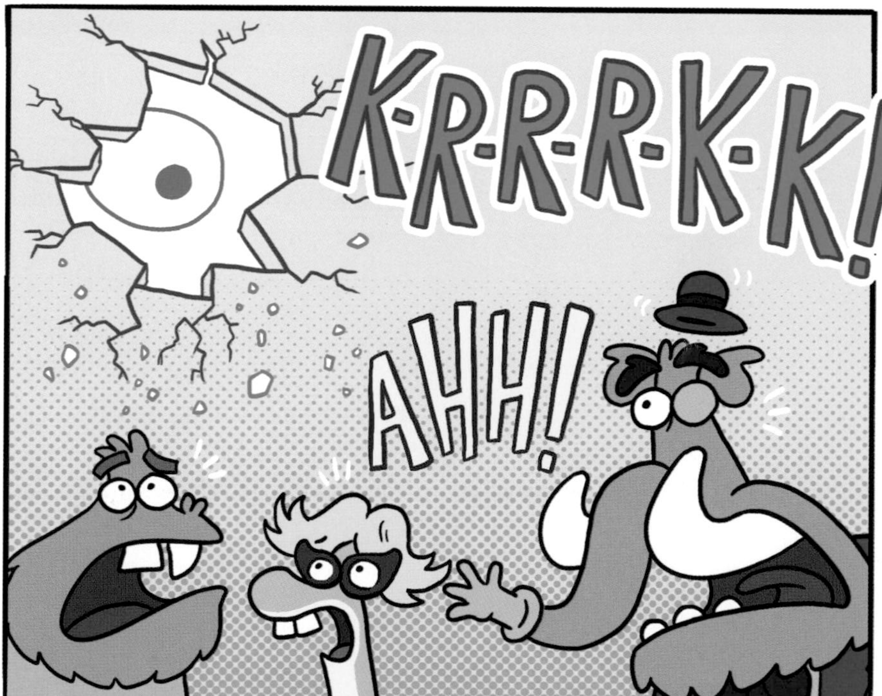
K-R-R-R-K-K!
AHH!

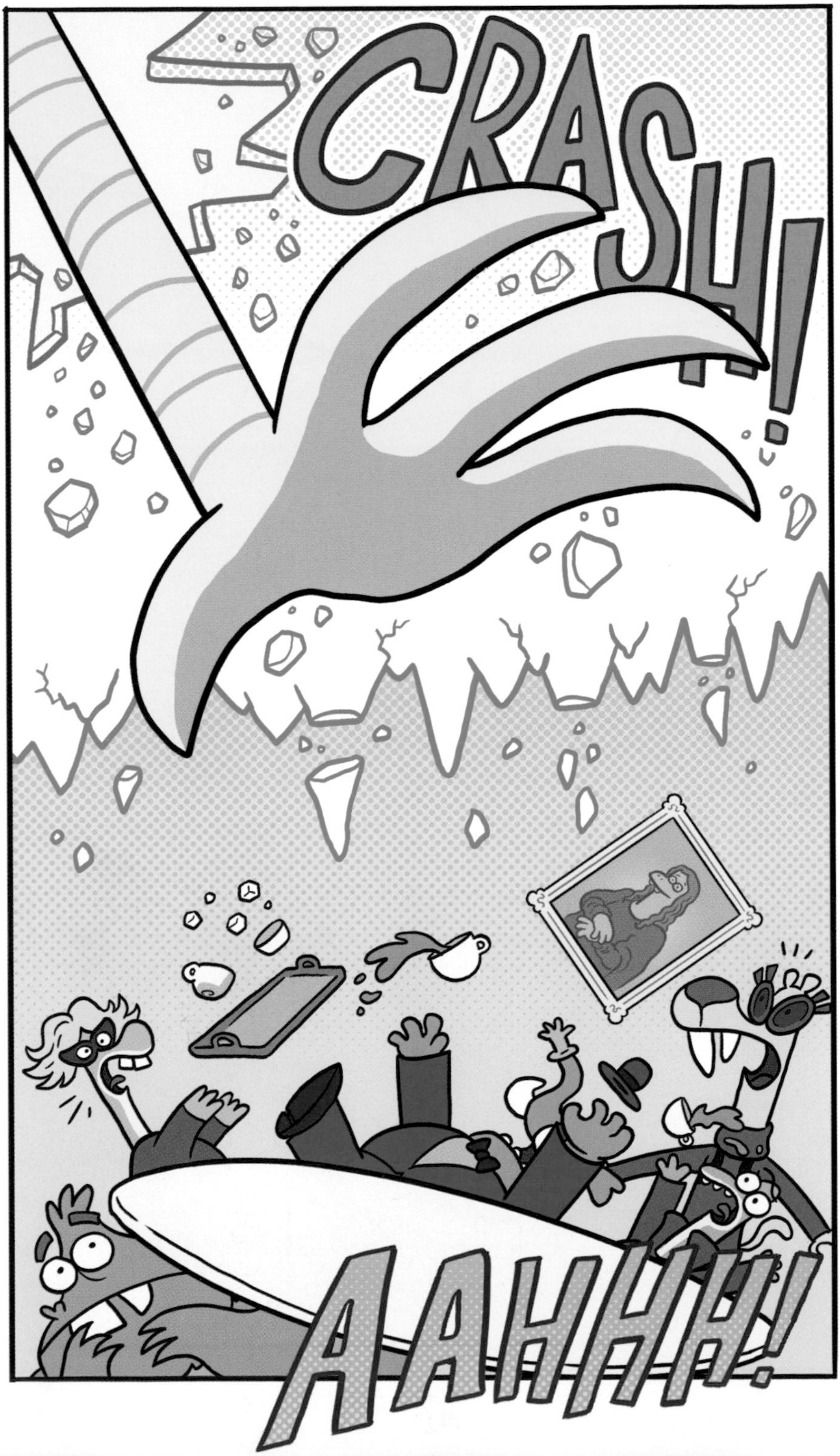
CRASH!
AAHHHH!

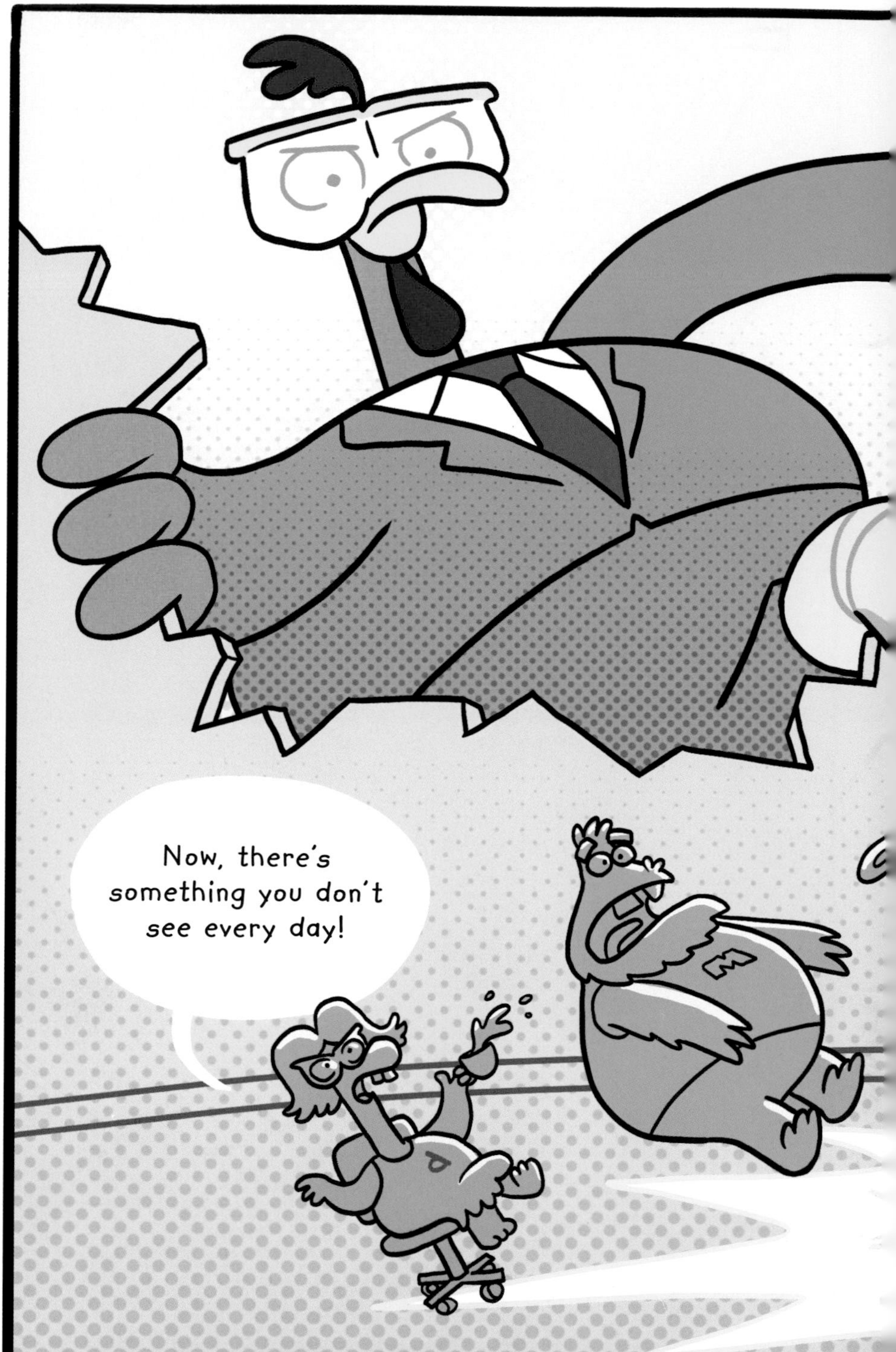
Now, there's something you don't see every day!

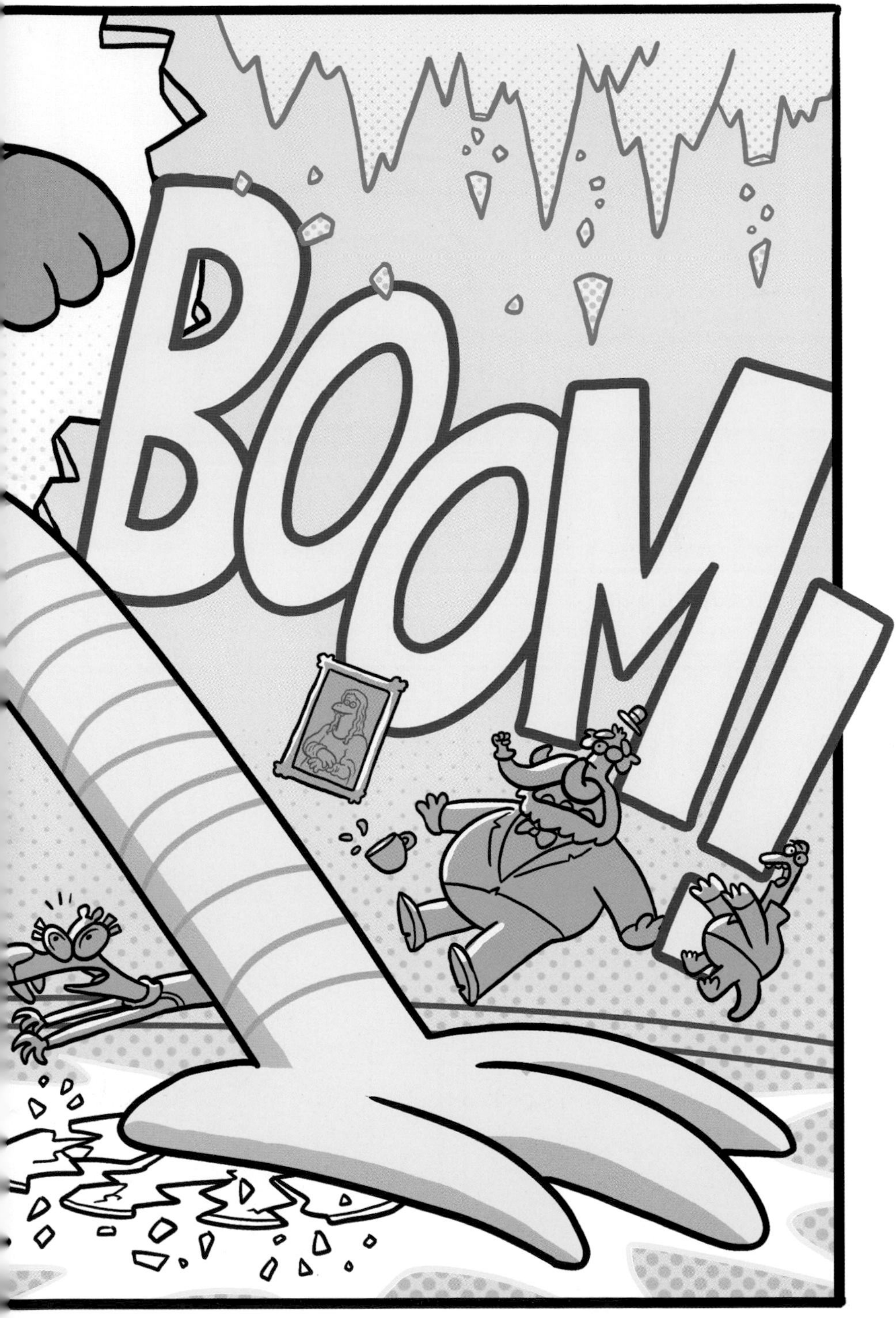
BOOM!

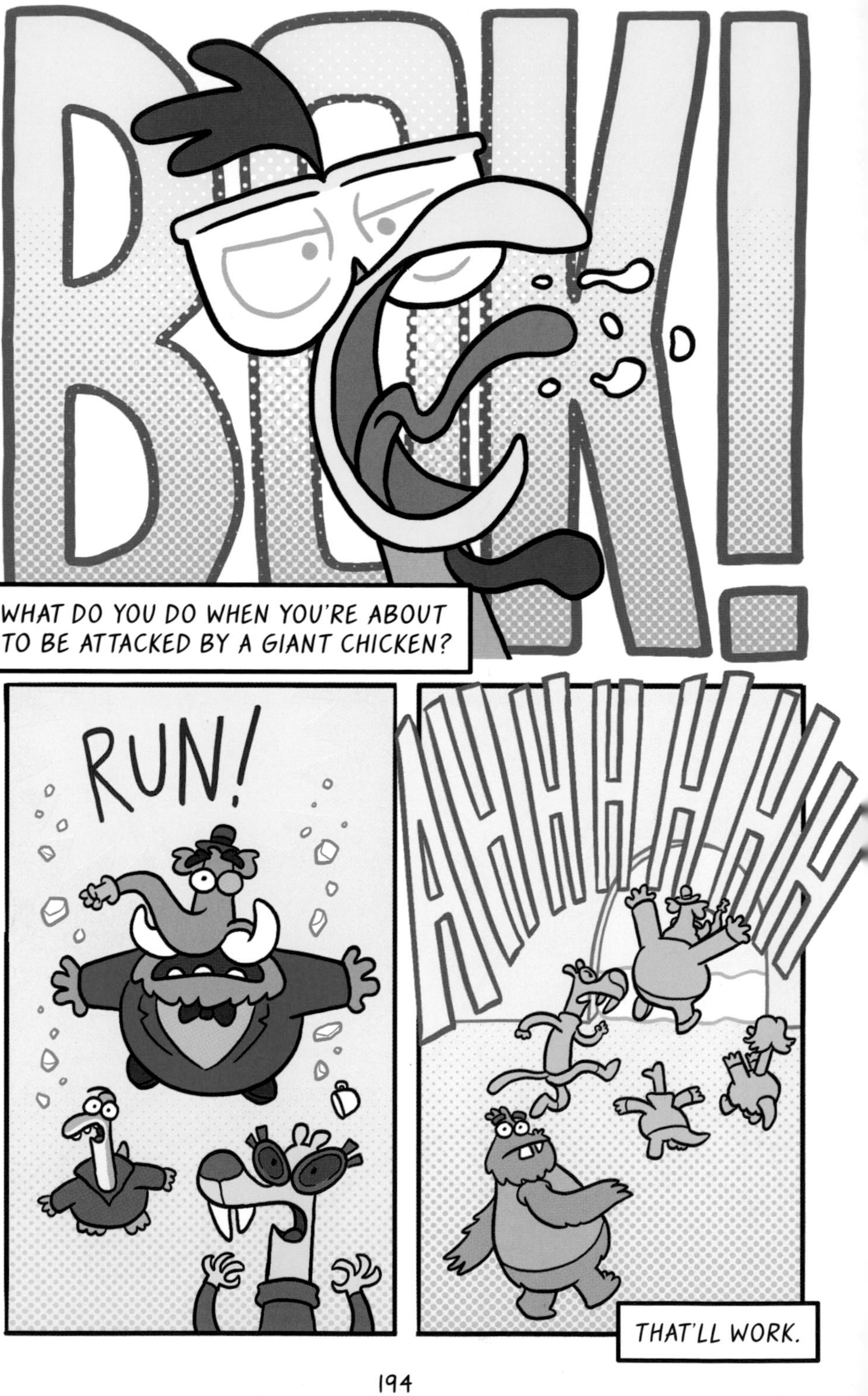
BOCK!
WHAT DO YOU DO WHEN YOU'RE ABOUT TO BE ATTACKED BY A GIANT CHICKEN?
RUN!
AHHHHHHHH
THAT'LL WORK.

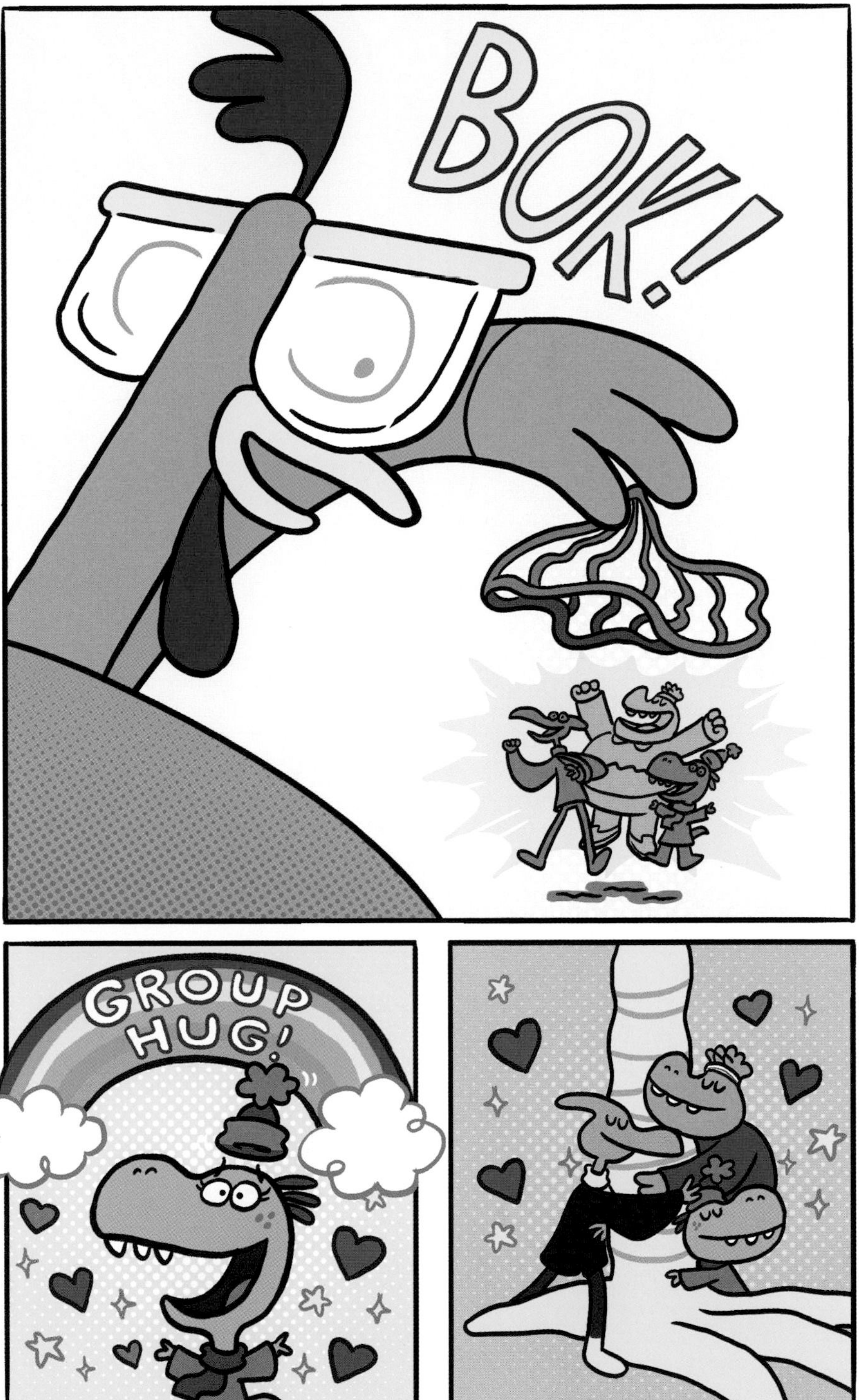
BOK!
GROUP HUG!

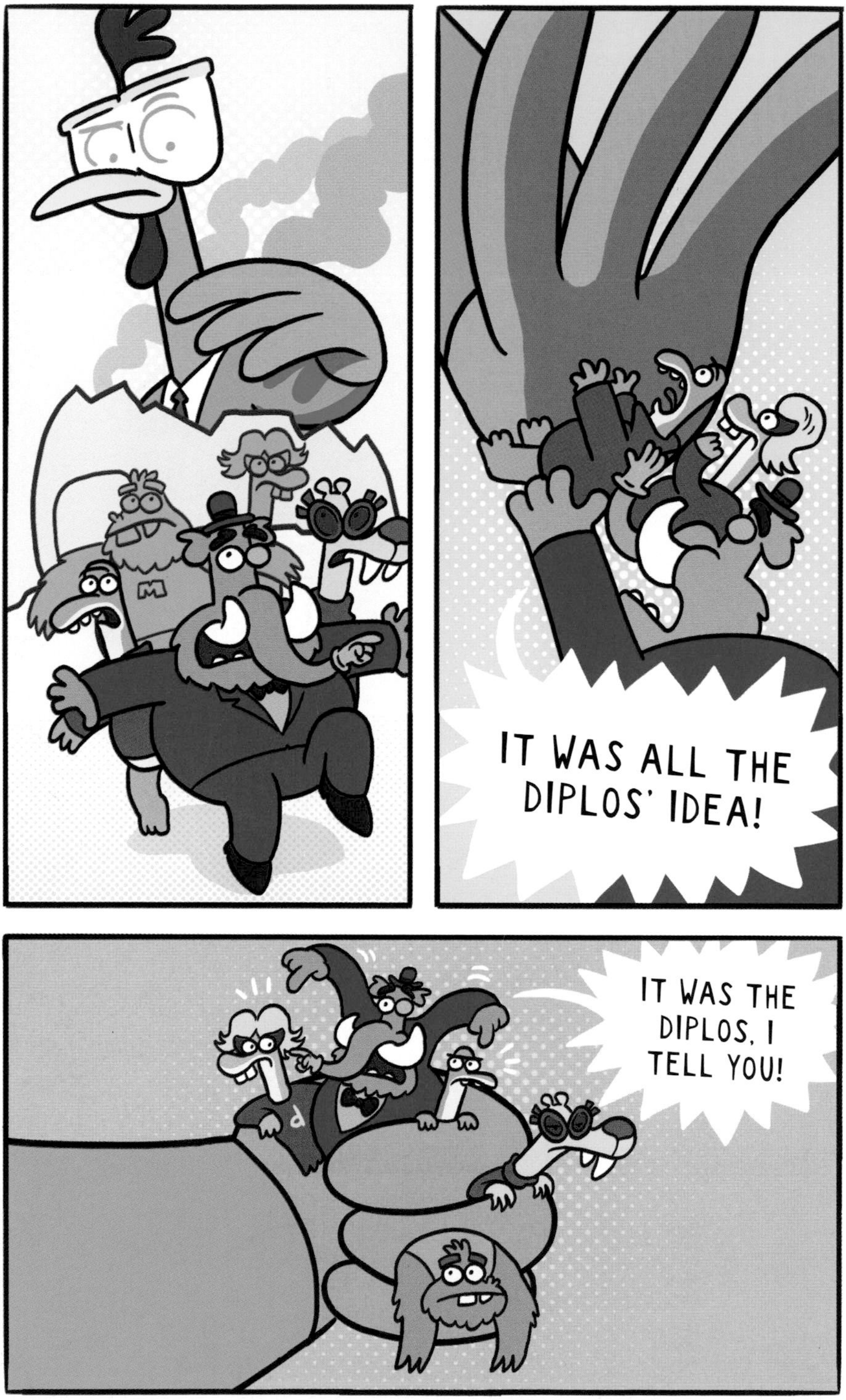
IT WAS ALL THE DIPLOS' IDEA!
IT WAS THE DIPLOS, I TELL YOU!

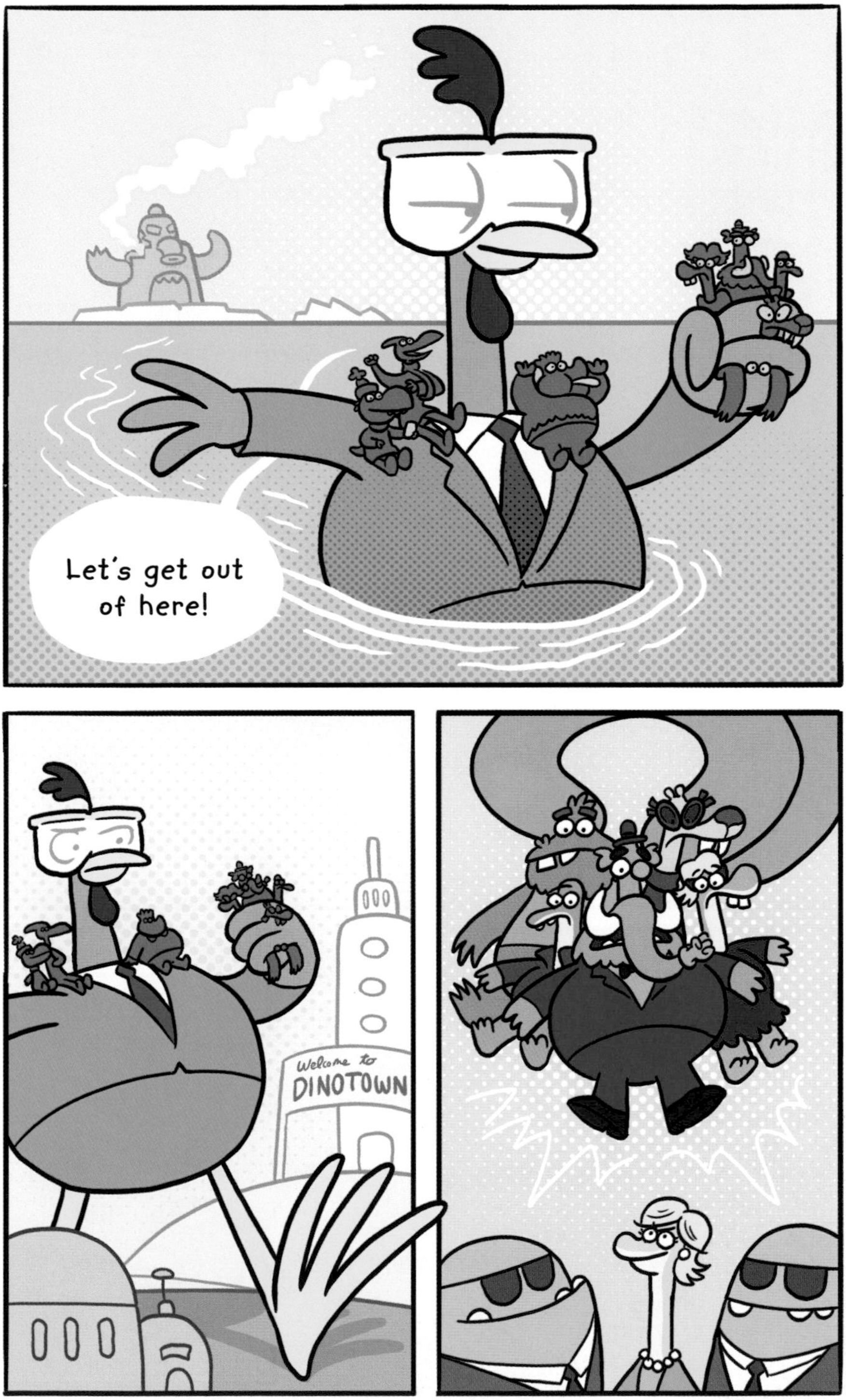
Let's get out of here!
Welcome to
DINOTOWN

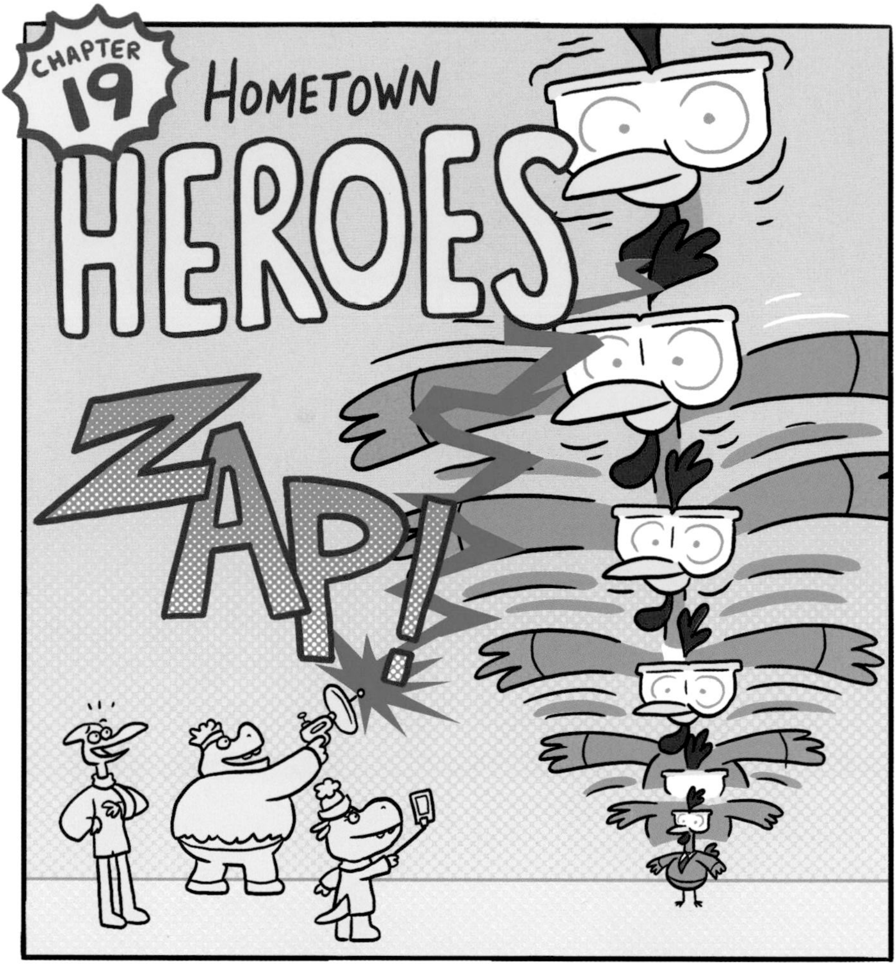
CHAPTER 19
HOMETOWN HEROES
ZAP!

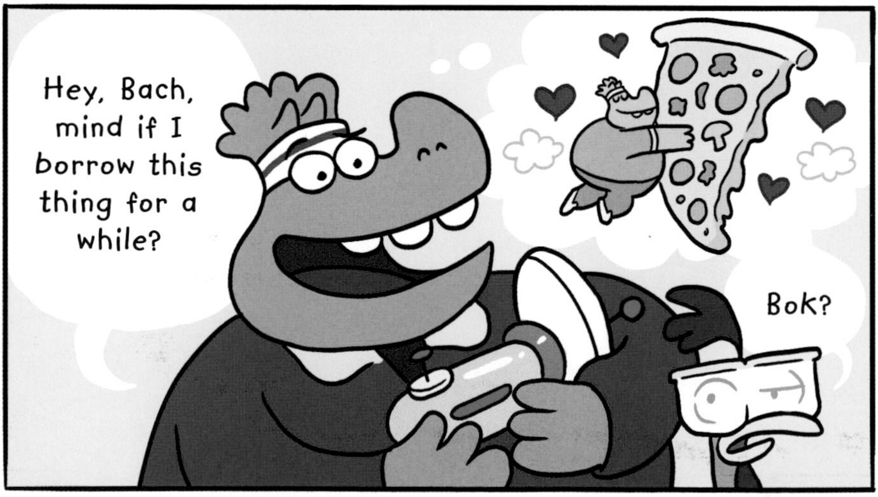
Hey, Bach, mind if I borrow this thing for a while?
Bok?

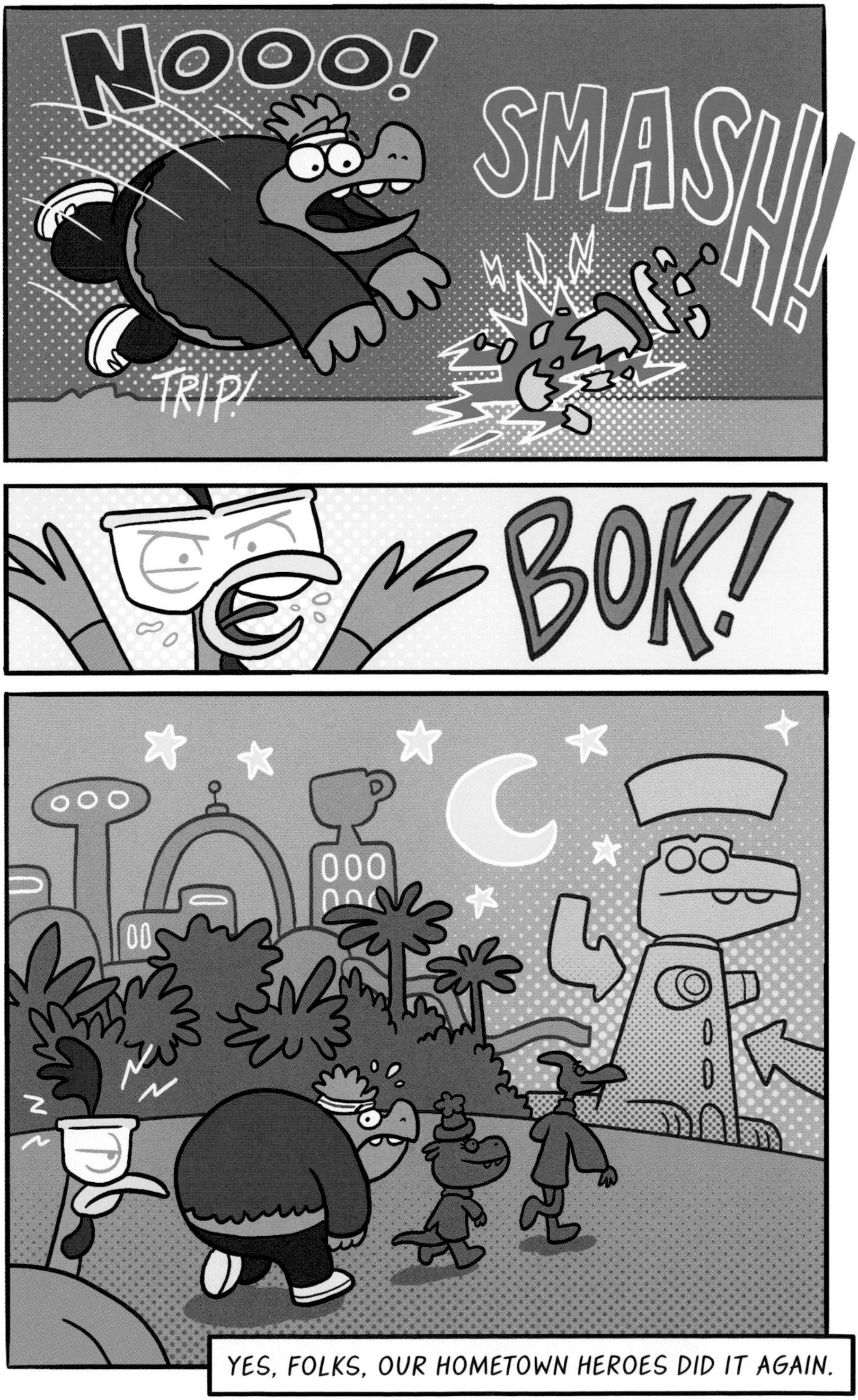
NOOO!
SMASH!!
TRIP!
BOK!
YES, FOLKS, OUR HOMETOWN HEROES DID IT AGAIN.

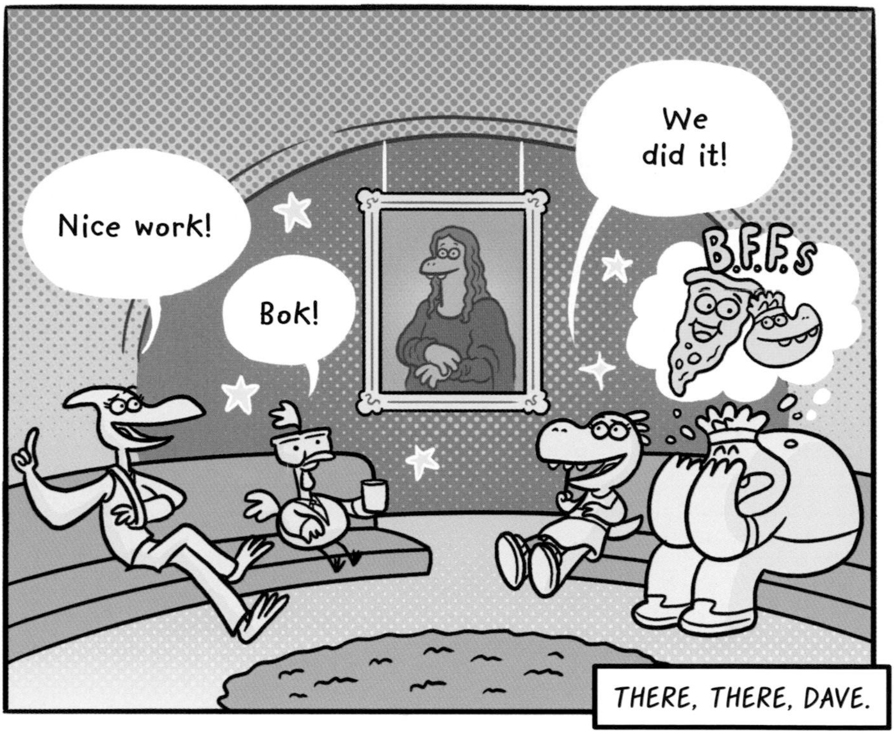
Nice work!
Bok!
We did it!
B.F.F.s
THERE, THERE, DAVE.

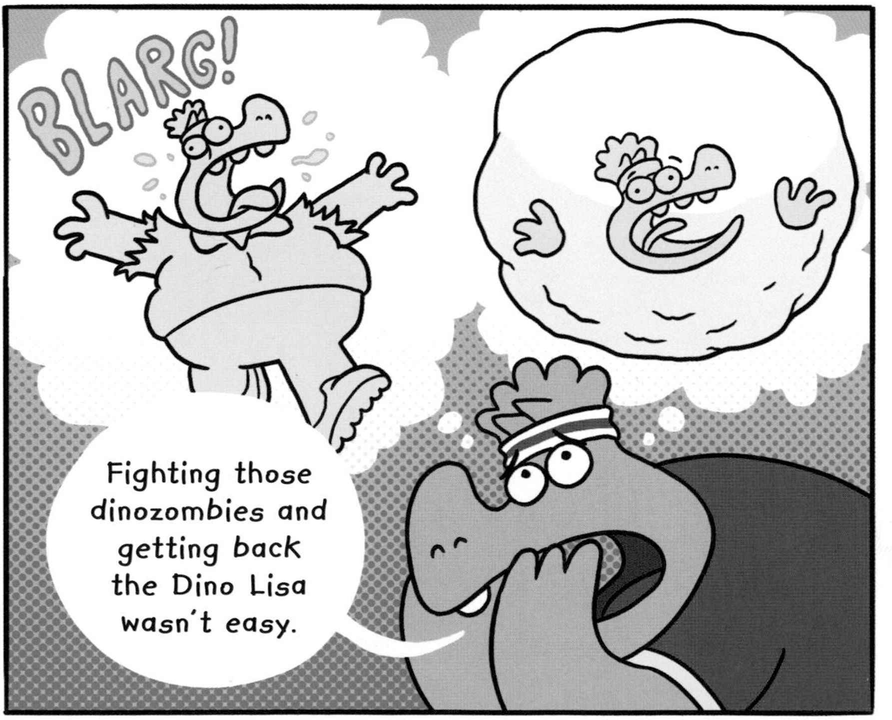
BLARG!
Fighting those dinozombies and getting back the Dino Lisa wasn't easy.

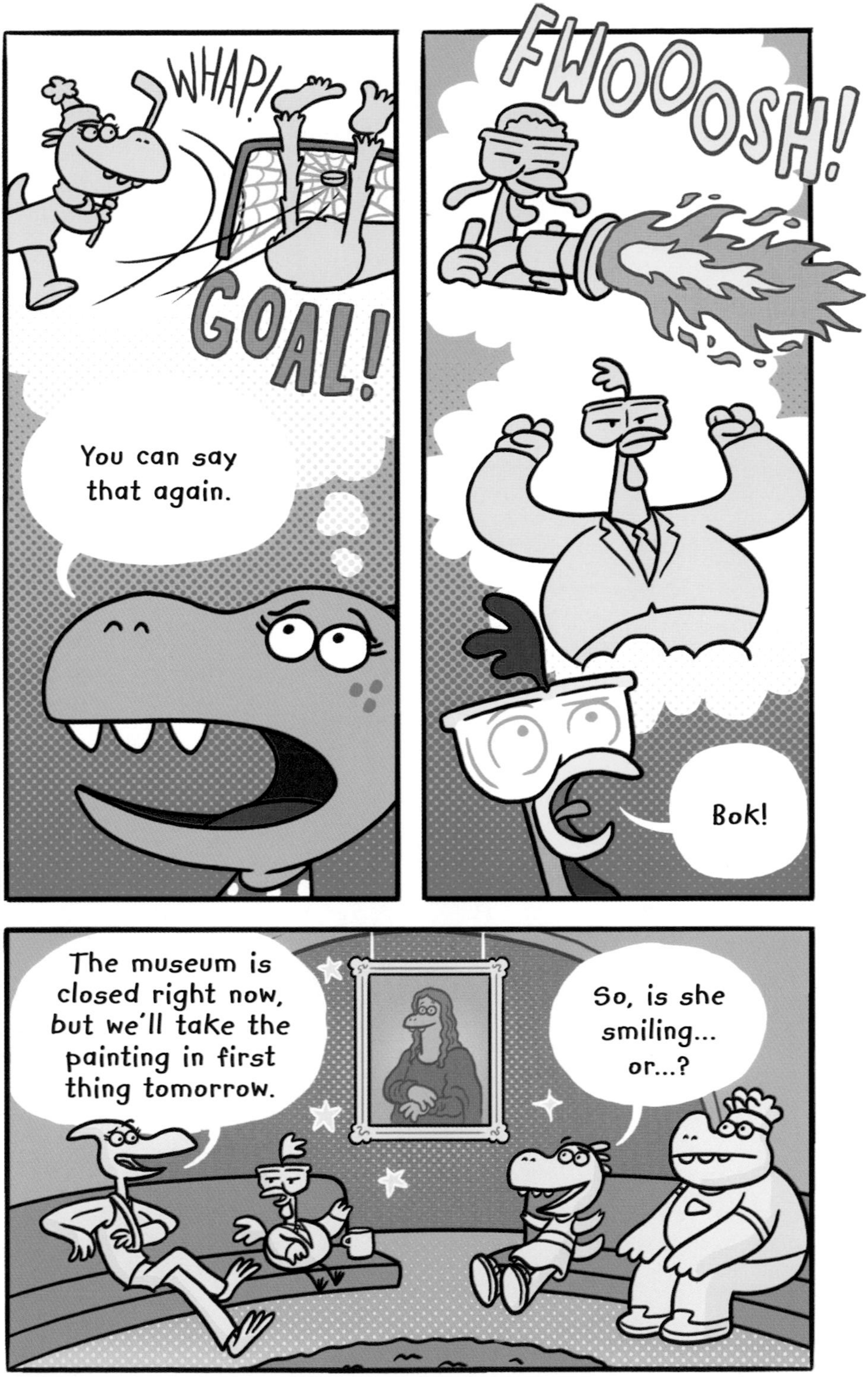
WHAP!
GOAL!
You can say that again.
FWOOOSH!
Bok!
The museum is closed right now, but we'll take the painting in first thing tomorrow.
So, is she smiling... or...?

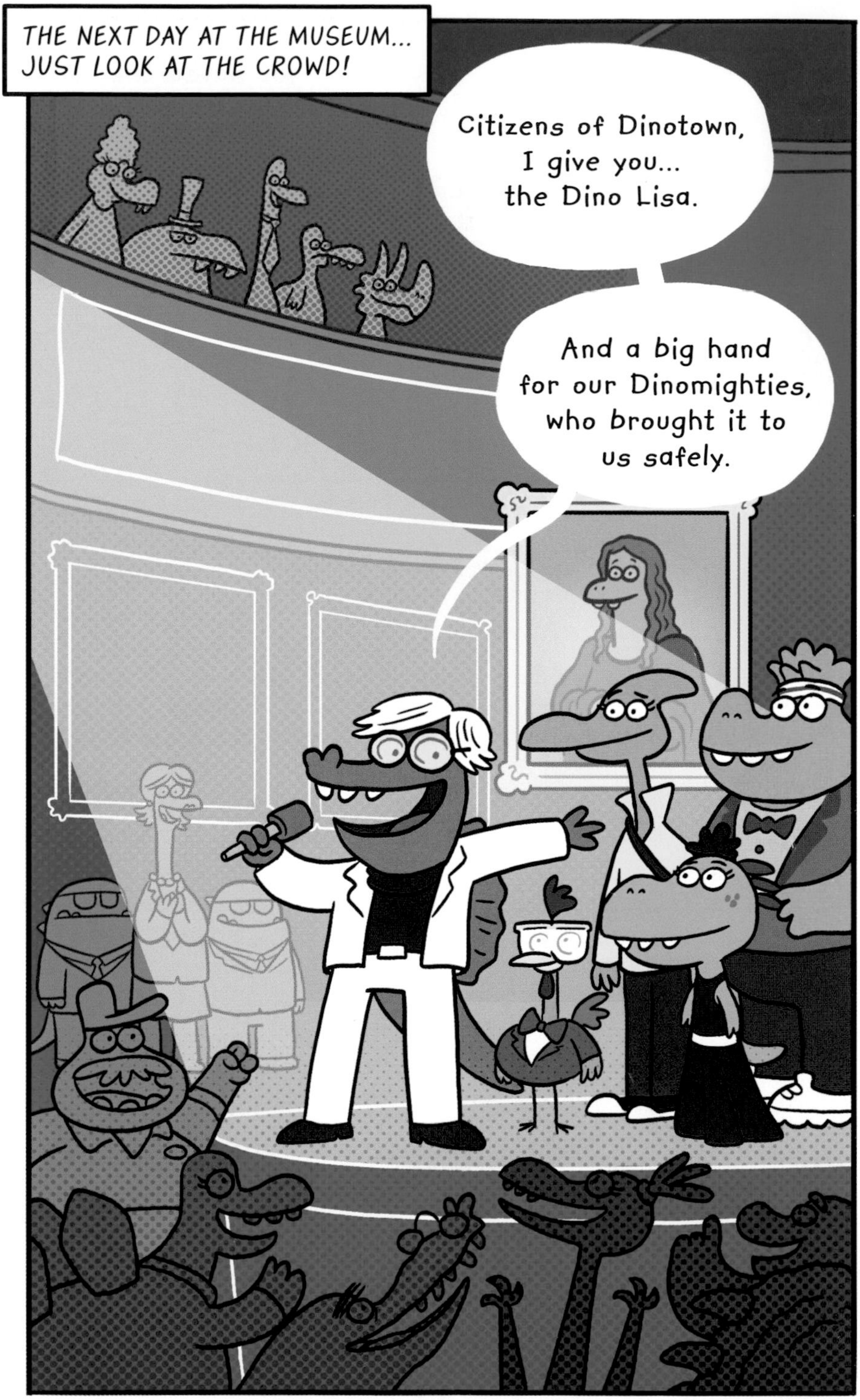
THE NEXT DAY AT THE MUSEUM... JUST LOOK AT THE CROWD!
Citizens of Dinotown, I give you... the Dino Lisa.
And a big hand for our Dinomighties, who brought it to us safely.

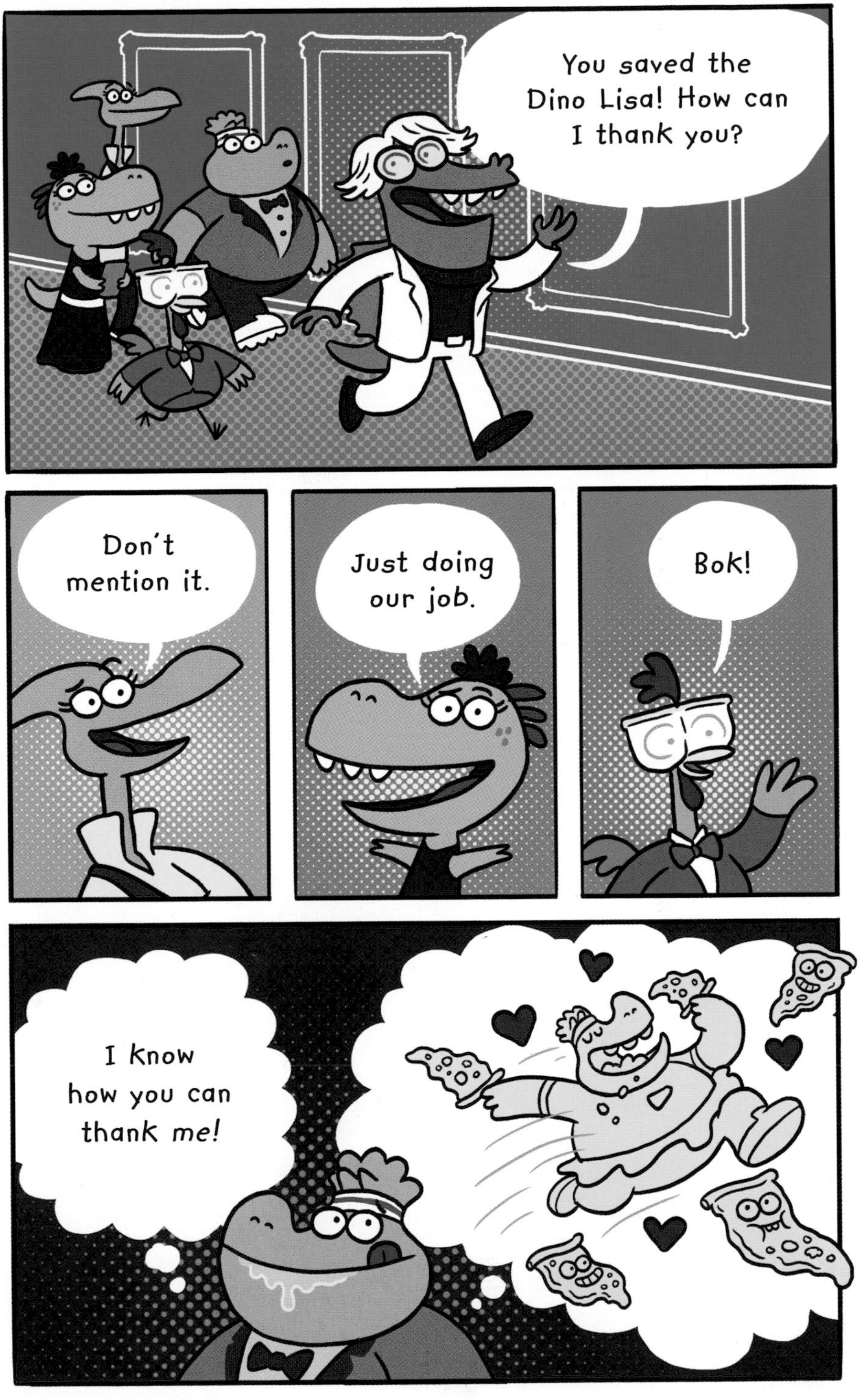
You saved the Dino Lisa! How can I thank you?
Don't mention it.
Just doing our job.
Bok!
I know how you can thank *me*!

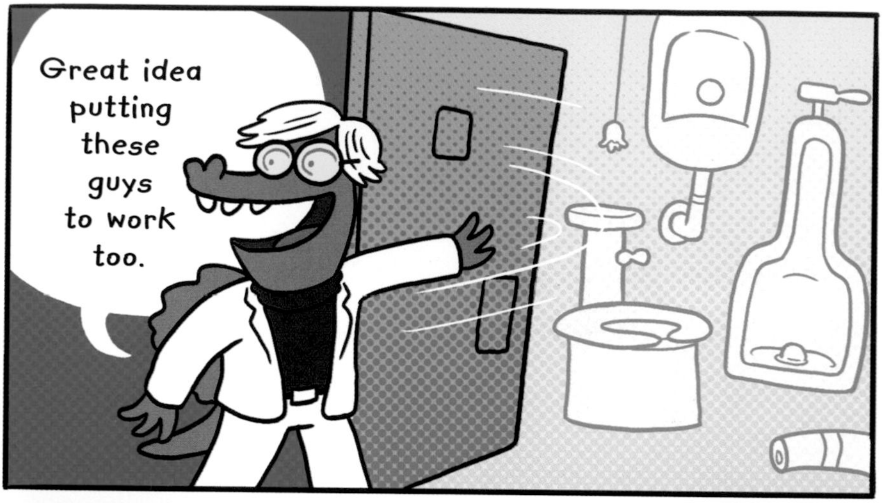
Great idea putting these guys to work too.

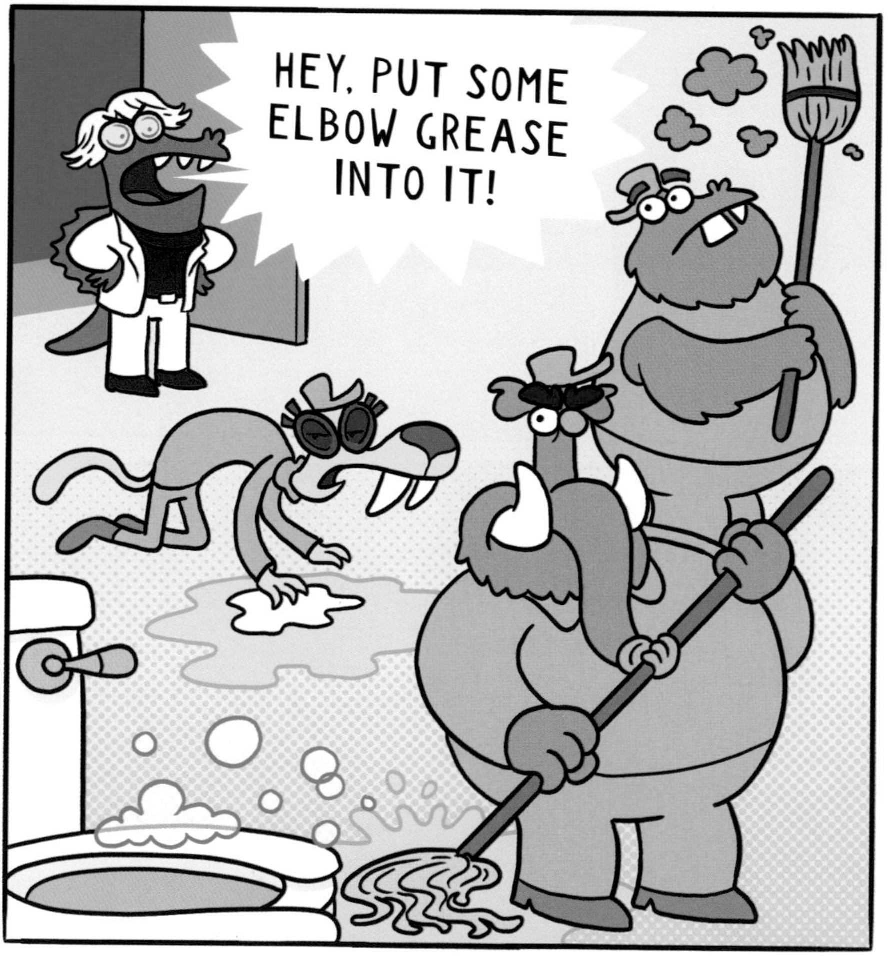
HEY, PUT SOME ELBOW GREASE INTO IT!

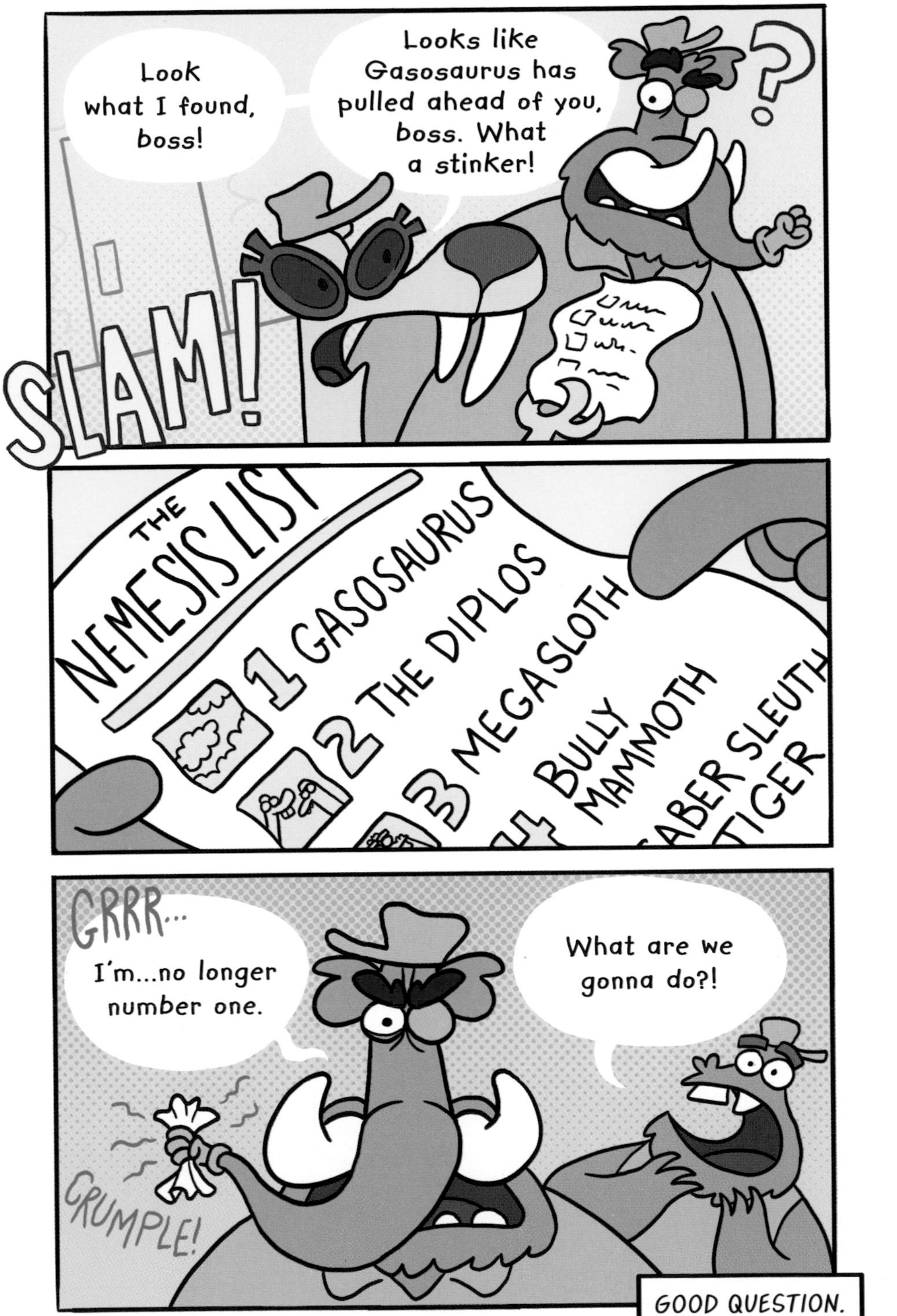
Look what I found, boss!
Looks like Gasosaurus has pulled ahead of you, boss. What a stinker!
SLAM!
THE NEMESIS LIST
1 GASOSAURUS
2 THE DIPLOS
3 MEGASLOTH
4 BULLY MAMMOTH
SABER SLEUTH TIGER
GRRR...
I'm...no longer number one.
What are we gonna do?!
CRUMPLE!
GOOD QUESTION.

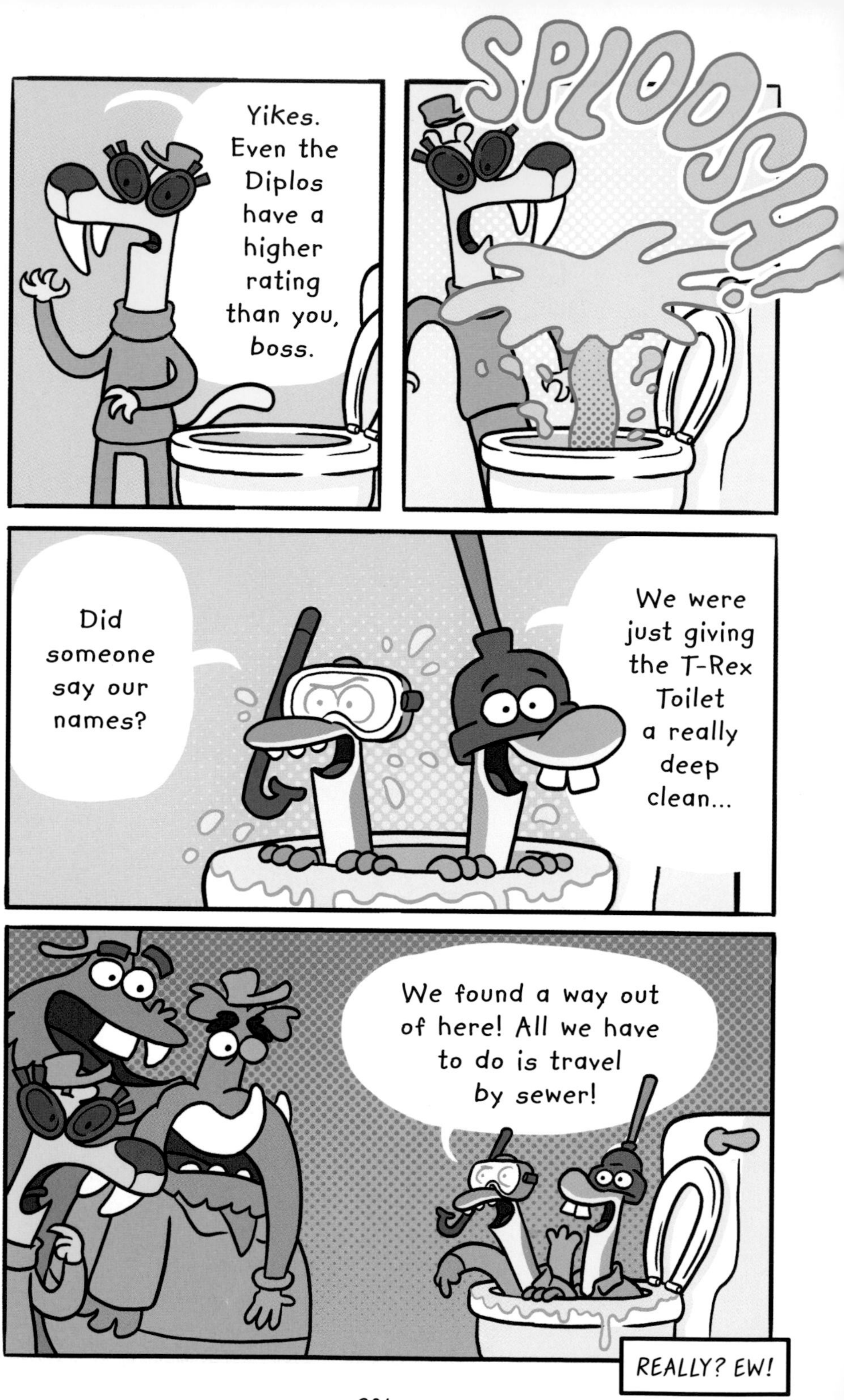
Yikes. Even the Diplos have a higher rating than you, boss.
SPLOOSH!
Did someone say our names?
We were just giving the T-Rex Toilet a really deep clean...
We found a way out of here! All we have to do is travel by sewer!
REALLY? EW!

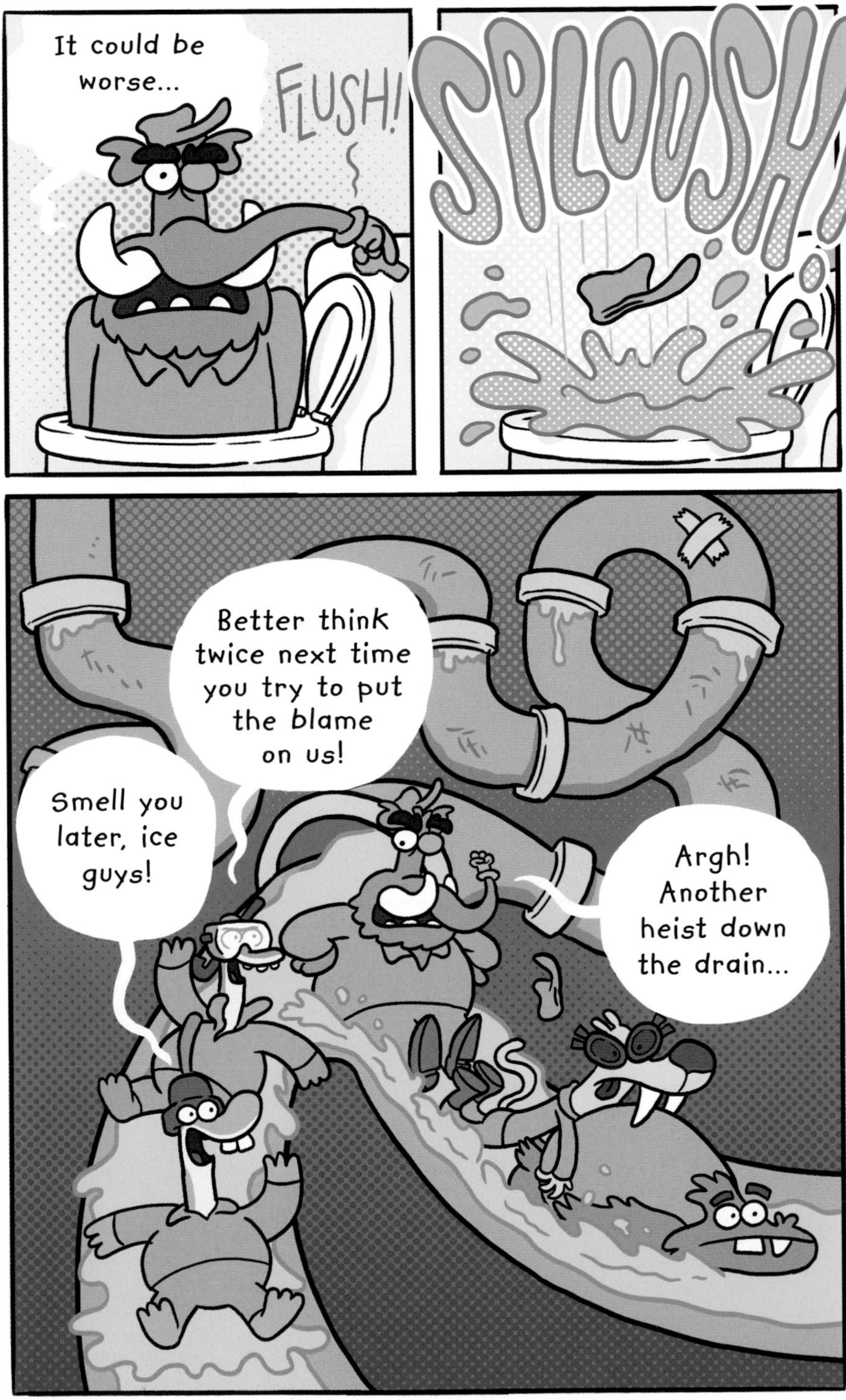
It could be worse...
FLUSH!
SPLOOSH!
Better think twice next time you try to put the blame on us!
Smell you later, ice guys!
Argh! Another heist down the drain...

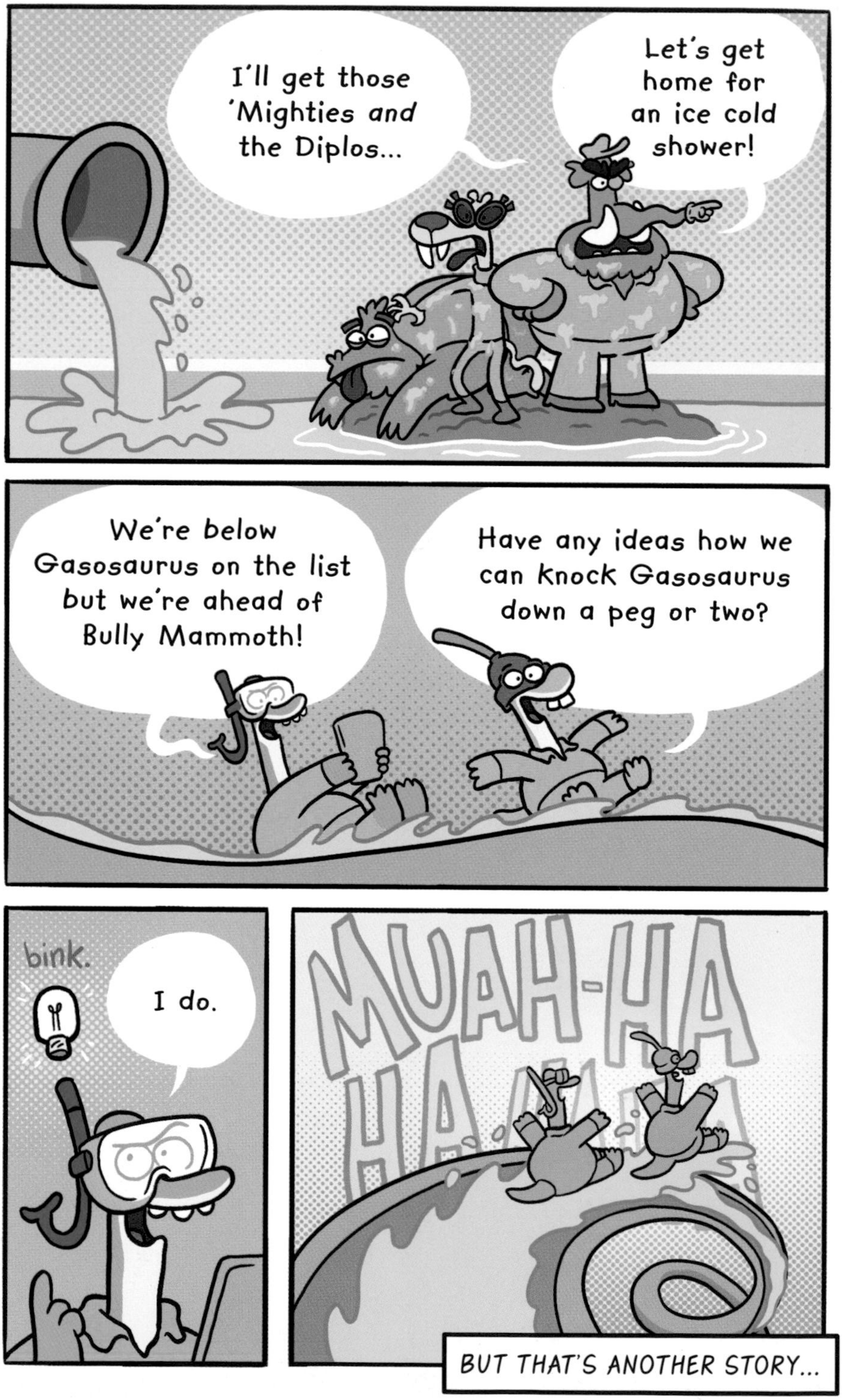
I'll get those 'Mighties and the Diplos...
Let's get home for an ice cold shower!
We're below Gasosaurus on the list but we're ahead of Bully Mammoth!
Have any ideas how we can knock Gasosaurus down a peg or two?
bink.
I do.
MUAH-HA HA
BUT THAT'S ANOTHER STORY...

# HANG ON...

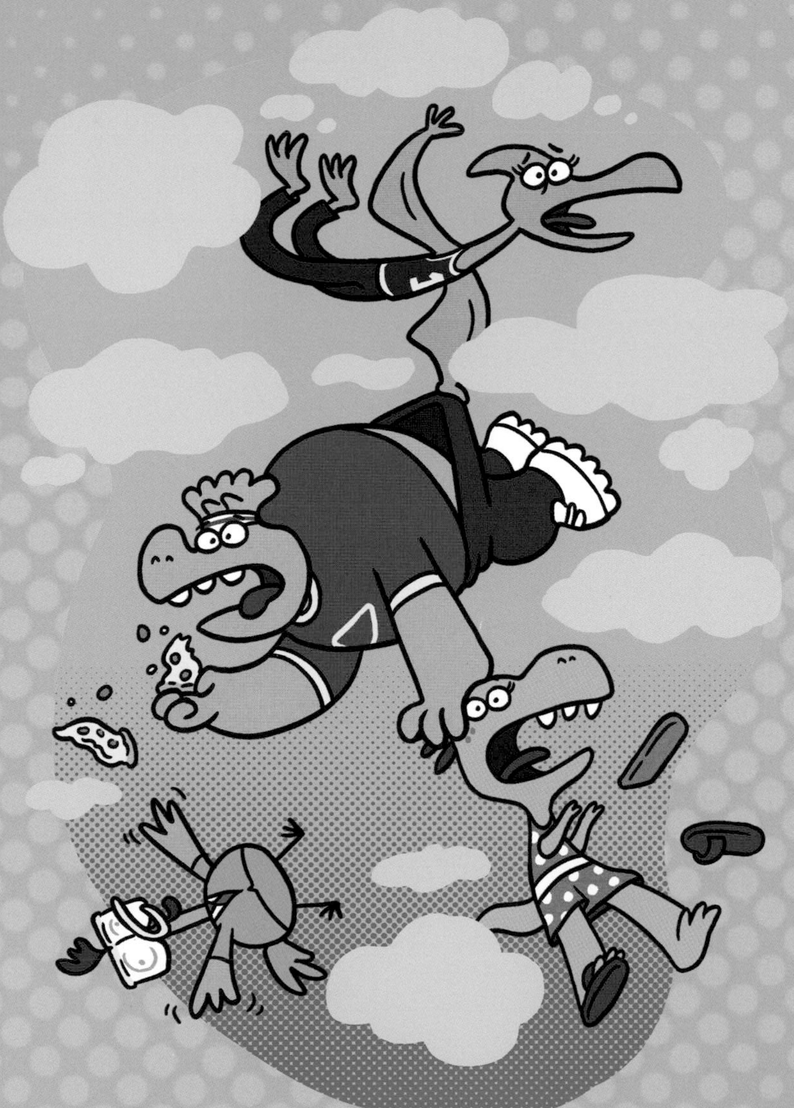

**BOOK 3: LAW AND ODOR**

**IS COMING SOON!**

**DOUG PALEO** IS A DINOMITE AUTHOR OF HILARIOUS BOOKS FOR YOUNG READERS. STONE IS HIS PREFERRED MEDIUM FOR ETCHING GRAPHIC NOVEL SCRIPTS. IN HIS FREE TIME, HE ENJOYS CAVE PAINTING, GOING ON LONG HIKES TO GATHER WILD BERRIES, AND OPEN-FIRE COOKING.

**AARON BLECHA** IS AN ARTIST AND AUTHOR WHO DESIGNS FUNNY CHARACTERS AND ILLUSTRATES HUMOROUS BOOKS. HIS INTERACTIVE, IMMERSIVE ART EXHIBITION TITLED <u>ALIENS, ZOMBIES & MONSTERS!</u> TOURS THE UK AND DEMONSTRATES HOW CHILDREN'S BOOKS ARE MADE. AARON LIVES WITH HIS FAMILY ON THE SOUTH COAST OF ENGLAND. FIND HIM AT MONSTERSQUID.COM.

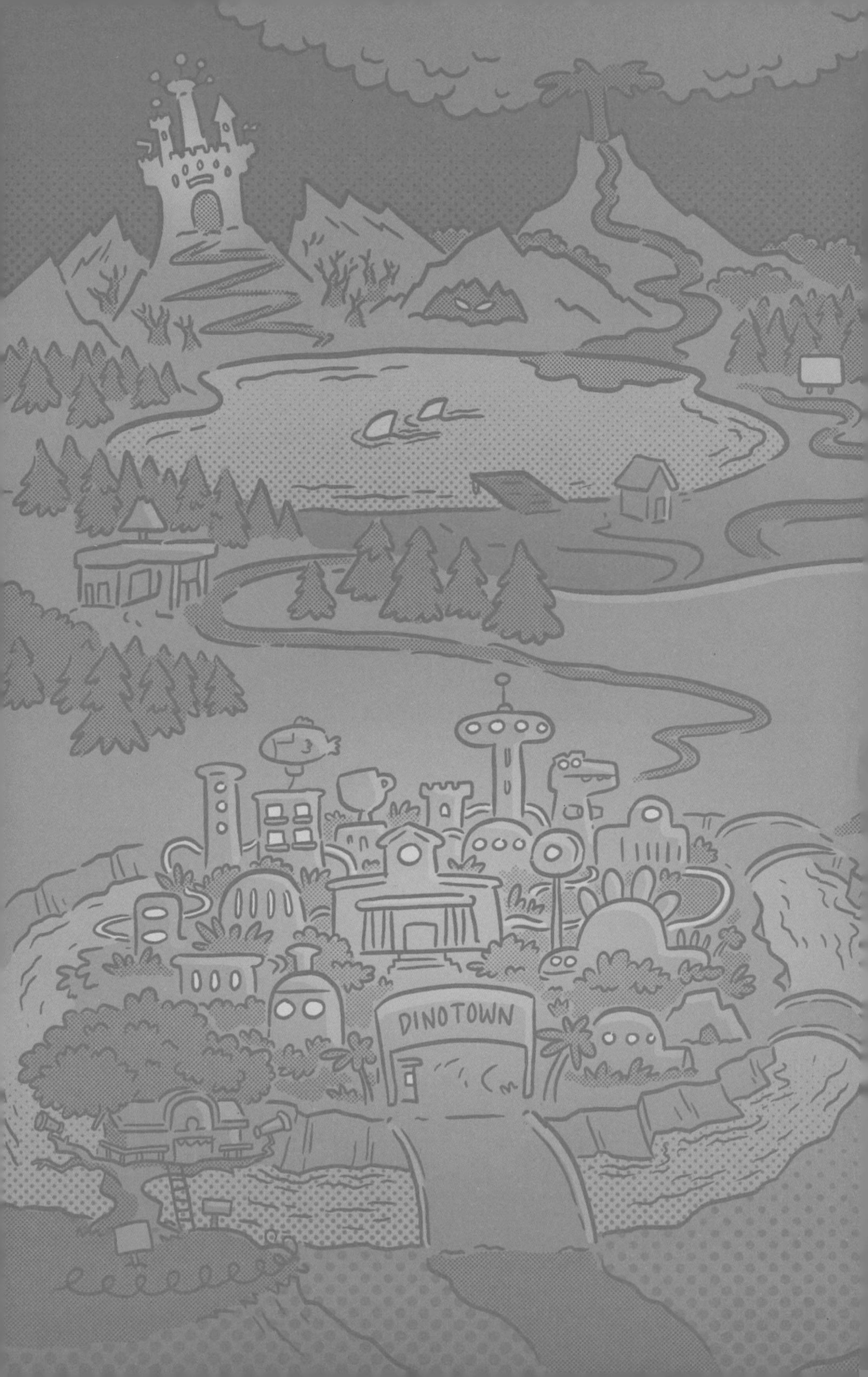
DINOTOWN